Praise

About the Carleton Sisters

"Dian Greenwood's intricately wrought tale of the family secrets and discarded dreams that divide the Carleton sisters brilliantly explores how even the smallest internal shift can begin an inexorable process of change. *About the Carleton Sisters* is as unflinchingly truthful as it is generous, funny, and expertly wrought, exploring the dangerous terrain of generational trauma through the lives of three unforgettable women. Both gritty and hopeful, this novel stayed with me long past the final chapter. I'm eagerly anticipating Greenwood's future work!"
—Michelle Ruiz Keil, author of *All of Us with Wings* and *Summer in the City of Roses*

"*About the Carleton Sisters*, Dian Greenwood's masterful debut novel, propels the reader forward with the drive of a train through California's Central Valley. In the fictitious town of River's End, the sisters gather around their dying mother in a mobile home full of secrets. A family long riven by betrayal and private resentments, they are locked in a struggle for connection and redemption."
—Joanna Rose, author of *A Small Crowd of Strangers*

"Dian Greenwood's debut novel, *About the Carleton Sisters*, hits one out of the ballpark with its depiction of three strong-willed sisters coming together to rally around their mother in her final days. Greenwood gives us a world rich in detail, honest in emotion and struggle, and multilayered in the complexities of reckoning with one's family of origin."
—Leslie Johansen Nack, author of *The Blue Butterfly*

"In the style of some of the best storytellers, Greenwood spins a tale about loss, poverty, and addiction that is laugh-out-loud funny. She paints a picture of three sisters reckoning with their lives in California's Central Valley that lets readers practically smell the musk of beer and sickly scent of gin wafting through an un-air-conditioned trailer. Like Fannie Flagg before her, Greenwood chronicles the drama and dark we encounter in life—and does so with a deft touch that ultimately leaves readers glad to have run into the Carleton sisters."

—Kate Carroll de Gutes, author of *Objects in Mirror Are Closer Than They Appear*

"Three sisters with multiple secrets—each telling her own story—keep this well-crafted novel moving forward in anything but a straight line. Complications, deceptions, a missing father, a dying mother—all this makes for the stuff of rich family drama. Dian Greenwood's novel reminds us of Tolstoy's observation that 'every unhappy family is unhappy in its own way,' which is precisely what makes *About the Carleton Sisters* such a compelling read."

—Judy Reeves, author of *A Writer's Book of Days*

"Dian Greenwood's debut novel shines a bright light into the shadowy corners of an unforgettable Central California family. Incisive, raw, and achingly beautiful."

—Laura Stanfill, author of *Singing Lessons for the Stylish Canary*

"Dian Greenwood's writing is precise, beautifully described, and full of heart and insight. And what's the best treasure of all in this complex, moving, and thoroughly entertaining book? The way she puts her characters on the page. How can you not fall in love with these sisters? Every last wonderful, snarky, sad, funny, wise, raging, captivating, broken, human part of them."

—Gigi Little, editor of *City of Weird: 30 Otherworldly Portland Tales*

ABOUT
THE
CARLETON
SISTERS

ABOUT THE CARLETON SISTERS

A Novel

DIAN GREENWOOD

SHE WRITES PRESS

Published 2023
Printed in the United States of America
Print ISBN: 978-1-64742-440-4
E-ISBN: 978-1-64742-441-1
Library of Congress Control Number: 2022920597

For information, address:
She Writes Press
1569 Solano Ave #546
Berkeley, CA 94707

Interior Design by Tabitha Lahr

She Writes Press is a division of SparkPoint Studio, LLC.

To all my sisters
And in memory of Penny

Summer 1954

They sat beside the creek, knees bent and the hems of their summer dresses trailing in the mud at the creek's edge. Crouching down, they mixed dirt with water until it became mud. Three sisters, three small heads concentrated over old pie tins and empty cans, a pile of leaves and twigs nearby to decorate their mud pies, the worst spoons Mama could find in case they lost them.

They didn't talk except to say, "I need the pie tin now." Not demanding or lording it over each other like they would if they were in their shared bedroom, where they hovered under the blankets pretending they were in their forts long after Mama turned out the lights.

Late afternoon light sifted through the birch trees while the Flieger boys hollered next door from their tree house. In summer, everything was possible. They could come back outside after supper and play run-sheep-run with the Brents who lived across the street. Or climb into the tree house when invited, the rope ladder always hanging down, always tricky.

Mud squished between Becky's toes. There were more tadpoles than she'd ever seen, not that she'd seen a lot. She was only four. If she told Julie, who was two years older,

Julie would say the tadpoles were hers; Lorraine, the oldest at seven, would yell at Becky for getting her dress wet. But Becky didn't care. She'd already peed in her under-panties, now wet from sitting in the creek water. Her back faced her sisters where she crouched over the water. The tadpoles, brown little things, swam helter-skelter near her feet. She'd imagined them green, like in her storybook. Like Julie told her they were. But these were brown, swimming around her ankles like they were playing ring-around-the-rosy. She was afraid that if she moved, they would disappear.

"Whatcha find?" Julie asked.

"Nothin'," Becky said. She lifted her dress and spread it over the water to hide the tadpoles.

"You got a frog under your dress?" Julie always knew when Becky was lying.

Julie raised her head. "Lorraine, over here. See what Becky found. A frog!"

"Did not." Now, they'd scare away her little friends. Like they did the bunny she found under Baby Walter's house, the one she kept teasing with carrots from the fridge and trying to get to come out again. Darned sisters.

"Go away, you're scaring the babies," Becky said.

"Lorraine, it's babies. Baby frogs. You better come."

"Why'd you have to tell her, Julie? You know she'll tell on me, then Mama will yell at me and I won't have the babies ever again."

Tears swelled in Becky's eyes and when she looked back in the water, the baby tadpoles were gone. All because of Julie telling. Julie always the smarty-pants. And she wasn't even the oldest.

Becky plopped back into the creek thinking she was sitting on the bank, but she wasn't. Now, she really had some-thing to cry about, water in her panties and the cold making her pee again. She'd for sure killed the babies.

"What did you find?" Lorraine said. She had a stick in her hand and she kept swishing the water and making it muddy. "What are you crying about?"

Becky's tears fell into the water. Then, the sob came up from her belly until it filled her mouth. "You kilted them. You kilted my babies."

"What's she bawling about?" Lorraine asked Julie. She stopped swishing her stick. "What was it you found? Tell me," she said. "Maybe I can get them back."

Becky looked up at her big sister, her tear-filled eyes full of hope. "You think they'll come back?"

"What were they?" Lorraine said.

"Babies," Becky said. She sucked in her breath. "Tadpole babies."

"That means frogs," Lorraine said.

Julie stood on the bank, her shadow falling over the creek where Becky's feet sat on the bottom, magnified in the water now that the creek ran clear again and Lorraine had stopped swishing her stick. "I didn't mean to scare them, Becky," Julie said. "I just wanted to see them."

When Becky looked up from the bank, she stared into the sun where Julie's head appeared to have a halo around it. "They were tiny," she said. "Brown."

"Maybe they'll come back," Lorraine said.

Mama's voice shouted from the back stoop. "Girls, it's time to come in for dinner."

"That means Daddy's home," Julie said. "Let's go and see what he brought us. Comic books, I hope."

Becky stood in the creek, her dress and panties completely soaked. "Mama's going to be mad," she said.

Lorraine reached out and took her hand, tugging until Becky stepped onto the bank. "Not if Daddy's home," she said.

Becky raced across the backyard, shouting "Daddy's home." Past the sprinkler, past their coloring books and colors scattered on the army blanket under the tree between their house and the Fliegers', past the rope ladder hanging down, past the garbage cans lined along the walk to the back door, and up the back stoop.

"Better stop," Lorraine said. "Take off your dress and panties. Mama won't want you tracking into the house."

Turning toward Lorraine, Julie right behind her, Becky said, "But Daddy's home. He won't care."

Then it was too late. Becky opened the screen door and rushed past them into the kitchen. By the time Lorraine and Julie came in, they were walking on wet spots Becky had left behind. Mama stood beside the stove. Daddy sat at the kitchen table, his lunch pail on the table and his overalls unbuttoned at the top. He was just taking off his boots and was down to his socks when Becky rushed to him.

Wet as she was, he scooped her up and set her on his lap. "How's my girl?" he said.

"You get down right this minute, Becky Sue, and get those clothes off in the bathroom. You hear me?" Mama said.

But Becky snuggled her head against Daddy's chest and gave Mama that *dare you* look she had when Daddy was there to protect her.

"It's okay, Dotty," he said, his hand stroking Becky's long and snarled red hair. "She'll change before supper." He raised Becky's chin. "Won't you?"

"Wash up, girls, we're ready to eat," Mama said. Turning toward Daddy, she said, "Becky, what did I just ask you to do?"

Instead of getting off Daddy's lap, Becky looked up at her father. She smiled the way she did when she was kitten-soft, waiting for him to tell her what to do.

"Listen to your mother," he said. He set her down on the floor and gave her rump a pat. "Get some dry clothes on, girl."

"Lorraine, you set the table after you wash up. Julie, it's your turn to clean up tonight."

Lorraine hesitated. "Yes, Mama," she said. But she kept staring at Becky beside Daddy's lap. Becky was Daddy's favorite, and they all knew it. Mama knew it, Julie knew it, and Lorraine knew it better than all of them.

Chapter One

June 1999

Lorraine

L unch and dinner specials didn't go on the chalkboard until I put them there. My best cursive, if I do say so myself, and I always took a certain pride when I'd finished, standing back and admiring the way I looped my c's and d's. That Friday, near the end of June—the fuzzy season in the almond orchards, my sisters and I always called it—I wrote meatloaf and tuna casserole and chicken-fried steak on the board in green chalk. The truckers would squawk for T-bones, but in the end they'd eat anything hot and fast to fill their gullets before heading up the pass and over the Grapevine to LA.

I pulled my apron off the hook. *Lorraine* in red cursive across the top, but everyone called me Laney, especially the truckers. Maybe it sounded friendlier. Friendlier than I am, to tell the truth.

Diego faced me in his dingy chef's hat and began to whistle, "Sweet Lorraine." After thirty years, it was our ritual. "You better get to it," he said. "I'm counting on you, sweetheart."

Alma, our overflow waitress, was late. One of her six kids had busted his leg. There's always something going wrong with one of them. Breeders, my sister Julie called them. That would be Alma. Also, Pastor Harmon's Pamela and Diego's nutty wife—all breeders. I'd shush Julie when she said that, but secretly had to laugh. Today, only Marie was there—no kids, like me—and she rolled her big cow eyes at me. Easy for her, she was at the end of her shift and she never worked a minute of overtime. Diego was partial to her big behind so he never insisted. Like a man, he had nothing but sex on his mind.

By ten thirty my armpits had sweat up to my pleated hanky and I hadn't had time to pee since I came on shift at six, having agreed to work breakfast until closing at ten, the Manteca–Lathrop rodeo likely the biggest tips of the year. Alma finally arrived with her too-fine, too-long hair in a net. She worked the counter, where we had the fastest turnover. Outside of daylong breakfast, only tuna casserole and meatloaf were left on the chalkboard and we still had the whole day ahead of us. In the kitchen, Diego shouted orders in Spanish, his usual late-morning conniption fit. Plus, José Luis was behind on dishes.

I worked the four booths at the side opposite the counter where the biggest orders came in. The drivers had bunched up so they could jaw with each other while an elderly couple leaned over their coffee near the window facing the highway. Just pie and coffee, they said from our best booth. Below the old lady's wrinkly neck, a single strand of fake pearls hung on the gray sweater that matched her hair. Nobody with real pearls came into Diego's, especially on a cowboy Friday. She skipped the ice cream on her pie and then ordered extra cream for her coffee. The six containers in front of her wouldn't do; she kept asking me to bring more. Folks like that never leave a tip.

I just wanted the day to be done, to be sitting on my bed cross-legged with my tips spread around me, unfolding the bills and counting them as soon as I put Mama to bed. A new total of three thousand dollars held promise within a few days' reach if we stayed this busy. I wet my pencil and wrote down forty-two dollars. Not bad for a single day. If I kept saving at this rate, I'd be able to get Miss America home from Vegas before Mama breathed her last. Let's see, fifty dollars for plane fare. Next week I'd have $3,050. Today, $2,905 in the total column. By the time I closed the brown ledger, my legs would already be cramping from sitting like that on my bed. The accounts book, back in my nightie drawer. In time, I could pay both Miss America and baby sister Becky twenty-five hundred apiece, their shares of the current appreciation in Mama's mobile home. That one sweet moment of the day made all the rest of this nonsense possible. After all, wasn't I the one who'd moved Mama into Sunny Acres? Paid the space rent? Hadn't I taken care of Mama these past years? My sisters hadn't done a darned thing to deserve one-third of Mama's anything. I'd never forgive those two.

"Take care of yourself first, girl," Mama always said. "Something I never learned to do." What she didn't say was, *After you take care of me.*

In the kitchen, I could only see the back of Diego's hat. But everyone in the diner heard him shout, "Somebody left the damn door open."

In the same moment I turned toward the front screen door, some woman in a yellow cowboy hat passed the cash register and headed for the only empty booth at the back. Never mind there were folks by the door waiting to be seated. Something about her, maybe the way the gal lurched, caught my eye and marked her as trouble. But I was too busy to do more than glance in her direction. She'd have to wait; my hands were full.

I was lifting pie onto two plates when someone behind me tapped me on the shoulder, right on my cutting arm with the knife poised and ready to cut. "Don't touch me. I've got a knife in my hand, understand?"

Short and skinny José Luis stepped back, looking at the knife like he was next. He pointed to the back booth. "That lady," José said, "I think she just threw up."

Jesus, help me; that was the last straw. "Get a bucket, José. With Clorox." Already, the stench, God almighty, the stench of vomit. It couldn't have been worse. Lunch and supper hours still ahead of us.

The woman's face and hat lay in a pool of puke. She'd already passed out, her face pointed toward the window. I lifted the cowboy hat off her head and chunks of vomit fell onto the table and all over the salt and pepper shakers. José stood behind me looking stupid with a mop in his hand and the Clorox bucket on the floor.

I took a rag from him and started to wipe the undigested mess now pooled on the table. When I lifted her head, what I saw under that yellow hat and red hair was my sister Becky's passed-out face. Lord God have mercy, I didn't know whether to smash her head into the table or yield to hysteria.

Right then, I felt like Job. The Lord was testing my limits, my sisters the scabs he'd blessed me with. Becky the worst. Every time and all the time, this family landed in my lap. Mama was dying and Miss America still paraded around in Las Vegas—dancing, she said—and, now Becky, my own baby sister, lay facedown on a table full of whatever she'd eaten last. If I could have, I'd have been down on my knees in Pastor Harmon's study, his steady hand on my shoulder as he prayed beside me. He might call this my truck ministry, but today I'd been assigned to hell.

"Call the cops, Alma," I heard Diego bellow.

Behind me, Alma had water glasses in her hand and her mouth hung open. She set the glasses on the counter and started to grab the telephone on the wall. I shook my head no as soon as Diego said cops. I gave Alma the *look*. Nobody survives that.

How would anyone at Diego's know this was my family? All the years I'd worked there, only Mama ever graced the diner, and I could count those times on one hand. "I don't care for him," she finally said, and that was that. Miss America, well, the place wasn't up to her standards.

Becky wasn't a blessed six weeks past her second DUI. Maybe that's why her husband, Kenny, took off. He hadn't wasted words when he called two days ago. "Gotta leave town," he said. "She's all yours." Men like Kenny made it hard to believe there were any good men left.

I stood with Becky's hair in my hand fighting my own urge to upchuck, but that wasn't me. I stifled whatever wanted to come out and went to work. I kept thinking back to the girl who brought me May flowers in a crepe-paper basket she'd so badly Scotch-taped together. "For you, Lancy, because I love you so much." Her small fingers holding on to the table, she'd waited for me to smile. Now, this.

The Lord loves a sinner, I said over and over to myself while, in the kitchen, Diego banged around his cast-iron skillet, the whole time, "Son of a bitch. Son of a bitch." I glanced up at him once and he glared back at me, his black eyes a bulge inside his head and his lips slobbery from cursing. If the customers hadn't been there, Lord only knows what he would have said.

His hands grabbed the service counter and he leaned over. "Get her out of here," he said. "*Now*. Don't bother to clean her up."

"We've got it handled," I hissed toward the kitchen.

I'd never seen such a mess. On her T-shirt, on the cowboy hat, and in her hair. My own sister, no different than one of those fallen-down skid-row men you see in movies. Except she was the girl whose hair I'd braided, the one I taught to play "Chopsticks" and make fudge.

The place was suddenly too quiet, and I had that burned-back feeling. "Coffee, Alma, coffee all around," I said, like this was everyday normal. I wiped at Becky's forehead, her eyes. I had to get her cleaned up and someplace safe before a longtime jail sentence became the next step.

Daddy. He was to blame. If Tom Carleton had sauntered through the door of the restaurant that minute, I'd have found a shotgun and blown the bastard to smithereens. It would have been worth the price of hell. The day he left, our family was wrecked in the same way Humpty Dumpty broke apart and, no matter how hard I'd prayed, the Lord hadn't been able to put us back together again.

Diego burst out of the swinging kitchen door. "Laney!" he said. "Get out of the way!" His beefy hands squeezed down on my shoulders before I could turn around. He'd never know how strong his grip was and this wasn't the time to tell him. All I could do was twist out of his hands.

Sweat in huge droplets ran out from under Diego's sweat-stained cap and down his broad forehead and into his graying and overly long sideburns. Diego was a big man and bulk-heavy and the way he eyeballed me, he would just as soon have picked me up with those meat hook hands and thrown me out of the way. "I'll get rid of her."

For the first time in my life, I did what my sister Julie would do. I lowered my head, awkward as that felt, and tilted it to the side, just so. I looked up at him from under my eyelashes, and smiled. *You're right*, my smile said, *whatever you want*. Then my voice got low, kind of whispery. "I'll take care of it."

My hands were sweaty and I didn't want to know about my armpits. Still, I played all my aces in that one smile. Like I was a fly looking down from the overhead fluorescents, playacting the hussy, nothing a Christian woman would do.

He stood there with his hands on his dirty apron. That

man had been waiting thirty-three years for that smile. You could tell he didn't know what to think once he got it.

I lifted Becky's head, the rag in my other hand, and finished wiping at her eyelashes and her nose.

"Wha's happening?" Becky muttered. Her eyelids attempted to open, but as soon as the words left her mouth, their heaviness pulled her lids closed again.

"I'll tell you what's happening," Diego said.

His big arms went under Becky's arms and then under her legs, his head sideways so he wouldn't have to smell her.

Becky lifted her head again and came eyeball to eyeball with Diego. "Who're you?" she said. Before he could answer, let alone swear at her, Becky's head gave way and fell over his arm. Out cold again.

"Through the kitchen," I said. I kept my voice down. Even so, a family that looked like hard times huddled by the cash register. The wise-sad stare of their boy, maybe nine or ten, said he might have seen this before. His mama kept her hand on his face, turning it away and toward the front door. Probably good people. Christian people. They'd made a mistake coming in here. The Stevens brothers out of Manteca picked their teeth while they leaned into the table and whispered. Likely telling dirty stories. Men like that don't act decent when they're away from their wives. But they knew who was boss at Diego's and who would have their tails out the door if they gave me any guff.

Cowboy hats and baseball caps were a blur as I passed in front of Diego, who carried the cargo. He couldn't argue as long as we kept moving, Becky being a lot more to handle than a hundred-pound sack of spuds. Past the stove and prep counter and through the kitchen to the outside door. I held the screen door open where, outside, the hotter-than-hell summer heat—having waited all day for the wind—waited for us with a vengeance.

"Put her on the bench," I said.

When Diego dropped her onto the outside bench, Becky lifted her head yet one more time. "Hey, take it easy, man," she said, her voice somewhere between sleep and a slur.

Becky's arms and legs hung limp off the sides of the bench, and her hair was an unbelievable mess of tangles and puke, her fancy yellow cowboy hat already in the dumpster.

"So, what's the deal with you and this piece of trash?" Diego said.

I pulled in Becky's arms and then her legs. All I could think about was her last DUI and what if the cops came and thought she drove here.

"Someone from church," I said.

"Church? Madre de Dios," he said. His hands held on to the hips of his dirty apron and his teeth chewed on the bottom of his mustache the way he did when he was mad or nervous. He kept reaching for her like he wanted to throw her in the dumpster along with the hat. He never met my eyes except for quick glances when he grabbed at his apron straps. Downwind, he reeked of the kitchen and his big body in the heat. "Just leave her here for the cops," he said.

Until the words came out of my mouth, I didn't know I would say them. "She's my sister, Diego."

Diego's eyebrows came together and his fat lips burbled, "Mother of God. This drunk is your sister?"

I glanced at my Escort in the parking lot next to a Swift long haul. The Lord says the truth will set you free, but some truths make you pretend you're invisible and not who you are the next time you walk into Walgreens or stop at Arco for gas. My hand shielded my face, and my eyes faced into the sun behind Diego's head.

That's when I touched his arm. Something I'd never done before.

My heart was never so alive and it beat into my temples. "We're going to put her in my car," I said.

His deep throat-clearing told me he wanted to argue, that he wanted the cops to come and take Becky away like she was any ordinary drunk. It was also possible he wanted this, like I did, to have happened to someone else, somewhere else. He kept clearing his throat, but he didn't say anything. That was the miracle.

Now, against everything I believed in, my full hand lay on his tight brown skin, the muscles hard beneath where the blue had faded on his old Navy anchor tattoo. I kept my hand there, like you would touch a child. A man-child. "I owe you big-time for this, Diego," I said. "You won't be sorry."

He looked down at me and then at my hand. His tongue reached up to catch his mustache, and his hands didn't come off his hips until he bent over to lift Becky.

Too late. The crunch of tires on gravel. The twirling red light fixed to the top of the black patrol car. Daryl and another deputy I didn't recognize stopped just short of us. "Gilbert Stevens from Manteca called," Daryl said. "I can see the problem, Diego."

Both men eased out of the car and quickly put on their hats. "We know this one," Daryl said, even as he looked at me. "Sorry, Laney. Got to take her in."

My face must have been the red of ripe strawberries. I didn't know whether to laugh or cry. There was no pretend left in me. I turned around as fast as I could and went back into the diner. Diego came right behind me, then past me and headed into the kitchen. I ducked into the ladies. "Lord God Almighty, why me?" I asked from inside the stall, my panties down around my knees. I bit my lip until I was sure it was bleeding. I pulled out my flip phone and hit speed dial to Las Vegas. "You'd better get your ass to River's End as soon as you can," I said into the recording. "Mama's dying and now Becky's headed to jail."

Chapter Two

Becky

Shackles, for chrissake. Did they think I was going to run off or kill someone? I was just an ordinary River's End drunk who got in trouble once in a while. At least give me that. And the geek who was supposed to get me out of here just stood there in his baggy trousers before a lady judge who reminded me of my mother. The same mad look on her face, her lips so tight it would take a crowbar to pry them loose.

Becky, girl, how could you get yourself in this pickle? Again. All because you wanted to get even with Kenny, him going off to Montana with the Misfits. Like he can do what he damned well pleases. So, what did you do? You took your parade to Sacramento, that's what you did. The credit card he didn't think you could find. That fancy cowboy store and five hundred bucks for a yellow cowboy hat to match your yellow Mustang. Holy shit. Talk about trouble. It'll be worse when Kenny gets the bill. Then you lost the damned hat somewhere that night. All you remember is the steak and baker, that guy behind the bar offering you his couch. After that, a blank. How the rear window of your Mustang got busted out and towed. How you ended up at the diner. No idea. But even that didn't wake you up.

I remembered the courtroom. The lady judge. The trucker who said I ran him off the road. Mean sucker. His red suspenders and one of those Carhartt shirts. Big arms like he could really do some damage. He made me glad I was surrounded by cops. He'd probably be too happy to come after my fat ass.

The judge looked down at me over the top of her glasses, just like Judge Judy. But none of those fancy neck things like Judge Judy wore. Frilly embroidered or crocheted things like Grammy made in front of the soaps. My geek did all the talking. Best if you don't talk at all, he said. Shit, I wouldn't know the outcome until after the hearing. The lady judge never crept close to a smile. Third time I stood there. She could make it really hard for me.

I wish Laney had been there. Someone on my side, not that Laney was. But at least she's family. Maybe the only one talking to me, Tits Up not yet back in town, though Laney said she was coming. Told Laney, not a word to Mama. She already had enough resentment to nail me in my coffin.

I was thinking back to when the three of us kids made forts with army blankets and played under the covers at night with those dollhouse lamps Daddy gave us. I'd never in my life want Daddy to see me the way I was today, standing in that courtroom wearing jail-issued jeans and an oversized T-shirt with metal cuffs around my ankles. Not the way Daddy would want to see any of his girls. If he'd stayed, none of this would have happened.

Goddamn, I'm not a loser. I'm not.

* * *

My banging on the cell door didn't do a damned thing. "Somebody out there," I shouted. "I need aspirin or Tylenol . . . something for this damned headache." I said it loud but not so loud I'd piss them off, hoping someone down the hall was sitting at the desk I could see from my bunk. Anything to get rid of the gal across from me, crying her damned eyes out all night like she was dying. Maybe she'd never been in the women's drunk tank before. Maybe she'd never lived under twenty-four-hour fluorescent lights inside winter-gray walls, where backed-up toilets smelled day and night, and if you weren't sick already, you soon would be. Not like I wanted to become a pro at this. Doggone Laney letting them haul me off from the diner like that. Not that I remembered a whole lot. Just that brute Diego she worked for, arms like a boxer. That's all I remembered before Daryl, same shit deputy as last time, closed the cell door. That grin on his face like he got me this time.

No watch. No purse. What the hell happened to my yellow cowboy hat?

"What are you crying about?" I shouted to the gal behind me.

When I turned around, she had the most pathetic look on her face. "My old man's left me," she said. She started sobbing again.

"You'll get over it," I said. "Mine does that all the time. He'll be back."

Not that I was sure of a damned thing. This was one of those times when you do and don't want them back. I sure as hell didn't want Kenny seeing me in here.

"Here's your breakfast," Daryl said. He was the only cop I knew who got away with a wad of Big Red stuck in his lower lip.

"Quit grinning like that, Daryl," I said. "I'll sic my sister on you."

"You'll be happy to know she's on her way. Said she's getting you out . . . asked if eight days had sobered you up."

"Smart-ass," I said under my breath. I turned toward my bunk where I could at least sit on that poor excuse of a plastic pallet and eat my biscuits and gravy. Peach yogurt. "Who the hell eats yogurt? I need coffee."

Roomie still clung to the bars. "You'd better eat," I said. "You'll feel better."

She turned and looked at me. "You been in here before?"

"A couple of times," I said. I lifted my fork, wondering if I could keep what was on my fork down. "Food's not as good as Denny's, but it's okay."

She started to smile and sat opposite me on her bunk. Opened the yogurt.

"You like that stuff?" I said.

"It's okay," she said. "I'm a vegetarian. I think there's sausage in that gravy."

A vegetarian in a drunk tank? I handed her the yogurt. "Here, you can have mine."

Daryl shouted from the cell door. "Your sister's waiting when you're done," he said. "Told me she has to be at work in forty-five minutes. Better get a leg on."

I set the tray on top of my bunk's rumpled blanket. "Let's go and get it over with."

Daryl grinned, the too-white cap on his front tooth catching the overhead light. "Wise choice," he said.

Down the long hallway, my yellow cowboy boots were stained with whatever I had in my stomach a week ago. I was tempted to ask Laney how to clean them but that would be begging for trouble. I was lucky she finally came.

In uniform, she had that prissy pleated hankie above *Lorraine* on her little pink pocket, pink everything else. She sat on a gray chair in an all-gray room, the same circles under her eyes, her hair pulled back with barrettes. It was the first time I noticed how gray she was getting. I was actually surprised her hair hadn't turned white living with that woman called our mother.

Hands folded in front of her, Buck's turquoise ring stuck out on her middle finger. All business, my sister.

"Howdy," I said, a lilt on the end like, *I'm friendly, you can be too.*

"Don't *howdy* me," she said. "You're in a peck of trouble."

She forgot lipstick, even that pale neutral color she usually wore. We're such a bunch, the three of us. If Julie, who I call Tits Up, was sitting across from us, she'd be done up to the hilt including false eyelashes, red lipstick, and her blonde hair all puffed up like she was a damned show dog. Nothing like the pigtailed girl who sat across from me on the grass when we played Barbies together. Of course, she had to be first to get a Ken doll.

"Like I said, you're in trouble."

"I got that part," I said. I straightened the shoulders of my oversized T-shirt like we were suddenly getting formal.

"They want to fine you two thousand dollars and put you on probation for four years. No driver's license except a restricted one for two years. You're also supposed to sign up and attend a county program where you'll have to go to a class once a week for eighteen months. All because of a second DUI and, this, your third arrest. If that doesn't work, you'll get one of the new ignition interlock devices you'll have to blow into just to start that pickup. That is, if Kenny even lets you drive, let alone pays the insurance on it. They also tacked on a hundred hours of community service. A nice way of saying you get to pick up trash along the freeway."

Holy shit. That woman judge threw the book at me. "That's the best that geeky lawyer could do for me?"

"You heard the judge, not that you were probably clear enough to remember anything. It's the judge who made the stipulations. 'Standard,' she said. Remember?"

All for a third arrest. My luck, no DUI. Not that Laney didn't strain saying words like *DUI*. Heaven forbid she ever said *shit* or even *damn*.

"Gotcha."

"Here's the deal," she said, her hands in front of her, her fingers fiddling with Buck's ring. She lifted her chin, her blue eyes right into mine. "I'll pay the two thousand," she said.

"You will?"

For the first time, I felt hope knocking on my door.

"But you'll have to sign an agreement that the money I pay for your fine will be your portion of the appreciation for Mama's mobile home when she passes."

"What?"

Her eyes never left my face. Her skinny lips held tight, a single hair on her chin that she never thought to pull wagged at me.

"Two thousand dollars?" I said. "That much from the old lady?"

"Your mother, Becky. She's your mother."

"Okay, okay. Whatever. That's a lot of money."

"That's what your share would be if you inherited it. And that's exactly what your fine comes to."

"I can't believe it! That's too damned much money for a fine if that's what I was going to get from the trailer."

"Your alternative is to go to the women's work farm for a year to work off the fine."

The shadow of a smile passed over her mouth when she said that.

"You know I'm not going to any damned work farm."

"Those are your choices. You either sign the agreement or they'll take you to the farm this afternoon," she said. Again, that shadowy smile. "Two DUIs are expensive. Three puts you in prison. This way, when you're at home you get to wear your own T-shirts. In the other two places you wear what they tell you to wear. Like what you have on."

"Okay, okay," I said. "If I have to listen to one more gal cry all night long, I'll never get straight."

Lorraine wasted no time opening her purse. She unfolded a piece of paper and straightened it on top of the gray table. Pulled out a pen and handed it to me. Good old fully prepared Lorraine. "There, where I put the *X*," she said. "Sign your full name. Rebecca Susan Carleton. I already filled in the date."

My hand shook and I couldn't believe how hard it was to hold a pen, let alone sign anything. Shit. If I wasn't in such a jam, I could have used that two thousand. Bought my own place, maybe an RV. Had my own dog. Finally got away from River's End. Then I could take off just like Kenny takes off. Wouldn't he love that? I'd pack up my Cabbage Patch dolls and the Raggedy Ann and Andy that Laney made me. Them and a dog's all the company I'd need. Maybe I should think again about the work farm.

The pen had its own idea. My name signed itself on the unfolded paper. And Laney was halfway out of her chair before I even finished.

She blew on the signature. "Don't have time to take you to your trailer at Stella's Landing. Here's five dollars for a cab. If you're lucky, they'll give you a provisional license after ninety days . . . so you can go to treatment." A smirk. "Whatever you do, don't leave town. And don't come near the diner *ever again* unless you're stone-cold sober. Just remember, there's no more money or rescue left in me. This better be the last time, Becky Sue."

She turned and signaled Daryl, who waited outside the door. "They'll process you at the front desk. Oh, here's the five bucks." Her eyes found mine. "You owe me."

I could feel the gall rise in my stomach. "I thought I just paid you plenty."

"Five bucks," she said. "You owe me five bucks."

Chapter Three

Julie

First light came through the bus windows in a haze of blue-black indigo just before the horizon turned the lipstick pink of a blotted kiss. Not unlike the pink and white oleander spilling over the median and separating the northbound and southbound lanes. The bus, the highway, and distant Sierras, everything ran north and south. Only telephone poles interrupted the Central Valley's cornfields and alfalfa, the straw-colored hills and rolling flatland. Everything the same noncolor it had always been, proof that nothing gets away scot-free. No matter what, everything lives for a while, then dies off.

I folded my red silk shawl around my shoulders. Early summer was as good a time as any to leave Las Vegas; the sun had already etched too many lines around my eyes, and the summer crowds were the kind of folks who love air-conditioning and cheap hotel rooms. For them, gambling wasn't just a moment's high, it was their future.

Not me. If Merce Cunningham was right and dancers are first-time souls, you never see tomorrow coming. Then one day you find yourself waiting in an airport or train station or bus depot, the one-way ticket in your hand, the bag on your shoulder, eyes straight ahead and you're into the dogleg turn you never expected. Whatever direction you thought you were going was dead-end done.

Two older ladies with the peculiar red of hennaed hair perched toward the front of the bus, their chatter too loud in all the quiet. They reminded me of Dotty, my mother. They were probably hard of hearing like she was. Through the window a solitary cypress stood at the edge of the field, where the slightest wind pulled its lower branches along the dusty ground, reminded me of a feather boa dragging across a lighted stage. The tree and my mother Dotty were alike, always steady, always there, until now. She was the reason I was on the bus, Lorraine's check for plane fare cashed in so I'd have a few extra dollars in my purse. The bus gave me time to think.

From where I sat, the taller men's heads rose above the top of the bus seats. A silver-haired fellow, tall like me, was the most obvious. He'd lifted his head when I got on the bus. His leather jacket hugged his shoulders beneath a crown of silver hair, the matching mustache. I was used to men staring. You can't avoid a woman who is six feet tall, with thick blonde hair around her shoulders and bracelets that jangle every time she moves.

I leaned back against the headrest. Who was I kidding? It took me five years of cocktailing to finally face the fact that Las Vegas is a kid's town, not meant for those of us starting the downhill side of fifty. Night after night I'd tell myself cocktailing was only temporary until the next trapeze bar swung into view. At least I didn't have to deliver cocktails with Lily anymore, her wrinkled cheeks and heavily lidded eyes hidden inside stage makeup and false eyelashes. A former dancer like me, she hadn't known when or where to move on either. Sweet as she was and full of advice she never took herself, time was working against both of us. Let's face it, I sure as heck didn't want to end up like her, my legs turning into skinny sticks while I pretended the skin wasn't falling down my face. Lorraine's call proved to be the push I needed to do what I needed to do: move on.

The air brakes hissed to a stop at the Fresno station and the bus, like a heavy and awkward elephant, lumbered into the back lot just past noon and a couple of hours before River's End. Over the Central Valley Bank, the digital thermometer blinked 103, a relief after Las Vegas.

The depot's windows faced the bus parking lot. Unlike the folks around me, I never used a back door unless it was a stage entrance. Hugging my straw bag, I was the last one off the bus. Breathe in, then out. Again. The smudged glass doors reflected my black sundress and long legs, my red high-heeled sandals, yes, along with the bunions and crooked toes, a dancer's dues. If I could walk onto Bally's stage in heels and a fifty-pound full-out feathered backpack, I could do this.

The door's weight surprised me, but not the smell of diesel fumes and rotting fruit in a trash bin. Inside, a disaster of broken glass and orange juice pooled above brown tiles where two yellow sandwich boards announced, *Caution, Wet Floor*. A long-haired attendant swished a mop, the juice simply transferred from one tile to another. He lifted his head briefly, the arch in his eyebrows and gawky stare evidence I wasn't who he expected. Welcome home, Julie, honey. Land of boxed wine and borrowed water.

Years ago, the train and bus station became home ground for my kid sister, Becky. I found her there once sprawled on a bench and listening to "Yellow Submarine" on her silver portable radio.

"Whatcha doing, kid?" I'd asked, though I could damned well see. Fourteen years old and smoking Newports.

"What do you think?" she asked, that tilt to her head trying to convince me she was cool.

"He's not coming back," I said. "For your sake I wish he would, but he won't."

"A lot you know," she said. "His dark glasses could come walking through that door any minute. So buzz off."

"Hey, hey. Calm the beast. I wish Daddy was here just as much as you do."

Poor kid. Why would he come back? Fruit and almond orchards and their roadside stands with cheap labor making somebody else rich hadn't kept me here either. Yet, for better or worse, here I was again.

The closed concession ended any hope of buying cigarettes. Forget coffee. I needed a cigarette in the worst way, but inside my straw bag my fingers groped my wallet and the makeup bag sitting heavy on top of my save-your-ass Snickers.

"Looking for one of these?"

The cowboy without his leather jacket. I'd already taken in the slow and easy stride above his lizard boots and the clichéd hand-tooled leather belt that said *Arthur* on the back. He shook the pack of Camels toward me and a couple of cigarettes leaned out. His hands were dry and wind tanned, clean but rough.

Any other time I'd have looked right past him. He was too much like Sonny, Husband Number Two. The innocent nod, a half-smile, the leather belt selling the Marlboro mystique. But I wanted that cigarette. "Thanks," I said. "Smoked my last in Bakersfield." I held the cigarette toward him for a light. "You're a lifesaver."

"Glad to help." He scratched a wooden match against a small box with *Red Fox Lounge* written across the top. When he held the match, he cupped his hands like he usually lit cigarettes against the wind.

He waited until he saw my cigarette was fully lit. After the first puff, I stood tall again, eye to eye with him.

"I saw you get on in Las Vegas," he said.

I took a slow drag. Something about him, maybe the hair on the back of his hands, or, like me, the fact that he looked like he'd seen more than his fair share of living, kept me from turning away. He lifted the match to his own cigarette and held it inside his palm. At least he wasn't one of those guys who pull their new Stetsons into a pose and pretend they aren't slumming from their accounting jobs.

"This doesn't look like home country for you," he said.

"Could be."

His lips were dry, and the longer I stood beside him, the more I thought about laced chaps and the saddle smell of worn leather. I nodded toward the closed concession windows behind us. "You wouldn't have an extra pack I can buy, would you?" I lifted a crisp Las Vegas ten from my wallet and held it toward him.

He pulled at the pearl snap on his blue and white gingham shirt pocket and shot me a smile. "You don't look like a Camels girl."

"You'd be surprised," I said.

He handed me a soft pack. His fingers were sandpaper rough when he pushed my ten away. "For a lady," he said.

I tucked the cigarettes and money back in my purse. "Thanks, mister."

He tipped his hat. "Ma'am," he said just before I backed away and turned to find the ladies.

Inside the station's restroom, fluorescent lights flickered against the ceiling. Add that to the Lysol that barely covered the smell of some gal's cheap hairspray. My back was sweaty and whenever I turned, I picked up the sour of someone else's drunken sleep on my arms.

Truth was, I needed a place to land, to start over. Except for Palm Springs, who wanted a fifty-year-old showgirl, a dancer? My big mistake was thinking men were an insurance policy. You'd have thought I learned my first lesson when Daddy left and Dotty ended up at Safeway wrapping meat just to keep us going. Add three husbands after that.

In the mirror, my white skin reflected gray in the fake light and, now, up close, you couldn't mistake the darker roots where my hair was growing. I had to pull myself together. Lorraine's message on the answering machine. "You'd better get your fancy ass back here. Between Dotty dying and Becky back in the can, I've about had it." Her voice broke on those last words. That's when I knew it was time. Dotty and breast cancer were one thing, Becky in jail another, but that crack in ever-strong Lorraine's voice signaled serious.

I straightened the shoulders of my dress. Yes, I looked like I'd spun off the merry-go-round, a middle-aged dancer caught in yesterday. Now, when I gazed into my gray-green eyes, the back of my hand following the beginning sag at the outer ridge of my jaw, I could still see that long-ago girl in her pink ballet shoes and first tutu. Naively, I thought the audience would never stop clapping and Las Vegas would always be mine, until that night Bunny, my manager, said, "You're done." I wet my fingers and tucked a blonde curl behind my ear. Settled the purse strap on my shoulder and turned toward the stairs, one last glance over my shoulder. If I learned anything from watching Bunny all those years, you keep going and you don't ever stop. Done doesn't mean over.

● ● ●

Back on the bus, I shoved my straw bag onto the seat beside me. Forget talking to anyone, especially after hours on a bus and family ahead of me. Dotty, always my biggest fan, would never know how tough it was last time I saw her in that brown recliner, the rooster clock still ticking in the kitchen, the same yellow Formica table. Like I'd never left, never lived beyond our Third Street house. Just the thought of her made me swallow hard to ease the knot in my throat.

"Mind if I sit?"

Before I could say, *Yes, I do mind*, the cowboy scooted his skinny butt into the seat next to me. I grabbed my purse and stuffed it between myself and the window. He looked past me toward the silos, one big smile and way too sure of himself. "Never been up 99," he said.

Sonny all over again. His hat hair and that boyish grin on a man's face that sets you up but eventually leads to disappointment. The skin under his eyes ridged into folds. With Sonny that meant too many late-night craps games.

"All these almond orchards?" the cowboy asked. His too-wide grin and straight teeth.

"They're walnuts."

The cowboy's skin was redder than I'd noticed when he lit my cigarette. Freckled on top of a natural flush, not too different from mine. He leaned across me toward the window. "Give me peaches and oranges, I can tell the difference."

Old Spice and cigarettes, a particular smell you never forget, lay heavy on his clothes. He gave me an observant eye. "I'd say you're more like a peach."

I glanced out the window. Even if someone had told me, I'd have never believed I'd end up on a Greyhound listening to lines pitched by a cowboy.

"You remind me of Natalie." He crossed his legs and the shank of his boot jutted into the aisle. "The way you carry yourself," he said. "Someone who likes nice things." He nodded at the wide silver bracelet on my wrist.

Except for a grizzled day-old beard and the lines around his mouth, I'd have sworn that it was Daddy sitting beside me. But Daddy wouldn't tolerate small talk or that Texas drawl. He warned me that guys from Texas always think they have something going on.

"Natalie, my daughter. That's who I meant," he said.

For a moment, something clouded his eyes. Maybe tears. I didn't want to ask.

"She would have liked this ride," he said.

"Yeah?"

It came out automatically before I could stop myself.

"Nuts about travelling. She liked road trips more than anything," he said. "Is that why you're on the bus?"

"Could be," I said. Road trips, who had time? All those years I was lucky the show went dark one night a week. If you were down for any reason, fifteen girls crowded the back door waiting to take your place.

"She had a VW camper bus. Travelled all over the country, even down into Mexico."

"Nice," I said.

He stopped, said nothing, just held his hands in his lap, a large agate ring on his right hand. Outside the window, the pink, fuchsia, and white oleander, now rampant, seemed too lush after the desert.

"She still doing that?" I asked.

He didn't answer for a minute. "No, not anymore."

I didn't miss the squeak in his voice. Figured I'd just hit a door he didn't want to open.

Now, peaches with their round globes hung inside the orchard's green trees. Why is it you go along minding your own business and bad things start to happen, the kind of things you always think happen to other people? Like Jessica, a dancer from Julian, Nebraska. Lost both brothers in a car accident and had to leave the show. Peter got AIDS and had to quit. Maybe what happened to this cowboy and his daughter. Bad stuff that happens to good people and makes you wonder what's fair and what isn't. Compound that with the fact that after a certain age, you start losing things. Then, one day you wake up and they aren't simply lost, they're gone.

The cowboy leaned into the aisle, those brown eyes again, the silvering hair and sideburns, a face as weathered as Nevada after a rainstorm. He didn't look at me directly but, rather, out the window toward the green and white freeway sign. Twenty-two miles to River's End. "Bet you work in Las Vegas," he said. "A dancer maybe? The big hat?" His hands lifted and gestured a fountain headdress.

"Was."

It was the first time I said *was*. The last word I imagined when Rita caught my headdress backstage. *Was*, now a hot burn behind my eyes. My hand reached automatically to cover my throat where the Carleton Curse climbed up my neck and onto my face. Whenever one of us, the Carleton women, became mad or upset or embarrassed, the Carleton Curse started as a flush at the base of our necks and spread up and into the scalp. When it came, it was just there, and never because you wanted it.

"With all the feathers?" he said.

"All the feathers."

"You must have been something."

Must have been. Outside the window, white sky hung over the Sierras along with a gray that comes with summer heat. More telephone poles. How can you tell someone, anyone, about landing in Las Vegas at seventeen, all-night lights and more skin than I'd ever seen. Lucky in a way, I started with a Clorox rag along the Tropicana's coffee-shop counter. What counted, though, was the afternoon I grabbed hold and climbed, one rung at a time, onto a silver ladder and into a disco cage, white fringe shaking off my boobs and tush, the clamor of slots below me and the shake, shake, shake they paid me for. Not on point and not New York, but I was dancing.

"You remind me of Max, my dog," he said. "He gets real quiet. Nose on his paws and all spread out."

"That's quite a compliment."

He leaned in front of me until I couldn't avoid his dark eyes or his thick, almost white hair. "I didn't mean to imply anything. You're just quiet. Thoughtful."

For a couple of minutes, I said nothing. Then, "Right now, you're here, I'm here," I said, not knowing where that came from.

"We're here," he said. "But this isn't home for either one of us."

My gray greens into his browns. "What is home?"

He looked down at his plumbing pipes and chain saw hands. "A Lakota man I once knew said that home is wherever you are in any given moment." He leaned in closer. His eyes were almost sad and his voice so low I could hardly hear him. "Actually, what he said was that the center of the universe is wherever you are standing."

Who was this guy, anyhow? And, what the heck did that mean? Outside the window, the green had disappeared and brown fields had taken over, giving way to a shopping mall with its Ross and J.C. Penney's. Further on, Costco. The bus crossed over the north- and southbound train tracks at Eleventh Street. We'd come in just past the afternoon freight from Bakersfield. In another hour the Sacramento would come through, if they ran on time. That's what Tom Carleton, my father, would say, train man that he was. Our whole life was planned around trains coming and going.

Folks around us reached for their backpacks and totes and held them close to their bodies. "Need to get my gear together," the cowboy said. "Nice talking to you, ma'am."

He stretched his legs into the aisle before he reached for the armrest and lifted himself out of his seat. For such a tall drink of water, he seemed agile and strong, the move too smooth for most guys his age.

I grabbed my purse from beside the window and unscrewed my lipstick. Peering into a small mirror, I drew the familiar outline on my mouth before pressing my lips together for the hundred thousandth time. Blush to my cheeks. I checked my teeth before running my pinkie across them.

Shoulders back, tummy tucked and neck high, I stood at the top of the metal stairs. Two deep breaths. The air smelled heavy with summer dust while, ahead of me, all twelve stories of the Red Lion kept its distance from the grain elevator. The elevator and loading docks at Dakota Avenue marked where the railroad tracks cut over past side yards waiting with empty boxcars. As strange blessings go, the stockyards had disappeared along with their awful smell of mortality.

River's End is no vacation spot, just a place where there's mountains to the east and west and a valley between stringing telephone lines together. An aqueduct heading to L.A. Most folks can't even tell you where it is, if they've heard of River's End at all. Like mothballs and damp basements, it reeks of the fifties the same way our Third Street house did. Trunks and boxes and shelves of canned peaches and dill pickles, everything old or homemade or hand-me-down. Once, harvests and trains and tomato trucks hauling their loads on Highway 99 tried to tell me this was where I belonged.

The cowboy, behind mirrored sunglasses with his Stetson shading his face, waited at the bottom of the stairs just long enough to tip his hat. "Ma'am," he said.

Chin high, I smiled my easy, generic smile. Another cowboy, someone I met on the bus, *Arthur* tooled into his leather belt. So what?

Then, like always when I get to town, I looked north along the tracks, past whatever storefronts had changed since the last time I was there, past the tall parking garage. My hand shaded the top of my round sunglasses, the afternoon sun blinding me. And there, beyond the smelly city buses and backpacks and big hair, at that place where L Street ends and Dakota Avenue takes over, the grain elevator stood at attention. Like a sentinel, its little red light on top wouldn't show red until the sun went down and the last light left the horizon. I had to laugh. If Lorraine was with me, she would have been the first to say, *center of the universe*. Just something we said when we were kids, like most kids say "home free."

A roller bag in each hand, I headed for the taxi stand out front while tires screeched along Ninth, the only downtown two-way street. Nothing had changed. Not the familiar bronze statue of the first pioneer that made this place home for people no longer here, or the train tracks that divided the town in two. Aqueducts and irrigation canals, smudge pots and harvest reminded me I was a long way from the Bellagio's blown glass and Fridays with Shirley at Caesars. I could have never imagined that twenty-five years in Capezios and fishnets would bring me back here.

Chapter Four

Lorraine

With effort, I pulled myself up from the kitchen table and moved toward the counter. It was close to *Wheel of Fortune* and tonic time. Five o'clock supper. I'd already torn the lettuce into the crockery bowl I'd bought for baking bread. That was before Dr. Strong laid down the law. Before Weight Watchers and counting points. If Sarah the Duchess of York could do it, so could I.

Outside my greenhouse window, the new houses across the field were already framed in and the roofs nailed on. When Mama and I came to Sunny Acres ten years ago, we thought we were moving to the country, to peace and quiet. Now, only a narrow and lonely fringe of field surrounded the mobile home park.

Becky. There was no way to save that girl, hard as I tried. A second DUI and now a suspended license. Yes, I paid the two thousand dollars. But that was the last straw. She wrecked Kenny's Camaro to earn her first DUI. I found her in the ER bleeding like a stuck pig. Head wounds do that. The whole mess ended up in the *River's End Journal*. For weeks, I could hardly meet the eyes of anyone I knew in Safeway, let alone at church, where everybody talks no matter how nice they smile at you. How I wish she'd gone to the work farm. Maybe she'd learn how to live the way the rest of us had to.

I rinsed the cutting board and tucked the rest of the lime into a plastic bag. Mama's squared-off bottle of Gordon's gin, the label blurred from freezing and thawing and marked by my finger and thumbprints, went back into the freezer. Something Mama saw on TV and now insisted that's where gin belonged.

Supper started and the dishes set out, my iced tea rested on the counter. It was the time of day when summer streams through the kitchen window. I tossed the salad even as the hot sun burned against my face. Like it or not, it was always me who got the calls no one wants to get and it was always an emergency. There were no men you could count on. Certainly not Kenny, Becky's so-called husband. It was just like him to take off to Billings. Some motorcycle derby gave him enough reason to leave her to me. Coward that he was, he might as well have dumped her on my front stoop between the red azaleas. More proof I'd never been able to figure out men.

Here I was, fifty-two years old. When did *I* get a break? The Lord knows I deserved one. Maybe a mission in Africa. China, even. At least a couple of weeks in Hawaii, though I knew Diego wouldn't let me go that long. Besides, who would take care of Mama and clean up Becky's messes?

The Carleton women, or the whole enchilada as Daddy used to call us, have been marked by men coming and going. You could say it started with him, Tom Carleton. An ordinary day, late spring, I was a junior in high school. Julie, a year behind me, was already wild. Becky was only a kid the day Daddy, lunch pail in hand, kissed us all goodbye and went off to the Southern Pacific roundhouse as usual. We should have known something was funny. He never left the house without his Dodgers baseball cap. Later that evening when the cap was still on the hook by the back door and he didn't show up for supper, Julie found his note on top of Mama's dresser. *Don't come looking for me*, signed *Tom*. That was all it said.

I gazed out past my rose garden toward the potting shed. Picnic table. With the field gone and new houses taking over, I'd have been depressed except for my plan and the Lord. He knew about problems and what to do with them. Like now. I grabbed on to the counter and closed my eyes just before I bowed my head. Lord, I need you to keep Becky sober. I was right in the middle of *Please, Lord, please* when, outside, a car pulled onto the paved pad below the window.

A car door opened and closed before high heels tapped across the pavement and what sounded like wheels backing out of the driveway. The car hadn't even turned around and headed out the main drive when the doorbell buzzed throughout the whole darned house. Only Mabel Peterson next door came without calling first. But Mabel didn't explain the car or the high heels.

Getting from the kitchen to the front door, I glanced into the living room and caught Mama pushing herself forward in her recliner. She waved the TV remote in the air. "Who is that?" she said. "We weren't expecting anyone, were we Lorraine?" Her voice followed me through the dining room where my new box-pleated drapes were still falling out, the wrinkles slowly disappearing. By the time I got to the front door, my heart was racing.

The late afternoon sun made it impossible to see through the door. It took a minute for the red spots to clear and for me to recognize the pair of Hollywood sunglasses staring down from atop a black dress only one person in the whole world would wear summer or winter. Red high heels.

"Miss Lorraine."

Julie lifted her hand and shoved the glasses up over her hair. The sun's halo behind her lit her blonde puff of hair into spun gold. Marilyn Monroe returned from the dead.

I opened the screen door. "You didn't tell me *when* you were coming."

"Nice welcome home, Lorraine." She reached down for a pretend hug.

As usual, we barely touched. But that's when I saw the gray half circles curved under her eyes and her skin faded to the white of my bedroom curtains when the sun is fully on them. With her hip jutted out and that pasted-on smile, Miss America had just arrived off national tour.

"I told you it would be soon," she said.

I stood there for a moment just taking Julie in. You'd have never thought this woman with heavy eyeliner was the same girl whose hair I fixed for her first Boy Scout dance, the same sister who went with me and Mama to buy Becky's school clothes at J.C. Penney's when Becky started fourth grade. The one I counted on to help me keep our family pasted together when Mama went into the Box and depression cancelled all hope for any future beyond sad.

There I was, already doing a slow burn. "Guess you'd better come in."

Send Miss America money for a plane ticket, Mama said. She's probably short on cash. Though we never talked about it, from past history we both knew money was the only way to get her here. And just look at her. The dress, the heels, those curls. Vegas oozed out of her. Boy, would Mama love that. Even as a kid, Julie would stand in front of Mama, hairbrush in Mama's hand while she brushed that blonde mane. A dreamy look would come into Mama's eyes just before she planted a kiss on Julie's forehead. No wonder Julie thought she was a princess.

Julie rushed past me and past her two enormous red

suitcases. The sick feeling in my stomach told me this was serious luggage and no weekend visit.

"Dotty," Julie shouted toward Mama. "Guess who just blew in from Las Vegas."

From the dining room, I watched Julie rock her hips into the living room, then stop in front of the recliner. It did my heart good to see Julie's shoulders cave and her arms hang down at her sides like her wings had just been shot off. In front of her, Mama's cheeks, sucked-in from chemo, might convince someone to ignore her now clouded blue eyes, but the wrinkled folds of her eyelids were so heavy and fallen it seemed Mama had become one of those dried apple dolls with a buzz cut of gray hair.

Mama lifted the remote where her too-skinny arms had gone flabby and were hanging out from below her yellow short-sleeved blouse. Still, the smile on Mama's face was one I hadn't seen in a long time.

I swallowed hard. Like always, the minute Miss America came home, her see-through black dress and big Mexican purse, Mama's eyes came awake. Mama finally found her voice, more croak than words since her last chemotherapy. "Lorraine, you said she'd never come."

"You know Julie," I said. "She's here and then she's gone."

Julie shot me a glance. But she didn't say anything. Probably just the shock of seeing Mama kept her mouth shut.

Julie reached her long, bare arms down around Mama's skinny shoulders while the two of them fawned over each other with *glad to see you* and *don't you look great*. The whole time I stood at the edge of the living room, my arms crossed and my insides a seething boil. Always the big shot, Julie could be counted on to give me a sinking feeling all the way down to my toes.

With her sunglasses still perched over her hair, Julie sashayed back to where I stood. "You didn't ask, but I'll have whatever you fixed Dotty," she said. "Except leave out the sugary stuff." She winked, like this was our private joke.

"Anything else you'd like, Your Highness?"

She kept that pasted-on smile going like her face would collapse if she didn't. "About six feet three, brown eyes," she said. "Not too bald and not too gray."

"Can't imagine you're asking *me* for that," I said. My hands on my hips were already balled into fists. "Must be hard times."

Julie glided past me toward the front door, but she never made a move to pick up her suitcases. Instead, she slid them across my new entryway tiles, probably scratching the finish. "You asked what I wanted," she said.

I stood there hoping she'd say something about how long she meant to stay. Mostly though, I didn't want to know. Julie and her conniving were worse once you knew what she was up to.

In the kitchen I took my time, the half lime rind up on the cutting board where my hand bore down hard on the knife just to steady my shaky fingers. The best thing that happened for all of us was Julie running off to Vegas. Not that I'd wish that on any decent girl, but decent never described my sister.

There was a time I thought I'd get out of River's End too, maybe Fairbanks with Buck. But not you, Lorraine, not Fairbanks, he'd said. "A gold camp is no place for a woman unless you hire on as the cook, and your tuna casseroles and spaghetti aren't real cooking, not for men. Besides, you'd never live in a shack," Buck told me. "Not the way you need nice things."

That was the day I gritted my teeth and said, this is it. River's End, Mama, and the mobile home, a real concession when all I ever wanted was a husband, a couple of kids, and an ice-maker fridge. Not big things, just ordinary, everyday things. A place where my kids would grow up and have more kids and I could bake Tollhouse cookies like grandmas do. But that wasn't happening, not in this lifetime.

Going through what I went through with Buck was bad enough. At least I wasn't sixteen and I never had to kill myself and my unborn baby, throwing myself in front of a train because of some man, like my best friend Rosemary Brewer did. The Lord knows I'd seen enough men slam the diner's screen door to last ten women. If it wasn't for Pastor Harmon, I'd have given up a long time ago.

I leaned into the lime and sliced down hard. The single shot of gin clouded the ice cubes just before I squeezed a lime wedge over the top. Satan and alcohol. Our whole family was plagued. Without me, we'd be a family of drunks. And if I'd learned anything in this family, you can't fight the devil by yourself. I poured tea over the ice in my glass. One teaspoon of sugar, then two, the way Buck always liked it.

In twenty years of waiting for that guy, not once did I hear him say, *I miss you*. More like, "See you come fall, Laney." His Boilermaker hat down to his black eyebrows, that grin I couldn't let go of, like his big arms and that voice soft in my ear whenever he said, "I think we're tired now, Laney. Time to go to bed."

I remember standing on the porch of his duplex that last time and waving, the yellow Land Rover disappearing around the bend, his arm out the window as reassurance that he was good for his word. The roses he left on the table, the note that said, *I'll be back*, was still tucked inside my jewelry box.

Mama's loud laugh nearly drowned the Round Table Pizza commercial in the living room. From the sounds of it, Julie was goading her on. Likely, with lies. Truth is, no one lives in Sin City and comes away unscarred.

Before I knew it, I'd tipped a fourth full teaspoon of sugar into my glass. What Weight Watchers didn't know wouldn't hurt them.

The fifth full teaspoon was in my hand, ready to go in the glass.

"Once on the lips, always on the hips," Julie said from behind me.

I didn't turn around. I didn't want to, especially when I could feel my neck getting red. Stay in charge, girl. Don't give in. I dropped the spoonful into the glass and gave it a good stir. I turned, my eyes on Julie's greens, steady as she goes, then gave her glass a shove across the kitchen counter. "Here's your poison," I said.

Julie sipped her drink, then wiped at her mouth. "Holy Christ," she said. "Put some gin in this thing." She pulled open my freezer door and yanked the gin bottle out by the neck.

"Not thirty minutes in the house and you're taking the Lord's name in vain," I said. I still held the knife in my hand and there I was, waving it at her face. "It's just like you to come here and get Mama all worked up. Then when she gets used to having you around, you're suddenly bored and out the door again."

Julie looked right past me and out the greenhouse window like I hadn't said a word. "Dotty tells me we're having a family picnic on Sunday," she said. "You never mentioned it when you called."

"There won't be any family picnic."

I don't think she heard me. She'd probably get satisfaction knowing Becky was on strict probation. As far as Julie was concerned, we were all an embarrassment, all of us sores on the face of Her Highness.

Julie took another sip of her drink. "This is more like it."

"Becky's not drinking anymore," I said. Not that I intended to say why.

Julie took a giant drink before she set her glass on the counter. "I don't care whether Becky's on the wagon or not," she said. "The only way *I'd* survive a family picnic is with a gin bottle in my hand."

She had to be the most selfish person I'd ever known. How dare she make light of our own sister. Someone we took care of. Held when she cried. Never mind the times we took her to Riverfront Park and told her to ask the cute boys if they caught any fish. Before I had a chance to say a word, let alone sip my tea, Julie pulled a pack of cigarettes out of that piece of gauze she called a dress. A silver lighter came out of the same pocket.

"There's no smoking in the house," I said. "Or have you forgotten that Mama has cancer?"

Julie never looked away from me. "I doubt cigarettes have anything to do with breast cancer." She just stood there while she put the flame to the end of her cigarette, before she smiled a half smile, a *gotcha* smile.

"Get that devil's stick out of here," I said. I reached toward the pack she'd laid on the counter but, just as quickly, she scooped it out of my reach.

Big as you please, she French-inhaled that cigarette, curling the smoke out of her mouth and into her nose. In one big puff, she blew the smoke toward my Comet-clean sink.

I fanned the air the best I could with my apron. "Didn't you hear me?"

I was *not* losing control, no matter what. I'd promised myself. Before Pastor Harmon and being saved, I'd have called her a pain in the ass right to her face. But I was a new, friendly Lorraine. A Lorraine who didn't swear.

Julie took another drag and blew it just past my face.

My hand went under the sink and around the can of Lemon Fresh. I aimed above her head, my finger on the button, and I sprayed in every direction.

"Get that shit out of my face," she screamed.

It did my heart good, like it always did, to see Julie get what she deserved. Even before our teens, she'd always had dance lessons, then figure skates—not Daddy's leftover hockey skates, like I had to settle for—the first to get a beauty-shop haircut, a manicure for her first dance competition. The one time Daddy came down hard on her, Mama softened the blow with "Now, Tom," and Julie wiggled out of what she deserved without so much as that angry tongue to the side of Daddy's mouth. She was Miss America long before I called her that.

From the living room, Mama shouted, "You girls at it already?"

Julie hiked her skirt up around her waist. Skirt tail in hand, she wiped at her eyes as if I'd aimed right at her. "Damn you," over and over through the skirt of her gauzy dress. Jezebel that she was, she hadn't even worn a slip, and those long, gorgeous legs stared back at me. Not a darned ripple anywhere.

"You could have blinded me," Julie said. "At least you can apologize."

I had to turn away. My blood pressure was sky-high while that woman had the audacity to think *I* should apologize. *When hell freezes over*, I wanted to say.

I turned around and crossed my arms. "This is my house and my kitchen, my rules, take it or leave it." My hands were shaking and I couldn't lift my tea. "Besides, caring means respect," I said. "Not something you'd know about."

Julie glared at me in a way I hadn't seen since high school when I caught her necking with Tony in the driveway, her blouse and bra off, brazen as could be. "Like you know all about respect," she said. She ground her cigarette out in my spotless sink, the sizzle enough to make me suck in my breath. "You need to get over yourself, Lorraine."

I took a step closer to her, my hands on my hips so she wouldn't see them shaking. "Ego and pride. That's what the Lord would say about you. You've never respected one damned thing that didn't have your name on it."

Right there, I'd lost it just the way I'd prayed I wouldn't. Damn Julie anyhow. I was fuming inside and guilty as sin.

She trained her drop-dead look on me and grabbed her drink, then sashayed right through the open kitchen door. The devil on parade.

Pastor Harmon said there are times when you have to say, *Get me through this, Lord,* and walk away. Easier said than done. Not even Becky could twist my tail the way Julie did. I should have hardened up after all those years at Diego's. But no, one little thing from Julie could set me off.

I slammed the refrigerator door. Of course she'd left the gin on the counter. She couldn't possibly turn around and put it back in the freezer. I should have never called her, just let her come back and find Mama dead. It would have served her right.

* * *

Mama waved her glass in the air. "Julie, honey," she said. "Come sit on the sofa so I can see you."

Mama had to push out her words like you'd shove a heavy box of groceries across the kitchen floor, her throat nearly closed off. Worse, her hearing came and went. She kept the TV too loud for conversation, not usually a problem for the two of us. But just when you didn't want her to hear something, she knew if a pin dropped.

"It's hot in here, Lorraine," Julie said. "Don't you have the air-conditioning on?" She smoothed the back of her dress and sat down. And wasn't it just like her to pull her skirt above her knees. You'd have thought she was Princess Diana ready for a *People Magazine* photo shoot. Later, she'd give me a lecture on varicose veins and why a girl should never cross her legs, saying *girl* like she'd never passed sixteen.

"Mama needs the heat," I said. "You can see she doesn't have any meat on her bones. Besides, I'd think River's End was an oasis after Vegas."

Julie's eyes remained narrow, seething and pointed at me. "I can't talk over *Wheel of Fortune,* Dotty."

True to form, she was only thinking of herself. I said nothing. Best to choose my battles and keep my blood pressure down.

Vanna White walked her slow exaggerated walk along the row of letters, their blank sides green behind her. She turned over three *e*'s to cheers and applause.

"Did you ever notice Vanna White never gets any older?" Mama said. She raised the remote in the direction of the TV and lowered the volume. "She just goes on pointing and smiling."

When Mama dropped the remote with a clatter on top of the metal TV tray, Julie jumped. "Maybe that's what women are expected to do," Julie said.

"Speak for yourself," I said.

Mama tilted her head back to see through her trifocals, first looking at me, then at Julie. She pointed her crooked index finger to just above my head on the wall behind me. "What do you think of the new Paris print?"

Whether Julie knew it or not, Mama was giving her the kind of test she usually saved for Becky. Because it was Julie, the whole thing made me smile.

Julie got up off the couch and stood in front of the framed print. She leaned close. "It reminds me of winter."

She had to say something. We all knew Mama.

"It's a rainy night," Mama said. "You can see it on the streets."

Julie stood on one foot, then the other, and leaned in closer to the print like she was supposed to see something she couldn't see. I have to admit, I loved watching her squirm, even if it was just for a minute.

"You like it, Dotty?"

"Of course I like it," Mama said.

"It's the kind of thing my husband, Dennis, would have liked," Julie said.

"We were talking about the print," Mama said. "Not some husband I never met."

Rule number one, don't cut Mama off. Number two, don't talk about somebody she doesn't know, especially Julie's husbands.

The Carleton Curse spread up Julie's neck and her lips tightened like she wanted to say something and couldn't. She waited a minute. "Was that something you picked out, Lorraine?"

"*I* did," Mama said. "It reminds me of Charles Boyer and Claudette Colbert."

Mama wasn't about to tell her the print was a Kmart special, old-fashioned buggy lanterns shining on rainy streets between French mansions, the Eiffel Tower in the right-hand corner. It was simply a bargain that filled the wall nicely. Whatever Mama thought about it, she was making up. I'd never heard her talk like this.

"I didn't know you liked Paris," Julie said.

"If you were around more, you'd know these things about me." Mama's fingers bent around the remote. Back into the air, the volume went up again.

I could see Julie getting steamed, her neck red, a sigh she didn't think I heard. Served her right. Julie needed to be put in her place and Mama was the one person to do it. I had a hard time keeping the smile off my face.

Julie stood and crossed to the side of the TV. She bent over and gazed at her photo on the TV console, her long arms hanging outside her flimsy sleeveless dress. Big hoop earrings and red high heels. What you'd expect out of Vegas. And wasn't it just like her to be mesmerized by a picture of herself.

Much as I hated to, I had to admit Julie was still so drop-dead gorgeous she could have been a stand-in for Olivia Newton-John in *Grease*; always full makeup, and her hair, tousled and casual-looking, had likely been arranged within an inch of its life, never mind she must spray the living daylights out of that mop with extra-fine hairspray. No Aqua Net for that girl. How she'd lived most of her fifty years in Las Vegas and still had to-die-for skin, I'd never know.

Julie smoothed her dress before she sat down again. "Dotty, I don't like the family picnic idea," she said.

Mama stared down at her thin wedding ring and fingered the curve of it, the design worn off for as long as I could remember. A full carat diamond engagement ring covered the plain band. The diamond, pear shaped, was the only jewelry she ever wore, most likely Daddy's way to impress his young wife. But she'd deserved it. She'd given up a bank career to marry him.

"The picnic was decided before you came," Mama said.

"It's only for supper anyhow," I said. I didn't want to spoil the show by admitting the picnic was already off because of Becky's probation.

Miss America threw her shoulders back and gave her head a little shake. Her big earrings brushed against her bare neck. "You know damned well Becky will never show up."

For once, she was right.

But this wasn't about her and it wasn't about Becky.

My conscience was clear. I called Julie right after Dr. Strong said the cancer couldn't be stopped. "It's important Mama sees you," I said. Julie didn't say anything at first, just breathed a big sigh into the telephone. She'd have to save a few bucks first, but she'd make it.

Mama, likely bored with the two of us, turned up the volume on *Antiques Roadshow*.

If you're like Mama and you've lived your whole life with disappointment and regret, not much matters outside of creature comforts. You could say the same about me. What's important in any given day is to have your coffee when you wake up. Your favorite TV shows. For her, a little gin in the late afternoon. Iced tea with extra sugar for me. Maybe the most excitement Mama knew was that day's guest on *Good Morning America*. Unless it was the soaps.

Julie gazed toward the dining room and the front door where she'd left her big red suitcases. "Tell me where I can park my things," she said.

"You can bunk with Mama in the other twin bed," I said.

Julie crossed her arms and hissed at me through her nearly closed teeth. "I don't think so! You damned well know that bed is too short for me." Her whisper spit on my arm and left spit dots on my white blouse.

I glanced down at my blouse, then up at Miss High and Mighty. My face froze the way it did in high school when I found out she'd borrowed one of my good Merino wool sweaters without asking.

Mama gazed over the top of her trifocals. "She can bunk in the big bed with you, Lorraine. It's longer."

My chin started to shake. First, Mama's glad-to-see-you smile. Now this. And after all Mama and I had been through together. The tough times, the things you never talk about except to each other. Never mind that I'd had my hands full taking Mama from her bed to the porta potty to the recliner. In fact, you'd have thought Mama was psychic. She'd been in bed two weeks straight until today, just before Julie showed up.

"This won't do," I said. "I'm the one who has to get up for work."

Mama's eyelids dropped to half-mast with her usual could-care-less look. "You'll work it out," she said to the TV. Nothing important had just happened as far as she was concerned.

"Have it your way," I said in Mama's direction. I'd get back at Julie, one way or another. Make her wish she'd only come for the weekend.

But that was the old Lorraine.

Family or no family, I got up off the couch without a glance at either one of them. Down the dark hallway to my bathroom, I locked the door. There, on the white rug in front of the bathtub, I got down on my knees. Closed my eyes.

Help me, Lord Jesus. You can see I'm trying.

The travel clock ticked on the shelf below the mirror while the toy poodles next door barked at the fence. I should have known it would be this way if Julie came back. Those big suitcases. She was moving in. *Shut up, Lorraine. Give the Lord a chance.*

Pastor Harmon's blue eyes came to mind. Blue eyes right to the bottom of my soul. His salt-and-pepper crew cut, the way he wet his lips when he talked to me. I'd have sworn his body was warm and praying beside me on the bathroom rug.

Pastor Harmon and being saved. My whole life changed the day I walked down the aisle of the First Covenant Church. Just as I am, the entire church alive with *Oh, Lamb of God, I come, I come.* Tears streamed down my face when I lowered myself to my knees and Pastor Harmon put his hands on my head, then on my shoulders. Big hands, warm hands that could heal the emptiness I'd felt for years.

After that, my whole world changed. Taking care of Mama became God's will. God's will spilled over to taking care of Becky. To those truckers who came into Diego's. Sure, they still got their coffee fresh and three eggs over-easy with a double side of sausage and hash browns. But *trust Jesus* is what I wanted them to get, not that I'd ever understand how you get to men.

Now, on the bathroom rug, I could almost feel Pastor Harmon's arm around my shoulders and his hand squeezing my arm. *Let Jesus carry this,* he said. *Let Jesus carry you.*

"Yes, Pastor Harmon," I said into the small room, the poodles now quiet. A sure sign.

My knees hurt where the bones poked through and my weight fell too heavy on them. Once up, I could see in the mirror that the red was leaving my face and neck. Still, the bags under my eyes had swelled to twice their normal size. I grabbed a fresh washcloth and ran it under cold water before I wiped the cloth against my cheeks and face and around my eyes.

If this is a test, Lord Jesus, I'm up to it.

Back in the hall, the Lord's face was in front of me and Pastor Harmon's hand rested on my shoulder. Toward the living room, past the dining room table and drapes, the plaques of young lovers on the wall, and straight ahead toward the Paris print. Pastor Harmon would remind me when to speak and when to hold my tongue.

In the living room, Mama and Julie turned toward me at the same time. You'd have thought I was Vanna White. I smiled at them the way Jesus would want. "Let's take you back to the bedroom," I said to Julie.

Julie's eyebrows arched like she didn't believe me. But she jumped up off the couch, and her heels clicked behind me on my ceramic tiles. I watched while she wrestled the larger of the two suitcases until she could pull up the roller handle. Then, against my will, I righted the other suitcase and pulled it toward the hall and straight back toward my bedroom.

"Slow down," Julie said. Behind me, her suitcase bumped against the walls. "It's dark in here."

Lamb of God who takes away the sins of the world. Pastor Harmon beside me. I'd have to repaint the walls, but I'd get through this.

I set her red suitcase under the window. When I pulled back the bedroom drapes to let in the late afternoon sun, light filtered through the sheers and onto the white duvet cover where my purple and sage-colored pillows lay perfectly arranged on the bed. I smoothed the duvet, taking in the pillows, my silk flowers, everything together the way they should be. *Blessings of the Lord*, Pastor Harmon would say.

Julie patted the bouquet of silk daffodils and irises I'd arranged on the corner table. "Martha Stewart in a double-wide," she said. A smile I didn't trust and that looking-down-your-nose tone in her voice.

I tried to imagine how I'd tell Pastor Harmon that I made room for her in my closet, gave her one of the bureau drawers.

Julie sat on the edge of the bed and bounced on the mattress. "Can't believe you still have this big bed," she said. "Thought it would have left with Buck years ago."

She'd hardly arrived, and we were in high school all over again. I couldn't help myself. Right into those gray-green eyes of hers, I gave her the disapproving look she deserved. "We all need to be grateful to have a place to lay our heads."

She nodded toward the wall. "I suppose you want me on that side."

"Actually, I'd prefer you were in Mama's room."

Julie grinned until I wanted to brain her. "You heard Dotty."

"You . . ." I started. I turned away to hide the heat on my face. Opening the closet door, I shoved empty hangers out of the way. I needed to remember who I was now. Maybe if she's here long enough, You'll find your way into her heart, Lord.

I gave her the bottom drawer.

Chapter Five

Becky

Outside my kitchen window, the kids next door, a girl of five and a boy about seven, colored at one of two picnic tables wedged between our two single-wides. Their faces were dirty and their clothes needed washing. Likely no one cared as long as they stayed out of their mom's hair. I knew how that felt. Didn't matter if I was in the creek hunting for frogs or playing Barbies with Julie on the side yard. As long as I didn't ask Mama for a damned thing, I was good.

I could barely move. I was so stiff and my hands shook so bad I couldn't hold onto a damned coffee cup. Had to grab the edge of the table, small as it was, just to get up from a chair. My trailer was a goddamn mess. What else was new. Three days of dishes stacked in the tiny sink, the curtain above splattered with spaghetti sauce or barbecue grease. That was Kenny's doing.

It was a good thing Daddy wasn't around. Not in a million years would I want him to see me like this, both of us wishing like hell that none of this had happened. "Count yourself lucky you just got a fine and treatment. Next time will cost you a long time on that plastic mattress," the judge said. Lorraine just stood there writing out the check to the bailiff, a damned *told you so* on her face.

There was no way I'd return Lorraine's calls, old bossy cow, nose in everybody's business. *Checking in*, she said on her phone message. Like she hadn't cheated me out of my part of the old lady's trailer. Well, she needed to get off my ass. I owed her nothing.

I jerked at the sound of heavy feet on the front porch steps. Kenny pulled back the screen door and his voice lunged at me just before his handlebar moustache and sad comb-over announced that he was home. "You still on your butt?" Boozer scooted past him and wagged his skinny black tail against my knee before he slobbered on my arm.

When I got up, my bare midriff showed my gut was even bigger after eight days of rat shit jail food. "Thought you'd never get here."

Kenny set the grocery bag on top of the table, right in my face. "Don't get pissy with me, lady," he growled. "You sit on your ass all day while I do it all."

"Yes, Lorraine," I said under my breath, not loud enough to start World War III, not with Kenny, not for the time being anyway. I was up shit creek; two DUIs and my driver's license suspended until they gave me a provisional . . . for treatment, straight there and home, they'd said. *That's what happens*, my geek lawyer told me.

I gave Kenny what he deserved, no smile and not as much as a glance his way. He wasn't the only one giving up something. Besides, if he hadn't skipped town for the Billings ride, I'd have never gone on a toot to begin with. Especially sorry now that I lost my new hat. Obviously, Kenny hadn't seen the bill yet.

"Unless you brought something in that sack for sand-wiches, we're down to week-old bread and peanut butter," I said.

Kenny lowered his head, his eyes right at me from just under his red eyebrows turning gray, the same as my hair. He looked at me that way whenever he was teasing or about to surprise me. "We're having grilled cheese and barbecue chips," he said. With that, he lifted a two-pound brick of cheddar from the sack and dropped it on the table alongside a loaf of white bread.

"Didn't go anywhere, did you?" he asked. He hacked at the cheese with his bone-handled hunting knife.

I threw up my hands, not that he'd notice. "Where the hell am I going to go? The mini-mart at the Tenth Avenue Bridge?"

Kenny stopped butchering hunks of cheese. "Good," he said. "There's nowhere you need to go."

I bit the inside of my lip. "Let's eat outside," I said. "I'll turn on the camp stove."

"Those damned kids are out there."

I headed for the door. "I'll deal with the kids."

Kenny was predictable, sarcasm and insults, but he stayed. Sure, I had to put up with his bullshit rallies and stay out of his way when he got loaded. But his staying was the thing. I can't stand being left.

At our picnic table, I pulled the cook stove out of the sun and into a patch of shade left by the overhead tarp. "Don't forget the margarine and mayo," I shouted in the direction of the screen door.

"I've only got two arms," Kenny said. He stepped out onto the porch, a sandwich on the palm of each hand, margarine spread thick on top and bottom and now on his hands. Too goddamned lazy to pull a plate out of the dish drainer, heaven forbid open the cupboard door.

If I matched his sarcasm, I'd pay for it later when the stars took over the sky and he was drunk or loaded on weed and started to grab at my titties wanting to make up. I wasn't in the mood. Hadn't been since I smashed up his Camaro and the first DUI. Now, every time he went for me, it felt like he was trying to get even. But if I know anything about guys, not being skin close fires them up. Kenny would never say so. God knows, I didn't want him to bring it up. We'd end up in a fight, me drunk and giving over inside a blackout haze.

I nearly forgot about the kids until I went for the mayonnaise. Both kids were so quiet and not six feet away, both of them with their heads down and not a peep, just coloring in their books. They sure could have used a bath. Probably something to eat. It wasn't right. Kids should never be that quiet.

"You guys had lunch?" I said.

"No, ma'am," the little girl said. Her stringy blonde hair hung around her neck. The little boy had dirt up and down his arms and a mean scrape on the elbow he'd propped on the table.

"Now, don't start, Becky," Kenny said.

I turned away from the kids. "They're hungry, for God's sake," I whispered.

"That's their mom's problem."

"You guys like peanut butter and grape jelly?" I asked.

A face and then a bush of hair that could have been a man or a woman came to the screen door of the trailer behind the kids, the body just a blob through the mesh. "Time to come in."

The kids stared back at me, their eyes warning me this wasn't good. Whoever was at the door, hopefully their mom, wasn't anybody I wanted to know, and whatever went on in there at night reminded me of being in jail next to that gal who sobbed until you wanted to strangle her.

I hated the look in those kids' eyes, hated how helpless it made me feel when they pulled their legs out from under the bench. Heads down, they wanted to go into that trailer like they wanted Chinese water torture. It was my fault.

"See, I told you," Kenny hissed in my direction. "Mind your own business."

What do you say to that? Nothing. Still, I knew how those kids felt. Damned if you do, damned if you don't. All I wanted to do was give them a little peanut butter and jelly for God's sake.

After lunch, we took our beater lawn chairs and walked with the two dogs down toward the vacant lot by the Tuolumne. Our Stella's routine, you could say. The smokes and lighter were mine to carry. Under his straw cowboy hat, Kenny led the way with a son of a bitch can of Budweiser. Damn that beer looked good. I could just taste it.

He gazed out across the river toward a snagged log stuck on the opposite side. "This is the life," he said. "A full belly, a couple of beers, and a good smoke." He grinned that big grin that made his handlebars go as wide as a longhorn steer.

"Easy for you to say." I nodded down at the weeds along the Tuolumne's bank. "You're not the one who's trapped here."

Kenny leaned right into my face, right in front of my sunglasses. "Get over it, girl," he said. "Maybe now you'll do it my way for a change." *Sure*, I wanted to say. *Like the way you finagled workmen's comp and sell weed on the side, or how you scored your blow for Billings. Sure, I should do it your way, asshole.*

Across the river, the afternoon sun hit the top of the oak trees and turned the leaves white. A couple of kids waded along the bank. They poked big sticks in the water, maybe looking for stuff that washed up on the shore like I used to do with Beano Giovanni and his little sister Sylvia. Whole afternoons we'd go into the shallows of the river. I'd have been killed if anyone told. Mama had always warned me about the bums who lived in the park. She was a fine one to talk. Never home to know the difference. Playing bridge when she wasn't working at Safeway.

The afternoon was so quiet you could hear birds high in the trees above and dragonflies buzzing close to the shore. I wondered what happened to the kids in the trailer, but Kenny was right; it was none of my business.

Kenny kept his eyes on the river. Once in a while, a secret smile came onto his face. Then his smile made a sudden turn to sour. "I'll never figure out how that old lady and sister of yours keep nosing into our lives. Damned broads."

I threw up my hands. "Damned broads who've saved our asses more than once."

Not like you'd have family come to the rescue, I wanted to say. But I wasn't about to say a word. Kenny's family, back in Nebraska somewhere, was what he liked to call *history*.

Kenny pulled down his cowboy hat to shade his eyes. Slouched in the chair, his beer belly hid his belt buckle. "We're fine just the way we are," he said. "Unless you're ashamed of us."

"A fine time to be saying that," I said.

Two days out of the cooler and I'd been fighting one big mad after another. Lorraine and Kenny, take your pick. If Kenny had any idea I'd stood to inherit anything, let alone signed it away, I'd have never heard the end of it. Now, staring at Kenny's gnarly hands with their broken knuckles, I wanted to say, *Just shut the fuck up for once*. But, hot as the seething burn that scorched my gut, I'd been down this road before, and I never knew when my big mouth would trigger Kenny's hand with that sawed-off finger.

Hell, it was the same old story. Make nice after the shit hits the fan, go along like nothing happened, until my being sober or him getting restless started the next tornado. Then, we'd go down and dirty and there'd be nothing left but the wreck of the wind. At least I wasn't drunk, and I could see it coming this time.

"You were the asshole who called Lorraine, said you couldn't pay the fine."

A storm gathered at the edges of Kenny's face. Red in the face and ready to blow, he grabbed a hold of that chair and then, you could have burned my ass, he looked across the river again like I hadn't just said *you were the asshole* and he didn't get red the way he did. Stared like we were sitting in some friggin' Holiday Inn or just stopped for a piss break outside of Green River, Wyoming.

"Lorraine's no friend of ours, that's all," he said.

I'd never seen him let go of something so fast, and it scared the shit out of me. What did he know that I didn't?

He leaned forward in his chair and put his hand on Boozer's black lab head—Boozer, the latest in a long line of strays Kenny picked up at the pound. Boozer and Johnnie Walker, the German shepherd, had stayed the longest.

"We're going for a walk," he said.

They took off down the grassy path, Kenny in his straw Stetson, Boozer lumbering along at his side. Just watching them walk away left me with an empty, disappointed feeling. Scared, really. I knew how to pick at him, to fight. But when he wouldn't fight with me, I started thinking he didn't give a damn anymore, like maybe he could get a piece of tail somewhere else without having to put up with my mouth.

Kenny is and isn't like Daddy. He doesn't have the same sweetness Daddy had. But he's put up with me for over thirty years, since before we got hitched in Las Vegas, through two treatments and more drunks than I can count. Now, two DUIs and jail. I've never kept a job and never paid attention to what's going on at home—our single-wide at Stella's Landing. The low-rent district, my sister Julie would call it. Bottom line, Kenny's been through just about everything you can throw at a man, and he's stayed.

Back inside the trailer, I put the cheese in a plastic bag and gave the crumbs a swipe onto the floor where the dogs would take care of them. At least I was home, jail a place I'd never counted on, a place I never wanted to see again.

Above my head, the Creeping Charlie was half-dead, probably weeks since it had a drink. The elephant plants along the floor grew so damned fast I couldn't keep up with them. Like the dogs. All of it was too much for a small trailer. Outside, the kids had come back out to the picnic table and were playing with a yellow Matchbox car. I hoped they'd finally eaten something. Goddamn people who had kids and didn't take care of them.

"Come here, Spanky," I said. The calico meowed near my feet and arched his back against my leg. Shit, you call one and all three cats show up. Maybe those kids next door would like one.

I bent down toward the under-the-counter fridge and found what was left of a half gallon of milk. I was just emptying it into the cats' bowl when I heard the little girl outside holler, then a clambering onto my porch. It had happened before. Voices squabbled, then shouted. By the time I got to the window, the old man who lived with those kids, raggedy-assed and long gray hair down his back, had stepped onto our porch and grabbed the little girl around the waist. The fat hag who never showed her face outside the trailer was on her front porch in leggings and what looked like a maternity top. She waved a baseball bat in the air. The little girl screamed and beat her fists on the guy's shoulders even while the boy, crying now, lost his grip on the old man's pants at the bottom of the steps. Meanwhile, the leggings hag swore a blue streak.

Johnnie Walker had come back without Kenny and was now through the broken screen in the front door and barking all the way down the stairs. Sure enough, Johnnie went after the guy's leg.

I was slow to see the guy held a gun he must have pulled out of his jeans. The minute he saw Johnnie go after his leg, he threw the little girl onto a pile of tires near their front porch. He raised the gun and took aim at Johnnie. By now, I was on the front porch, crazy as a witch. "Leave my damn dog alone," I shouted. "Johnnie, come back here."

The little girl disappeared around the side of the trailer, but the boy, hidden under the picnic table, was exposed as hell. The bitch, their mother or grandmother, whatever, stopped dead still on the front porch, that baseball bat momentarily at rest on the railing.

About that time, Kenny came around the corner, Boozer out ahead of him and on the attack for the gun guy from behind. Gray Hair didn't know whether he was coming or going. First, he waved the gun at Johnnie, then at Boozer. He didn't even see Kenny.

Kenny, smart guy that he is, started to call off the dogs, not loud like you might get somebody mad, but just loud enough, like you wanted things to stop being so nuts. "Johnnie, Boozer." Each time, Kenny's voice got low and controlled, like it gets when he's backed into a corner. "Boozer, Johnnie." The dogs backed away at the sound of Kenny's voice. Me, I was scared shitless. Someone or something was about to be shot.

"It's okay, man," Kenny said low-like, his hands facedown in the direction of the gun guy like he was trying to calm the situation. "My dogs ain't gonna hurt you."

"He was up on our porch," I shouted.

Gray Hair stepped back toward the pickup, but he never turned his back on Kenny. He sailed onto the passenger seat, then slid across and started the damned pickup. He aimed the gun through the window—not at Kenny, but at the two dogs. Then, like the guy had second thoughts, he pointed the gun at me.

I pissed my pants. Honest to God, right there on the porch, the hot pee ran down my legs. The giveaway smell a puddle on the porch and all eyes on me. Kenny stared at me like he was about to see me blown away. I started to bawl.

The guy grinned. The gun, the grin and, goddamn, I couldn't look away. That's how scared I was. He had the engine going before he dropped the damned gun onto the seat like he'd just made the biggest joke in the world. I have to hand it to Kenny. He stood still as a statue in a wax museum. Dead still. The dogs beside him. I didn't dare take my eyes off him.

The guy shoved that piece of shit truck into gear and lurched forward. He was going straight for Kenny. But Kenny's too smart for that crap. He and the dogs jerked aside just enough to let the bastard pass. Otherwise, he stood his ground, his hands on both dog collars. Just watching Kenny stand there with his dogs, in control and the cool that says *don't fuck with me*, his glance at me, not like he was mad or disappointed but like he was watching out for me. He stood still and watchful like that until the asshole made the turn to go out of the trailer park, but not before Kenny shoved his arm in the air and gave the guy the finger he deserved.

Chapter Six

Lorraine

F inally, a breather. Mama and I were just getting started with gin and tonic time and a *Wheel of Fortune* we'd taped the previous week that she wanted to watch again. Nothing unusual, my shift at Diego's ended at three, and I had the usual stop at Safeway. I was no sooner in the door when Miss America, dressed to the nines in a cut-too-low slinky red blouse and a gauzy black skirt, those red high heels, said she needed the car. Must have surprised the heck out of her when, smiling, I handed her the car keys without a fuss. She'd soon find out that I never bothered to get gas and the car was down to fumes.

Settled on the sofa with my iced tea, I picked up my needlepoint. Without a word, Mama raised the remote and shut off the volume even as Vanna White—a new dress for every show—started her usual sashay down the row of green-sided letters.

"I need to talk to you about something," Mama said. She gazed off in the direction of the closed dining-room drapes.

This had to be trouble. Mama dictated or pronounced, she never said she needed to talk. In the past she'd spend hours at the kitchen table smoking cigarettes and drinking coffee just before she made her announcement. Like after Daddy left, she stared endlessly at the rooster clock as though it was sending her telepathic messages. She only got up to empty her ashtray or pull a fresh pack of Winstons from the fridge and pour herself another cup of that awful burned-up coffee. When her bottom-line came years ago, I wasn't a guppy, gawking like Julie and Becky did. "As far as I'm concerned, your father is dead." That was that.

Mama set the remote down on the metal TV tray, carefully, not her usual toss along with the clatter that followed. She grabbed hold of her glass with both hands, necessary now that she was growing weaker each day. She lifted her drink to her lips, her eyes never leaving the drapes until she turned to speak to me. "I've been thinking about the mobile home."

Just the words *mobile home* tied, then double-tied, a knot in my stomach. I didn't say a word, couldn't trust myself. We'd never talked about the mobile home since I took back her notarized signature to Bill White, our attorney. *Divide the appreciation in the mobile home three ways. Until you move out.* Not to my liking, but I never said a word. *You get the furniture and what's inside,* Mama had said. Forget that this was my home and not some prize she planned to dole out equally in the end, unjustly in my opinion, giving equal parts to my two sisters who deserved no consideration. One way or another, I'd buy them out—Becky no longer in the running—even while my tips savings accumulated. That's what kept me going.

Her eyes, cloudy with cataracts, stayed on me now, steady as she goes. "I want to change the will."

I tried to swallow what felt like a hard-boiled egg stuck in my throat and unwilling to budge. "Change what? Everything was settled ten years ago."

"Things are different now. You know, the mess with Becky." She stopped. Didn't say anything for a moment. "Since Julie's come home, I've been thinking." She'd probably been rehearsing this speech during long hours in front of *Days of Our Lives.* My gut told me that I was in for an unexpected turn.

Her eyes went back to the drapes behind me. "I want you to take out an equity loan against the mobile home and give some money to Julie. Call it 'advance inheritance' or whatever you want, she needs our help."

"What the heck are you talking about?"

She raised her hand in my direction. "I'm not finished." She paused. "I want Becky off altogether. She deserves nothing."

My needlepoint fell to the floor. She had no idea Becky had already been paid off. That I was out two thousand dollars of my own hard-earned money. "What do you mean 'equity loan'? Even if we can get one on a mobile home."

"You're smart. You'll figure it out, Lorraine." She lifted her glass with both hands, her eyes back on the TV screen now. "Point is, she needs the money, and I want to help her. Better now than when I'm dead. Besides, you're still working. You can handle a small mortgage."

You're still working. You can handle the mortgage. I sat there fuming, my needlepoint useless, which was just about how I felt. A working machine, that's all I was good for. God darn it, the old Lorraine would have been on her feet and yelling, *Like hell, I will.* What the heck was Mama going to do? There was no way she could get up out of that old smelly chair of hers without my help.

Mama gazed down at her hands, the ringed hand over the top of the other, the veins on the backs of her hands like raised rivers running at odd angles. "You and Julie will be the only beneficiaries."

My hands sweated in a way they hadn't for a long time, and my chin quivered out of control. *Take it easy, girl,* I said

to myself. *Go slow with this. Remember, the Lord's your witness.*
I grabbed hold of my iced-tea glass to steady myself. I was
already orbiting outside my body, the panic rising like flood-
waters. To tell the truth, I hated Mama right then. Hated
every minute I'd dragged her to Dr. Strong or called in her
prescriptions. Each and every night I left my bed to shove
the bedpan under her behind. I was drowning, and she'd just
pushed my head under water.

Help me, Lord Jesus. Help me!

The Lord knows I'd scraped together everything I'd
saved just to get Becky out of jail. She was finished, done as
far as I was concerned. But increasing Julie's share meant I
was losing what ground I'd gained paying off Becky. That
was *not* in my plan. "Everything was settled years ago," I said.
"Julie will have her fair share when the time comes."

"But that's what I want to change," Mama said. "She
needs it now."

The heat in my face must have been a volcano because
that's what it felt like inside. "Julie hasn't done a darned thing
to deserve an advance. She can do what I've done. Get a job.
That simple. If anything, Julie owes *me!*"

"She needs our help," Mama said. "It would only be fair."

"Fair! What the heck is fair? To give Julie more? It's only
fair because you adore Julie."

I shouldn't have said that. But we all knew it was true,
everything unsaid over the years.

Even as her eyes searched the drapes and ceiling, my blood
pressure was at a boil. Mama knew I was right, and she was
smart to keep her mouth shut. I'd only gone off on her one
other time and that's when she decided, on her own, to stop her
blood pressure medication. Said she didn't need it anymore.
Never a thought about the fact she could stroke out any minute
and go into a coma, that I'd have to pick up the fallout.

"Yes, Becky's a handful," I said. "We all agree on that.

Your feelings about her are well-known to all of us, Mama. But what in God's green earth has Julie done to deserve special consideration? Has she made your toddies and your supper? Cleaned or shopped or kept you safe and well cared for? Has she held your hand when you got scared?"

Not a word from her. The volume back up as though we'd just taken a break so I could make her another toddy. Her eyes telescoped back on Pat Sajak and whoever that creep with the glasses was who had just spun for the jackpot.

Up off the couch, I grabbed the remote, then spun around and turned off the TV.

"What the hell do you think you're doing?" Mama said.

"Just what it looks like," I said. "We're going to have this out right here, right now."

"Sit down and act civilized," she said. "And give me back my remote."

"We are borrowing nothing." Back on the couch, I tried to calm myself by grabbing the needlepoint. "I've worked my ass off taking care of you, Jesus forgive me for saying that." A quick glance at the ceiling. "I've stayed on at Diego's and put up with that slob for ten years longer than I should have so we'd have a few nice things—the drapes and new tile entry, a new sofa, a bigger TV. Julie's been doing only what Julie wants to do since the day she was born, and now, because she's told you a couple of stories about her so-called glamorous life, you want to cut Becky out altogether and give Julie a bigger share. My answer is no! Absolutely, without a doubt or second thought, no! Unless you want Julie to take over and be your caretaker. Your power of attorney. Your nurse at midnight and first thing in the morning."

"No, I don't want Julie to take over," Mama said. She drained her glass and held it toward me for the second round.

I motioned in the air, pushing her glass away. She could darned well wait.

She pulled the glass back but she didn't put it on the TV tray, likely holding out for the possibility I'd change my mind. Her eyes glanced toward the TV, but her head was decidedly bowed. I'm sure she'd expected some reaction from me, just not as steamed as I was right then.

"Julie's a little down on her luck is all. Said she's been cocktailing the last few years since they let her go at Bally's—her age, that was the reason. Needs to get on her feet. Just thought we could help."

"So why the heck isn't she cocktailing here? Tell me that, Mama. She hasn't even *looked* for a job. She doesn't even try, and that's the part that frosts me."

"She's keeping me company," Mama said.

"Yes, she's got you watching those horrible makeovers. No wonder you have nightmares and wake up at all hours. Sometimes she fills your tonic, but let me remind you it's not Julie stooping over to clean the bathtub and toilet, to mop the kitchen floor. No, Julie's remained the honored guest since she arrived."

Mama didn't have a leg to stand on. She knew I was right. If Mama wanted to make a change, she'd have to pull herself up out of her chair and down the wheelchair ramp to the car. It wasn't going to happen.

She leaned back in her chair, her head floppy against the headrest. We sat like that for five, ten minutes, the rooster clock in the kitchen marking time and the only sound in the house.

Buck's face that last time appeared in front of me. The same pleading eyes I saw now, the long silence. Fifteen years I waited for him, before and after the abortion. "You know I can't marry you, Lorraine," he'd said from the plaid sofa he bought at a used-furniture store. He'd sat on the very edge when he shook his head. "You know how I am. Come spring I need to hit the road again."

The Carleton Curse invaded my neck. I didn't know whether to laugh or cry or scratch his eyes out. "After all this time, you finally came to this conclusion?" I'd said. "Where the hell do you think that leaves me?"

I remember shouting, "I've waited and waited like you asked me to. I've let go of ever having kids of my own while waiting on your sorry ass. Now, *you're not the marrying kind*. Like that excuses you from never growing up. Get the hell out of here. I never want to see your face in this town again. Go live in bloody Alaska for all I care."

That was the end of all I'd hoped for, dreamed about. He left me with Diego's and an apartment I couldn't afford. Then Mama talked about selling the Third Street house. "We'll buy a mobile home," she said. "Together."

Together. Ten years together. Her thousand dollars down and me paying the small monthly mortgage and rental space. Now, this.

You could have shot me dead on the spot when Mama finally turned toward me. Never, except right after Daddy left, had I seen tears gather in that woman's eyes. I had to look away. My hands were sweaty and that hard-boiled egg was back in my throat.

"Whatever you say," was all she said.

Don't ask me how, but I wasn't losing this argument, tears or no tears. Julie, her photo the dark angel on top of the TV console, wasn't going to win this one. I'd earned the right to have some things my way for a change. Besides, I had the Lord on my side. He knew. Pastor Harmon, my last prayer at night and first in the morning, knew as well. Unless Julie had put Mama up to this and was going to haul her off to the attorney herself, things would remain the same. Unless Mama had already made out a handwritten will. Damn that Julie.

Chapter Seven

Julie

On the second Wednesday of the month, Dotty's social security direct deposit was due in the bank. Lorraine insisted I go with her to Safeway to get what she called *supplies*. You'd have thought we only got off the farm once a month. If I hadn't needed butter lettuce and fresh fish, two items that never saw the inside of Lorraine's shopping cart, I'd have never gone.

In River's End you plan your day around the trains if you want to go downtown, especially at noon when the freight from Sacramento heads south loaded with rice or grain or whatever is growing at that time of year. Over fifty cars, a good ten-minute wait. I'd forgotten once, chewing the inside of my lip and drumming the steering wheel for what seemed like fifteen minutes. All it takes is once or twice and you learn. The same with the northbound six o'clock from Bakersfield. If you're meeting someone downtown for dinner, you make the date for seven o'clock. In other words, *after* the train.

But typical Lorraine, she couldn't gauge herself with the rest of the world and left the house in her rattletrap Escort at

five minutes to twelve. Lucky for her, the noon freight out of
Sacramento was late and just then heading toward the Dakota
Avenue crossing, coming toward us but a good five blocks
away, far enough that the crossing's safety arms hadn't yet
come down. You could predict the engine's timing. Lorraine
slowed unnecessarily and stopped. A string of cars honked
behind us, and I couldn't blame them. You didn't even need
to floor the gas to get across the tracks. But not Lorraine.
Hand on her seatbelt, she let the car idle as if we had all day.
Forget the honking cars or the fellow in the produce truck
raising his fist out the window. We were on Lorraine's time.

Trains and railroad tracks and sitting there with Lorraine,
our whole family history wound in and around these same
trains. Somehow, they seemed both necessary and dangerous. Before Daddy left, I'd lie alone in bed at night and try
to imagine that first step over the rail and onto the ties, then
standing there in the face of an oncoming train. I was barely
a teenager when a pregnant Rosemary Brewer, our former
babysitter, did just that.

I know she heard the train. We heard it every night, give
or take five minutes, coming from the south at suppertime
along the tracks behind our Third Street house. Seated at the
head of the table, Daddy would follow the second hand as
it made its arc around the circle of Grandpa Teddy's pocket
watch. "Right on time," he'd say. Or, "Later than it should
be. Damned Charley missed it again," which meant Charley
Rupp took too long out of Fresno.

Lying there in bed, I would imagine Rosemary's feet
crunching the gravel as she stood between the rails, maybe
five minutes, maybe not. The early dark. The waiting. She
would have been alone, except for the wind blowing during
that time of year when the trees are done with their leaves
and winter is right around the corner. She had to see the train
coming, the train and the engine's roar on a black November

night. It was already too late by the time the one-eyed engine picked up her plaid winter coat. The light's beam blinding her at the same time as the awful sound of the engine, then the whistle when the engineer saw her and yanked hard on that first, then second, then third blast, the shriek of brakes, steel on steel. She didn't move. Wouldn't. The whole time, the terrible hiss and screech and no way to stop. Rosemary and the engineer knew that. Hoped it wouldn't happen. The whistle, again and again, until everything inside Rosemary's body vibrated with the engine, the monster locomotive right at her. More screech and hiss and vibration just before the pitch black and a quiet she'd never remember.

I'd never asked, but I suspected that's why Lorraine wouldn't take a chance and cross in the face of an oncoming train. She was the one who took Rosemary's death the hardest. My best friend, she'd said over and over.

* * *

The Safeway parking lot sat right where our Third Street house used to be. The same road, the same sidewalks we'd walked to school. That day, midsummer, midday all those years later with Lorraine, the familiar sour of dairy cows seemed to come off the pavement along with the Central Valley heat.

There I was in my hibiscus-red sheath and red strappy high heels, all dressed up for Safeway. Lorraine, ahead of me, crossed the parking lot, her head bent over her grocery list in her old-lady denim skirt and white orthopedic sandals. The Nun, I once called her. There was no way you'd think we were sisters.

I overtook her in three paces and she had to hurry to keep up. She pointed to the rows of shopping carts. "Get one of those," she said.

That older-sister thing never dies, and Lorraine simply wasn't a battle worth fighting. I yanked a cart loose from the lineup. "Just so you know, I'm working on a plan," I said. Slipped my sunglasses up and over my forehead. "After Mama—you know, I'll be out of your hair before you know it."

The look on her face made me want to smile, just before she said, "Maybe in the meantime you'll have some luck finding Husband Number Four."

I shouldn't have been surprised, but an old sting shot through me just the same. "Not that you'd know anything about husbands," I said. Not nice, I know. Just one more sign I needed to find a job and get the hell out of Sunny Acres, the weekly savings withdrawals more painful every time I went to the bank.

The cart's metal wheels squealed against Safeway's tile floor. I usually made do with a small plastic handbasket. In fact, I couldn't remember the last time I wheeled a fill 'em up basket, having to dodge on-the-loose kids and old ladies who stood mid-aisle like they'd forgotten why they were there.

"I thought you were here to *help*," Lorraine said. Her lips, wrinkled like Dotty's, somehow matched the little cross earrings that dangled beside her cheeks. When she opened her purse, the color of old limes, all you saw was a tidy packet of Kleenex, her brown wallet, and a small Bible. Somehow, Lorraine had stalled out between Diego's diner and the convent.

She hooked her wire-rimmed glasses behind her ears and pushed them up on her pug nose, the chain hanging in wide loops around her face. She rummaged in that joke of a green purse and pulled out a once-silver lipstick case. Uncapping the tube, she twisted up the too-pink lipstick, its well-worn, decided point aimed at her thin lips. With the case's small mirror in front of her, she drew the bright pink on the small *o* of her mouth. Must be a special meat cutter she hoped to see.

As I followed her up and down the aisles, her rear end and too-long skirt revealed how Lorraine's backside had spread since I was last home. You'd think she'd have read a women's magazine now and then in her fifty-three years. I tried, as diplomatically as I could, to suggest tunic tops or a longitudinal stripe to camouflage those hips, but she never listened. Get pissed, yes. Listen, no.

Where we went wrong, I don't know. Both in our early teens when Daddy disappeared, we started going in different directions about the time I began high school. Boys, maybe that was it. She could hardly get a date, and there I was, seventeen and the Almond Blossom Festival Queen waving from the top of a white Cadillac's back seat while she sat huddled in a stocking cap and football blanket with Mama near a curb in lawn chairs. Even Becky, a twirler, was in the parade. Mama waved both hands in the air as we drove by them, but the look on Lorraine's face was one I'd never forget. Not the usual set to her jaw when she was secretly judging me. Something else, the downturn of her mouth, an unmistakable sadness that left her looking as old as Mama.

Add the thirty years I'd lived in Las Vegas, someplace on nearly everyone's map, where men knew the difference between Armani and Dockers, where sequins and long legs and perfect breasts were standard fare and putting on your makeup every day wasn't a question. Private jets and limousines were as common as folks from LA or Dallas or Tokyo looking for excitement, for glamour.

Our lives never regained the footing we enjoyed as girls who skipped rope and played hopscotch together, or made up musicals performed on our front porch. Whatever we lost, we'd never been able to find it again.

I pushed the cart down the aisle, Lorraine ahead of me, tossing in white bread and Campbell's soup, 980 mg of sodium in every serving. She showed me some cholesterol-lowering margarine. She probably thought I didn't see the Pepperidge Farm chocolate chip cookies or the Ben & Jerry's chocolate chunk ice cream.

Folks turned and stared at my dress and sandals. These were the moments I once loved most, the moments I lived for. One fellow in particular, his trousers and tasseled loafers, the kind who shave their heads to disguise baldness, likely a salesman for plumbing supplies, gave me the not-so-subtle up and down. *This* is what hot looks like, I would have once said. Today, I smiled at what I wanted to believe was a compliment.

Past Cap'n Crunch and Cheerios. Toilet paper. A couple of small boys played tag in the aisle. Potato chips, giant liters of sugar water. Lorraine took a sharp right toward frozen foods and stopped. The Carleton Curse came up and out of her white collar. Her chin trembled, the dead giveaway. She quickly folded her grocery list, but she was too distracted to put it in her purse. She began to fidget, not knowing what to do with the list in her hand.

A white-collared clergyman stood in front of frozen foods, a salt-and-pepper buzz cut with an extra clean line on his neck. He pulled the door aside and reached into the case. Lorraine lowered her glasses and let them drop from their chain against her chest. She faced the freezer case, her list hand stopped midair while she waited for him to turn.

Until now, I'd never seen the sun come through her eyes since the day Buck asked her out for the first time. The corners of her mouth lifted and she leaned, unaware, toward where this man stood. The Carleton Curse spread its full flush from the base of her neck up, and gave her color and life. She was as pretty as I'd ever seen her.

Now I understood her agitation and crankiness since my return. Because Lorraine wasn't someone who even liked men, just a woman who works around men every day, never seeing them.

This fellow was the kind of tall that makes you stare the same way people stared at me. At least six-four, he was slender enough, but his kind of handsome came with his height and a rounded, perfect U-shaped jaw. From the way Lorraine's chin quivered, this guy held an invisible silver chain that ran from his hand to Lorraine's neck.

He must be the source of all the Jesus stuff. Maybe God had nothing to do with it. "So, that's the Holy Father."

Lorraine wet her lips and pressed them together. "Pastor Harmon. A father with five kids and six hundred followers," she whispered to me. "And, here he is, grocery shopping."

He lifted a package out of the freezer case with the longest fingers I'd ever seen. He had no fat on his bones, yet his mouth, seen from the side, was full and pink. The missus must be someone you'd describe as nice, who stayed pregnant—five kids—I could just see her high-necked collar and loose-fitting skirt while she fixed the pastor his pork chops.

The tremble remained in Lorraine's chin when she stepped closer to the freezer case. At the same time the good pastor turned to lay his package in the cart, he saw her. "Sister Lorraine."

He Who Belongs To Jesus was one big smile and blue eyes the color of deep water, like Dennis, Husband Number Three. He bent down toward her, his Crater Lake blues coming at her like he was seeing her in the buff right there in Safeway. Whatever was between him and The Boss, it wasn't just down on your knees in prayer.

Lorraine's little cross earrings danced above her shoulders. "Julie's the one I told you about." Tough Lorraine, her chin shivered against her will and her eyes shined teary-bright. She had no idea she kept twisting her grocery list until it was about to come apart in shreds. *Lovebirds* was the only way to describe what I saw in front of me.

Pastor Harmon nodded toward me in a polite way, like he would tip his hat if he had one. The intensity with which he'd studied Lorraine disappeared and he became guarded behind a new formality. "Sister Julie," he said, "I've been hoping you'd come home."

When I reached out to shake his hand, my bracelets jangled like wind chimes. For such a big hand and long skinny fingers, his grip was sweaty and made me want to let go. "Will we be seeing you at Bible study tonight?" he said.

I flipped my hair over my shoulder. "Probably not."

Lorraine's extra-wide smile just moments before became strained, her lips pulled tight at the same time she attempted the called-for pleasantries. "Julie will stay with Mama," she said. "She's failing again, and I don't want to leave her alone."

My mouth must have gaped. Three weeks of twenty-four-hour days in Lorraine's Clorox-clean kitchen and her bedroom with its fake flowers, the living room where *Days of Our Lives* turned into *Jeopardy*. There was nothing for me to do except, much as I loved her, watch TV with Dotty and tell her stories about Las Vegas. Now, would I babysit Dotty while Lorraine went to Bible study?

"Sorry, I have other plans," I said.

She turned away, refusing to hear me, just like in high school when she'd promise to take me shopping in Sacramento but planned it for Saturday mornings when she knew I taught ballet class.

Still, I had to be happy for her. As far as I knew, there'd been no one in Lorraine's life since Buck—the pregnancy at seventeen and the abortion in Oakland should have been the end of him. But Lorraine could never let go of anything, whether it was shoes she'd outgrown, a dated skirt, or Buck Walters. She waited fifteen years for him to marry her—if you call watching TV and getting him another beer a relationship. They didn't dare live together, not in River's End, not Lorraine. Dotty told me that one day when Buck knew she was working, he left a dozen red roses with baby's breath at Diego's before he drove off to Alaska. Afterward, she should have joined the Poor Clares convent.

I pushed the cart ahead of me, away from Lorraine, her all-too-proper preacher and their supermarket tryst. I strolled past the seafood case with fresh halibut steaks, the white filets nearly lost in a bed of crushed ice. Pink shrimp clumped together, their black veins showing through. Then larger, gray-shelled prawns. I'd never figure out why Lorraine bought frozen when there was good fresh to be had. It seemed any pleasure life presented to her had to be denied. How sad.

A sudden ache brought back Fridays with Shirley at Caesar's. Oysters on the half shell. Cocktail dresses and chandelier earrings. Moët & Chandon. "So, who is that guy you're dating?" Shirley once asked. "The guy with the silver Porsche."

"If he lasts two dates, I'll tell you," I'd said. We both laughed.

Dating wasn't easy with two shows a night involving five costume changes. The lights blinded me so intensely that I couldn't see who was in the front row. But Chuck or Ralph or Connor could see me. That's usually how it happened. A backstage note to the tall topless blonde, second from the left end.

Shirley and I would dish about Bunny and the new younger girls she'd hired. Shirley's daughter, my namesake, was ten now, probably had a brush in her hand, trying to deal with the same blonde mane I'd started with. For old time's sake, I bought a half pound of prawns.

I turned down the liquor aisle. As Dotty and Becky well knew, alcohol was the only reprieve while living under Lorraine's dictates of *let us pray* and *we don't smoke here*. I pushed the cart past wine labels called Smoking Loon and Cherry Hill. Places like Sand Springs, Raven Ridge. Shed Horn. I was mid-aisle when I saw the Charles Krug Merlot on the top shelf, but even with an extra three inches in my heels, I wasn't tall enough. I considered stepping up on a shelf when a man stepped in front of me.

"Let me help," he said. I thought I recognized the small white lettering on the back of his cobalt-blue T-shirt but, without my glasses, it was impossible to see.

He turned to hand me the bottle. Only in that moment did I see *Dukakis Construction* in two-inch white letters on the front of his T-shirt. He grinned. "Julie."

Just seeing him standing there, it was no surprise I escaped with him in his red '66 Chevy before caps and gowns the last June of high school, the clutch popping as we rolled down the hill that predawn morning, my eyes on the side mirror where I spotted Dotty stooping to retrieve the morning paper from the front porch.

"I'll be damned," I said. Tony Dukakis, gray but still lean, that lovely lower lip and a single dimple in his right cheek I'd know anywhere.

He held the bottle toward me and laughed with those black Greek eyes, the nails of his squared-off fingers lined with Sheetrock dust. "This is what you wanted?"

I reached for the bottle and, for just a second, the back of his extra-large hand with its rough skin rubbed against my hand. Even with construction dust and a Band-Aid on his palm, these were the hands I craved at fourteen. In that moment we could have been at the Tuolumne River or necking in Riverdale Park. All the bad boys I ever loved started with Tony Dukakis.

His eyes were on my face, my hair. Thank God for the dress, my red strappy heels. A flush of heat warmed my neck and shoulders. It had been a long time since I'd wanted a man with the old wanting I felt right then.

"Kind of fancy for the grocery store, aren't you?" he said.

One breath, a second. My hand went to my throat where the Carleton Curse worked its way up my neck and into my face. "You know me, Tony," I said. "It's always showtime."

The Sand Crane Motel in Las Vegas, just months after being named the Almond Blossom Festival's queen. "We'll have three days in a real motel," I'd told him. With Tony, the promise of sex, Jim Beam, and 7Up in the room, before and after and in between, kept him focused before we left the motel room for Denny's or the nickel slots. Until I stabbed my index finger with a safety pin the night I ran out on him. My new yellow spaghetti-strap dress, the suitcases packed, maybe a crack of light from the bathroom door. Except for my shit, I'd have been out of there before he woke.

We had to pull our carts out of the way to let a woman and her young son around us. We were just close enough in that single moment, I caught a whiff of Mennen above the tobacco smell on his clothes and on his skin. His sideburns seemed whiter. His eyes were on my face, and there was no mistaking his jaw kept working like he had to hold on to himself or who knows what would happen. I glanced down at his cart. A giant package of T-bone steaks and a six pack of Bud Light, Dr. Scholl's corn pads, and Preparation H. Pampers lay beside a couple of rubber nipples wrapped in plastic and a case of what must have been baby formula.

"Tony Dukakis, the new father?" I joked, trying to recover my stage smile.

"Grandfather."

I'm sure my mouth fell open. Yes, I noticed the small Buddha belly that lapped over Tony's belt. But nothing compared to the gerbil cage in my stomach.

His face relaxed with that one word. "It's great, actually." He pointed to the nipples. "They're for my daughter Julianne's son, Anthony. We call him Little Tony."

"You've been *domesticated*, Tony," I said.

"It's called love, Julie." The river lines deepened around his mouth. "Something you wouldn't know about."

My mouth went hot. This was the sucker punch he wanted to land all those years ago.

I couldn't look away from the kiss shape of his mouth. His hands on his forearms and those big arms you never forget. *Fuck you*, I wanted to say. Instead, I started to pull my cart to go around him, even while the dark centers of his eyes reminded me of the trees near Riverdale Park. The back seat of his Chevy.

"You look terrific," he said. "I'll give you that."

I squared my shoulders and stepped back, pulled the cart away, my bracelets jangling against metal. Forget him. I was around him and past, headed for Lorraine, wherever she was.

Chapter Eight

Lorraine

I was late. Alma had been working both the four booths and the counter. The minute I grabbed my apron off the hook and glanced toward the kitchen, Diego was up to his pits with three frying pans going and José Luis acting as prep cook today. "Glad you could make it," Diego said, a snarl in his curved lip, his mustache recently trimmed. That was a first.

"Got a shit load at home," I said, the words out of my mouth before I realized what I'd said. Cursing. That's what Julie's being in the house had done to me. Her skinny butt waltzing around in red high heels. I pitied the next guy she snaked with her lasso. By the time he woke up, she'd be gone and he'd be pulling himself out of the hurricane's wreckage.

"I'll take the counter, Alma," I said. We both knew the biggest tips came from the booths.

She stopped, her hands loaded with breakfast plates, and she looked at me, her hairnet covering one ear and her eyebrow pencil having missed the mark on her left eyebrow. "Sure?" she asked. We both knew that my giving up the booths was the only apology she'd get out of me.

"Sure," I said. I grabbed the Clorox rag and started wiping up the end spot where someone had spilled coffee, the back of his cowboy hat the only thing I saw except for the ring of sweat that had made its way through the rim. "Hot out there," I said to no one in particular.

"Got another catsup back there?" Randy, a regular, asked. He held the other bottle upside down and kept squeezing, though he'd made his point.

"Give that to me," I said. Doggone Alma. Part of her job was to make sure all condiments were filled at the end of the dinner shift if she was working last night. Which she was.

A fresh catsup on the counter and a nod at Randy, which was all he deserved. He came in here every morning, his golf cap covering his bald head, and he took up a counter stool for a minimum of two hours, jawing like he owned the place. Wanted his coffee cup filled and refilled until the cows come home. I wiped around him and lifted the salt and pepper in front of him, hoping he'd get the hint.

"When's Goldilocks coming in?" Diego shouted from the kitchen.

"When do you think?" I shouted back. "We don't have enough butter lettuce to satisfy Her Highness."

"I'll buy a case if she'll pull back that screen door and take over where Randy's sitting just so I can look at her while I cook."

"Fat chance," I said. "You'll never get Randy off the stool."

I quickly turned and gave Randy a big grin like Randy wasn't the butt of our joke.

"Who's Goldilocks?" he asked Diego.

"Laney's showgirl sister. You should see her, Randy. Unbelievable. If we had her working the counter, we'd have a line out the door half a mile long."

"Maybe she could take over for me," I said. "Then I could parade around in high heels and fancy skirts."

Diego whistled. "I'd sure love to see that, Miss Lorraine. Might get me to run away from home."

"Don't hold your breath."

"Damn, now I want to see her, whoever the dish is," Randy said.

I lifted his empty plate and removed his coffee cup. "Good luck with that, Randy. We don't quite fit her standards."

"I'll do whatever it takes." He rubbed the two-day growth on his chin. "Could stand a little lift in my life."

I bet you could, boring as your life must be, but I said nothing. Just wiped the counter in front of where he still sat. Then checked the chalkboard. Chicken-fried steak, meatloaf, and pork chops. Nothing erased yet. That was a good sign. Even if we got a rush at lunch, there should be plenty for the supper crowd, lighter and mostly local.

"Marie called in sick," Diego said, loud enough for the few remaining customers to hear. "You'll have to stay through supper."

"Can't," I said. I didn't dare look at him. He'd put some guilt trip on me, the two of us having to go out the back door to wrangle it out.

"Alma's got kids," he said.

Sweet as I could, I turned toward him. "I've got Mama. You know that."

Rather than shouting like he usually did. "Why don't you send Gorgeous in. Will lift our spirits, like Randy said, and make supper go faster."

"Hell, I'd have to stay," Randy said.

You can all go straight to hell, I wanted to say. But of course Lorraine, who found Jesus at the First Covenant Church, would never say those words. Sweet as I could, I pasted on the smile Julie taught me. "Wish I could help out, Diego, but you know what I live with."

"Somebody has to work supper," he roared, his good mood gone as quickly as my smile.

"Maybe it's time you train José Luis. For emergencies, of course. Besides, I'll be here until five to get things rolling," I said.

"Alma," he said. "Can you come back at five for two hours? I'll pay double time."

Double time. All of it into the fund. That son of a gun.

"Sure, Robbie can sit with the kids for two hours," Alma said. "Not a minute past seven though, okay?"

"Are you sorry now, Sweet Lorraine?" Diego rubbed his fingers together. "Double time and maybe a bonus."

"And would you be the bonus?" I asked.

He dropped his glance. We'd played this game for so long that our lines were scripted. But today I wanted to give him the finger so badly, I could hardly stand it. I had to duck my head under the counter and count to ten, something Pastor called an intervention. "Jesus, help me," I whispered out of earshot. "I don't know how much more I can take."

◆　◆　◆

Julie pranced behind me into the kitchen. "Poor Dotty, it's sad that her life has come down to soaps and talk shows." She pulled out a chrome chair, then scraped another across my newly waxed linoleum just to elevate her feet.

I kept my head down and ran the head of broccoli under cool water. "Yes, it's sad," I said. "I think they call it *life*."

Ever since Julie arrived, all Mama talked about was Julie this and Julie that. More than ever, things seemed odd between me and Mama, and the bile of seeing Mama's changed attitude kept seeping up from my stomach.

"What happened to the Dotty we knew when we were girls?" Julie fluffed her skirt and pulled it to just above her knees. "Remember when we spent hours paging through photo albums? Dotty, always poised and standing tall in her suits and smart shoes, dressed to the nines outside the First National. Her bank advancements. Even when she ended up at Safeway, she could still laugh and joke with us."

I stayed focused on the broccoli. "Mama's sick, Julie. You can see that. Even when she stays up late with you, she's asleep most of the time. Add all the pills she takes and you never know who you're going to get from one minute to the next."

Julie crossed her legs on the opposite chair. "Guess I hoped she'd be full of fun, that she'd be laughing at least some of the time."

I closed my eyes and waited a moment. "That was before cancer, or have you forgotten?"

"You're right, getting sentimental isn't a place I usually go." She stared past my head and out the greenhouse window. "We were talking the other night about you taking me to J.C. Penney's to buy my first bra. Remember that?" She looked down at her hands, following the length of her fingers with the opposite hand. "I remember how proud I was. Finally, I was a woman."

I reached for my best knife, meant to separate the broccoli florets. "If Mama could have, she would have taken you."

Neither of us said a word. Like our silence, the truth took up another chair at the table. Who wanted to remember hurried dinners of fish sticks and oven-fried potatoes, nobody saying a word at the table for fear of riling Mama after an eight-hour shift on her feet.

I kept my head down, my eyes following the knife. It was hard to admit that the woman sitting at my kitchen table once doubled as my sidekick. To recall those days when the two of us were old enough to mother baby Becky, to babysit our little sister on Saturday nights when Mama and Daddy, arm in arm, left for dinner and dancing at the VFW Club.

After Daddy left, Mama disappeared into the Box—what we called their bedroom—and told me later he'd probably run off with someone else. After Mama said that, I made it known to Becky and Julie that they should never mention

Daddy's name again. Since then, Mama and I remained close until she started this changing-the-will business.

"You have no idea what it's like to come home and find Dotty all shrunken up and crabbing about things she never gave a second thought to before. She's not only sick, she's *old*, Lorraine. That's the worst of it."

Little did Miss America know that when she came a month ago, Mama snapped out of her old depression and what I thought was her final decline. These days, she practically slept in the recliner just to be in Julie's company. Never mind I'd been running my feet off the last ten years for her and the only thanks I got was, "Is dinner ready, Lorraine?" But with Miss America in the house, the air-conditioning went back on, forget the expense, and Mama kept the TV volume down on *Good Morning America*. The Princess was still asleep. Now, this past week, Mama could barely get up before *General Hospital* in the afternoon at one o'clock. Until Julie spouted off today, I thought nobody else noticed she was headed back downhill.

"When you don't get things the way you want them, you just pray harder," I said.

Julie studied my hands. "You'll have to do all the praying," she said. "It's not in my repertoire."

She kicked off her new red flats, exposing her ugly bunions and the crooked toes she probably meant to hide. At least she had a flaw or two. I hated to admit it, but I was glad when I saw them. Still, I couldn't get past those red painted toenails, a sure sign she was ready to reel in some man. What else was new? Even in River's End, she flounced around in her flimsy skirt and peasant blouse way too low, off the shoulders.

I rinsed the broccoli and set it on a towel. It was the small comforts that counted. The steady *tick-ticking* of Mama's red-tailed rooster clock over the stove. Today's afternoon sun for one thing. Even the way it fell directly onto Miss America's legs where she sat filing her fingernails. Just like Buck, despite the obvious, she was full of big dreams, all talk and no show—except for her dancing. I had to give her that.

"What are you making? Broccoli casserole?" Julie said. "You know cheese will kill you, Lorraine."

I lifted my knife in the air and looked at where she'd now hiked her wide turquoise skirt halfway up her long thighs, all dressed up for an outing, a late afternoon movie or some other reason to borrow my car. Her legs were completely exposed and there wasn't a vein to be seen. What deal with the devil had that girl made?

"I wasn't fixing this with you in mind," I said.

There I was, doing my best to get supper started when Miss America inched up behind me and started to pull her precious butter lettuce and organic whatnot out of the fridge. Then she elbowed her way to hog the sink.

"Can't you wait? I'm fixing supper here," I said.

Her separate salad with her premium organic vegetables, a measured tablespoon of imported olive oil and balsamic vinegar. Her broiled halibut. Always, her special this, special that. Like she was scolding me without saying a word. Now, those raised eyebrows at my broccoli-cheese.

"For Pete's sake, I need to wash a few things, Lorraine."

I moved my cutting board farther down the counter. "If you're going to cook tonight, I'd appreciate you cleaning up after yourself," I said. A nice, even voice. Not nasty or mean like the old Lorraine, who would have chased Julie down over a messy pan in the sink.

"I swear, Lorraine, you're getting as crabby as Dotty."

Dumbfounded, I had to swallow the bitter taste that crept up from my stomach. Balancing the broccoli head on the cutting board, I took the butcher knife and brought it down hard and clean through the thick stem. My neck tightened every time I thought about Julie owning half the mobile home.

Julie stood there, probably ready to tell me a better way to chop broccoli. Under her gaze, I chopped faster, almost forgetting what I was doing. Had to be nerves. Pissed wasn't something a good Christian woman was allowed to feel, let alone admit.

She yanked open the fridge and grabbed her specially corked French lemonade. When she pulled an ice tray out of the freezer, she cracked the cubes and then dropped most of them into the sink. "Damn it," she said. "I can't believe you don't have an automatic icemaker."

Knife in hand, I flinched like I always did when she cursed or accused me. "You're complaining about *my* refrigerator? Where there isn't a lick of room for *my* salad? After you've taken *my* car and left the gas tank empty? Ooh, let's not skimp on *your* five-dollar bottle of French lemonade."

"My, my, what's twisting your tail today?" She reached into the cupboard over my head for one of my best ruby glasses. To say she towered over me even in bare feet like Daddy once did is an understatement. But I was the one with the butcher knife.

She stood beside me and sipped her drink, calm as you please. At least she had the good sense not to get too close. Still, she was in my way.

With the cheese grater in one hand, I pressed the cheddar hard against the ragged steel grate. "If you're going to stay, which it looks like you are, I hope you plan on getting a job and contributing a few dollars to this household," I said. "Maybe then Mama won't annoy you the way she does."

Julie said nothing, a whole other world inside her silence. She eased along the counter and back down at the kitchen table where, again, she propped both feet on the other chair. Like always, she only heard me when it suited her.

I sliced along the red length of a salad pepper until I had finger-length strips. Then, three strips at a time and evenly matched, I minced the lengths into squares. "I'll tell you what's twisting my tail," I said. "Mama's on her last legs and Becky, our sister—whether you like it or not—has just survived a jail cell. All you do is complain about ice trays."

She looked at me for the longest time. "If Becky was in jail, she landed there all by herself."

"I expected you'd say something like that." I lifted my head and bore my eyes right into her. "Truth is, there's a world around you, Julie. With other people in it. Imagine."

Say what she liked, I'd never give up on Becky. One of my first prayers in the morning and my last prayer each day, after Pastor Harmon and Mama. Becky could depend on the fact I'd never stop reaching out. A phone call just to check in. One day I actually took a Bible to her trailer. She wouldn't let me near her. I don't know when I've felt so helpless. She remained proof that this family was on a downhill slide, working its way one more inch toward hell every day.

Miss High and Mighty lifted her glass of precious lemonade. "If you think she's going to stay sober, you're crazy, Lorraine." She hesitated for a few seconds. "I suppose both DUIs made the newspaper."

I shook my head in disbelief, automatically picking up the red onion and propping it on its side. "Aren't you something?" I said. "To you, sisters are as disposable as the cotton pads you use to remove your eye makeup every night."

Julie glanced at me with those gray-green eyes and that perfect mouth. "My, my, how you exaggerate." She tipped her glass back in a long swallow.

I kept my head down. "The fine was two thousand dollars."

She leaned toward me. "What the hell did she do?"

My voice dropped lower. "Assaulted a police officer."

Julie's head went back and the laugh that came out of her mouth was a cross between a scream and a hoot. She couldn't stop. My neck and face felt hot with sudden heat, and I had that old sinking feeling inside. It wasn't just the shame of Becky's charge, but more, Julie was laughing at us, her family, in the same way she'd laughed at the Ringling Brothers' clowns in the center ring when we were kids.

She'd just proved we were all lost souls.

I lifted the knife and brought it down hard against the onion. Off with the ends and outer husk. "Becky said all she did was drive to the diner from The Portals. She doesn't remember the police."

Julie pulled herself straighter in the chair, those eyes pointed right at me. "You didn't pay the fine."

The solid bulk of the butcher knife's handle came down and down again. Another and another slice of onion until I was close to the end. My eyes blurred until I had a hard time seeing what the knife was doing.

"Took out a personal loan," I lied. My nose was running.

"Against the mobile home?" Julie said. "Without my say-so? Dotty's?"

The butcher knife bit hard through the last of the onion. "Becky's had the least chance of any of us," I said. I could still see her small, skinny body as she waded in the Tuolumne River while Julie and I flirted with boys. Becky was always the pest we had to drag along while Mama worked. Now, Miss High and Mighty, without my say so.

The TV got louder in the living room, then just as quickly, it went silent. "Where's my dinner, Lorraine?" Mama shouted.

"In a minute, Mama."

Julie's eyebrows shot up. "Does Dotty know?"

"Not really," I said. "The mobile home is collateral."

"You hocked our trailer?" Julie said.

Heaped on the cutting board in three separate piles was a mess of red pepper and red onion and broccoli. I picked up the knife, to do what, I don't know. The Lord had already cataloged my lie. "We're talking about our sister," I said.

"*You* were talking about our sister."

My blurry eyes leaked tears I couldn't stop even while the knife's handle lay solid in my hand.

"Lorraine, I'm talking to you," Mama shouted.

The knuckles of my hand turned white where I held onto the butcher knife. It was one thing to deal with Mama after I told her about Becky and the latest arrest, now Miss America was nothing but grief.

"Finish your toddy!" I yelled.

Julie glanced over her shoulder in the direction of the living room. "Let's look at this realistically," she said. "Becky's only going to do it again. That's what she does."

Her tone, almost soothing, caught me off guard. This might look like a peace talk, but I knew Julie better than that. "Let me tell you something, Miss Fancy Pants," I said. "I'd hock this entire mobile home outright if I thought it would help someone in my family."

Julie must have bit down on a piece of ice by the way her jaw tightened. "Over my dead body," she said. "It's not yours to hock. It's Dotty's. It's all of ours, really."

Who was this woman the Lord set down in my life? "That means Becky, too."

She snorted. Mercifully, she kept her mouth shut.

I rested my hands on the cutting board and took a deep breath.

"Lorraine?" Mama shouted again.

"I'm coming, I'm coming." But I didn't move. Couldn't.

Courage, Lord. Hold my tongue. The gall that Mama recently insisted on dividing the mobile home two ways had taken up residence as a heavy, dull space in my stomach. I didn't need to make matters worse by letting the latest cat out of the bag.

Julie dropped her feet to the floor and leaned into the table in order to get up. She was halfway to standing when I put the knife down.

Her face was stern, those perfect eyebrows scrunched. "I can't forgive you for hocking the only asset we have."

That did it. Eyes teary from the onions and my mouth half-open, I picked up the pulpy mound of onion and broccoli and my arm was in the air before I knew it happened. A fistful of red onion flew straight at Miss America, her flouncy skirt and French lemonade and her hair-sprayed curls.

Julie stood there and stared down at the green and purple mess that streaked her white blouse and ran down her turquoise skirt. Before she could say a word, I let go of the red pepper, my arm in the air and my aim right at her. It was the best feeling I'd had all week.

Onion and broccoli and red pepper goop fell off Julie's blonde hair and onto the floor and onto her bare feet. She started to say something just before I picked up the scraps left on the cutting board and heaved them. Like a dummy, she glanced from the front of her blouse and skirt to where I stood, not six feet away.

"You've lost it, Lorraine. Just like Becky." She lifted one hand and then the other and began to wipe at the mess in her pretty curls and on her forehead. She pushed her hair back from her face and threw her hand at the floor like she couldn't stand to feel the wet and near-slimy vegetables on her fingers.

Mama shouted from the living room, her voice peevish. "What's going on in there, girls?"

My chest heaved. One voice inside me laughed its fool head off. *Finally, she got what she deserved!* But another voice chastised: *She's your sister. What were you thinking?*

Julie's mouth finally closed, but her lips went tight the way they do when she's thinking about how to get even. Chin down, her eyes stayed on mine.

I reached behind me for the dish towel. When I felt it in my hand, I took a couple of steps toward her and extended the towel.

Julie's glance moved between the towel in my hand and where the knife lay on the counter, like she couldn't predict what might come next, and she was afraid to turn her back on me. She gave her hair one last shake as pepper and onion and broccoli fell down her arms and dropped from her skirt. She edged toward the back door.

Jesus help me, I loved it. I couldn't help myself. I started to laugh. Just the sight of Miss America under siege made my day. But in the same moment, I realized what I'd just done, nothing a Christian woman would ever do. It was crazy. Crazy, like Becky, and now like me. What was happening to all of us? Was there nothing to hold us together except this mobile home?

Mama's voice again, softer, gravelly. "What's going on in the kitchen, Lorraine?"

Julie backed into the screen door and pushed with her butt. She was gone out the back door just like that, the front of her skirt, her blouse, her hair a sight she could have never imagined. The screen door closed on its hinge, the last sound I heard before she disappeared.

I stood over the mess. Red juice and green all over my white counter, all over my waxed floor, and it ran down the opposite wall. But the sight of the vegetable goop covering Julie's new red flats made me laugh again. Julie may have had all the luck from day one, but today was my day.

"Lorraine!" Mama shouted. "I need my supper!"

"Coming, Mama."

Chapter Nine

Becky

K enny stamped out his cigarette butt on Lorraine's front stoop. There we were, waiting for Lorraine to open the door. I held my cherry Jell-O with fruit cocktail close to my chest along with that dried onion and sour cream dip I made just to show them I could. No empty hands or store-bought crap this time.

Kenny smoothed his comb-over. He'd bellyached all the way from Stella's Landing. "Sundays are for beer and TV, not playing nice to some old bitch who hates my guts."

"Knock it off, Kenny," I said, "It's only for an hour. I just need to prove I can do it."

He gave me the once-over. "An hour. Can't deal with it any longer."

He had no complaints. He had his half rack of beer under his arm. The only way I could get him to come. We'd been down the same road with my family too many times and, today, he needed to give me an A for effort. I rang the door-bell again and leaned on the buzzer longer than I should have. Knowing Lorraine, she was up to her elbows in potato salad.

To tell the truth, I was too scared to come alone. It would be the first time I'd walked into the old lady's house sober since I ran away with Kenny at sixteen. Never mind I'd been up half the night watching *Perry Mason* reruns just to get my mind off this picnic. Fussed for a whole hour with my hair, finally pulling it back into a ponytail. I was a wreck. The dye that was supposed to be Red Seduction turned into an orange mess. What did I expect, Kenny was half-drunk when he dyed my hair. Then there was Candi, my new treatment-ordered sponsor's words running like ticker tape in my head. *Families are as dangerous as bars*, she said. But, Becky being who Becky is, I was determined to get through this picnic or die trying.

When the door finally opened, the old lady's voice came through the screen door even before I saw the blue of Lorraine's eyes. "Can't you hear the damned doorbell?" She was likely in the living room on her throne. With my luck, I'd hear that voice long after she was dead—which, from the sound of it, might come sooner than I expected. Lorraine kept saying she was failing fast, some bullshit about this being her last summer. Lorraine was always over the top when it came to family.

Lorraine tugged at her blouse when she opened the door. Her face was bloated as hell, and she was fatter than ever— or maybe I just hadn't noticed. Never mind I was a little porked-out myself, though with my good legs, I could still wear cut-offs. I could have been a showgirl too if I'd wanted to. *All tits and legs*, Kenny always said about me. My being thick in the middle never stopped him.

Lorraine grabbed me by the shoulders and kissed my cheek hard. "Praise the Lord, you're okay," she said. She held me away from her, staring at my boobs. When I looked down, I saw the jellyfish blob of a melted Hershey's bar on the right tit of my tank top. Sugar, you know. Anyone who'd been to an AA meeting or two can tell you, off the sauce, into the sugar. Sugar and caffeine and nicotine were all those AAs cared about.

When push came to shove, I wanted to believe Lorraine was on my side. Except for those seven days and eight nights in jail and signing the papers she shoved under my nose so I could get out of that hellhole. The last time I saw her, or I should say she saw me, was at that damned jail. Since then, it had been *Jesus this* and *Jesus that* and *let us pray* until she riled me so much I told her to get the hell out of my face.

"Hi," she said to Kenny. "You can bring that stuff inside." Like he was the grocery boy for Christ's sake. Still, unlike my dear sisters, I had a man and one who stayed.

When Kenny pushed past her, she raised her arm to take the Jell-O and the back of her hand clipped his mustache. He'd spent a good hour waxing that thing to get the ends to curl like a cat's tail. Once red like his hair, his mustache was nearly gray now that he was pushing fifty. Besides his Harley and me, his long mustache was his man-pride. Because of Lorraine, it now bristled and curled, crooked as hell. He banged the Buds on the counter and tore the carton open.

"Mama will be glad to see you," Lorraine said.

Horseshit. I knew it and she knew it. I was the brat she and Daddy spit out when they were trying to keep things going between them. It didn't work. Things went south after he left and the old lady always blamed me for his leaving. Imagine, I was a kid. No wonder I ran off with Kenny after I turned sixteen.

Lorraine put my Jell-O mold down beside her green crockery. There should be a law against people who wipe their counters as often as she did. I was afraid to even walk on her damned floor, let alone leave a dish in the sink. And I didn't want to be around when she found Kenny's cigarette butt on the front porch.

"Where's the movie star?" I asked.

Lorraine glanced at me, matter-of-fact, like she could care less. But I didn't believe it. Not for a minute. Any time of the day or night, she'd know where Julie was, what she was doing, how much it cost.

"In the bathroom primping," she said. "Where else?"

Kenny had just hoisted his beers off the counter, about to put them in the fridge when Lorraine got in front of him and grabbed the carton. "I'll do that," she said. She stuffed the beer cans onto the bottom shelf. "What have you been up to?" she asked Kenny. Like she gave a shit.

"Guarding the White House," Kenny said. He pulled his Marlboros out of his T-shirt pocket and started to reach for the BIC lighter in his jeans. I grabbed his hand and gave him that *don't you dare* look. Lorraine would throw a shit-fit twelve miles long if he lit up in her kitchen.

Lorraine was bent over, pushing around the catsup and mayonnaise and what looked like potato salad in the fridge. I didn't miss the Whitman's Sampler toward the back on the second shelf.

"Thought I told you Kenny was riding in Montana," I said. Might as well practice my social skills like they taught us in treatment.

"One day you're going to break your neck," Lorraine said. She was talking from inside the fridge. "How many years have you been doing those motorcycle derbies?"

Kenny's finger was on the pop top. "Rally," he said. "But nice of you to care." He snapped open his Bud. When he cracked the beer, spray flew up in the air and all over the kitchen. Most of it landed on Lorraine's neck and back. "Oops," Kenny said. He stepped back, trying to hide his grin, and he nearly bumped into me.

Lorraine turned around as slow as you can turn. She came up out of her crouch in the same slow motion. I'd have given five bucks just to let go of the laugh dying to break out of me. But not with that Holy Hannah look in her eye.

Kenny sucked off the top of his beer. His crooked mustache

was coated with foam, and his mouth was puffed out with that first big swallow. Damn, that beer looked good. I'd have given anything for just one fat gulp to quiet my nerves.

I grabbed the towel that was looped through one of the cupboard handles and handed it to Lorraine. She wiped at her hair and the back of her neck without taking her eyes off Kenny. You don't fuck with Mother Nature.

Still, Kenny could drink his half rack while I had to do it straight. Jail and now outpatient. Crossroads said I wasn't serious enough for the Big House. Only the day program and AA until I got thirty days away from jail. That's probably why Candi said I couldn't handle coming to the old lady's so soon. Hell, I was ready to jump out of my skin. Staying sober might not be worth it except that going to jail again was worse.

I stuffed one plastic bag inside the other. "How long has Her Highness been hanging out this time?"

The last time I saw Julie was fifteen years ago when Kenny and I spent five hundred bucks to go to Vegas and finally get hitched. We saw her show, tits out and nothing to the imagination. She skipped out afterward with her fancy boyfriend and his slicked-back hair, just so she didn't have to party with us. Bought the champagne and got the room comped, but that was as far as she'd go. Like we were riffraff and she wasn't my best friend, the one who organized our Pollyanna games and let me follow her around at the playground when we got older.

Kenny's grin didn't hide his black lower front teeth, what happens when you chew too much Big Red. But he'd never hear that from me.

"Can hardly wait to see Tits Up," he said.

I reached out and smacked his bare arm, the sound so loud it startled me. But it was Lorraine's loud guffaws, despite covering her mouth that surprised me most. Kenny had caught her off guard and once he saw Lorraine laugh like that, he let loose with his deep bass holler. Lorraine laughing her fool head off made my day until she looked over my shoulder, past me and Kenny, and right in the middle of laugh-until-you-cry, you-know-who had come into the kitchen behind us.

I shouldn't have been surprised. Julie always had a way of looking younger than me. I hated like hell to admit that, even to myself. Makeup, heavy liner around her eyes below perfectly arched eyebrows, blonde curls still wet from the shower hanging down on her shoulders. A full red skirt. Big tits in a lacy peasant blouse.

"I thought I heard my name," she said.

"Hey, girl," Kenny said. "How the hell are you?" He grabbed Julie in a big hug, tattooed arms around her waist and his head nearly buried in her tits due to him being all of five-seven.

His Harley-grease hands were all over Tits Up, something prissy Lorraine would never let near her. Not Julie. She'd stoop any way to Sunday to be fawned over by a man. For me, my heart was pounding so loud I felt the flush behind my freckles. Right then, I could have used a straight up, vodka double.

Kenny held on to Julie's shoulders, a shit-eating grin on his face. "God, are you a sight," he said. Coming from Kenny, that's the best it gets.

"Hi, sis," Julie said. She slithered out of Kenny's hands and took a step toward me, her arms out in front to hug me.

I backed away. "So, you're in River's End," I said. "Slumming with the poor folks."

She tried to smile, but her lips tightened with the strain of it. Those gray-green eyes showed disappointment, like I was supposed to bow down to the queen or some damned thing. I'd missed my cue.

Kenny, beer in hand, opened the back door. He lit his cigarette right there in the kitchen.

"Don't you want to go in and say hello to her first?" I nodded toward the living room where we could hear a Tide commercial. I was already doing a slow burn with him and we'd barely landed.

He grinned. "I'll take my chances out back."

I lifted the sour cream dip out of the sack. "Asshole," I said to Kenny's back. Julie stood in the doorway, a stupid grin on her face. This was probably the best show River's End had to offer. I could have slapped her.

Lorraine took the dip and bent down, her wide ass facing me in front of the fridge.

There was that awful feeling again, the worst part of getting sober, like my bones could break just from the weight of standing. That and the nakedness. Like my skin had been stripped off and I was standing there, a goddamned skeleton with my bones going every which way. If someone even blew on me, I'd hear myself splinter into a broken heap on the floor.

I peered into the fridge over Lorraine's shoulder. "You only got diet Coke?"

"I thought you'd bring your own sodas," Lorraine said.

All I could see was the butter dish and cottage cheese, Kenny's Bud. "Brought Squirt, but I feel like a Coke," I said. "Something with caffeine and sugar. How about those chocolates you've stashed in the back?"

"Why don't you say hello to Mama," Lorraine said. "I'll fix you some nice iced tea."

Saving the Whitman's for herself, the bitch. "I guess," I said.

"I'll go with you," Julie said.

Under my breath, "Isn't it bad enough having one big sister?"

The half smile on Julie's face reminded me of the snake. Curled in the air, his yellow length with the black stripe down his back. I must have been five or six when Roger Kline chased me, the snake's jaw pried open between Roger's fingers. I ran as fast as I could, but it seemed as though I wasn't moving. I can still hear Roger's breath coming down heavy behind me and his feet slapping the dirt path.

Julie had been ahead of me with her girlfriends. She turned around and, just like that, she grabbed Roger's arm where he held the snake. Without a twitch, she yanked that snake out of his hands and turned it back on him. She chased Roger all the way into the creek and, with one strong arm, she threw the snake into the air. Before you knew it, that snake was wrapped around Roger's neck. Talk about a howl worth hearing. Afterward, Julie bent down and hugged me. "You don't ever have to be afraid," she'd said.

Now she nodded in the direction of the living room. "Dotty's still in shock that I showed up. You, she's expecting."

Julie had called the old lady Dotty since I could remember, high school anyhow. Somehow, she got away with it. Me, I didn't call her anything. She was my mother, yes. But it seemed there was no love lost between us. I looked too much like Daddy. My red hair. The freckles. I had his brown eyes too. Julie walked in front of me, her long skirt lifting above the strappy sandals, all six feet plus another couple of inches if you counted her red high heels. Forever onstage. But at least Julie and I had some life in us.

The old lady was mumbling to herself, the remote in her right hand where it grew out of her crooked fingers. I'd swear it had been planted there.

Julie stepped aside and when she did, I stood there feeling naked as hell.

"We're all here, Dotty," Julie said. "All of your girls."

"I'll be damned," the old woman said, her eyes narrow. "When did they let you out?"

I'd known that look since Daddy left. After that, anything soft or warm in that woman went straight to hell. How can you hold something like that against a kid?

"Dotty?" Julie said, probably the only one who could get away with scolding the old lady.

"Just being honest," the old woman said.

She lifted the remote and the volume went dead. "You know what I mean," she said. "How was jail?"

"I'm in treatment," I said.

"Treatment," she said. "Is that what they call it nowadays?" Her plastic remote clattered against the metal TV tray. "You know you can die getting sober?" she said to Julie. "I heard it on TV."

Just being in the same room with someone, even if she's your mother, who hates you that much and you're trying to talk to her, trying to reach into the dark tunnel of what might have been, it makes your mouth go drier than dry. The urge, right then, for the easy burn of a vodka slider, the only thing to make it go away.

You can divorce your family, Candi liked to say. A hell of a lot she knew.

"It's not every day you get *all* your girls to keep you company," Julie said.

The old lady kept staring at the TV even though it had gone dark. "Did that man come with you?"

"Out back," I said. "Having a beer and a smoke. His name is Kenny and we've been married fifteen years." I couldn't remember the last man she liked. Maybe Buck, Lorraine's old boyfriend. Though, like Daddy, he was smart enough to get the hell out of town too.

"Probably better he stays out there," the old lady said.

Out back was where I wanted to be. Look at this place. The living room was nothing but brown furniture and beige walls. Lorraine's fake flowers—autumn all year long—on her perfect dining room table where we never sat. The whole place was like a bowl of oatmeal. Just like Lorraine. No swearing here and gospel with your gravy.

The old lady stared past me toward Julie, like I wasn't even there. She raised her glass toward Julie. "Happy day when you came back," she said.

Hell. What was I? Week-old fish? Anyway, it was plain Julie didn't come to see the old lady. It was something else, probably waiting for the will. She always had an angle, even while she sat there with that angelic smile, her eyes all shiny. Probably high on something. Downers most likely. I could have used a few myself.

Julie looked over at me from inside her trance, a half smile on her face like Danny, my Lahaina man, when he's in the bag. She smoothed her skirt and leaned over to look at one of her legs. "It's good to be back," she said.

That's the way they always talked. Nicey-nice. What I wouldn't give for a little honest talk in this family. No wonder I never came home sober.

The old lady raised her glass and pointed it toward me. "So, what the hell did you do to your hair?"

I pulled at the orange mess. Nice of Julie not to mention it. "It's the latest style, don't you like it?"

"Maybe you should give up dying your hair," she said. "Nothing wrong with natural."

Not like she'd say that to Julie. "So, what's happening with you?" I said. It was an old trick I learned in bars to get free drinks. People love to yak about themselves.

She leaned forward in her recliner, her eyes on me. Her hands grabbed at the arms of the chair, fingers bent into their crooked shapes. She still wore her narrow wedding ring with the full carat diamond beside it, the diamond I'd always wanted and would get, even if I had to wrestle it from her. "What you see is what I do," she said. "I sit. I wait for Laney to bring breakfast, lunch, and dinner. To take me to the john and wipe my ass. Now, aren't you glad you asked?"

"Thought you liked to shop at Ross," I said.

"Those days are over. Even the soaps bore me to tears," she said. "Getting so old I can't remember what's happening from one episode to the next."

In the mirror above the TV, folds and wrinkles covered her neck. I tried to imagine an arm, hers, around me inside a baby blanket. Those hands with all their ugly veins feeding me, changing me. She had to care once, sometime. Now, antsy, I scooted toward the edge of the sofa so I could get up with the least motion.

"Where are you going now?" the old lady said.

My hands were under my butt, ready for liftoff. "Need to make a phone call," I said.

"You just got here," the old woman said. She pointed the remote at me. "Who the hell do you need to call?"

"I need to pee," I said. "Is this a test?"

"First it's the phone, now it's to pee," she said. "Make up your mind."

I didn't wait and I didn't look back once I was on my feet. I knew that down the hallway, in the bathroom near Lorraine's bedroom, I'd found some Vicodin once. Not where I was headed now, much as I wanted to. The phone next to Lorraine's bed. That's what I needed.

I punched in the numbers. The phone rang and rang. Candi, pick up. Pick up, for God's sake.

On the eleventh ring a man's voice said, "Howdy." By the time Candi came to the phone, from the garden she said, my snot and slobber were all over the phone.

"I can't do it," I said.

"Becky, is that you, hon?"

Only grunts came out of my mouth. "Hold on," I said.

At first, I couldn't see the damned tissues; the place was such a mess. My God, Julie'd left a cyclone trail all over Lorraine's bedroom. A red satin nightgown and those feathery streetwalker slippers plus a big suitcase hogged the floor under the window. Looked more like a move-in than a visit. Holy Hannah must be going nuts.

On top of Lorraine's dresser, the only neat place in the room, sat a box of Kleenex.

In the mirror, I looked like something from a horror film. Mascara ran in twin rivers down my cheeks. My hair had come undone and that god-awful orange mess hung around my shoulders.

"You must be at your mama's," Candi said. "Now, sit down, hon, and just breathe while I talk to you."

Over the phone I could hear her shuffling around. All I could do was wait, which I'm not good at, ever. "What's the booze situation?" she asked.

"Kenny brought beer," I said. "You said his drinking was none of my business. But I need something. I need something really bad."

I was and wasn't listening as she babbled some AA drivel about my thinking being the problem. It was all horseshit and I wouldn't be talking to her if Crossroads hadn't laid down the law about a sponsor or no treatment.

"Go to a meeting," Candi said. "I'll even pick you up and take you there."

"I can't go to a meeting at suppertime," I said. "I'd never hear the end of it."

"Call me then before you leave your Mama's," Candi said. She hung up.

No way was I ready to go back into the shark tank in the living room. I stood at the dresser. Toward the back sat our only family photo, an old-fashioned black and white. All of us. Daddy's long fingers around my waist where I stood beside him. I could almost feel his arm and his warm hand holding me, like I always remembered. Now, if you piled orange hair on Daddy's head and smeared mascara down his cheeks, we'd have been the spitting image of each other.

A new sob came up from my belly, the kind where there's no way to stop it. I kept staring at Daddy's hair combed back in that old-fashioned pompadour. Smiling. I reached out and touched his smile, my fingers against the glass as though I could get back a part of him. His teeth were white and shiny, like mine, our same freckles. Then I couldn't see him anymore, the tears streamed down my face along with that awful emptiness that came over me when I cried like that. I had to wipe and wipe to get the tears to stop. His face, that smile. His coffee breath in the morning before I left for school. The smell of Lucky Strikes on his camel-hair sport coat before, out the door, he and Mama went off dancing on Saturday nights. My head fell forward and, in that moment, I wanted to die from loneliness for him.

I had to snap out of it. This crying and carrying on was just what the old lady expected. And, strangely, she didn't even look mean back then. Her brown hair fell onto her shoulders in a pageboy and, like always when she dressed to go out, she wore a black dress with a string of pearls. She smiled like all she wanted was the family in that photo.

Those pearls. One time I sneaked into the old lady's room and tried them on. Seemed like I spent an hour on the damned clasp and then was so afraid someone would walk in and find me there. Must have been the same time I tried on Mama's dress, the rough silk sliding over my head in dress-up, the sweet pea smell of face powder inside her dress. Knowing Lorraine, she probably had the pearls stashed in a shoebox and thought we'd forgotten them.

In the photo, the full carat diamond overlaying the wedding band on Mama's hand stood out more than ever. It was their tenth anniversary. I don't know why I remembered except Daddy had just given her the ring that she still wore.

We three girls stood between and behind Daddy and Mama, my red pigtails down around the tiny heart locket Daddy had given me. None of us knew it would all change, would all get lost. But someday I was going to get mine—that ring. I'd show them.

                       *   *   *

The backyard seemed the only safe place to go.

"Get off your ass and help me."

I'd come from behind so Kenny didn't see me. He turned around, his eyes big with surprise and his mustache twitching. There were shiny wet spots on his cheek where I spit my words at him, and his reddish-pink tongue flicked this way and that inside his mouth. At least we were alone.

"Get me some Coke," I said. "Before I start working on your beer. I'm just about to lose it."

"Sure, baby," Kenny said. "I can do Coke." He was up and off the picnic bench faster than I'd seen in a long time. He tipped back his beer and drained the can before he threw it into a black plastic bag he'd draped over the end of the picnic table. "You sit right here and have a smoke," he said. He rubbed the stump of the pointer finger he'd chopped off in woodshop, stroking that finger like he does when he's nervous. "Stay away from that old alligator."

For me to stay sober this long, jail or no jail, was a miracle. After the first treatment, I'd been drunk within a day. Only stayed sober a week the second time.

The sky was the oyster shell–white it gets in July. Even with the afternoon sun baking my rear end, being outside and away from my so-called family calmed me. Lorraine's roses, especially the silvers, were all open. I reached over and touched one, the petals like soft rubber. Weird like that, her only Mister Lincoln stinking up the whole backyard. When I leaned down to smell it, I felt like a kid, back in summer again, back in the time of the family picture, Julie and me with our hollyhock dolls in the oak tree shade at the Third Street house. I chose pinks and was the fairy princess. Julie went for red, of course, already practicing her queen-of-hearts routine. It was sweet when I thought about it. She was nine. That means I was about seven.

From near the fence, I smelled lighter fluid where Lorraine's neighbors, the Petersons, had lit the barbecue. Their damned poodles sniffed and barked at the fence bottom. Anything that yips like that should be shot. You can always tell that people with small, red-ribboned dogs inside their big fancy cars think they're better than everybody else.

"You ready for company?" Lorraine said.

Just when I had a little peace and quiet, Lorraine stood there behind the old lady's wheelchair at the top of the ramp. Damn. Even though the old gal was a lot skinnier than when I last saw her, the wheelchair almost got away from Lorraine when she came down the incline.

"It's too hot out here, Lorraine," the old lady said. "Are you trying to give me sunstroke?"

Lorraine maneuvered the wheelchair toward my side of the picnic table until the old woman was under the plastic awning and out of the sun, facing me with those big creepy sunglasses she wore over her trifocals, sunglasses that made me think of movie aliens.

"You keep Mama company while Julie and I bring out supper," Lorraine said. She turned to go back inside.

Goddamn.

"Keep your pants on, girl," the old lady said. "Lorraine already gave me a lecture about being nice." Her creepy sunglasses shielded her eyes. She straightened her yellow blouse with her twisted fingers, and then righted the diamond over her wedding band. Her eyes swung in my direction. "You going to get a job now?"

My cheeks were red, I knew it. *Don't react*, Candi would say. I lit a new cigarette off the one I was smoking.

"I bet Diego could use some help at the diner," she said.

I walked over to the garden tools on the potting bench against the fence and fingered Lorraine's well-used garden gloves. I sorted through the drains looking for an ashtray, anything to keep me occupied and away from her.

"Will you please sit down?" the old lady said. "Why is it that no one listens to me anymore?"

Under the overhang, the sun became shadows, but the heat didn't go away. "Maybe because all you do is complain," I finally said. In one hand, I held a clawlike hand trowel. In the other, a clay drain for my smokes. Somehow, they had to get me through the afternoon.

She lifted her alien eyes. "You going to stay sober this time?"

The claw's handle fit into my palm, the weight of it solid, a comfort. "It all depends," I said. I turned it over in my palm, feeling the prongs for sharpness. It wasn't always like this, her riding my back and bitching at just about everything. There were those times when I was a kid and she would twist my hair into French braids and give my back a quick rub with the palms of her hands to let me know she'd finished. You'd have thought she was almost proud of me.

For a minute or two, neither of us said anything. Then old man Peterson came out and started that baby talk to those stupid mutts. The smell of their steak cooking on the barbecue made me hungry, distracted. I didn't hear the door slam or Julie's footsteps on the wheelchair ramp. She came from behind me and lowered a big bowl of yellow mush onto the table. My family's idea of potato salad.

"Jesus, you nearly gave me a heart attack," I said.

"Push in that bench so I can bring out the other stuff."

"I need to go back inside," the old lady said. "It's too hot."

"Hold tight, Dotty," Julie said. "I'll bring you another tonic to cool you down." Julie turned and walked back up the wheelchair ramp. In the sunlight, the outline of her long legs came through the gauzy red fabric. There wasn't even a shadow of panties, let alone a slip. No wonder Kenny drooled all over himself. Men sniff out that kind of thing.

The old lady lifted her gin and tonic to her mouth. She didn't even try to hide her loud slurp. "Too bad you can't have one," she said.

There it was again. The feeling like my bones were melting in the sun. Like I had no skin. Pretty soon I'd be the same as that mushy potato salad. "Kenny went for Coke," I said. I sat down on the bench with my back half-shielding me from her, the gardening tool in my hand. I began to claw the table, white scratches showing through where the prongs pulled against the soft gray wood.

"What the hell are you doing?" she said.

I pulled the claw, back and back again. The connection between my arm and the wood felt better every time.

"Stop it," she said. "You're making me crazy."

Down and across the table from her, I reached the claw in her direction, my fist clenched and my hand tight around the tool. I pulled along the length of the table. The claw was solid, doing what it was supposed to do. For the first time that day, I had a chance.

"Why did I always have to get so loaded to come here?" I said.

She lifted the empty glass and the ice clicked against her wrinkled lips. "There you go, feeling sorry for yourself again," she said. "Just like always."

"What the hell do you know about *sorry*?" I said. I stood up and took a step toward her. The claw was in my hand.

"You're just like your father."

My face felt as tight as my hand, and I was holding on for dear life. All I had to do was take four giant steps forward to catch her throat just right. I couldn't stop the quiver I felt in my hand or the hot sting I'd never counted on getting hotter behind my eyes.

"You never could stand how much Daddy loved his girls. Loved me."

Eyes on the rings, she kept straightening them like they'd get away from her. "Both of you, nothing but disappointment," she said.

The moment she said that, a numbness came from something I'd always known. The truth we never said, why Daddy left, why she hated me. A hurt that went so far down I couldn't even go there. I had to step back. "I'm better off at an AA meeting."

She snapped off her sunglasses and glared at me from those watery blue eyes. "Good," she said. "You can hang out with all the other weirdos and whine together."

My arm was up over my head before I knew I'd let go. The gardening claw in the air and headed right at her head not six feet away. I wanted the claw to find its target. At the same time, I dreaded it would. As luck would have it, the old lady ducked. Good thing, because that claw would have caught her right eye and right temple. She let out a scream that made my blood stop.

I turned and walked up the wheelchair ramp as fast as I could. The first thing I saw in the kitchen on Lorraine's sterile counter was the bottle of Gordon's Gin. Beside the gin were Lorraine's best ruby-red glasses she only put out for fancy doings. I grabbed the nearly full bottle, the gin freezer-cold against my sweaty hand.

Julie stood by the sink, the faucet running full blast, and Lorraine was fiddling with the kitchen radio. She'd hit the volume button wrong. The kitchen was now louder than loud and as crazy as where I'd come from.

Fuck them. Fuck them all. I stood there, waiting for the *no* voice in my head to go off. But it didn't. Inside my hand, the bottle's gin was cold, the clear run of water. Harmless, that's what I wanted to believe. I poured gin into one of

Lorraine's good glasses and picked up the glass. There was the weight of the glass and the gin inside. I held the glass up to the light. *Just something to hang onto*, I said to myself. Already, my mouth watered from the smell of juniper, the gin's slippery legs sliding against the inside of the glass.

After Daddy left, I was just the pain in the ass they had to consider for school lunches and what's for dinner. Julie was off dancing and Lorraine babysat after high school and through the supper hour for Maxine, next door to the Third Street house. No one was around except me and the old lady. Plus, her constant visitor.

"What's going on?" It had to be Lorraine who said, "Becky?" The water stopped and Lorraine had flipped the radio's off button.

I held the glass at eye level. I could already feel the gin's warmth slide down my throat. Then everything would be all right again.

Candi was probably right. Drinking again would be like diving off the deep end when you can't swim.

Sunlight came through Lorraine's kitchen window into the red glass. My eye was level with the oily line of gin and the sun warmed my hand, and then my wrist. Like the day I knelt in the dirt, bent down beside Daddy. He'd told me to drive the tomato stake into the ground. I remember there was dirt on my hands and under my fingernails where we'd been working. His one hand lay heavy on my shoulder while he held the stake with his other hand. My own small hand was wrapped around the mallet when I turned and looked up at him for just a second, my brown eyes into his brown eyes. In the space of his smile, my steady hand brought the mallet down hard. As the stake sank into the soft, black earth, Daddy said, "My girl."

"Becky? What're you doing?"

Another voice, "Hush."

The screen door slammed. Flip-flops on the linoleum. There was a hand on my arm, just before Kenny's grease-lined fingers came around in front of me and reached for the glass. "Easy, girl. It's gonna be okay."

Chapter Ten

Julie

My spangly silver bracelets razzled as I headed down J Street, a place I didn't normally walk, my black skirt and red blouse reflected back in shop windows and the Red Lion Hotel's automatic doors. My French heels clicked on the pavement. A deep breath in, then out.

Past a secluded restaurant with the smallest sign, a black limo parked in front. Probably the nicest place to hang out and I was tempted but, no, it looked too intimate. I needed someplace fun. Like that place across the street. Café tables lined the sidewalk and white-aproned waiters passed in and out of French doors. I could hear show tunes floating out onto the street from an inside piano. The Blue Moon was perfect.

Because it was summer-hot, the dinner crowd had gathered outside, groups of gals and some couples close together at tables near the street. Inside the windows, a baby grand took up the far end of the bar. Opposite the piano, empty white-clothed tables lined the front inside windows facing into the August sun. A young waiter with a closely shaved beard stood beside the door smiling at me.

"Outside," was all I said. My generic smile.

The waiter nodded, his light blue eyes direct. The sun at four o'clock, high off the western sky, gave me the late-afternoon feeling that comes at the end of summer before the day moves toward evening. That same sun reflected off the waiter's white shirt and shined back at me.

"For one?" he said.

"For one."

The waiter returned. "It'll just be a minute," he said. "Can I get you a drink?"

"Glenlivets," I said. The thought of the Scotch's mellow warmth was just what I wanted.

I stood in the doorway, staring toward the golden sky. Ginkgo trees lined the street with their fan-shaped leaves blowing in the breeze. The waiter, carrying my drink, led me to a table at the far end of the sidewalk away from the couples and groups.

The first sip of double Scotch went down almost too smoothly. For a two-glass champagne gal, I couldn't believe I'd come to this. Alcohol was Becky's remedy, Mama's. Now, in River's End, it was beginning to look like mine.

Was this what happened to women growing older, especially alone? The extra glass of wine at dinner, the secret desserts. A way of staving off the fact of sitting by yourself in front of the evening news, then closing the drapes against the day, against the possibility someone might see the faraway look in your eye that confessed to missed possibilities. Like Lily. Her stories about Las Vegas's beginnings. "I'll never be able to leave," she'd said, her tray tilted and the two glasses precarious at the edge. "This is all I've known." Except for finding another man, what was there? The tray, the fishnets, the crowd. Truth is that when you're busy gliding in a predict-able direction and your soul is not yet honed to the wisdom of age, you blindly follow the next impulse until someone like

Bunny looks up at you from the bottom of the stairs and says you're done.

Some folks can start again, some can't. Maybe that's what Lily was saying.

The waiter returned after several minutes. "Another double?" he said.

"Another," I said hoping my ten-dollar bill would cover the tab, Lorraine's credit card hidden in the glove box paying for gas.

The waiter picked up my empty glass. My eyes followed him when he turned and walked away, his slender frame disappearing inside the restaurant. Reminded me of Lance, Husband Number One. The same self-assurance, a certain sideways look in his eye. Lance, my Elvis look-alike lying against white sheets, his black hair mussed. My ebony screen with an etched heron behind him. Before the wedding chapel at midnight on New Year's Eve.

"You're ravishing, Mrs. Jordan," he'd said when he kissed me after the *I do*s. Ravishing was all that mattered at nineteen when I'd secured my first gig in the Tropicana line.

"Do you really think we can live in my studio apartment?" I asked an hour later.

"Why change what works?"

What works, then doesn't. Alone in my bed six weeks later, the wedding ring nothing but a prop that went into my jewelry box. Yet, the same old dissonance sneaks back, that waiting for something, for someone, to happen. Such a sentimental fool I am. If I could be more like the leaves, just doing what leaves do when summer breezes cool off the day and all you have to do is wait for the Scotch to deliver its promise.

The sun felt welcome on my face and against my sunglasses. The dry wind lifted the ginkgo leaves as they touched each other, first a flutter, then the sound of satin or silk. No Lorraine here. No Mama. God forbid, Becky.

A touch on my shoulder. Someone who thought they knew me well enough to put their hand there.

I turned, my eyes facing into the sun, my hand up as a shield above my sunglasses.

"Las Vegas," the voice said. "Didn't think I'd run into you again."

The very same Arthur with the hand-tooled belt. Camels in a soft pack. The cowboy I met on the bus but dressed in a suit and tie this time.

I barely glanced at him but, rather, kept my eyes on the trees across the street. "Thought you were just passing through."

"No, I had business at the hotel. Thought I saw you from the lobby. I'm glad you didn't go too far."

The trees. The sun at seven o'clock. Was it the sun cutting through the ginkgoes or the fact that the cowboy lived in a world outside of Sunny Acres? My eyes aimed toward that place on the horizon where, eventually, the red light on top of the grain elevator would shine inside the night sky.

"Can I buy you a drink?"

Two fingers over the top of my glass. "Afraid I've had more than my fair share."

"How about dinner then?"

"I don't even know you," I said.

He laughed and his mustache lifted over his upper teeth, white and straight except for a chip on one of his two front teeth. "You probably know me better than most people do."

For the first time, I removed my sunglasses. I looked into his eyes, the gold specks inside the brown that I'd seen on the bus. "Dinner's probably good considering how much I've had to drink."

"Do I need to catch up?"

I laughed, for the first time in a long time. Laughed until my head went back. "You tickle me despite myself," I said.

"It's probably not a good idea for both of us to get sloshed."

When he grinned at me this time, there was something else going on in his eyes. I'd swear it was a kind of sadness. "How about I have one double to catch up and ask the waiter for a menu," he said.

That sadness in his eyes said what I felt, as though all my years had landed on me at once. Maybe the same sadness along with a haunting question. How do you start again when you come from where I'd been? Glamour every night. Men in silk jackets, their nails buffed to a shine. Other dancers like me with their tight bodies and secret sadness, always the question of how long this would last, who was waiting to replace me, when would Bunny fold her hands on top of the desk and shake her head before she said, *No contract this season.*

Arthur pulled a pack of Camels out of his shirt pocket, and his Old Spice floated between us when he reached for the ashtray. Daddy's scent, his spice, familiar as the roundhouse or roughhousing on the living room floor. Arthur offered me the pack.

I took the cigarette, noticing how his white T-shirt showed through his dress shirt behind the brick-red tie. His lighter flamed under the end of my cigarette, and his hand cupped the flame, the white hair nearly invisible on the back of his hand. Never once did he look away from me, the circles and crow's feet surrounding those eyes and, just above his mouth, the brush of his white, well-trimmed mustache.

He lit his own cigarette and tilted his head back before blowing a smoke ring into the air. "Care to tell me what's going on with you?"

"There isn't anything going on." I glanced from the back of his hands to the ginkgo. "Maybe I should leave."

"You can," he said. "But you'll miss a good two-step partner."

Why that made me laugh, I don't know. "Now you're talking."

"I asked my question all wrong," he said. He blew another smoke ring. "What I meant is . . . and, I realize it's none of my business." He found my eyes and held them for what felt like a long time. "Why *did* you come back?"

My laugh was nervous this time. "Maybe I'm looking for home."

The waiter set down menus, Arthur's drink, a double gin, the smell of pine reaching across the small table. The waiter gave me the eye as though to ask if this guy was bothering me. I nodded. "A friend," I said.

"Thank you," Arthur said after the waiter left. He raised his glass. "New York steak's good," he said without looking at the menu, his eyes too serious for my comfort.

"Alright." I could hold that gaze too.

"Home is one thing. Honest is another."

"Agreed," I said. "Now, it's my turn to be curious. Why are you here and why dressed up?"

"That's fair." He flicked his growing ash into the ashtray. "I'm an almond broker. Here to meet with some of the orchard growers."

"Business," I said. "So, why the bus? I'd think you could fly easier, faster."

A flush I recognized crept up from his neck and into his face. He looked down at the agate ring on his third finger, the silver mounting shiny as though just polished. "I'm afraid of flying."

At first, I wanted to laugh. On second thought, that sounded mean. Even cruel, considering his apparent embarrassment. I leaned across the table, closer to him. "You're honest," I said. "I like that."

"Honest," he said. "Is that something that's hard to come by in Las Vegas?"

"Depends on who you're talking to."

He stubbed out his cigarette and looked past my head. Then, at me. "So, let's start there."

The gingko trees, the brick building, the grain elevator in the distance. "Maybe I'm scared too."

How we moved so quickly into serious territory was beyond me. Maybe that's the kind of guy he was. Full of surprises. Not anyone I would ever pick out in a crowd, dismissing him as uninteresting and not worth my time. But there was something about him. Maybe the honesty. Maybe the just-for-fun gal was melting away as I got closer to my fifty-first birthday. How would I, could I, know? River's End, a cowboy, someone who wanted a real conversation.

I took a drag from my cigarette and, almost immediately, the Camel made me light-headed. The ginkgo leaves had stopped shining now that the sun slid behind the brick buildings across the street. Inside, the piano played "Hello, Dolly" and, out of the corner of my eye, I could see a few people gathered around the copper-colored sequined dress of a female pianist. Above the street traffic, the sky behind the grain elevator glowed with orange and pink streaks while a halo of light surrounded the tall building. The whole thing was squared off like a vertical angel against the sky. But it was still too early to see the little red light on top of the grain elevator.

Arthur's white hair was whiter now that the sun had left the table. He dragged on a new cigarette, the orange fire glowing red. Waiters came and went, the tables changed. The street traffic became heavier and louder with the oncoming evening, unlike the quiet between us.

He stubbed out his cigarette. Arthur leaned in, his elbows in his shirtsleeves on the table, his face about a foot away from mine. He looked down at his plumbing pipes and chain saw hands, his words so low I almost couldn't hear. "I'm glad I found you again." His voice matched his eyes, sad, with crow's feet bearing down hard. Inside those black-to-brown eyes blazed all the hurt that comes from living long enough.

For a gal as lost as I'd felt, I could only say, "I'm glad you did, too."

He put his hand over mine, his touch light and almost not there. But still, it was his touch, the way it crowned my fingers, the certainty with which it lay heavy. "Would you like to dance?"

* * *

Arthur's hat highlighted the brothel-red leather under the dome light and created a gray circle on the back seat of his supposedly rented, factory-shined fifties Cadillac. He stood beside me even while I watched his hat on the back seat. His shoulder was up and under my armpit before I knew it happened. I wouldn't even be in his car and he wouldn't be here now if I hadn't turned an ankle on the curb when we left the Blue Moon. If he hadn't been there to catch me. All those years of dancing and being careful not to get injured and, now, my first real night out in River's End and I nearly took a fall. It was embarrassing. After all those years in Las Vegas, there I was, practically on my butt except for the quick catch by a man I barely knew.

Arthur closed the car door and the dome light disappeared. With my back against the cushy seat and the engine rumbling under all that red leather, the last place I wanted to go was Sunny Acres.

"Where do I take you, pretty lady?" he said.

Laughing, but not really laughing. "Take me with you."

He pulled the gearshift into drive.

"The only place I'd take you, Las Vegas, is home."

I couldn't tell you why my breath caught in my throat. It wasn't him. And it wasn't the drinks or my foot or the late night. Or even River's End. It was that lonesome feeling again, the one that comes in the darkest part of the night or early morning, an empty you can't define.

Plus, I wasn't used to being turned down.

He didn't talk and I didn't talk after I gave him directions, the freeway off-ramp signs speeding past, white against green or green against white, depending on how you saw them. It didn't matter. All I knew was the numbness that had come with the end of this evening. It definitely wasn't my foot, much as my ankle hurt.

A short four blocks off Texas, his headlights hit the Sunny Acres sign. We were now in the trailer court with its fake wood sidings and speed bumps, the swimming pool and its metal awning that Dotty called the cabana.

"You're reading this all wrong, Las Vegas," he said.

"My name is Julie," I said. "Here." I rolled down the window. The smell of roses mixed with night-blooming jasmine mixed with leather. "Pull up to the hedge."

I scooted as close to the door as I could and reached to open it.

"No, no," he said. "Let me." He cut the headlights and was out and around the back end of the car even as I pushed the door open.

"I can do it myself," I said.

"Hold on, Las Vegas," he said. "Don't be stubborn."

With that, he reached around and under my arm until he had a firm grip on my waist. His hand and arm were stronger than I would have thought, his grip both firm and gentle. My pain became buried in the hollow between his neck and shoulder where the remnants of worn-out Old Spice and a too-long day lay against his skin. We stood there, not moving, his arm propping me up.

"If you can just get me into the house," I said.

"Maybe it's easier if I carry you."

My laugh became filled with wanting and not wanting what he suggested. "Just hold on to me until we get into the house."

It was dark on the stairs. No porch light, and the awning erased the stars and half moon. We'd never be able to do this without waking Lorraine and Dotty.

I grabbed the screen handle and pulled. After Arthur pushed open the door, the odor of fried onions and garlic, Lorraine's natural remedies for Dotty, surrounded us. "Welcome to my house," I said.

The night-lights helped us avoid the dining room table. "Straight ahead," I said. "Put me on the sofa."

I pointed to a large shadow resting against the wall. "There," I said. "Coffee table in front." But I was too late. We both heard his knee bump against it.

He buried his face in my shoulder. "Shit."

"You better put me down here," I whispered.

He was just about to ease me down onto the sofa when the dining room lights went on behind us. "Julie? Is that you?"

Arthur did a half turn. "Got a sprained ankle here, ma'am."

Lorraine's hands went deep into the patch pockets of her robe. Her hair was smashed on one side.

I pulled my head around Arthur. "Stepped off a curb downtown," I said.

Lorraine's mouth seemed to shrink as her chin started trembling the way it does when she's anxious or upset.

"This is Arthur."

"Ma'am," he said, nodding his head. There was a twitch in his shoulders, like he was supposed to shake hands. But his arms were still full of me.

Lorraine looked right past him. "Set her down," she said. "Let me take a look."

Before I knew it, Lorraine had turned on every damned light in the living room. Then out of her robe's patch pocket came her glasses.

My ankle was swollen, but otherwise my foot looked normal if you count the fact that I ruined my good French sandal.

Lorraine kept pushing up her glasses. "Need to get ice on this."

Then she moved out of the light.

Arthur looked first at my foot, then at me.

My French heel was still in my hand. I'd been holding it since we left the car.

"Don't look so sad," I said. "It's just a sprain."

The crack of ice trays and water running came from the kitchen. Arthur leaned down and, I'll be damned, his lips, slightly chapped and half-open, touched mine. Gin hung on his breath when his mouth brushed against mine.

He was only there a few seconds. But the slight wet of his kiss was still on my mouth when Lorraine cleared her throat behind us.

"Need to get in there," she said.

Lorraine lifted my foot onto sofa pillows. She took an ice pack and wrapped it around my foot. The freeze of it went from my skin to that just-before-you-go-numb, eye-watering cold.

Lorraine covered me with Dottie's purple afghan. She never looked up and she never nodded.

"How much did you have to drink?" she asked.

Miss Inquisition. "It's been several hours," I said.

"She had a couple of Scotches," Arthur said.

"Did you ever think of taking her to emergency?"

"No, ma'am," he said. "Didn't look that serious."

"I don't suppose it did," Lorraine said.

She shook her head at me. "Too much swelling now." She gave the afghan a tuck. "I'll get you a Vicodin. You can sleep here."

She moved to stand up and her robe flapped open. There was no mistaking her Winnie the Pooh pajamas. She grabbed at her robe to close it. She stood there, holding her robe, not moving, not looking at anything but my foot.

Arthur tipped his head toward me. "Night then," he said. "I'll call tomorrow to make sure you're okay."

The bus station in Fresno two months ago. *Arthur* on the back of his belt. There was nothing about him that I saw the same.

A strange heaviness landed in my chest. "Arthur," I said. He turned. His hands on his slender hips. "Yes, Julie?" "Thank you."

Chapter Eleven

Becky

F riday afternoon and no idea how long I sat in Kenny's damned pickup on Ninth just staring up at the sign for The Portals. Wanting to go inside and not wanting to go inside, not quite happy hour at a bar I called survivor's paradise. A Coke. Yes, a Coke wouldn't hurt. Just a howdy-doody Coke and out the door in a half hour. What was the harm in that? Besides, what else was there to do in August when the sun was boiling your behind and your old man took off on a ride to Montana?

It was dark inside, the kind of dark that said home, but with a weird edge. Like I wasn't supposed to be there but I wanted to be there anyhow. I eased onto the barstool next to Danny, my best drinking buddy. "A week ago, I tried with that family of mine," I said. "Went to their fucking picnic and all I got was a ration of shit." I screwed up my mouth the way the old lady does. "'When are you going to get a job?' that woman who calls herself my mother wanted to know. I should have known better. All of them, looking down their noses at me, drinking their gin and tonics big as you please.

Just because of my lousy probation. Can you believe I lost my damned license?"

"Thought you said you drove here," Danny said. His cigarette smoldered in the ashtray. He lifted his empty glass and nodded at Ray Barnes, the craggy-faced longtime owner and bartender. Ray delivered Danny's drink pronto, never having to guess with me and Danny. Both of us drank vodka tall with a squeeze of lime to give it juice. Now, my second Coke. What're you going to do?

"Well, yeah, I have to drive," I said. "I'm calling that piece of shit pickup a farm vehicle."

The only light inside The Portals came through the partly open door and the two wagon-wheel chandeliers, the bulbs on dimmer switches. Near the bar where we sat, a jukebox played Patsy Cline's "I Fall to Pieces" to an empty dance floor.

"Don't kid yourself, sweetheart," Danny said. "It's the moms who call the shots until the day they die."

"What do you think, Ray?" I said. "You think the moms of the world are going to run us off our barstools?"

Ray tossed a lime slice into Danny's glass. He avoided looking at both of us. "You'll never be driving Peterbilts, I can tell you that."

Fuck him. I waved my cigarette over the top of my glass. "How about one of those," I said pointing at Danny's drink.

"Thought you were on the wagon," Ray said. He kept wiping that glass like his life depended on it.

"That was before I came in here," I said. I slapped five bucks on the bar.

My back faced the door, a way of thinking no one saw me in there, yet every time the door swung wide, a ray of sun bounced off the mirror in front of me. That's when I'd see my ponytail too loose and the gray streaks taking over the red. But one thing stayed the same. The deep V-neck of my T-shirt showed off my good tits. I might never dance topless like Julie, but I wasn't some hag you couldn't stand to look at. And, believe it or not, I could still drink as much as I wanted without looking like one of those gals with bloat, their guts holding them back from the bar. If I ever got like that, I swear I'd quit drinking.

I eyeballed Danny in the mirror. A native from Lahaina, which sounded exotic as hell, he never changed, skinny and wrinkled as he was from living off sun and vodka. "It's the dads who make the difference," I said. "If they hang around."

Danny lit another cigarette off the one in the ashtray. He grinned at me, the one front missing tooth I forgot about most of the time right in my face. "Doesn't matter if they hang around or not," he said.

Didn't surprise me, his saying that, or him, sitting there studying his drink like it was a damned crossword puzzle, his slept-in Hawaiian shirt and curly black hair that hadn't seen a comb the whole time I'd known him. He just wanted the world to go away. That was Danny. But I liked him well enough, especially in profile. His small nose and mustache made him look like Burt Reynolds before Burt lost his hair. Couldn't imagine what he'd be like in the sack, if he could even get it up. Said he'd been married once and even had a kid he lost touch with years ago when he stopped paying child support. Pissed me off when he told me that.

"Your old man probably never ran off," I said.

"Yeah, he did. He died."

Took me a minute to sort that one out. "Died or ran off, which is worse? Just goes to show, you can't count on anyone. They all leave you in the end," I said.

Danny nodded toward me, his dark eyes in mine. He closed them for just a moment. "Know whatcha mean," he said. His glass found his lips and he swallowed. Then, turtle slow, he turned toward me head on. "Lucky for me, my stepdad was different. Took over a KFC franchise before he keeled over."

I gave his blue BIC lighter a whirl on the bar. "Lucky you, whatever that means. All I've got are a few memories, nothing to hang on to."

I glanced into the mirror. Couldn't believe I was turning forty-nine this coming April and, there I was, sitting at the bar like it was my job. I lived in a single-wide by the Tuolumne with two dogs and three cats, always waiting for my old man to come back from some motorcycle rally hundreds of miles away that I didn't want to know about.

"Why's your dad so special that you miss him so much?" Danny said.

I had to think about that. I'd missed him for so long that it was hard to know why anymore. "He always called me *my girl*. That was something."

"I could call you that and doubt I'd get the same lonesome I hear in you."

"He took me fishing. Every Saturday morning, just the two of us."

Danny closed his eye where the smoke from his cigarette curled back on him. "That's somethin'," he said. "Never had that or anything close to it."

"Just me. The only one of all his girls," I said.

It was my job to pack the sandwiches while he got the gear together. "Need to be quiet so we don't wake the others," he'd whisper. The smell of fish guts already on the overalls he saved for fishing.

"All we got is bologna and white cheese," I told him.

"Perfect," he said carrying his old shoes to the car. "Don't worry about mayo or mustard. We'll be so darned hungry it won't matter."

Two slices of white bread, extra bologna and cheese for him. Just plopped the sandwiches in a paper bag, no waxed paper or anything for fear I'd wake the others and ruin everything.

Danny looked at me with a smirk curling his mouth. "You're too serious."

"Damned right, I'm serious," I said. "I haven't worked at a job longer than two months since I got married and got my GED."

Danny caught my glance in the mirror. "I've never worked," he said. "Sure, a couple of stints as manager at my stepdad's KFC, but we both gave up both times." He laughed and the missing tooth made the black hole inside his mouth bigger.

"You think it would have been different if your real dad hadn't died?"

"Suppose so. He went to the Naval Academy, was a Navy pilot. Mom said he was hot shit. He wouldn't much like the way I've lived."

Dim tears glazed his eyes. Now he was my Danny, the real Danny. The times I liked him best. No more bullshit. It didn't happen often, and I was sorry about that.

He started to slide off the stool, but I grabbed his arm. "Don't go," I said. My voice was just above a whisper.

"Yeah, sure," Danny said. He caught my eye in the mirror. "What's up?"

"Just asked myself the same question, that's all," I said. "You know, what if my dad had stayed around. How things might have been different."

I couldn't look at him just then. There was too much going on inside me that I didn't understand, maybe didn't want to feel. Like some dark jungle, so overgrown I'd never get through it, even with a machete.

"So what if he'd stayed around." Danny said.

"I would have tried harder. Finished school. Got a real job." I stubbed out my cigarette. "He liked a woman combed and made-up, looking nice in hose and a skirt." I looked into the mirror. "He'd have been disappointed in me."

"Why'd he leave?" Danny said.

I nodded toward his Marlboros and waited for an invitation. "My old lady ran him off."

Danny shook a cigarette loose and offered it to me. "Ever see him again?"

"No, but I've always had the creepy feeling he comes back into town every now and then. Incognito," I said.

Incognito was a big word, and I liked the roll of it on my tongue. I blew a smoke ring over my head. "Did you ever do that? Go back and see your kid?"

Danny shook his head. "Nah. No point, really," he said. "Her mom would just want money."

Right then, I didn't like Danny. Didn't like what he'd done to that little girl.

"Stand by Your Man" filled the silence between us. At the end of the bar, Ray lifted glasses out of the dishwasher and stacked them on a towel. He was probably getting ready for happy hour. A backwards-hat guy leaned on the jukebox, otherwise there was only one other couple sitting in a booth at the side, behind us. Business was slow, even for a Friday afternoon.

Danny nodded in the direction of the restrooms. "Be right back."

Danny was right. I was too serious. In the mirror I pulled the loose strands of hair around my face, fixing them in a Julia Roberts look, the kind of look Kenny went for when I was a kid.

My hair like that reminded me how once, during our early-love time, Kenny asked me to cross Wyoming on the back of his bike. "Hang on, sugar," he'd said. I remember the roads were mostly straight and the land around us was dry with the boring brown of grazed fields after winter. Every so often you'd see a herd of antelope in the distance. They'd stop, their ears pricked into the wind, and they'd wait. When they heard the motorcycle's engine, their white tails puffed out just before they turned to run. "Scared the shit out of them, didn't we?" Kenny said into his helmet speaker. I remember squeezing his back to let him know I heard him, the smell of his leather jacket all I cared about, the wind in my face and sagebrush everywhere.

One night on the Wyoming plains we pitched a tent beside a creek, then, sitting close, let the fire go down slow. Like a damned cave, dark around us and nothing but stars up above. I was sober that night when Kenny took my hand. He just about gave me a stroke, like the five shooting stars I counted. His rough-skinned hand around mine like he cared in a way I hadn't felt since we first got together. Every time I closed my eyes to make a wish, I wanted that night to go on forever. Anyhow, that's how I liked to think of that time. The next morning, we headed for Independence Rock. Nothing but a mound of granite sticking out of ragweed and buffalo grass, but the horizon went on and on in all directions, the sky like arms, and me, holding on to my man, even feeling a tear now and then, from the wind maybe, or just from being behind Kenny. I felt really small again, almost like Daddy was there.

Danny climbed back on the barstool, his legs wide as he straddled it from behind. "Been thinking about you and that so-called husband of yours," he said. "Why's he so damned special you always wait for him like this?"

I threw my head back and laughed. Danny could tickle me sometimes. "Who do you think pays for these drinks, honey?"

We both got quiet for a minute. Just his asking that made me wonder. Why was I always waiting for Kenny and why didn't I ever ask if I could go with him? Because he never asked me to go, that's why. I reached for Danny's Marlboros and shook a cigarette loose before I lifted the blue BIC toward the end of my smoke.

I turned around toward the jukebox. The backwards-cap guy was dropping quarters into the slot and the next thing you know we had gonna take a sentimental journey, gonna set my heart at ease.

"Hate that shit," Danny said. "We need something to wake up this place. Give me a couple of those quarters." He slid off the barstool, then held out his hand and took the quarters I'd been collecting as a tip for Ray.

When he walked toward the jukebox, he reminded me of Uncle Dale, Aunt Naomi's husband. The dark mustache and skinny legs. Sometimes he'd be quiet for the longest time. But, unlike Uncle Dale, Danny never went off on some damned story I'd heard a thousand times before. Uncle Dale and Daddy always drinking too much when he came around, telling their war stories. One night, Uncle Dale and Aunt Naomi, the old lady's only sister, disappeared from the house where they lived next door to us. We never saw or heard from them again.

"I like you better when you're not so serious," Danny said. "Think we should go to Cliff's tonight and have a steak. After all, we're here to party before the next disaster hits." He laughed, and the black hole of his missing tooth had become part of his charm.

I tossed my ponytail in the mirror. "I gotta go slow. Shouldn't be here to begin with," I said. "Drinks hit you too damned fast when you've been on the wagon. Already lost count."

The next round was followed by another, the barstools more comfortable with each new drink. I kept putting off the awful moment I had to get off the stool just to get circulation back in my legs and butt, then hope I didn't fall down and embarrass the hell out of myself.

I should have known certain things. Like when the light outside the door slides away and Patsy Cline is first choice on the jukebox. Especially when Danny reached for my knee and his hand crept slowly up the inside of my thigh, something he'd never done before. I should have known we were tanked, and it didn't help that the place had gotten so full of people that I had to lean closer just to hear him.

The next thing I knew, Danny had me off the barstool and into "Folsom Prison," which he'd started playing over and over. We were dancing right in front of the bar, my body all slithery with my arms and legs every which way and that marshmallow feeling like the rest of the world had gone away.

Felt good to forget my problems. But to say Danny and I were anywhere close to sober would be a mistake. I was lost in shimmy shaking, my breasts against Danny's chest and my hair wet where my ponytail had come undone and my short shorts kept riding up my butt. We were so drunk at that point, we were lucky to stand.

A clawlike hand grabbed my arm and yanked me back. "I'm home, sugar."

Who knows how long Kenny had been standing there. Or how long it had been since I stopped to look in the bar mirror for someone I should have been looking for. Between the booze and the reddish light, I'd melted into the music.

Kenny didn't wait for his words to register; he jerked me away from the dance floor. That's when I realized he wasn't going to catch me or hold me up, my legs like rubber and my head floppy all over the place. "Kenny, you shoulda called." My tongue felt swollen and my words were too thick. "You shoulda let me know."

"And ruin the party?" Kenny said. His hands, rough and scratchy, bit down too hard on my arm. First, he propped me against him, then he backed me away from the bar and threw my butt into a chair, where I landed hard.

Drunk and scared shitless, I completely lost track of Danny. If he'd been smart, he'd have been out of there. The last time, Kenny threatened to cut Danny into bite-sized pieces for Boozer and Johnnie, starting with his cock.

Kenny moved closer to the bar, his shoulders hunched forward and his hands out in front of him. "Now," he said, "what worthless piece of shit would try to steal another man's wife?"

Beside and behind Kenny, all I could see was a haze of leather and studs, neck kerchiefs dirty from too many days on the road, and belt buckles that glinted in the light from the overhead wagon wheels. The Misfits would never let a brother down. Never.

In front of me all I saw was Kenny's back and, past that, Danny's face, his mouth mostly open and a look in his eyes I'll never forget. Like he was watching a twister blow toward him, his hand behind him feeling for the barstool. There was no pretending this wasn't happening. Maybe Danny was thinking about how much distance he had between the barstool and the back door where we both knew Ray took his breaks. Maybe he thought about the gun Ray kept behind the bar.

The only sound was Elvis's backup electric guitar and Elvis singing "Are You Lonesome Tonight." Nobody breathed. Kenny's voice, husky, in what sounded like a whisper but wasn't. "C'mon, baby," he said to Danny. "Meet me."

I held onto the chair for dear life, my jelly legs and arms hanging limp, but my head scared straight and as sober as it could be. This was the worst thing that could have happened. I had to make Kenny believe I only came here an hour ago, the trailer baked to a summer crisp and the air conditioner broken. Danny was just an accident. After all, I couldn't stop him from hanging out at The Portals.

Danny backed away, like a cat caught in a corner with nowhere to go. I could barely see Kenny's fists, but I knew they were balled up and waiting to make contact. I kept hoping someone would tell him to cool it or come and stand between those guys. Anything to stop the sound of skin against bone, then the crack of bone against bone. But the

Misfits weren't going to stop it. And the other scumbags in there didn't have the guts. Whatever happened, I needed to hold my head up to see what I'd have to apologize for later, my mouth in the permanent shape of regret.

Someone, probably a regular, shut off the jukebox. Then Ray stepped in front of me, having come around from the other end of the bar; his shoulders and his back blocked anything I could see. Ray's hands were on his hips, his deep bass an echo away from my face. "Alright," was all he said.

Without turning around, Kenny barked, "Get the fuck away, man. He's mine." Then his voice got low and smooth as river glass. "You shoulda known, you son of a bitch."

I could just make out Danny's face between the bulk of the two men. His eyes were wide and his lower lip shook like Lorraine's when she's pissed or scared. Pussy that Danny was, he reached his arm around toward the bar, but he never took his eyes away from Kenny. Danny was in that in-between space, maybe just for a second or two before all hell broke loose.

"I told you once," Ray said. "Back off." Ray's bulk and height towered over the two men like he could spread wings and everything would disappear.

Kenny wasn't backing away and he wasn't stepping forward, his arms red from riding in the sun and his neck in need of more than a day's worth of burn ointment and aloe. I was glad I couldn't see the crazed smile he gets when he's holding on by a thread. I just wanted to disappear. But the whole time, with all the lights on now, I might as well have been in jail. Or the lineup in the police station when everything's dark except for those glaring overhead lights and you don't know how the hell you got there.

"This is *my* place," Ray said to Kenny. He took another step toward Kenny's back. "You're not gonna fuck it up and I'm not calling the cops. You take this party outside or someone will pay."

The menace in his voice sobered me fast. I knew about Ray's gun, Danny knew, and Kenny was smart enough to know that Ray wasn't fooling. But Kenny kept inching forward until he was practically in front of Danny.

Even from where I sat, drunk as I was, I heard Danny start to wheeze like he does when he's going into an asthma attack.

Louder this time, "You hear me?" Ray said.

Kenny, as if against his will, turned to say something to Ray. That's all it took. Danny was around the end of the bar and out the back door we both knew was just down the hall to the johns. I heard the door slam, the echo of it filling the room.

"Son of a bitch!" Kenny shouted. He did a full body turn toward Ray. "Now, see what you've done, you cocksucker? You let him get away!"

"Get out," Ray said. "And take this piece of shit with you."

My mouth hung open, and my sweaty hair was stringy and all over the place, my clothes plastered to my body. I started to look around to see who Ray was talking about. It wasn't until I felt the stare of all those Misfits that I knew the piece of shit was me.

I can only say that being stuck with Kenny at the end of this day was about the last place on this damned earth I wanted to be. The last place any woman would want to be. And if I could have sneaked out the back door right then, if I even thought for one minute I could ease out of there and into the pickup, especially if no one saw me, I'd have locked the doors and just camped out until I finally woke up again. The happiest drunk on earth.

But my luck had run out. Simple as that. The first time in my life there was no one and nowhere to go. I might as well have been back in that gray jail cell with the piss-yellow light. Anything would have been better than where I was.

I waited. That's all I could do. Just sat there, hunched over, like I needed to protect my chest or some damned thing, a target that waited for the next shot and not a weapon in sight to save myself. Someone was going to tear me limb from limb.

Everybody else was waiting too. Ray was a tall blockade in front of me, and Kenny, somewhere in front of Ray, snorted the way he does when he's buying time. Shit. I'm sure it wasn't more than a minute but it felt like an hour, the stalemate like the silence in the bar, a thick haze and going nowhere.

Kenny stepped aside and turned on me. I'll never forget the look in his eyes. Like that judge, his eyes full of hate or something in the same family. He snickered, right toward me, but he never took his eyes off me, his handlebar wide and sweat coming through his kerchief, a slick of it on his forehead. His eyes burrowed into me until I thought I'd melt right there in that chair. Slowly, like I'd disappeared, he lifted his chin and gave Ray the biggest shit-eating grin I'd ever seen. "Piece of shit is yours, man. You can have her."

My mouth opened and I could feel something, a word, some argument hang at the back of my mouth, but my tongue wouldn't cooperate. No way. My brain did not want to let that sound out. In that moment I realized I could buy the farm right there and I'd never find the breath again to tell the story. Piece of shit, the better way to go. Leave it at that.

Kenny's backside headed for the door, his arms around Rat and Jasper, two of his buddies. With their helmets under their arms and the rank smell of what they'd left behind, they were out the door and eaten up by the night. The door came back on its hinges until there was nothing, only quiet inside. Ray turned and, from where he stood, way the hell up over the top of me, he looked down. Just looked at me, the lines around his mouth longer than long, and he never said a word.

Chapter Twelve

Julie

The four o'clock LA to Sacramento caught me at the I Street tracks; the dull and loud train whistle roared at me with the train's approach. I could just see Daddy pulling on the hip pockets of his coveralls with his thumbs. "No damned reason to be late," he'd have said. Loved that Daddy always wanted to be king of the trains.

An old feeling that wasn't late July heat and wasn't the train settled in my stomach, the same feeling I had as a kid from the other side of the tracks. The wrong side, like now. Look at me. I lived in a trailer court and drove Lorraine's old Escort that rattled along without a speck of air-conditioning. The déjà vu you never see coming.

Though my makeup threatened to run, I'd stayed away from the house as much as I could after Lorraine's meltdown and Becky's snag in whatever the court mandate said. The library sometimes, today a movie. Anyplace where the air-conditioning worked. There'd been no callbacks from Palm Springs or the LA clubs where a couple of gals had gone. Work should have been at the top of my agenda the minute I hit town. However, with Dotty still hanging on—a hospital bed now taking up space in the living room—the mobile home had become even smaller than it was before.

Dead ahead on the east side of Tenth Street, I was surprised to see a bail bondsman's neon lights and security gate had replaced the Rexall where I drank a thousand cherry Cokes with my dance pals back in the day. Across the street, the old Outrigger Hotel was boarded up, its windows plastered with paper and graffiti. When had that happened? What stayed the same was the pink Southern Pacific Station and the grid of one-way streets. It was a small town like other small towns, the kind you forget when you're on your way to somewhere else.

Home nearly eight weeks was a record for me. Three days max, that was my rule. My longer stay simply underscored how different Lorraine and I were. Had likely always been. My spontaneity—eating when I was hungry, going out when it struck me—let each day take care of itself when I wasn't working or in rehearsal. Unlike me, Lorraine lived by notepads left conspicuously on the kitchen table. A weekly menu on one. The shopping list on another. Like laundry on Mondays and ironing on Tuesdays, they carefully outlined her days until you'd have thought we were back in a time when women hung those Monday through Sunday hand-embroidered dish towels on the outdoor clothesline.

The next thing I knew, I'd pulled into a parking spot in front of Downtown Dance, my old dance studio, someplace I hadn't been since I left for Las Vegas. The same white stucco walls needed paint, the oversized ballet shoes—pink cutouts—still hung away from the Shriver building, though the black sign's background paint had chipped and faded badly. The fake Spanish door—older, more beaten up—was further confirmation of small-town neglect. *You can't help where you started*, Tasha, my old dance teacher, used to say. *It's where you go that counts.*

Inside the entryway, the odor of fresh-cut wood from some construction project or repair permeated the rather large, squared-off foyer. I was struck by a funny disconnect between the lyrical quality of the upstairs music and the foot-falls—the missed beats, too muffled and heavy for kids. Must be adult beginners.

A crazy excitement pushed me up the staircase. At the top of the stairs and down the corridor, the same exit sign glowed neon red. New plate-glass windows opposite the studio revealed the old Raymond Hotel. As girls, we'd hang out on the roof looking for hotel guests who hadn't pulled their drapes. Every once in a while, we'd get lucky and see someone naked or half-dressed. When we did, they were good for a whole afternoon of laughs at the Rexall.

Through the glass door I could see a dozen or so women in mostly black leotards, late forties or fifties with gray or dyed hair, close to the familiar barre and opposite the long-mirrored wall. They were practicing *tendu*. Front, side, back, their arms in second position but with the benefit of the barre. Only the younger women toward the middle—a runner, from the looks of her legs, next to a too-thin blonde—stayed focused on the teacher and maintained time with the music. Others, close to my age, had no waists, and their legs were too heavy to lift with any grace. Unlike Las Vegas, crow's feet and sagging skin weren't a crime in River's End.

The studio and the students reminded me of why I'd left the Central Valley in the first place. If I was too tall for New York ballet, I'd go somewhere flashier, not as snooty as New York. What can I say? I was seventeen and mad at Tasha, my teacher, for telling me the truth about my skill level and the likelihood of professional ballet. Nearly thirty years later, it was Las Vegas that held my memories of opening nights and rehearsals, the backstage and dressing rooms, each club like a new city. Even now I could feel the excitement pounding in my legs at the thought of everything I'd lived and danced. Not just how to hold myself and when to blend in or step out in a chorus line. I learned how to go after what I wanted and make hard work pay, spotting that fixed point, onstage and off. Auditions for new shows, new casinos. Pressure was a given, so I depended on simple things, like pulling my shoulders back and making my neck tall. To own all six feet of who I was. Big breath in, then slowly, release. Again. Toe out, I stepped forward. No matter how scared or frustrated I was. The minute the lights came down and the curtain went up, the first wave of adrenaline hit my stomach—music, lights, stage, and the rush, in that order. Once into the first number, I wasn't thinking anymore. The routine was already in my arms and legs. Down ten or twenty stage steps balancing a thirty-pound headdress in heels. No problem. The headpiece riding high above a fifty-pound backpack in a full-out feather fan. I was pearls and rhinestones and ostrich feathers and little else, my hinge walk holding me steady each step of the way down.

Standing in the hallway outside the dance studio with Philip Glass music on the other side of the wall, I suddenly felt out of place, that sense of something lost. The awkward and lopsided swans inside mimicked an old tension I felt creeping into my shoulders along with a too-familiar impatience and a longing that filled my chest. It had been over five years since I danced, let alone taught, and I suddenly envied the poor teacher hidden by a partial wall I didn't remember being there.

The sun shot down through the high windows and bounced off the schoolroom-style hanging lights. Two paddle fans attempted to move the air. Still, sweat bled through the backs of the women's lighter-colored leotards. I leaned into the old trophy case standing next to me. Row after row of trophies lined each shelf, the bad light and the glass doors so smudged with fingerprints and dust I could hardly see the names. My trophies must still be in the back where I'd put them the day before I left town.

My earrings and curls reflected back from the glass doors along with my hollow cheeks and longer face, the lines around my eyes a dead giveaway to the years that crowded between that once-young girl and the face in front of me now.

A rustling skirt. An impatient and familiar voice, the Russian accent. She clapped her hands. "No, no, no."

Why that voice surprised me, no, *shocked* me, I don't know. She should have retired long ago. I leaned too hard against the windowed dance studio door and the same squeaking hinge from years ago gave me away.

The students, already stopped, turned in the door's direction. Tasha. Her long purple skirt swayed in a full arc, and the same impatient arms flew up in exasperation, a gesture I knew all too well. Her breasts, fuller with the years and added weight, pushed against the scooped neck of her leotard. The same hoop earrings brushed her shoulders where her lobes hung low, like they'd been stretched with fishing weights. Nothing surprised me more than her full gray curls.

The Carleton Curse heated my neck and ears. You'd have thought I was five again and just caught talking to the dancer behind me.

Her hand poked inside her skirt's fabric. She reached for her glasses, and when she pulled them out of her pocket, they were the same black-rimmed glasses she always wore.

"Excuse me," I said.

"Julie?" Tasha said.

At first, I blinked at the sound of my name. I stood away from the door, my head high and my neck long. First breath in, then out. That last time at seventeen, under these old hanging lights and high windows, I'd thrown a towel in her face before I walked out and slammed the door. My smile now felt weak, embarrassed.

"Wait for me," Tasha said. She turned toward her students. "All right, let's see that eight-count *glissé* across the floor again. Arms in second, and don't forget to start with the right foot."

They tried again, but they couldn't coordinate their arms and legs and they kept missing the beat. At last Tasha clapped once more and brought the session to a merciful close. The students, looking relieved, grabbed their things, their feet heavy on the stairs and their gym bags bumping against the outside walls of the stairwell. Tasha walked toward me, wiping at her forehead with a makeup-stained towel. Her deep sigh exhaled into the room's quiet.

We must have been a sight to the one student who eyed us through the plate glass window. Though always slender, I'd grown even taller since seventeen, while Tasha had lost height and added weight. She had to reach up in order to wrap her arms around me. But her arms, warm with body heat and sweat, felt familiar and welcome.

I pulled back. "I never knew you did adult ballet."

"You do what people want," she said. There was sweat on her neck where the skin had collapsed into folds.

She turned back from waving to the last of her students. Deep lines trailed her mouth, and there was heaviness in her jowls I hadn't noticed before. Why I'd expected her to look the same, I don't know.

In the old changing room, a half-dozen hooks caught the drape of Tasha's skirts and leotards. I found the single chair in the corner and perched on the edge. Tasha dropped her skirt and tugged at her leotard. "Remember when you and I and Joe McKenzie all changed in this room?" I said. "Sometimes all three of us at the same time, sliding into corners or turning our backs?"

Tasha faced the mirror opposite me. "He's done well for himself," she said. "Best supper club in town." She seemed to mentally sort a jade blouse that hung on a hook next to a pink one. The tops of Tasha's thighs had remained tight, the one thing dance gave us that didn't go away.

Watching her reminded me of that first time I stood dwarfed in front of what seemed a giant of a woman, her black curls shaking in the sun from the overhead window while she instructed the five-year-olds we were, my small, sweaty hand gripping the barre. A *tendu*, *plié*, *relevé*; the strain to get it right.

She stepped out of her leotard and her breasts, no longer supported by Lycra, dropped heavily toward her waist. When she leaned over, the skin on her arms hung away from the bone. "You need a stronger stomach, girl," she said. "This is what seventy-two looks like."

Tasha's arm swept wide and she clipped my ear when she reached for the jade blouse. "You're not still dancing in Vegas, are you?"

"Sure," I said. Only out-of-towners called it *Vegas* rather than Las Vegas.

"Vegas kept you trim," Tasha said. "I'll give you that."

"It gave me everything," I said.

"Why is it I don't believe you?" She looked at me like she had a way of testing what she just said.

I dug around in my purse until I found my black patent lipstick case. Mirror in front of me, I drew the lipstick along my bottom lip, then the top. Pressed my lips together. A single breath in, then out. "Still principal in *Jubilee*," I said.

"Good for you," she said. "At fifty-one that's no small feat."

I squirmed on my chair, wondering how she remembered my age and why I needed to lie. No point in digging this hole deeper.

"Let's go to The Durango for a steak," she said. "We don't even need a car."

"Sure," I said. "Anything's better than *Wheel of Fortune*." For tonight, Dotty would have to be disappointed.

Tasha took the same purple skirt I saw in the studio and hooked it in the back before belting it with a wide silver belt, a style Tasha had always worn. "Help me fasten these beads."

In the light's glare, I stood behind her and began to right the clasp, the turquoise and jasper beads heavy between my hands. I leaned in closer, my shadow hiding the light, the smell of dance class still on her neck.

Her eyes met mine in the mirror. She patted her hips. "What you see is what you get. Eventually, even you, Julie."

* * *

My red heels tapped against the parquet floor in the otherwise quiet dining room. The leather booths were Wednesday empty except for a few couples and four guys. At the edge of the dance floor, some fellow's head bent over a twelve-string guitar while he played classical music. Small lamps lit the tables, a single rose leaning out of a crystal vase on each linen tablecloth. It could have been LA or San Francisco or even Las Vegas.

At a table against the far wall, our waiter seated Tasha first. The eye sparkle and the shine on her wet lips told me this was the most excitement she'd had in a while. "Two gin and tonics," Tasha said to the waiter. She shook her head and laughed. When she did, her earrings became lanterns embedded in wide silver bands.

"Tall for me," I said. "Extra lime."

After the waiter left, I leaned into the table, my eyes on hers. "You haven't changed," I said.

Tasha's head went back. Her laugh lit the center of her mouth with its gold crowns at the back. "It's not like you to be polite, Julie," she said. An old tic pulsed under her right eye, more pronounced than before.

My purse clasp claimed my attention as a way to avoid the heat on my neck. She'd always called me on my half truths; I'd just forgotten.

Our waiter set the first drink in front of Tasha.

"What brings you back to River's End?" she said. "Your mother hasn't died, has she?"

"Her breast cancer is back," I said.

Tasha folded her arms across her chest. "Bad?"

My glance went toward the table's small lamp. I don't know why that grabbed my throat, not something that happened when I was around Lorraine or even sitting with Dotty. "Lorraine's in charge," I said. "You know how that is."

Tasha's hands, with their liver spots and wrinkles, bobbed the lime in her drink, her finger the focus of her attention. She was maybe five years younger than Dotty. She glanced up at me. "You're like a well-pruned tree." She held her glass midair, waiting for me to lift mine. "To my success story," she said. Her amethyst ring caught the light when her glass tapped mine.

Lucky or unlucky, Tasha evolved into my other mother, nothing like the woman Dotty became in her house slippers and white chenille robe. A morning shuffle to the coffee pot on the stove. All that talk about the career she'd given up, who she could have married and where she'd be now.

Not Tasha. She was low-cut peasant blouses and artsy earrings. New York–trained, she ended up in River's End with a Southern Pacific guy like Daddy. With or without a man, she never looked back, and she never cared what people said or thought about her.

She sipped at her drink, her heavy beads hanging at the puckered skin on her chest where the cleavage had once been smooth. "Let me see your legs," she said.

What the hell. I scooted my chair back from the table and pulled my skirt thigh-high. I lifted my leg into the space between us. My leg hovered midair with my red sandal above the light from the small lamp and nearly on top of the table. I tilted back on my butt and brought my other leg up alongside it. My skirt was nearly around my waist.

She leaned back. Her head went from side to side. "Legs are everything," she said. "Faces disappear onstage."

This wasn't what we talked about thirty-some years ago when legs were a given and faces got you there.

Her finger stirred her drink, the ice cubes going around and around in their own slow dance. "Does Dotty mean you're staying awhile?"

I looked down at my drink. "Probably," I said. "How about you? How long are you going to teach?"

"Somebody has to pay the bills."

"You could have married again," I said. "Had somebody else pay them."

She lifted her glass into one long swallow. "Not me," she said. "Men are just for fun." She wrapped her fingers around her cold and sweating glass. "Men weren't your ambition either. All you wanted was a big stage."

Tasha fished the lime out of her drink and put it to her lips. Squeezing it together, she sucked on the juice. Her lips puckered into a thousand tiny lines. "Joe should have gone with you to Vegas," she said. "But you had that no-good Tony."

Yes, Tony. My ride to the rhinestone choker and ostrich feathers.

Tasha waved to the waiter. "Want to teach?" she said. "It's time I got out."

At first, I said nothing. Eyes on my drink, a deep breath in. After five years of no luck and waiting for something to happen. "Sure."

Her brown eyes were too shiny inside the folds of her eyelids. "I could have told you this was where you'd end up," she said.

The couple at the next table, their legs entwined under the table, was the only place to look. My throat, tight again, made it hard to swallow.

Tasha shook the ice in her near-empty glass. "No one had what you had."

"You had it." I sucked an ice cube.

"Once," she said. When she shook her head, her earrings became lanterns again.

Awkward, not sure where to go with this, I said, "Was I thirteen or fourteen when we went to New York to see Martha Graham and Nureyev?"

She raised her hand in the direction of the bar. "You could have gone there if you'd pushed harder," she said.

"New York was your city."

"It could have been yours."

"My tits were too big and I was too tall for ballet. You said so yourself."

"If I did, I was teasing," she said. "I don't remember saying that."

Stunned. A whole life, a career based on what now appeared to be a casual statement. Did she even know what she'd done to me? That last scene in the studio stretched before me now, the seventeen-year-old girl I was with her blonde ponytail and black leotard, the towel in Tasha's face when she said too much breast, too tall. The same heat on my neck and face now, the same disbelief.

The waiter's shadow fell across the table lamp. He set down new drinks.

After what she'd said years ago, I'd have given up if at thirteen I hadn't rummaged through Daddy's sock and underwear drawer, snooping for money or cigarettes, when my eye caught the edge of a slick colored brochure sticking out at one side. That Las Vegas showgirl, her hand on her hip, the long rhinestone earrings and a white feather poking out of her seed pearl cap. I was mesmerized by the white bikini tops and bottoms, the white tail feathers flaring behind her and all the way down to her heels. Beautiful. I could do that.

"I wanted heels," I said, conviction in my voice. "Long trains and feathers."

Tasha's hands went around her glass, the red fingernails weaving together. Her liver spots were darker in the dim light. There was a time I envied her hands, was inspired by them, especially overhead, poised like the neck of a swan.

"You don't do anything unless your whole heart's in it," she said. "I give you credit for that."

On impulse, I reached out and took Tasha's hands in my own. Her fingers were thick and warm. The multiple rings hard. One breath, a second. What could I say? My career, how could you? My eyes on her liver-spotted hands. What was the point? A lifetime of dance was over now. But she was the beginning.

I kept holding her warm hands with their hard rings. My fingers kept rubbing against the silver bands, not really knowing what to say. The swell roiling inside my chest with all those mixed-up feelings, something I couldn't trust. Still, my eyes couldn't leave hers even though I felt the heat of long-held tears.

Her brown eyes, both sad and shiny, came closer. "You're just like me," she said. "You always were."

Chapter Thirteen

Lorraine

J ulie's white legs stretched out bare under the black skirt on the spare seat in front of her. She'd pulled her skirt past her knees and mid-thigh, her legs spread apart in the heat, never mind the folks gawking when they walked by the downtown Coffee Carousel on K Street. This was our first casual outing away from Mama and the mobile home and, as always, she flaunted herself. Sometimes she embarrassed me so much there was nothing to do but what I was doing, gaze across the street at the new county offices, the four-story stucco showing orange in the afternoon sun. I just hoped no one I knew saw us there.

"I should have taken Dotty to Las Vegas," she said.

I sipped at my iced coffee, feeling the August air against my skin, my throat. "And you'd have done what with her? Left her sitting alone in an apartment while you gallivanted all over town?"

Julie tucked her hair behind her ears. "Dotty would have loved Las Vegas. Cher and Rod Stewart," she said.

"Wayne Newton. There's always something going on. Always excitement."

The old me would have pounced on that. *You think your shit doesn't stink?* But that wasn't me anymore.

"Mama would mix with Las Vegas like polka dots and stripes scrambled together," I said. I could just see Mama, and it wasn't pretty; day after day, an old lady with her white plastic beer cup full of nickels in front of a downtown slot machine. What a disaster.

"River's End might not be the Mandalay Bay," I said. "But it's calm and steady and you know what to expect."

Julie's Hollywood sunglasses zeroed in on me, and her mouth took the shape of a smirk. She didn't have to say a thing. I knew what she thought.

We sat like that for a while, not saying anything, and I was thankful for the breeze blowing down K Street. Julie probably didn't notice the blue hyacinth that stuck out above the yellow marigolds in front of the convention center. We might not be the MGM Grand or her precious Bally's, but look at that waterfall and those magnificent trees, forty, maybe fifty feet tall. The Red Lion to the west, the convention center on the east, everything balanced the way it should be.

"Tell me, what's so special about River's End?" she said.

"Almond blossoms in February. Every February. You know it's that time of year when you see them. And peaches at roadside stands in July," I said. "Peaches and the smell of peaches. Every July, that smell and that taste—juice running down your chin. We don't get them all year long, so it means something." I picked up my iced coffee. "What about those times we picked up mica between the railroad ties when we were kids?"

"You really get off on nostalgia, don't you, Lorraine?"

"Since when did you get so high and mighty? There was a time when being Almond Queen was the peak of your success." She wasn't going to derail me. "It's not just the orchards and the town," I said. "It's a feeling that you *belong*. People care about each other, and you care about them."

Julie set her plastic glass down on the wrought-iron table and mercifully crossed her legs. She gazed toward the new county building. "I had that in Las Vegas," she said. "For a long time, I had that."

"Then you know what I'm talking about. It's about caring enough to take someone to the dentist or, even at Diego's, if someone is down or in trouble, you can be a little nicer." An edge of old anger rode behind my words. I could feel it there and I had to watch my mouth. "Some stuff you have to put up with. Like at home. Cleaning Mama's porta potty or soaping her down on her shower stool." Just imagining Julie leaning into the shower, her precious curls at risk to the shower spray made me want to laugh, but it wasn't a ha-ha laugh. No, she'd never be able to handle what I'd put up with the last ten years.

"With Dotty, you can pay someone to do that," she said. "But I wouldn't."

Julie sipped at her drink. Kids with piercings and tattoos hurried toward the Saturday matinée at the multiplex next door. A father and his small boy, hand in hand, walked past in their matching Cougars baseball caps. "No bright lights, no action," she said. "Afraid I'd die on the vine here."

That's what I'd expect her to say. People without faith in their lives never take the first step toward being human. Entertainment is what they live for. Something happening. Because inside them, nothing's going on and the Big Empty terrifies them. Right now, maybe because I refused to argue, I could see through my sister and what I saw was one scared woman.

"I suppose this is my town the way Vegas is yours," I said. I sat forward in my chair and leaned across the table. "Once we had fun here. Swimming in the Tuolumne or Saturdays shopping at Rexall. Remember our front-porch plays? Setting our hair together in the bathroom?"

Julie couldn't hide the half smile that crept into her face. She hesitated before she said, "That's before I knew there was a bigger world."

I stayed forward and whispered so no one would hear me. "I wish just once you'd have something good to say about the place where we grew up, a place that's been good enough for me and Mama and Becky. But, no, you had to run away just like Daddy. Like home is a trap. I've never understood either one of you."

She gazed at me with that wide-eyed stare of hers, the heavy black liner around her eyes and those hoop earrings against her shoulders. Right off the set of *Grease*, except for those dark circles under her eyes. That was her.

"Speaking of home," Julie said. "How much do you think it's worth?"

Who'd believe someone could still shock me at my age, but my sister took the cake. Took it home and frosted it. "It's my home," I said. "That's what it's worth."

"Come on, Lorraine," Julie said. "You're too practical. You've thought about the cash value."

An angry heat fried my neck and face and I didn't want to know my blood pressure right then. "It's not up for discussion."

"It's one-third mine," she said.

"One-third of the appreciation is yours. That figure was determined a few years ago."

"Small details," she said.

I grabbed my purse off the table and rummaged around until I found my lipstick case with the mirror, my face matching the color of Julie's red purse. If she only knew about the dictate from Mama, she'd be gloating. I pointed the lipstick at my mouth, careful to keep my eyes on the small mirror.

"I have the right to know, Lorraine. I'm part of this family too."

"When it's convenient," I said. "Like now. Assuming I'd sell."

"You'll have to sell. Becky and I will want our parts," she said. She opened her purse, a shoulder bag the exact color of her red shoes. "Or you can buy me out. However you want to do it, so long as I get my share."

"Well, if you're so concerned about what things are worth and we're sitting here like we're on vacation in Frisco, I'd like to know when you're going to pay your third of the rent or go back to Vegas. You're no movie star, Julie, you're fifty-one years old. You can't just sit in my lap and freeload."

This had been coming for some time. I was sick of her stuff all over my bedroom and bathroom and now, with Mama all the time in the living room, there was no place to go and be alone.

"You're telling me to leave? Is that what you're saying?" she said. "You have no right."

"Okay. Fine. You spend the next year wiping Mama's— and I'll go work as a topless dancer in Las Vegas."

"You? A showgirl?"

All Julie's old River's End fillings, including the gap from a molar pulled when she was fifteen, showed as her head went back and she laughed. Despite the caps or crowns or implants, whatever she'd done, nothing could hide her crooked lower teeth. I bet none of her uppity Vegas friends ever told her that.

Still, there was something about her laugh, deep and breathy, always contagious, even now when I was the butt of her joke. There was no way I couldn't laugh with her. This whole conversation was ridiculous. Mama living in Las Vegas and Julie wanting to sell the mobile home. Not in my lifetime.

We both heard the train whistle at the same time. The freight cars clicked in succession along the tracks a few blocks behind us until the weight of the cars hit a sudden connect when the brakes screeched. An old sound, a familiar sound— the bells clanging at the crossings—drifted toward us, the on and on of the trains, half a dozen times a day. Like the Tuolumne River, they came and went from one invisible place to another. Sometimes, like now, the train made me stop and stay quiet like when I was a kid standing below the tracks on Third Street, our house shaking and the windows rattling the way I imagined an earthquake would shake. I'd listen to the whistle, at first an echo, far away and sad. Before you knew it, the sound and shake of the train could swallow you. We'd be sitting at the dinner table when the Bakersfield six o'clock came through and Daddy would pull out Grandpa Teddy's watch with all the dials. He'd listen to the train while Julie and Becky and I guessed the number of cars. After the train passed, Daddy would say who won by how long he timed the train. At least she hadn't forgotten that.

Neither Julie or I said a word until the train disappeared along Second Street. There wouldn't be another until supper and, by then, we'd be back at River's End, gin and tonic time all over again.

"Fifty-six," Julie said.

"Closer to fifty-one."

Trains since the beginning. The railroad tracks with their mica and pink quartz crystal. "They always remind me of Rosemary," I said.

Julie fanned herself with a napkin, her sunglasses like binoculars on the traffic where nothing was happening that I could see. "Rosemary," she said. "Things gone wrong."

"You were the one who found the stains on the tracks. Those shreds of what was left of her. Talked me into going with you up the embankment to look."

Julie lifted her glass. "Rosemary was a good lesson for all of us. Leave them before they leave you." She took a long last swallow, the ice having melted except for a few chips in the bottom.

Julie was right. Rosemary's death taught us something I should have learned before I got tangled up with Buck, then let it go on so long. Oh boy, wasn't she right. Even though what Rosemary did was a sin in the eyes of the Lord, it was a lesson.

I remembered pointing down at the stained tracks like blood was a bad word when Julie found what could have been a tooth or maybe a bone splinter. Tiny pieces of what looked like chicken fat. She came toward me with her so-called prize lying on the meat of her palm. I thought I'd upchuck right there.

About twelve and thirteen at the time, we never told anyone about that day. Why would we? No one in our family wanted to talk about a sixteen-year-old girl, only a few years older than me, and her baby not yet born.

"So, tell me about this Pastor Harmon you're seeing," Julie said.

I could feel my blush reach into my forehead within the next half second. "How dare you!" I said. "He's my pastor who happens to be married and a very nice man. He's helped me more than you could possibly understand."

I sat straight in my chair while my feet searched for my sandals. This wasn't something I wanted to talk about with her, now or ever. I gazed toward the other side of K Street where the hyacinths had started to wilt in this awful heat.

Julie leaned forward until I couldn't ignore her. The whisper in her voice matched what I'd call a leer and made it seem like we were accomplices. "Don't tell me 'that's all.' I saw you at the supermarket. Do you think I just fell off a tomato truck?"

I could feel the bricks and mortar fall into place, those eyes that wanted to see through me. Not that she'd ever let me see inside of her. No, she'd dig around until she had one up on me.

"I'm surprised you're interested," was all I said.

"This celibacy thing of yours is crazy, Lorraine. Life is short, and then it's gone."

I had to look away, six motorcycle cops in a row stopped at the light. Julie always had to have a man somewhere. She'd bragged to no end about who and what they were and how they took care of her. Now more than ever, she needed somebody somewhere, if only to buy her French lemonade and butter lettuce.

"Speak for yourself and your own so-called celibacy," I said.

If she knew, really knew, that Pastor Harmon was the perfect man for me, she'd be scheming and suggesting ways I could steal him from Pamela. The Lord knows, as much as I wanted that man in my life, I wasn't going after someone else's husband.

"You never have to worry about me being celibate," she said, a smile that showed the deeply curved lines around her mouth. "I haven't spent half my life waiting for some man to show up."

That would be Buck. And Julie too. Two kinds of people in this world. The stayers and the leavers. We might as well be two different species.

"Why do the ones who leave always think they're the winners?" I asked.

My breath escaped in a big sigh, though our table was quiet again. All you heard were the cars stopped at the light on K Street. Then someone peeled out. Close by, a girl on her cell phone pleaded with her mom to pick her up. We listened without listening.

Julie tipped back her drink until the remaining ice chips jammed against the plastic lid. She set the cup back down. "Somebody has to leave," she said. Serious and far away, something I hadn't seen before. "With men, it's like that. It's good while it's good, and then it isn't."

She laughed, but it wasn't her usual laugh that came up out of her belly and caught me in its wake. It was more like the laugh after you've cried so much you're all dried up and you can't cry anymore.

Shadows hung on the county offices across the street and the day looked different than it had before. For just a minute, Julie had let me see what I call the lonely place. No one can go there with you, especially when it gets so bad you feel you could break apart or, yes, even step in front of a train. The ache that keeps calling you from that time you thought you'd always be across from him, the one you loved, at a table or just riding in the car. First, their profile, then their eyes focused out the window like they didn't even know you were there. Or you were getting out of their car and you looked back one last time. They'd said something to you, it didn't matter what and, even while they talked, the sadness set in. Because when they were there, they weren't there, and whatever you had between you was over. All you had left was that invisible sadness that connected to their face and went right into a place in your chest that got tripped whenever you remembered them.

It happened to me, and I could see it happened to her. But unlike her, once was enough. Besides, whenever someone saw my sister, beautiful and desirable—her old dance partner, Joe, even Tony—she had a power I never had. But the real question was: Did it make the leaving easier to know you'd done it yourself? It didn't look that way—only that you wanted to believe you'd been harmless. That was the wage of sin, right there.

"I'm sorry," I said.

I said it really soft, not to disturb what seemed broken in her. Life did that to us, gave us pieces that would never fit back together no matter how much you angled them this way and that. The whole mosaic or mirror or picture you might have had was wrecked for good.

Chapter Fourteen

Julie

By five o'clock, the river was ripe with the marshy smell of heat and garbage. Like many towns divided by a river, one side is for folks who protect themselves with gates and security patrols, while the other side is for the rest, the worker bees and the disenfranchised. The minute you crossed the Tenth Street Bridge over the Tuolumne, the road dissolved into two lanes, both narrow and windy. Forget sidewalks. A couple of boarded-up houses edged Riverfront Road and, farther down, a burned-out shell with busted-up garbage bags and trash all over the front yard served as the welcome wagon.

I must have been crazy or bored, maybe both, to agree to go to Becky's. "Kenny let her come back home. But, still, we need to check on the situation," Lorraine said. "It's the least you can do. Remember? She's *our* sister." Always that twist on the end, meant to put me in my place.

Stella's Landing. The brown letters scrawled across the chipped yellow paint of a beat-up wooden sign. The driveway's broken pavement bounced my tail good until my tush practically grazed what became a gravel road.

Single-wide trailers lined the river side of the road, opposite a couple of old Airstreams hunched next to a converted
bus. A stenciled manager's sign, in sun-paled red, leaned
against the window of the only double-wide, its green flower
box filled with summer zinnias and lupine and miniature dai-
sies. The orange and purple and yellow against the green
refreshed the otherwise dreary trailer park.

I slowed down to duck potholes and keep the gravel from
spitting against the windshield. Shadowed by late afternoon
sun, all these junkers spelled depressed and pathetic. If you
wanted to stay lost, this was the place to go. No one would
come looking for you here.

A dilapidated dumpster overflowed with black plastic
bags and the stink of whatever was in those bags while three
or four folks crowded around an old gray beater with the
hood up and some guy leaning into it, his jeans halfway off
his rear end and the crack of his hairy butt exposed.

A slew of kids ran barefoot in the middle of the street. You'd
have thought there wasn't one functioning adult alive in here. If
there was, they were probably stoned or drunk from the looks
of these kids in their bare feet and mostly naked bodies.

Becky told me to watch for a clothesline pole and a
couple of picnic tables. They were just beyond where those
folks were performing surgery on the beater. Close to a
converted bus, the sagging ruin she'd described as her trailer
had seen all nine lives. The windows featured hanging-all-
over drapes that would have given Lorraine heart failure,
let alone the aluminum foil taped inside the window about
halfway up. Sunny Acres Mobile Home Park was a resort
compared to this.

On the stoop, a black garbage bag overflowed with beer
cans. I hoped they were Kenny's, but there was no way to be
sure. A clay planter housed dried stems of what looked like
flowers from a season or two ago, and the screen door had

been kicked out at the bottom. On the back of a tablet in the window, the number 44 had been written in black crayon.

Not in a million years would I confess to family in this place. Just one look at the trailer filled me with both disgust and a strange kind of pity. How in the hell did someone, someone who was my own blood, my own baby sister, get this low? It was one thing she dropped out of high school and ran off with the deadbeat she married. Then, again, I suppose the folks who crowded the slot machines and leaned over the poker and blackjack tables, those who spent their money to see our shows, belonged to someone, were loved by someone, at least once, even when they fell off the edge and couldn't crawl back onto the blacktop again.

I parked on the gravel, just a couple of spaces away from the beater and its friends, and I checked my watch. It was half past five when my knuckles connected with the door frame. I'd stay exactly a half hour. I took a first deep breath, then a second.

I'd barely tapped the wood and Becky opened the door. She must have been watching for me. Shorter by just a few inches, Becky stared at me through the wire mesh, a purple elastic cloth tie barely holding her hair back. She could have been a ghost, her hair, more gray than red since the picnic, now hung in long strands around her face. Her big smile, too wide, immediately made me suspicious. She held on to the door handle from the inside. "Look who's here," she said.

"Hi," I said. Even from outside the door, a mangy German shepherd bared his teeth in welcome. I pulled my red purse tight against my hip as if to protect myself. "Your buddy thinks I'm the filet mignon he's been waiting for," I said.

"Never mind Johnnie," she said. "Short for Johnnie Walker." Behind her, his low growl warned *don't you dare*. Becky laughed, and the black gumline of a capped tooth reminded me she was capable of taking care of herself. "He's always that way," she said. "Boozer's worse, so I've got him tied up out back." She grabbed the dog's collar and pushed against the screen until it was wide enough for me to step over the doorsill. "You quit being such a tease, you coward," she said to the dog. "These critters do love me."

I stepped inside, careful where I put my feet down, and I never took my eyes off her dog.

"Protection's a good thing in this dump." Becky pointed toward the crowd around the beater. "Those guys wouldn't know class if it bit them in the ass." She took in my black dress and the red shoulder bag hugged against my side. My open-toed red shoes. "I didn't know we were dressing."

She let go of the screen, and that's when I noticed her bare belly stuck out between the denim shorts and purple tank top. Daddy would have croaked to see his little girl now. For me, this was the scene you avoid at all costs, like the news clips and humanitarian relief promos you toss in the trash after just a glance. I didn't know whether to be polite and stay, or trust my gut and leave.

The faint odor of cat pee drifted above the stained sofa with its faded floral pattern where a pile of unfolded laundry had been heaped from God knows how long ago. At least I wouldn't have to sit there. Closer to the kitchen, I spotted one slightly cleared-out place at the end of the sofa. A black leather skirt had been flung over the sofa's back. Under the laundry pile, a pair of yellow cowboy boots lay scattered on the floor. I thought I was messy. Now I could imagine how Lorraine felt about sharing a room with me.

Cats came from everywhere. One tabby assumed an Egyptian pose on the empty armrest. Eyes like golden marbles, he was taking it all in. Another one, black with one eye missing, crouched on the back of the sofa. Coming out of the kitchen, a calico, bloody scratches alongside its nose, rubbed his back against the cabinet as he made his way toward me.

Becky swatted at the two cats on the couch. "Get off you guys; give the gal a break." She bent over the sofa and grabbed hold of the laundry in one big armload before she moved the whole pile toward the opposite end of the couch, then kicked the boots out of the way. "Go ahead and sit down," she said. "Just don't lean on my skirt."

Fat chance. I didn't even want to sit. What if there were fleas or bedbugs? And the tiny kitchen opposite was nothing but living compost.

Under my butt, the couch was an odd mix of bulges and the too-soft lumps of broken-down foam. The minute I sat down, the black and tabby cats assumed their previous positions, and the calico rubbed against my leg. Meanwhile, Johnnie, the dog, lay at my feet, part of his belly over the open toes of my flats.

"A little vodka and tonic?" Becky asked.

At first, I was so stunned, I said nothing. Wasn't Becky on probation? Damn Lorraine, she had to know Becky wouldn't stay sober. Oh, I'd get her for this. Then, again, what did I care if Becky decided booze or that burned-out biker was her deal. I wasn't a cop. Still, she was my sister and I did care, if for no other reason than that.

Becky didn't wait for an answer. She grabbed a purple glass from the dish pile and set it on the counter before she poured in half a glass of bargain-basement vodka. "You've never been to my place," Becky said. "What do you think? I call it recession-proof."

Behind the counter, she laughed at her own joke, but the whole time she watched me while she fixed the drinks. The long and loose strands of her hair fell around her face. She picked up two ice cubes and plopped them into the purple glass.

Besides her mess, big-leafed, vinelike plants that looked like elephant ears grew in row after row of standard gardening pots until they formed pyramids and threatened to strangle the place. In each corner, Creeping Charlie hung down from the ceiling in macramé hangers making my skin crawl with claustrophobia. She couldn't possibly see how depressing this place was and still live in it. Hell, I'd drink too if this was my life.

"Me and Kenny always talk about going back to Vegas," she said. "But we never go anywhere unless it's to move." She lifted an ashtray of cigarette butts and opened the door under the sink. "Shit. He never took out the garbage," she said. "Men, you ask them to do one damned thing and it's too much." She closed the door again. Was she waiting for him to come back from Pocatello? Again, I thought about how little I did around River's End. Princesses. Both Becky and me.

Becky came around the kitchen counter until she stood in front of me, an unlit cigarette hanging from her mouth and an ashtray balanced on the flat of her lower arm. Awkwardly, she held both drinks in her hands. Her fingernails, with the same chipped orange nail polish she wore to the picnic, were now bitten to the quick and the cuticle was bleeding. She handed me the purple glass. "How's the foot?"

My foot was the last thing on my mind. "Fine," I said. I gazed down at the red flats. "I'm working at my old dance studio. Two beginning ballet classes and a private student."

"Working already and you just hit town," she said. "Lucky you."

She made it sound like I was one of the select few ordained to work. Outside of cashiering at a convenience store and a short gig as a motel maid on McDowell Avenue, my fallen-by-the-wayside sister seemed allergic to work, at least according to Dotty.

Never would I have imagined this was where innocent, lonely little Becky would end up. Whatever slack I'd cut Daddy, this was his doing.

Her orange glass had no ice and was nearly filled to the

brim. She carried a folding chair, the cigarette still in her mouth. "You've got to be resourceful when you live in a small space," she said.

Or drunk. Or crazy.

"Not that you would know." She hooked her little finger in the air. Likely making fun of me. "Trailer life depends on decent weather," she said. "It's hell in the damned heat and worse in winter. Always, the narrow walls and mess inside are enough to make you nuts."

We all need to be an expert on something, even if it's trailer life. I glanced down at my watch. Fifteen minutes to go.

With the cigarette in her mouth, Becky reached for the orange glass she'd set on the kitchen counter, but jammed it against the counter's edge, spilling her drink into the ashtray and onto her knee. "Shit," she said. When she wiped at the spilled drink, I noticed flea bites covered her lower legs. She'd scratched them until they bled.

She kept trying to hold her now-lit cigarette propped in the air, like she had to impress me. Then she looked down at my feet like she'd just noticed them. "God, your feet are all messed up," she said. "Some guy do that to you?"

I pulled in my feet but it was too late. There was no way to hide the bunions and knobby bones, even with red toe polish. "They're dancer's feet," I said.

Becky took another cigarette out of the pack, then held up the one still burning to light the fresh one. "You did something, though," she said. "You got out of this shithole."

And in ten minutes, I'd do it again.

She reached forward with her pack of generics and dropped them on my lap. "Have a cigarette."

"Gave them up." I set them on the arm of the sofa.

"What did you do that for?" She reached over and took them back.

"They give you wrinkles."

Becky's laugh emphasized her black gumline. "Who gives a shit." When I didn't say anything, she quit smiling. Her eyes got narrow and her mouth shut tight. "Guess that's a big deal for someone who makes a buck with their looks."

Her face was too many country roads. Nearly forty-nine, she'd let cigarettes and sun and booze carve lines in her forehead and around her eyes that reminded me of Curtis photos of old Native women who lived their whole lives in the sun. Already, her eyelids were as droopy as Dean Martin's. Most likely, she never gave it a thought and figured miniskirts and yellow cowboy boots would carry her to the grave. All I could feel was sad.

She stubbed out her cigarette and stood up. "Want another?"

The dog had completely taken over my feet and the cats, the calico and the one-eyed, sat on either side of me like bookends in a macabre movie. Any minute I'd get up off the sofa and ease toward the door.

I glanced inside my glass where I'd only managed a couple of sips. Maybe there was still a chance. A year or two sober, who knows who she would be. As a kid, a sweet shyness would come over her whenever she came into the bathroom where I was putting on makeup. She'd stand there and hold on to the door, her questions tentative, adoration spread across her face.

The dog let out a bark that made me jump, Becky too. Her drink slopped onto her knee when the dog shot up off the floor and headed through the screen. "Damn dog," Becky said. She wiped at her knee before she laughed a sideways laugh. "He's doing his job though, just like I taught him."

Becky started to take a fresh cigarette out of the pack. "I've always been pissed you didn't take me with you, ya know," she said. "Left me behind just like Daddy did."

Take me out and shoot me. The Carleton Curse, its giveaway redness, radiated up my throat and into my cheeks.

"What makes you think I owe you a damned thing?" I said. "You had the same chance I had. Sure, Daddy left. You get over it. I left town and got stronger. You made a choice, same as all of us."

You'd have thought I slapped her. Her mouth opened but nothing came out. Then, following a strange silence, she said, "I looked up to you. I thought you were my friend."

For a moment, I knew she was right. Summers, the two of us with our Barbie dolls on the army blanket under that big tree where the Fliegers built their tree house. And down by the creek wading in the water looking for treasure. Even after I ran off, I'd send her postcards. Elvis and the Beatles. So long ago, yet a heaviness in my chest reminded me of those times.

She sat there looking pathetic, that stupid orange glass, her barely lit cigarette and knees that should be covered at all times. My sister. The same mom and dad. How did stuff like this happen? Sure, Daddy left. But how did she let it take her down?

"Yes, once we cared a lot about each other, helped each other," I said. "You could have done something different too. So don't go laying your *sorry-me* on my shoulders."

"Speak for yourself," she said. Her mouth curled around the words. "*Land of the Lost* has a new tenant." She dragged on her cigarette. "All your bullshit about Frank Sinatra this and Rod Stewart that. Mooching off Lorraine and the old lady." She started to stand. "Think I haven't figured it out? Everybody's hip to you."

The heat on my face became hotter as it moved into my scalp. "You don't know what you're talking about." I grabbed my purse and stood up.

Becky's ash had grown beyond the slight curve that held it. The ash fell onto the carpet, but she didn't seem to notice. She started to laugh, but it came out half snarl. "You're over the hill, Julie, darlin'," she said. "Just like me. I know it and you know it."

I stood in front of her slumped shoulders and flyaway hair. I pointed at her face, her hair. "For someone who's just had their butt saved one more time, you've got a lot of room to talk."

Becky closed one eye and took a drag on her cigarette. "All your hoity-toity ways. You're a loser now too." Then she laughed a laugh that shook her boobs and her belly.

Insult to injury, I found myself hitting at fleas, real or imagined, on my arms and on my legs. "I'm getting bit to hell."

A snotty half smile covered her face. "Welcome to my life."

Damn Lorraine! I pulled my purse into my side, ready to head toward the door. But, just my luck, her mangy dog clamored back through the screen and hunched in front of me, a growl rumbling from deep in his throat as he showed me all his teeth. Becky just stood there looking like she'd won, whatever that meant. The cats, who followed my every move, jumped back onto the couch, back onto the pile of laundry except for the one-eyed cat rubbing his back against my legs.

"Call off your dog," I said. "I can find my own way out."

Becky's drink was tilted in one hand with a fresh cigarette ready to light in the other. "You coward," she said. "I tell you the truth just like AA says I'm supposed to and you're too scared to hear it."

My mouth was hot with my own spit. In front of me, all I saw were the yellow teeth of a mangy German shepherd.

"Cool it, Johnnie," she said. "Let the bitch go."

It wasn't until I sat my butt down in Lorraine's Escort and locked all the doors that I dared breathe again. As I drove out the way I'd come in, the rearview mirror caught the overflow dumpster and the beater's friends, all bent over the hood except for some bearded guy in a bandana who smirked at me while he humped the air.

Chapter Fifteen

Lorraine

Sex was in the air. At least between Laura Winston and Wayne Killgallon, the two teenagers in the far back seat of the church van, suspiciously hidden behind the other six kids. I saw it the minute Pastor Harmon pulled into my driveway at Sunny Acres to pick me up for the August Fresno Revival. We should have split them up. But, for once, I didn't want to bother. Let things take their course.

The day promised to be what I imagined heaven would look like, minus those eight kids, of course. Pastor Jack Harmon and I were the real kids, playing hooky from school and off skipping into the wilds of Fresno. He'd bounded onto the front porch that morning, a navy-blue polo shirt and khaki trousers. How young he looked, how carefree. A man who never went anywhere without his white clergy collar and a black shirt, dress slacks. He bent forward to grab my overnight bag, his hand around mine before I realized I could let go. His skin, so soft, unlike those rough and crusty clubs Buck called hands. And that look on Pastor Harmon's face when he stood back up, all six feet four of him. Those blue eyes. His soul looking into my soul. This was the kind of man a woman wanted in her life.

I must have changed what I was going to wear at least a dozen times before I settled on my usual denim skirt and a sleeveless flowered blouse. A pink sweater to throw over my shoulders. I didn't want him to think I was silly or overly excited. This wasn't going to be any different than all our other times together. But I'd stood in front of the mirror at least two hours, as bad as Julie, worried about how I looked and in agony over my rear end.

Up front and happy riding shotgun, I sat next to Pastor Harmon as he drove, bathing in the scent of his aftershave, clover or fruit, I wasn't sure which. He'd nicked his chin shaving, and that seemed kind of sweet. His left elbow leaned on the door's armrest, though he curled around toward me as if he wanted the best advantage for talking. Soft organ music on the radio, that classical-sounding stuff I never listened to, but just the right touch, though I was sure the kids would have preferred the grind and blare of their own music. As Pastor Harmon's chest and shoulders faced in my direction, so cozy, I did the same, my body turned slightly toward the van's center island. For once, I thought, forget the kids in back. Mostly boys, five of the eight, and all of them brats, especially Wayne Killgallon who needed the Lord in his life the most. I wasn't having any of his smart mouth, especially the way he kept saying, "Looks like you're getting it on, Miss Carleton," and then he'd wink, hinting that Pastor Harmon and I were talking about something other than prayer and being of service.

The whole ride to Fresno, I noticed the countryside after Ceres, flat with rolling hills to the west, the summer's brown taking over the fields, the corn stalks tall and the corn getting ready to be picked. I'd missed seeing that. This was my first vacation away from River's End, away from Mama, since she fell ill a year ago. The freedom of it! No Becky, no Julie, no Diego. The last time I went anywhere overnight was when Buck took me that one time to Alaska on the Alaska-Canadian Highway. That was fifteen years ago, the quiet on that long road, that particular night we slept in the tent and listened to the loons. The cabin outside of Whitehorse was the place where we talked about going back for our honeymoon. I was happy then, very happy. Like now. The Lord knows, I wanted to trust what was happening, complicated as it was. Sun on my lap and blue sky overhead. Pastor Harmon's blue eyes and salt-and-pepper crew cut. The smell of him and that little cut on his chin. Happy to be going somewhere, anywhere, even if it was only overnight. Besides, this would give me a chance to talk to Pastor Harmon about Mama's decision to change her will.

"Julie going to be okay with your mama?" Pastor Harmon asked.

"Or, vice versa." I laughed. Dry fields out the window. A silo. "It's been so long since I've been away, I don't know how to act."

"You deserve this, Lorraine. Besides, we're doing the Lord's work," he said. "That's justification in itself." He seemed more relaxed, his long fingers wrapped lightly around the steering wheel where just minutes before they'd been on my shoulder. "I don't know if I told you before, but I'm glad you offered to come on this trip." He glanced at me with a smile, his eyes scrunched up like he meant it. "It has to be a lonely life for you, Lorraine. Taking care of your mama and now your sisters as well."

"Funny, I never thought of it that way," I said. "It's what I've always done."

"No time for yourself. No one to help you, to keep you company."

"You mean Mama? She's always there to keep me company."

"I don't mean your mama—you know what I mean. A companion for you, someone who can love and take care of you. *Appreciate* you."

A warm rush went from my stomach, up into my chest and through my neck, right into my head, reminding me of the night I was saved. Up out of my seat and down the aisle to *Oh, Lamb of God, I come, I come.* Tears streamed my face that night, and I remember feeling lifted on angel wings. "You're never going to forget this," he'd said then. "You'll be part of me and the Lord forever." Words I could live by, especially since they came from Jack, his given name and one I only said to myself.

A nice name, Jack, and one you don't hear very often. Jack Harmon. Maybe not a name you'd think of for a man of the Lord. I'm sure it suited him better in his roughneck days in the Wyoming oil fields. From his profile, the sharp forward chin and longish nose, I could just imagine him in the hot sun, his shirt off, jeans hugging his hips, sweating over one of those dirty oil rigs. That devilish glint in his eye I saw just now, hinting at something fun and naughty you could only guess. He was a boy then, he'd said, and he didn't have the Lord in his heart yet. He spent all his time drinking and dancing and fooling around with women. He never said fooling around with women, but you could imagine. The sound of Jack was friendly and familiar like the direction we were moving in.

The sun through the windshield came right into my eyes. I'd forgotten my sunglasses, even though I'd bought new-used aviators at the Goodwill especially for the trip. I pulled the sun visor down and, in doing so, the visor mirror flipped open. I needed more pink on my mouth, but I wasn't about to pull out my lipstick case. I'd just have to keep my lips wet with my tongue.

"We'll be in the big tent all afternoon and into the evening," he said. "You know Denise Lawrence is meeting us at the church."

Oh, for Lord's sake. That black-haired phony from Manteca with big boobs and clingy dresses. Just because her father was a deacon and big contributor to the church. She was young enough to be my daughter and a good fifteen years younger than Jack Harmon. "I didn't know Denise went to youth conferences."

"Normally, she doesn't. But I asked her as a special favor." He glanced over at me. "She's wanted to get more involved. Laura?"

In the rearview mirror, his lips pulled tight. He was talking into the far back seat. I looked into the visor mirror in time to see Laura Winston's blush. She'd probably been caught with her hand where it shouldn't be.

"Maybe you want to switch with Evan and sit up here behind me?" Pastor Harmon said.

I didn't have to turn around to know Wayne Killgallon was behind this. He and Laura Winston had been going at it since freshman year. If they hadn't already gone all the way, it was a miracle. And her mother, Luanne, wasn't about to put Laura on birth control pills like Mama finally did with me after Buck and the Oakland ordeal. I could have told Laura about the shame you live with the rest of your life. But I would have been giving myself away.

Jack turned to me, his head tilted just the slightest, and his blue eyes caught mine. He winked at me, a wink that tells you you're in on what's going on.

I nodded, *Sure, that's why we're here.* Chaperones. But I also took his wink to be a sign, different than duty calls or quick hugs on the front porch after he stopped to pay his respects and pray with Mama—except she'd refused to have him in the house since Julie arrived. Then, recently, at the annual meeting, he said, "Lorraine Carleton, stand up." My neck must have been red enough to fry Diego's eggs. "Do you know this little lady single-handedly put the annual bazaar together?" Applause. Heat on my neck. "Fifteen hundred dollars for the Indian orphanage outside Pierre, South Dakota."

After that, Mama's second diagnosis happened and Julie came back and Becky landed in jail. Unplanned as it was, I'd had to bring in a hospital bed right after I had it out with Julie in the kitchen. Now, Mama lived twenty-four-seven in front of the living room TV. Once she was planted in the living room, especially with Julie in the house, Jack and I hadn't had our usual time together. Today, heading toward Fresno was the first time in seven weeks and five days since we'd been semi-alone. Even at my age, there are times you can't make that wanting-a-man thing go away no matter how hard you try. Like the blue sky and the hot sun landing on my arms, the van rocking down 99, it was a natural thing. Meant to be. Same as the abundant fields this time of year out the window. What was the harm? It wasn't a sin to notice kindness and beauty, natural human urges.

Just after ten, we pulled up in front of the Everlasting Fellowship Church in southwest Fresno. The kids' duffels and suitcases banged against the seats and then the van's door as they unloaded far too much luggage for an overnight stay. Laura and Wayne were the last ones off the van and never said a word, though Wayne gave me his usual bold stare. The kids would be sleeping in the church basement with chaperones from the Fellowship Church. Still, Jack and I were responsible, and Laura and Wayne were a matter of personal concern.

After Wayne slammed the van door shut, Jack turned over the ignition. "We got them here safe and sound. Let's see where we're supposed to sleep."

He drove about eight blocks from the tent meeting to the Motel 6 on Frontage Road where the Fresno church had reserved rooms. I realized that Jack and I would probably stay in side-by-side rooms. I don't know why that got me excited, but it made my stomach jump, and I started feeling light-headed. Side-by-side rooms with an adjoining door. Locked, of course. *Stop it, Lorraine. Don't be a fool. Jack's married with five kids. He belongs to the Lord.*

But right then our physical closeness in the van matched our spiritual closeness. You see, spiritual love comes straight from God, and what we shared was a common faith. When it came in such an attractive form, who was I to complain?

The excited feeling stayed in my stomach while I watched the shadow of Jack's navy-blue golf shirt and khaki trousers through the motel window, his elbows resting on the high counter of the office. That giant tall he is, his hands invisible from where I stood in the sun, yet I could imagine that little mole on his scalp near his right ear. Dumb me, without my sunglasses, I didn't have a clue about what was going on except I kept thinking they had to be side-by-side rooms. The older woman at the front desk, her hair perma-nented like Mama's before chemo, kept looking out at me while Jack talked to her. When his head bent down and his forearms went flat on the counter, I knew he must be signing for the rooms.

Jack came out of the office all smiles. "You're in 118," he said. "Ground floor, right on the end." He put his hand against the back of my arm and guided me toward the van. Then he helped me in, the length of his hand warm under my forearm when he opened the door on my side. He gave me a boost, his strength something I hadn't expected. When he put the key in the ignition and smiled at me in that certain way of his, you'd have thought we were on our honeymoon.

I could have asked where his room was, but I was too embarrassed. For Pete's sake, I couldn't even look at the man without blushing. I took the key he handed me, his fingers brushing against mine, barely brushing and, still, a thrill all the way up my arm.

He drove to the parking space in front of Number 118. He came around and opened the van door, taking my elbow and helping me down the long step. Just the feel of his skin against mine sent shivers through me, his fingers so certain and strong, yet gentle, like he knew I was a woman and not some sexless old biddy as Julie suggested.

Jack seemed more serious once we got back to the church. Maybe he was expected to preach, certainly to stand with other pastors up front when folks came forward in the service. His brow wrinkled when he helped me out of the van, and he never really looked at me again now that we were with other adults. Kids were everywhere, sitting on the church planters and steps or right on the cement walkway. Every once in a while, I'd spot someone with a nose ring or pink hair or studded leather jacket in all the heat, but there were so many kids that the weird ones got swallowed up with the ordinary. Except Wayne Killgallon, his jeans so low you didn't miss his gray and maroon striped boxers.

Then, wouldn't you know, coming toward us was Denise— who drove separately, thank the Lord—in a white eyelet dress, of all things, and as tight as her skin. In the sun, you could tell she dyed her hair, that giveaway shine. A pair of red high heels Julie would wear and those same big, tarty earrings Julie liked. Bad enough I had to live with this at home.

Denise threw her arms around Pastor Harmon's neck and pulled his tall body down until, in front of God and everybody, the other pastors, the kids and a respectable woman like me, she kissed him on the cheek. Left one pink lipstick ring there.

"When did you get here?" Pastor Harmon asked. "Saw your car near the Sunday school."

Her car happened to be a bright blue BMW convertible her daddy bought her for college graduation. Now, she was showing off, especially in front of the kids, and Pastor

Harmon hadn't yet figured out her seductive ways. Needless to say, the steamed heat rising up my neck had nothing to do with a hundred and five degrees that August day.

Julie told me twice not to wear the denim skirt, and now I wished I'd listened to her.

Pastor Harmon pulled his hanky out of his back pocket and wiped at his cheek. He bent down and smiled at Denise like there wasn't anyone else around and he had something private to tell her.

Finally, she turned toward me. "Oh, Miss Carleton," she said. "I didn't see you standing there."

"You nearly stepped on my foot," I said.

Drama queen that she was, her brown eyes got as big as Alma's chocolate custard pies. "I'm sorry," she said. But sorry was the last thing on her mind.

"If you'll excuse me, I need a word with Pastor Ford before the afternoon begins," Jack said.

Both Denise and I watched his navy-blue shirt wind through the crowd of kids. Denise turned to me. "Are you one of the chaperones sleeping in the church?"

I closed my eyes against the sun, against the white flash coming off her dress. "No," I said. "I'm a little beyond sleeping on church floors."

"You know I volunteered for the basement." When she laughed, her silver earrings flashed in the too-bright sun. "Pastor Harmon suggested it because I'm so young."

A kid chaperoning kids. No wonder Wayne Killgallon was so helpful. Maybe he thought he was going to get a piece of this pie.

"Excuse me," I said. I'd relocated the navy-blue shirt. This jezebel was *not* going to get me off track. "I need to catch up with Pastor Harmon."

I didn't wait for her response but turned away and pushed through the crowd of kids. Pastor Harmon saw me coming and nodded toward me just before he broke away from Pastor Ford. He headed in my direction like he expected me. Together, we walked through the tent flaps at the beginning of "The Old Rugged Cross." Someone handed Jack a hymnal, as if we needed it.

Inside the new white tent, folding chairs pointed toward an altar at the front, beneath which a long roll of carpet like a hallway runner had been spread—for people to kneel on, I suspected. Loudspeakers lined both sides and the same in the back. Fans churned everywhere. A large screen hung above the altar, and the video camera sat on a tripod at one side, not to interfere with people coming down the aisle for altar call. Just in front of the screen and behind the altar, a huge cross had been suspended from the central support beam of the tent. Purple banners inviting the Lord's children waved from the crossbeams throughout, but even the huge fans whirring in every corner couldn't touch the heat. Everything else was about the business of being saved.

Jack held the hymnal open between us, his long fingers wrapped around the pages while his wedding ring shone gold against the blue cover. Even while we sang *on a hill far away*, my mind slid back to the motel, anticipating our side-by-sides. Until Denise, I'd never thought much about what Pamela, Jack's wife, had to put up with: flirty and loose women like Denise making a pass at her husband all the time. Most women know how to behave. But all it takes is one bad apple. That would be Denise. She was with us today, right in the front row.

My physical closeness to that man made it impossible for me to think of anything else, especially when his arm brushed against mine from time to time; my skin was so sensitive to his touch, I swore I could feel the hair on his arms touch the hair on mine.

All day and into the evening I kept my distance from Denise. You couldn't miss her; that white dress made it easy to track her. And she stayed away from me, maybe the same bad vibes going both directions. I did notice that Pastor Harmon got really quiet. He probably had something on his mind or he was deep in conversation with the Lord. I wasn't expecting it when he left my side and moved down the aisle toward the altar.

I'd dealt with women like Denise all my life. In high school, girls were always after Buck from the time he showed up sophomore year. Senior year, he became the football team's star quarterback, and I had to constantly defend my territory. Maybe his shyness attracted the girls. In the end, to keep him close, I went all the way with him.

You could tell when evening had come by the gold-and-orange glow outside the open flaps of the tent. And I can't say all that happened in the tent that night except that Laura went forward for the altar call. Maybe a guilty conscience, but I was glad she did. She needed the Lord to protect her from Wayne. She made me so proud that my chest warmed and my eyes teared up when I saw her rise out of her seat and head toward the central aisle, her brown ponytail hanging down her back as she walked forward with folded hands and knelt in front of Pastor Harmon. I have to say that was the second happiest I'd been since the day began and I first sat next to Jack Harmon in the van.

Before long I got filled with the spirit, what with everyone going forward and the excitement of five hundred people in a fervor for the Lord. I walked toward the altar, almost floating, like the Lord had pulled me out of my seat and angels held me by the elbow. I could finally give myself fully to the Lord, that feeling of letting go that started in my stomach, reached up toward my throat and down toward my toes. That's how I knew it was real, the Lord's spirit taking over my body. Whatever was lifting me didn't have a particular face or even a form. It could have been the brown fields or the blue sky. Maybe it was all of that *and* the Lord. I only knew that I didn't have to do a thing but wait to be led.

I was in a state as close as I may ever come to feeling the Rapture.

Once, Becky told me she took LSD and got pretty crazy. I wasn't crazy, just full of bliss and divine inspiration inside a lightness, a weightlessness I'd never known before. Any grief or worry I'd had at seven o'clock this morning disappeared, and the world was suddenly a bigger, quieter place.

After the meeting, I walked outside the tent for fresh air. The sky was a halo of summer light from the west where the sun hadn't yet gone down. The August heat seemed so still and quiet, a relief really, after the excitement inside the tent. Somewhere, the kids were getting settled. Such a relief I didn't have to chaperone them. Such freedom. Such God-happiness, I called it. Looking up at the heavens my only thought was *Thank you, Lord, thank you for my sisters. For Mama. For Jack.* It was the first time I used Pastor Harmon's given name directly to the Lord, a testament to my life being so full, full of what it should be.

A faded orange had just left the sky when Jack walked through the tent's wide opening. The morning's easy look on his face had disappeared, and there was something solemn around his mouth, his eyes. I wondered what had happened to him.

Without a thought, I took his arm. "Ready?" I asked.

He looked down at my arm linked through his and, for just a second, his eyebrows furrowed and his body stiffened. He had to be deep in conversation with the Lord. So I slid my hand over the warm skin of his arm and pulled it back to my side. I was rewarded with the deepest, most sincere smile.

* * *

By now the sky was full of stars, no longer orange or even the faintest navy blue, and a half moon held court just above the horizon. At the motel, still not a word between us, I pulled on the van's door handle to help Jack in opening it. But once he shut off the engine, he sat mute in the driver's seat and draped his arms over the steering wheel. He made no move to go anywhere; instead he looked straight ahead at the three numbers on the door of 118. Then, with a quick glance at the neon open sign hanging high in the office window, he reached down and jerked the handle on his door. He turned toward the open door and swung his long legs out of the van and down onto the parking pad.

I didn't wait but climbed down out of the van by hanging on to the door in order to find that one long step with the toe of my short foot. The key was already in my hand, and I was headed for Number 118. The van door slammed behind me and Jack's feet walked heavily on the asphalt. The only light hung off the end of the building and shone like a spot onto the last two doors, Numbers 117 and 118. I'd already fit the key in the lock where the blue plastic tag dangled and brushed against the outside of my hand. As I turned the lock, I felt Jack Harmon standing right beside me, my overnight bag the only thing between my knee and his leg.

For some reason, I reached down and grabbed the bag's handle from him, and my hand touched his at the same time he let go of my bag. Now I had the weight of the bag to myself. In that moment, I looked up to where the light shined behind his head. I couldn't see his face, just his head bent forward and his long arms propped against his hips where his hands held on.

I'll never know what got into me. But I wanted that man, one way or another. And when you have that kind of wanting in your heart and you're fifty-two years old and you've just been in spiritual rapture, you're crazy-possessed in a way you only consider long after the fact.

I dropped the bag and heard it clunk on the pavement. Then I reached my hand around Jack's neck, and felt the damp of his close haircut where it disappeared inside his collar. I pulled him down toward me, my mouth open and ready. I kissed him so hard I surprised myself.

The whole thing happened before I knew it happened. Before Jack Harmon knew it happened. So surprised, he didn't even resist, his lips dry from the day and partly open, pressed tight against mine. I couldn't see the look on his face, but his long arms came up out of nowhere and his fingers dug into my arms and squeezed hard. He practically shoved me aside. A big shove, like I was the devil. He pushed me with such force that my shoulder hit against the partly open door and threw me into the room. I remember one lamp burned on a bedside table and the flowered bedspread blurred as I stumbled, then fell, and something inside me gave way like you see in the movies when someone falls down a well shaft or an unseen cavern. They're falling through space and they have no idea if or where they'll land. The only thing they know is the drop and nothing to grab hold of, to hang on to. They're doomed to spend eternity falling through space like some astronaut who had his lifeline cut, forever certain he'll die slowly through endless falling.

On the floor, my legs, hip, and arms burned against the carpet before the heat of shame flamed up my neck and into my face. I was so stunned I didn't know what had happened.

After such a long time of having nothing and no one, all the goodness I'd held up to the Lord including the church bazaar and Bible study and home visits and riding in the van with those snot-nosed kids, my faith, my new life foundation going forward, fell out of me and onto that walked-on, diseased carpet. High as I'd felt before, that's how low I fell. I started to cry. It didn't matter that Jack Harmon asked if I was hurt or tried to pick me up or even that I shook his hand free from me after he dared come into the room. Bad enough I'd made a fool of myself. He didn't have to knock me down.

"Lorraine, I . . ."

"Don't say it. There's nothing to say." I wouldn't look at him. He'd said it all with that big shove. No, he could stand there until kingdom come, I wouldn't move until he left and shut the door behind him.

That was the longest minute of my life. How could I have been so stupid to think he'd be attracted to someone like me. Someone plain and hard-working and normal, no different from Pamela, his wife. Like boiling oil from a cauldron, shame washed over me and wouldn't let me go. I had been so lifted up and, now, I was shattered like a hollow clay idol. "Go. Just go."

The door closed behind him. The sound like a prison door closing.

Chapter Sixteen

Julie

The assault from an alien buzz blasted into the dark bedroom from the white, glow-in-the-dark Big Ben on the side table, the big hand on twelve, little hand on three, a streetlight shining through white sheers. That moment, I did and didn't know where I was. Yes, Lorraine's bedroom, but no Lorraine. Some reason I was supposed to wake up. Supposed to do something. Then I remembered. Dotty, alone in the living room, the hospital bed. She was the reason for the alarm in the middle of the night.

"Make sure she's still breathing," Lorraine had said. Her little cross earrings had danced against her cheeks. "It's your turn." The van, a church retreat and tent meeting in Fresno with Pastor Harmon, whose smile a Crest commercial would love. "Only for overnight," she'd said. But her trembling chin gave her away.

My hand grabbed my silk robe, and my long legs and feet found my mules on the side of the bed as I steadied myself into standing. The silence and smell of sickness inside this family catastrophe made gin and Ambien and ten hours of sleep the only way to survive.

Since June when I returned until mid-July, Dotty's life had been day after day in her brown corduroy recliner, the TV and TV tray, toddies and dinners in front of the tube. Then, just weeks ago, came the hospital bed into the living room, her toddies and dinner sitting up in bed, me and Lorraine in the kitchen, a home health nurse, finally, two. Recently, no toddies and no dinner. Just this.

Dread, I was filled with dread. The living room was the last place I wanted to go. Seeing Dotty like this, anyone old and fragile as hell, with no way to reverse the course, made the thought of approaching the bed, of having to touch her withered folds of skin that rolled beneath my touch, of having to do something as simple as lift her head for a sip of water, those eyes that leaked all the time and her protruding blue veins made me cringe. God forbid this place I never wanted to go myself, let alone visit.

The night-light along the hallway guided my slippers with their white fur ruff. Past the bathroom with Lorraine's obscene glow-in-the-dark cross. Past Dotty's room and its pervasive smell of urine and ammonia. If it was me, I'd rather go fast in a car crash. Or go off someplace alone like a wounded animal. At the very least, fall into a long sleep, one day here, one day gone, rather than end up a drugged and leaking semi-corpse. None of this hovering nurse and tiptoeing-around business for me.

The closer I got to the living room, the louder the buzz-grunt of the oxygen machine beside Dotty's hospital bed. With the sofa and coffee table crowded against the far wall and the recliner jammed into the corner next to the three-way floor lamp on low, the living room had become an in-home ICU.

Night-lights beamed the bed's shadow along the carpet. Yes, I was supposed to walk over to the hospital bed with its cold chrome railings and gizmos and take care of Dotty like this was everyday normal. But nighttime was different from middle of the afternoon—the walls, the light, the smells—everything took on a menacing tinge. "Look at the level of the IV drip," Lorraine had said, "and then at the pee container." The Boss had even spread a picnic oilcloth under the two-gallon plastic jar. "You might have to empty the urine," Lorraine said. "The mixing bowl is there to catch the drips."

Dotty lay asleep under the bed's white expanse of sheets, a white blanket, and a baby-blue mask covering her face. According to the doctor, she wasn't getting enough oxygen on her own. Above the mask, her gray-white hair bristled against the pillowcase like a field of two-inch stubble after a light winter snow, when spring's green is still far off. It had started to grow back, so thick now you could no longer see the pink skin that once showed through her scalp. Thank God they'd given up on the cancer drugs.

Besides her peculiar hair, there were her blue-veined hands, her left in particular with its wedding rings where the hand lay on top of the white cover. How strange she'd never taken them off. Maybe a strange mix of loyalty and revenge. Who knows.

From its stand next to the bed, the clear plastic upside-down bag hung half-full, half-empty beside the wheeze of the machine and the intrusive bed that took up most of the living room and all of our lives. Like a still-life painting, the well-placed pee jar told you that what was inside you was coming out, and this was what it looked like. Half-full, the pee jar stared back at me.

To think in the end, we're all just a bag of skin and bones reduced to the in and out of tubes and a buzzing machine, the pee jar the final indignity.

Dotty lay quiet, her head taken over by the plastic oxygen mask, something I could have lived without seeing. I'd spent my entire life looking past the wheelchairs and walkers in the casinos. Like a foreign tribe, they comprised a species from another planet you glanced at quickly before turning away.

Dotty, under the white sheets, under the thin white blanket, her hands folded and her eyes closed, lived inside that pasty skin. Not that I wanted her to die. Tough and sometimes mean as she was, she never took the chances she had. After those early years as a bank teller and the promise of management, her life became a series of steps between the laundry and ironing and cleaning up, one task after the other, one paycheck to the next. She'd ended up at Safeway just to make ends meet, and she probably thought she was lucky to scrape together enough money from the Third Street house to get to Sunny Acres. She had social security and whatever Safeway paid her for retirement, maybe a couple hundred dollars a month. At least she had that and, much as I hated to admit it, she had Lorraine who was willing to take care of her. But it wasn't fair. You survive your whole life to end up emaciated and repulsive to the touch. You can't bear to see yourself in the mirror, let alone have anyone else look at you.

While the bloating in her upper cheeks gave her a softer look under the shaded light, her mouth below the mask was too still, too gray, as if her blood was leaking out and what remained was a cast-off shell of who she'd been. Only the oxygen machine's white noise drowned out the awful middle-of-the-night quiet.

The last time we'd talked, I'd told her about the all-night parties after the second show, all the girls together, usually Thursday, and not at the big casinos, but the clubs on the west side that only the locals knew. About joking with the strippers at Chippendales. She actually laughed. Then, late at night, after Lorraine went to bed, Dotty would lean back against her pillows, a serious, soft look in her eyes. "Tell me about Sinatra, Julie," she would say. "What was he like? Was he romantic?" I told her about the time I sat on his lap for a publicity stunt, another time Bunny brought him backstage to meet the *Jubilee* dancers and showgirls. Afterward, that softer than soft gaze was still there in her eyes. You'd have thought she was sitting on a cushy chair in Old Blue Eyes' backstage dressing room, a gin and tonic beside her, chatting with him before his second show. That's when I knew romance never dies. As long as the pulse kept going, no matter how old you got or how long it had been since someone touched you in a special way, that first tingle erased years of long-tossed calendars.

I stepped closer to the bed. Not that I wanted to, especially to watch her so dependent on the oxygen inside that mask, let alone to know how she was doing. My God, I just wasn't the person for this. And I'd never get used to who Dotty had become, let alone the meanness acquired with age in some folks, her cheeks sucked in with the weight loss, her eyelids so wrinkled and heavy I wondered how she could open them. Her nose was webbed with spider veins I'd never noticed before or paid attention to. Dotty wasn't just old, she might as well have been in a pine box already.

Looking down at the woman who lay on the bed, my shadow across her one remaining cancer-filled breast, she was still the woman who first called Tasha, who pulled me up the long staircase to the dance studio, who braided my hair and dreamed big dreams with me. "If you want to dance, you'll dance," she always said.

The living room was too dark and quiet without the TV blaring and Dotty's toddy glass or remote hitting the metal TV tray. If Dotty had been awake, really awake, she'd be straight up in bed watching the *Today* show or Oprah Winfrey or Wayne Dyer. I suppose when you come to where Dotty was, you want to believe anyone who hints of hope. Like Lorraine and her Jesus, that ridiculous glow-in-the-dark cross.

Like me when I put on makeup and snug my dress against my hips before showing my face to the world. Hope, hope, hope. What we live for.

Dotty lay so still she scared me. I couldn't tell if she was even breathing against the infernal sound of the machine. My throat caught and I could feel the dreaded heat behind my eyes when I reached out, my fingers with their pink and rounded nails against the swell of her blue veins. Reluctantly, I lifted her age-spotted hand gently as I could, the cold of her skin now in mine, and her bones too close to the surface. My throat filled with something I couldn't swallow and that hot sting behind my eyes threatened to take me to a place I didn't want to go. She was more than a body that took up space under a three-way bulb, her bumpy veins and the long bones down her fingers, the skin so thin I wondered if it would tear from my touch. Yet I was afraid to let go. What would happen if I lost her?

In the end, this is where we all go, a land of withered fruit and dry winds that suck the tears and sweat out of us. Cold that's just below the skin where the blood has slowed to a trickle and there will never again be enough warmth to rekindle whatever fire was there before. For Dotty, for me, for any of us. Maybe for her, this was okay, dying in a trailer in Sunny Acres Mobile Home Park, Number 15, fifth space on your right after the swimming pool and cabana.

When I turned to go back to bed, a grunt came from behind the mask and Dotty's hand twitched, all the tubes coming and going, creeping along the top of the covers. Her crooked fingers grabbed at the sheet. I'd waited too long. All I wanted was to check on her and go back to bed. Lorraine should know I wasn't any good at this.

Dotty pulled the oxygen mask away from her mouth, her lips chapped under the mask's blue edge. Her eyes, the milky blue they'd become, scrunched under the three-way on low.

She was afraid. Even I could see that. And while I'd prayed she couldn't see me, it scared me to see her scared. Maybe she didn't know where she was. Or something else had her. Her fingers kept pulling at the mask. "Away," she said. Or something that sounded like *away*.

She pushed the oxygen mask to the side of her face and off her nose. My heart pounded in my throat and my mouth went dry. I didn't know what to do. I forgot where I put the number for the home health agency, and there wasn't anyone around except the Petersons next door and their yappy dogs, quiet now in the night. Dotty, don't you dare die on my watch!

Shoulders back, neck tall, one full breath. A second. "Here," I said. I lifted her head and felt for the strap under her now thickening and coarse hair. The elastic band had to be easy enough to find, her hair as short as it was. Besides, what was the point and why did it always have to be what Lorraine wanted or said? Why not just take off the mask and do what Dotty wanted?

Dotty's fingers clawed at mine, and she scratched my hand where I tried to remove the mask. "Take it off," she whispered.

"Hold on," I said. I fumbled with the elastic and then the clip, but her fingers kept grasping at mine. "Dammit, give me a chance."

Her hand, blue veins on top and a dark two-inch round bruise from a previous needle stick, went around mine. Her crooked fingers lay cold on top of my sweaty hand. I pulled them loose and started to ease the mask away from her face. My head was down, in close. I didn't want to hurt her. "Dotty," I said. "It's okay, I'm here. Julie."

I reached out and lay my hand on her arm where the cold came through her skin into mine. I kept my hand on her thin and wrinkly skin even though my impulse was to pull back. Dotty was the one, the one who gave me permission to live the life I'd lived. That's why I was here, why I was standing beside her bed.

Dotty's old eyes, now teary, blinked, and blinked again. Her lips opened slowly and her tongue curled in an effort to speak. But what came out was only a grunt of what it might have been. Behind her head, the in-and-out wheeze of the oxygen machine stayed steady, a sound you could count on. That close in, I could smell iron on her breath. The metallic smell of dying.

Tears leaked down her lined and wrinkled cheeks. Still, the shine in her eyes remained. "Tired," she said.

I touched her cheek with the back of my hand. Her skin was so dry and rough against mine that my own hand seemed young and soft by comparison. When I turned my hand over and stroked her forehead, it was cold. Too cold. My eyes, still fresh from sleep, were caught off guard with a now familiar sting. I swallowed but my throat felt too thick.

I reached for the chrome of the hospital bed, maybe to steady myself, maybe to feel something solid and real. Nothing mattered, really, only Dotty's eyes leaking tears down her face and into the pillow.

"Here we are," I finally said.

I lifted Dotty's head to pull the pillows closer under her neck where they'd slipped away. But when I tried to pull back, her hand wouldn't let go of mine. From the way she held on to my fingers, her grip so tight it pinched, and from the look in her eyes, all I saw was the loneliness of being on board that last train into a black tunnel from which you'll never return.

I panicked and tried to pull away but she was too strong. Finally, I got her fingers loose. "I'm not going anywhere," I said. I reached down and wiped at her tears with my fingers.

Right then, in a moment when time stands still, something was slipping away, something important I'd nearly missed. The tears I'd been fighting fought to the surface. I remembered the day I arrived, she'd said, "If you were around more, you'd know these things about me." She was right. I'd missed knowing who she really was, still clinging to the image of her from my childhood, her housedresses and trim slacks. I had no memories of what it had been like for her these past years, let alone her hopes and dreams for herself. Because this woman, no matter what Lorraine or Becky or I thought of her, was not only the beginning, but the *over* for the family we'd been. When she went away, a big piece of me—my memories, my sense of family—would disappear as well.

I lifted Dotty's head, then the pillow to fluff it. Dotty grabbed at my hand.

"Hold on, tiger," I said. "Give me a minute."

I lay her head back down, my fingers under the rough gray hair, her head a weight against my hand. Inside her blue eyes, the pupils, just moments ago so milky, had grown dark. She was falling someplace inside herself.

I couldn't help but remember the time Lorraine took Mama to Memorial Hospital during the first cancer scare. That would be eleven years ago, before Sunny Acres, before Lorraine moved in with Mama. The hospital had instituted new smoking rules and the only designated place you could smoke was at a prescribed distance from the automatic doors. There I was, at the side of the building and right in the sun, without a bench to sit on, standing beside a cement post that was supposed to be an ashtray.

At that point, I didn't give a damn. The feeling inside my gut was empty and raw, like now. That constant churning at the thought of losing Dotty then, after the mastectomy on her left side. Yet, it was a relief to be away from the ICU, with its curtained walls and gurneys, rubber soles squeaking on linoleum. They didn't yet know if they'd found all the cancer.

For days, Lorraine and I had hovered beside the ICU bed that held a gowned body and oxygen mask and her still-hefty arms. Above the bed, green-line monitors stared down at us. As long as the lines zigged and zagged, she was still with us. I knew that much.

At that point, we didn't think she was ever coming home.

While I stood against the building next to the ashtray, I recall being glad I was alone. That is, until I saw The Boss, no sunglasses, just her usual denim skirt and over-blouse to hide her sugar belly, come toward me through the hospital's automatic doors. Her gray hair, even then, was nearly white in the sun and that lime-green purse she couldn't seem to part with hung off her arm. Lorraine was the last person I wanted to see right then.

She marched toward the shaded smoking area like that was her job. She'd hardly caught her breath when she said, "They asked me if I'd sign for them to pull the plug."

At first, it didn't register, the pull-the-plug part.

Then I lost it.

"Since when is it *you* they ask, *you* who makes those decisions?"

You could say I caught Lorraine in the whirlwind of my own despair. I couldn't stop myself despite the look of stricken sadness on her face. "First, I don't want Dotty to die, at least not here," I yelled. "A hospital is a place where people don't know you and doctors only see you their way. The clean beds are meant to camouflage the smell of sickness. Worse, this is no place to say goodbye, whatever the hell that means."

Lorraine, those cow eyes and the trembling chin, looked like she'd turn into a spring-swollen river if I kept going. Her mouth opened and her voice was a whisper that nearly disappeared in the whoosh of an overhead plane. "I didn't say I'd do it. I only said they asked."

I'd never forget the look on her face. Or the drop inside my gut that went all the way down when I realized that, just like me, she was having her own hard time.

That happened before we knew there'd be a reprieve. But you could say it set the tone, the dress rehearsal for where we were now, death's same anteroom. Now, I wanted to feel that sympathy or sadness or care, whatever I felt the day she said *I only said they asked*. We'd all grown so far away from each other. Now, without Mama to navigate the world between us, I didn't know if we'd ever get back what we knew as girls, whatever *that* was.

Lorraine and Becky thought the trailer had kept me here. Truth was, I needed a chance to start over. Had hoped for it. Now I realized I'd ignored what was real, what was important or, at the very least, postponed what that might be. Still, I wanted to deny my shortsightedness, the twinge in my hip on the left side that said dancing as I'd known it was over and, yes, the more than occasional hot flash. But there, inside Dotty's eyes, I could no longer deny what was real, what mattered: Mama and a family I'd disowned. As her cloudy blues stared up at me, I suddenly felt cheap and small. I had to look away.

Dotty's fingers pinched me with a strength I hadn't expected.

"What? What do you want?" I asked, the sound of panic in my throat.

She fell back against the pillows and closed her eyes. Then she let go of her grip on my hand and her head rolled toward me, away from the light and into shadow. Though her face had dimmed, she seemed to really see me for the first time.

The oxygen mask off her face, she wheezed and gasped, but the thin bones and wrinkled skin of her hand were stronger than I would have imagined. She tightened her grip again. "If only I could have seen you . . . dance. Just once more."

Only once. At Becky's poor pathetic wedding. Before I left The Trop. A topless performance with my mother and sisters and brother-in-law in the audience. I recalled the self-consciousness I'd never felt onstage before. Embarrassment. Whatever it was, I ran off with some guy afterward. *Jubilee*, the big show at Bally's, was the one she should have seen. But I never asked her to come.

"You made me proud," she croaked.

I felt a clutch in my stomach all the way up to my throat. I didn't trust myself to say a word. Instead, I squeezed her hand. How selfish I'd been.

"Like yours," she wheezed. She tried to lift her head, her neck so weak I put my fingers under it. Maybe it was the angle I was standing, bent over as I was. But her head weighed down my hand. With her eyes directly in mine, "I wanted a life like yours," she said.

This was what it came to. All those dreams and longings, the wishful thinking, the life we hoped for, and it was never what we imagined it would be. It was just what it was, a blessing or a tragedy, depending on how you saw it.

My throat constricted, and any sound at all would release a blockade of tears. I squeezed her hand again, no longer sure I'd ever had the answers. Would ever have any answer—not to the simplest question—just her skinny fingers in mine and whatever strength we could muster between the two of us.

"No more," she hissed.

"What, Dotty?" I asked. Even as the words came out, I knew she meant the bed, the mask, the tubes. The ongoing white noise of a silence that was never really still.

"Pillow," she said. Her voice was more of a whisper, like she couldn't push the breath through her throat anymore. I leaned in closer. "Pillow," she repeated.

My hand felt the bottom edge of the pillow to make sure it was under her neck. "What about the pillow?"

She tightened her hold on my hand, and her cold and crooked fingers clenched mine.

"You want another pillow? Softer? Harder?"

"No," she hissed with a deep sigh, exasperation really. "Don't be stupid."

The hair went up on the back of my neck. "You want the doctor?"

She held my hand against her flattened chest where the one breast had been removed and, now, her other diseased breast had nearly disappeared somewhere beneath her skin. In that moment, I couldn't escape the irony of my own breasts and the doors they'd opened. I tried to pull my hand back from hers, but her fingers dug in deeper. She wasn't going to let me go.

Her blue eyes seemed brighter, even bigger. "The pillow," she repeated.

I leaned over her, closer in, her iron breath in my face and her wrinkly skin crevassed with the wet of her tears. This wasn't happening. Not to her, not to me. Maybe I wasn't really awake. Didn't she know I wasn't brave, I wasn't loving, I was the wrong person? Why not Lorraine? Because she was a Christian?

Her fingers dug into my arm. She closed her eyes. "I can't," she said.

The pillow. Her words, *you made me proud*. I couldn't just turn around and leave, imagine none of this was happening.

"Do it," she whispered. "Oh, God in heaven . . . please, help me, Julie."

It was her eyes. They wouldn't let me go. Not then, not now.

But a pillow out from under her head? Something inside me said no, it can't be me, I can't do this. To be alone with what I never wanted to be alone with. The sting burned behind my eyes even while she stared back at me, the three-way a pinpoint somewhere in the room reflected back from her blue eyes. Her hand, her grip pinched mine. We were past the *might have been*s and *if only*s.

That's when I knew I'd stopped breathing, my hand now sweaty where I held her too-cool hand. The blue mask lay against the pillow. The pillow.

Her eyes were never as alive as they were then. Her coarse hair scratched rough against my palm and those familiar blues never left my face as I pulled the pillow out from where I'd undone the mask. Her mouth had a slight tremble, but the firmness in her chin told me she was certain.

Right then, I didn't know what to say. So I said the only thing that came to me, the only thing that made sense. I got down close to her face and, almost in a whisper, my eyes in hers and hers in mine. "Thank you, Mama."

Her neck moved ever so slightly as she nodded yes.

Years ago, I remembered her sitting at her chrome kitchen table with the yellow Formica top. Her elbows rested on the table and cigarette smoke curled above one hand, while the fingers of her other hand looped through the coffee cup holder. Even then, I could see the ache in her mouth and in her chin. Her eyes held all the sadness and disappointment she never wanted anyone to see. Her sitting there like that said more than all the secrets she'd ever carried with her.

God help me, I lifted the pillow.

Chapter Seventeen

Lorraine

All the way back to River's End in time for the ten o'clock Sunday service, Pastor Harmon had Wayne Killgallon sit in the front seat beside him. No talking. Not so much as a glance in the rearview mirror where I sat next to Laura, her book the main event. They were the longest three hours of my life. He even took me home first, instead of the kids like he'd done before. In fact, he went out of his way to drive past the church and into the Sunny Acres driveway. He couldn't get me out of that van fast enough.

The minute I stepped onto the front porch, I was grateful to be back. My home, my sanctuary, the place where I was certain to find peace. As I opened the door, I smelled not only the familiar smell of sickness, but the reek of cigarettes. In the kitchen on top of my white tile counter, Mama's gin bottle lay empty on its side while, facedown and passed out at the kitchen table and stinking of booze, sprawled Julie.

I hadn't even dropped my overnight bag and, already, I wanted to brain her. I'd left for one night and what did I get? She smelled like Becky when she's been on a toot. I lifted her head by a hank of her thick blonde hair. "What the heck's going on here?" Shouting, like I was at Diego's. That long hair in my fist, I wanted to yank it out. I was that mad.

She lifted her chin inside my hand. Just as quickly, her eyes rolled back in their sockets and her eyelids retreated. There wasn't a sign of life in her.

"You're drunk," I said.

I might as well have been talking to the chair. Suddenly, I was afraid to go check on Mama. Somehow, it seemed easier to get something out of Miss America, passed out and slobbering on her arm. "Julie, what happened?"

Not a word. She may as well have been dead.

I tore into the living room, my heart about to beat its way out of my throat. Mama's bed was empty. The pee jar and baking bowl had tipped on their side; the plastic picnic tablecloth and carpet were soaked. The IV stand, like a lone and defeated soldier, hung its bag and clear plastic tube down onto the carpet. The hiss of the oxygen machine, steady the past few weeks, was silent.

I don't know if I screamed or my voice got stuck in my throat. Mama, gone, and there was nothing left but a mess all over the living room. I had no one to blame but myself. If I hadn't convinced myself I was serving the Lord by going to Fresno, when it was myself by way of Pastor Harmon I was catering to, I'd have been here.

In the kitchen, Julie, her arm under her head, lay snoring. "Wake up, dammit," I screamed. "Wake up before I give you something to drink about."

Still, no sign of life from Julie. Coffee. Black coffee. Full-strength caffeine. Get yesterday's beauty queen awake so I could find out if Mama had taken a bad turn and been carted off to the hospital. I both dreaded and hoped that's what happened.

I ran the pot under the faucet and had a devil of a time getting the black crust off the bottom where Julie let it burn.

Then, while the coffee pot spit and brewed, I went back into the living room. Even with light filtered through the closed box-pleated drapes, Mama's bed stood unbelievably empty. Everything I counted on day after day—Mama's tonic time and *Wheel of Fortune*, the evening casserole, what kept me anchored and solid—was gone in that moment. Though things were getting worse every day, I'd never imagined an empty bed. And never did I think I'd come home after the one day I left town overnight in more years than I cared to count to find Mama gone. I sat down, defeated, and I started to cry.

Leaving Mama with Julie was the worst decision of my life. With tears still wet on my face, I grabbed hold of Julie's hair and shook her dead-to-the-world head even as I stood there in the kitchen sniffling. Behind me, the coffee maker spit as it dripped. I poured what was made into a cup and tried to shove it between her lips. "Where's Mama?" I shouted. But I might as well have talked to the wall. Julie moaned, barely opening her eyes, drool leaking across her arm, and mascara smeared under her eyes and down her face.

Gentle wasn't on the menu that day. I pulled a chair up to the kitchen table and grabbed Julie's shoulder. I shook her good. "Wake up," I shouted. "For God's sake, wake up."

She turned her head in my direction and gave me that eye-roll business, her eyes not open for two seconds. I reached under her chin and lifted it. Doggone, if she hadn't drooled on my table as well as all over her arm. I could have slapped her for that alone.

Her head started to move like she was trying to get away from my hand, but my grip was stronger than anything she could shake at me. "Drink this," I said.

A good four mini-swallows were all I could get down her. I gave her a rest for thirty seconds, then more coffee. The whole routine over and over until that half cup of black coffee, no sugar for her, thank you very much, was gone.

She started to blink and finally kept her eyes open for a few seconds. "Where's Mama?" I said. "Where'd she go? Where'd they take her?" Now that she sat up, her red kimono fell open and, Lord help me, her naked breasts hung between her and the table. "What the hell happened?"

Julie shook her snarly blonde curls the same way she did when she tried to come out of the Vicodin I gave her after she turned her ankle or the cowboy stepped on her. Straight at me, those full-on gray-green eyes without a sign of anything, not even being drunk. "She's dead."

"Dead!" I screamed. "What do you mean dead? I left for one night!" It couldn't be true. "She was fine before I took off," I shouted. "They said she'd be okay." I got right in Julie's face. "I trusted you."

Her eyes were open, steady on my face. But no one lived inside her skin. "They came at six," she finally said.

"Who came at six?"

"911." She sagged back and closed her eyes. "Took the body to Greenfield Mortuary."

"Shit," I said. I was half out of my mind. "Not there. That's the most expensive place in town."

"Fuck Greenfield Mortuary." Julie raised her head and laughed that crazy kind of laugh before you cry. "Mama's dead."

Mama's dead still didn't register.

"Damn you, Julie. Mama should have gone to McClinton's. I can dicker with old man McClinton." All these years he'd come into Diego's, crazy about Diego's scrambled eggs and corned beef hash. Then I realized it was absurd. Mama was dead. She was dead! "Did you check her? Did you check her monitor?"

"I checked her."

"When did you do that?"

She was just sober enough to look me square in the eye. "Three in the morning, just like you said."

"So when did you check again?"

"Six. And she was dead."

I felt my knees start to give and wondered if I should sit down again. But that was too much like giving in when rage had taken hold and insisted on having its way. Right over her head and in her face, I yelled, "One damned minute I leave town in the last ten years, and you screw it up. I wouldn't be surprised if you're lying too. Likely you *never* got up in the night and you're just telling me you did."

Something like pain crossed her face. Julie started to stand, but she was wobbly and had to hold on to the table to keep from falling. She tried to hold her head up, to look me in the eye, but every attempt to pull herself more erect failed. She began to crumple where she stood.

Watching her start to fall brought me back into myself. Someone had to be responsible here, and it sure as heck wasn't going to be her. "How'd you know she was dead?"

"She'd pulled the oxygen mask off her face." Julie's lips remained thin and tight like they do when we argue. That goes all the way back to when we played dolls in our bedroom, before Becky was born. "She wasn't breathing. I called 911." She more or less folded back onto her chair. "Leave me alone."

My chin shook with frustration, and a sigh came from the same place where I was fighting more tears.

Head down as if talking to the table, Julie mumbled, "They said she'd been dead for a couple of hours."

Helpless was all I could feel. "I should have never left her," I said. "Should have never gone to Fresno."

"She was going to die sometime, Lorraine."

Julie's words hit like she'd slapped my face or slugged the breath out of me. It was my fault. I should have never chased after that shifty, deceitful Pastor Harmon, was the truth of it. Mostly, I should have never pretended I wanted to be with those brats. I was being punished for Jack Harmon, and I knew it.

Julie's shoulders began to sag. She turned away, avoiding my eyes, and she started to rise again. She attempted a step toward the mudroom and patio, probably to smoke one more of her fags. But the minute she moved to turn around, she collapsed at the waist. That's when she started to bawl.

I got around the table in time to half-lift, half-drag the crumbling mess of who she'd become back toward my bedroom. Still drunk and now on a crying jag, she moaned and hit the walls in the hallway with her dangly arms. I had to tighten my good right arm around her waist or she'd have flopped right over. By the time I pushed her onto the bed and lifted her long legs in after her, she'd passed out again. Just as well. I didn't need her bawling on top of everything else. Tempted to leave her uncovered, I pulled up the sheet anyhow.

I stood in the doorway looking back at her, my *other* drunk sister. "Damn you," I said. "Both of us, really."

She was past hearing me, past much of anything that day. Her blonde curls spilled all over my pillows. Thank the Lord I'd covered her, or her red silk kimono would have lay wide open revealing her titties and her privates. Likely, that's how she was dressed when the medics came. Mad as I was and drunk as she was, there was something else. A downturn to her mouth like she was still crying where she fell across the bed, even passed out.

I turned and walked back down the hallway, glancing at the cross in the bathroom. Where *was* Jesus in all of this? Yet even after everything that had happened, I wanted to call Pastor Harmon. Instead, I called Becky's place. No one answered, not that I expected her to, especially now that her jailer, Kenny, was out of town again and I was supposedly in charge. Just the same, I left a message that said I needed her to call me.

Still wearing my clothes from Fresno, I drove to Green-field. It was likely too late to stop the process, but I was determined to dicker with them about the cost. "Where is she now?"

"Downstairs in the prep room," the slick undertaker in his dark suit said. "Do you want to see her?"

"Not necessary," I said. I avoided his eyes, his face, that fake sympathy they put on to keep their business going. Besides, I'd rather remember the way she was the last time I saw her. Maybe I'd live to regret that decision, maybe not. It's what I decided.

"I can tell you right now, there will be no embalming. No casket. Just cremation," I said. No funeral. No service. "Who would come?" Mama had asked. "A cardboard box and into the fire." I don't know how many times I said the whole church would turn out, that people cared. But no, cremation and a walk through an almond orchard. *No Jesus.* Those were her last words on the subject.

"I want to talk to your father, Mr. Greenfield, about the fees," I said. "I may want to move her."

"A reason?" he asked. His bushy brown eyebrows went up like this was the most surprising thing anyone had said to him in a long time.

"I can probably get a better price at McClinton's. Personal friend," I added to support my case.

He shrugged his pinstriped shoulders. "Your choice," he said. "But you'll have to pay for transport both ways."

Damn, they get you coming and going. And damn Julie. If she'd had two brain cells synapsing at the same time, I wouldn't be in this fix. "I need to see the figures," I said.

He closed his eyes and nodded like, *Sure, whatever you say*, but you could tell he was seeing dollar bills fly out the window and was likely pissed. So what.

"I'm sure we can come up with a fair price," he said. "Less

work for us." As though he had to somehow get in the last licks. For himself. For Greenfield.

He directed me to a waiting room with dark and plushy furniture, organ music piped in from somewhere and a sickly sweet smell, faint, meant to cover up something you couldn't see.

Funeral homes are lonely places. The dark room and organ music above the awful quiet made me want to leave. Worst of all, Pastor Harmon wasn't there. The only person I'd ever called a friend besides Rosemary. Now that Mama had died, my wanting him and his friendship was the biggest wanting I'd ever had. Never would I have imagined walking through Mama's passing alone. He and I were supposed to stand together as he blessed Mama's forehead with Jesus's spirit. Afterward, we'd pray over her sadly dead body just before he took my shoulders in his strong hands, before he pulled me against his chest, his fingers resting in my curly hair.

Then Fresno happened. I wasn't thinking about Jesus when I reached up and kissed Jack Harmon outside the motel room. Or when his mouth opened and he kissed me back like he'd been waiting. Before he pushed me away and wiped the back of his hand across his mouth. Before he gave me his preacher look. I'd never forgive him for that.

Now, forget about my sisters' help, forget about funeral expenses. I'd given up on Julie and Becky a long time ago. Once again, I was doing it on my own, the whole thing the way Mama and I discussed. Lucky for me, we never did get the will changed in time. But Julie and Becky would never need to know that. Unless Mama spilled the beans. Probably not, she went downhill so fast after that talk. So the only way to deal with those two was no chitchat and business as usual. They'd see. No more home-cooked meals. No offers of iced tea. Forget the gin. They'd never find that in my freezer again.

The funeral guy returned. Nodded what was meant to be reassuring. "We have an indigent fund," he said. "We'll cover the expense except for a box for the ashes. Will that be acceptable?"

Mama wouldn't have liked the indigent part, but she wasn't here to argue. That was that. The whole thing was settled. It was a good thing I came *and* I came alone.

That night I sat alone in the kitchen with my leftover broccoli and cheese casserole and, sure, it hurt. Julie, still sprawled on my bed in a drunken stupor, might have been desperate enough for some of my casserole when she woke up. Just as well she was out of it; she could fix her own damned supper.

Much as it broke my heart, the Lord had made no inroads in this family. Now even I had stepped too far away from him. Way too far. And the aloneness I felt sitting at the kitchen table was too much like the day I told Buck I was pregnant and watched him walk away. We were in the high school gym late afternoon, long after everyone else had gone home. Head down, he walked back into the locker room and left me standing there in the middle of the gym floor. End of conversation. Now, Pastor Harmon. He'd said forgiveness was for those who were sorry, but I was only sorry my attention hadn't been welcomed by him. I was ashamed, I wasn't sorry.

All of Sunday, Julie moped around in her Queen of Sheba satin robe. She never said anything. In fact, she avoided being in the same room with me. That was just fine. She wouldn't have the guts to run out on the funeral, not that there was going to be one. Still, I expected I'd see the last of her in about a week.

When Pastor Harmon finally called, I must have been out on the patio watering the roses. "I'm so sorry, Miss Carleton," his message said. Call him if he could help. Like I was a stranger, someone who just happened to stay for coffee and donuts on Sunday, someone you talked to about the peach harvest or water shortage. My finger was solid and determined when I hit the delete button.

Monday, around noon, Becky called. In a soft voice, as gentle as I could, I said Mama died in her sleep on Sunday. In less than an hour, Becky roared into the driveway in Kenny's rickety pickup. "So, she finally went, huh? Were you there? What's for lunch?" Before long, Becky was hunched over one of my egg-salad sandwiches wearing her usual short shorts and her boobs practically in her plate. That girl wouldn't know how to dress right if you drew a picture. "So, when's the funeral?"

"There's no funeral," I said. "Mama's request."

She shook her head; that mop, undone as usual, hadn't seen a brush since I last saw her. She looked right past Julie. I probably hadn't heard the whole of that episode at Becky's trailer.

"What do we do now, Laney?" she asked. "Where's she going to be buried? Will there be a headstone? Have you thought about what it would say, Laney? Will it say *wife of*?" Nonstop, she talked like she was high on speed, which she probably was. She'd use anything to stay loaded. With her, you never knew who you were going to get. Whoever it was, it wasn't someone you could stand to be around for very long.

In the living room, my sisters sat as still as pruned rose bushes. You had to wonder, who were these two? An over-the-hill topless showgirl who thought her poop didn't stink and a slovenly drunk who didn't wash her clothes or dress right. You'd never know we came from the same family.

Becky, finally quiet, her rear end in a dining room chair—no one seemed to want to sit in Mama's recliner—stared at the Paris print behind where Julie and I sat on the sofa. Julie, even in the house now, wore her Hollywood sunglasses all the time. I told them about the cardboard box. The small pine box for ashes. "There won't be a service," I said. "Just an almond orchard."

The words weren't out of my mouth before Julie tore off her glasses. Her eyes swollen, yes, and dark circles had left their mark below them. Drama queen that she was, she put her face in her hands and started to bawl.

Well, she should have been crying. First, she didn't pay attention when Mama passed, then she got drunk afterward. That was something *Becky* would do. Still, I'd never seen her cry like that. Not Julie. Always the first with a wisecrack or know-it-all smile until you wanted to smack her. Maybe I'd been too hard on her. It wasn't her fault really. She was right; Mama had been dying for a long time.

My hand reached out and touched her arm before I could stop myself. Julie's warm skin lay under my hand. When I glanced up, Becky was staring at us, gawking really, her mouth open and her brown eyes like cats' eyes when you catch them in the dark. Becky, her hair pulled back in the same scraggly ponytail, had swollen bags under her eyes too. Toxins. Likely from everything she put into her body. That girl could use a good dose of Kaopectate.

Somewhere in that gaping toward me and Julie, her mouth turned up into a half smile, the same weird smile I'd seen her switch on when she asked *were you here?* Becky started shaking her head at me, her eyes half-closed in some pretense of sympathy. Like, sure, Laney, you do whatever is right. We need to be kind to Julie. She's taking it hard. And whatever you arranged at the funeral home, Laney, that's fine with me.

I bowed my head. "Let's pray."

It was the first time I felt like a hypocrite. Praying when I was so damned mad at Jesus and Jack Harmon I could have breathed fire. If Julie and Becky knew what happened in Fresno, I'd have been hooted out of the family right there. But in the name of respect for Mama, my being the only one who had any so-called religion, it was up to me, just like everything else, to say a prayer.

I left my hand on Julie's arm, and I'd have sworn her sobs came into me right through my hand. To my surprise, she didn't try to shake me loose.

"Sweet Jesus, take this cup of sorrow from us," I said.

My one hand in my lap, the other on Julie's arm, I caught the three-way lamp on low out of the corner of my eye. The drapes were pulled closed as always, with the afternoon sun filtered through the fabric's weave. The three of us in the living room like the day of the family picnic. Mama would have been sitting in her recliner, watching reruns of *Antiques Roadshow*.

"We're gathered today for the sake of our mother," I began. I didn't expect my throat to get so tight or my mouth so dry I could hardly speak. But I had to go on. If I didn't, no one else would take over. "Each of us has our own cross to bear," I said. "Mama's suffering was long and just what it was. The worst is over. Bring her comfort, Lord."

I didn't have a clue who I was praying to or if there was anyone or anything to pray to. The words sounded like empty shells with no echo in return. What faith I'd had fell out of me and onto that diseased carpet in Motel 6 just nights ago when Jack Harmon gave me that shove. All my life, one foot in front of the other, I took care of what needed to be taken care of and never looked too far to the right or left since the day Daddy disappeared. Cursed. That's what I felt in that moment. And if there was a God somewhere, he didn't have my name on his list. None of us Carleton women, really.

Except for Julie's sniveling, the house was as quiet as it had been the morning I walked into the living room and found the empty hospital bed. It was the awful quiet that makes you jittery. You start thinking about supper or what's on TV or wouldn't it be nice to have iced tea right now, just to fill the empty space. Always, Mama's rooster clock *tick-ticked* from the kitchen. I wanted this to be over, probably as much as Julie and Becky did.

Julie started to cry again, and her sobs came through my hand from so deep down she couldn't stop them. Wouldn't you know, in the middle of Julie's bawling, Becky belched.

"Becky," I said. I gave her my look. "You, of all people, whatever you felt about Mama, she was still our mother. Doesn't she deserve more than a gutter belch?"

Becky quickly folded her hands and glanced up at me, her face strained to look serious even while temptation hid behind her seemingly angelic smile. "Sorry, Laney."

"The Lord giveth and the Lord taketh away. Amen." We were done praying.

No one said a thing. We just sat there, the afternoon stuffiness around us since I'd turned down the air-conditioning, the rooster clock seeming louder than usual from the kitchen. So this was it. One day here, then gone. There'd been no divine intervention, whatever that would look like. Truth was we were all vulnerable. Just a snap of the fingers and we could be snuffed out, or simply fall from grace like I had.

Julie was already up off the couch, her Marilyn Monroe kimono nothing but a tail flying around the corner as she disappeared down the hall. Becky, across from me, chewed her bottom lip like she was still high on something. After that day she came into Diego's, I couldn't tell anymore when she was sober and when she wasn't. The booze smell today could be this morning or last night or the day before.

Past the pleated drapes and the young lovers on the wall, I headed into the kitchen as if led by Mama's rooster clock. Sad to say, I wasn't sure there was any *home to Jesus* for me, for Mama, for any of us. No more Mama, no sister love to speak of. Nothing but the numbness I'd felt these last two days and the place where we were right now, Number 15, fifth space on your right after the pool and cabana. A summer tornado had come out of the blue and lifted me right off my foundation; it had left me in a state of regret and scattered me ten miles in every direction.

Chapter Eighteen

Becky

I climbed into Kenny's hunk-of-junk pickup and got my ass out of the old lady's house as fast as I could, driver's license or no driver's license, and I headed for the Greenfield Mortuary on McDowell. I needed to do what I'd been meaning to do all along but never had the chance. I'd be damned if I was going to let the old lady's dying screw it up. Right then, I wanted a drink so bad I was ready for mouthwash, but I'd promised myself that once I got what was mine, I'd find a way to give up the booze. If I didn't, the old lady would have won. "Worthless," she'd said the day of the picnic. "That's the only way to describe you." Which is why I was moving into the old lady's room with Julie. I needed insurance against booze; being with Julie and Lorraine could give me that. Mostly, though, I needed to get that ring. It had to be on the body or somewhere in the house.

I watched the speed limit, never going over twenty-five, on the lookout for other cars, kids on bikes, old ladies pushing grocery carts. And cops, always cops. The last thing I needed was to land my ass in jail again.

The whole time at Lorraine's, I'd thought about nothing but that damned ring. Daddy's ring. That diamond on the old lady's finger. He gave it to her before everything went downhill. Those sisters of mine could fuss over that old lady all they wanted, but I knew the truth, and the old lady knew I knew. I deserved that ring and I was going to have it.

But what if they'd already taken off the rings? Or Julie took them before they hauled the old gal to the fermenting parlor? I couldn't ask a question like that without giving myself away, duh.

Sweet Jesus. Take this sorrow from us.

Sorrow, my ass. It was a relief.

What I couldn't believe was how Tits Up went into meltdown. She'd always been the old lady's favorite, no matter what Lorraine wanted to believe. Still, it was hard to figure why she was taking it so hard, unless she was worried about her stake in the old lady's trailer. This was the longest she'd stayed around River's End since high school. I figured she'd have been long gone by now.

Those belly sobs coming from Julie were real—the kind that scared the hell out of me. Once they got started, they never wanted to stop. Treatment's where I learned that. Right in the middle of Jesus this and Jesus that, Julie jumped off the couch and got the hell out of there. Since I'm such a heathen, Lorraine must have figured it was time to go straight to *amen*.

Not one tear from Lorraine. What a hypocrite. "I'll check on Julie," was all she said.

At Greenfield Mortuary, the guy who answered the door looked like the geek the court gave me, a dark suit and gray tie, but this one was younger with one of those smooth radio voices, and his head was bowed, sad-like. I didn't believe it for a minute.

All I could hope for was that Lorraine or the mortuary missed the rings. Not likely, but I'd find out one way or the other. That diamond was mine!

"That's my mother in there," I said. "Dorothy Carleton. I need to see the body and say my goodbyes."

"I'll need some kind of identification," he said. "We have to follow state guidelines."

Just looking at me, he could see I didn't have a purse and no wallet sticking out of my back pocket. I was ready to fight, then thought better of it. I smiled at him, that sickly sweet smile I've seen on Julie's puss when she wanted something from our mother that she knew could start an argument. Smiled like my life depended on that smile. Cocked my head just so.

I lifted my hands and opened my palms, my arms outspread between us. "You can see I've been so overcome with grief that I came here immediately. I don't have a thing on me," I said. "Is there something I can sign since I don't have my purse?"

"You don't have a driver's license?" he asked.

"No, my husband dropped me off on his way to work."

"What's the name then?"

"Rebecca Susan Carleton," I said, a sad look on my face. "You wouldn't deprive someone of last respects, would you?"

"Of course not," he said. "But we have rules."

"I understand. As I said, would it work if I signed something for you?"

"Let me go and check," he said.

The guy left me standing in the spookiest room I'd ever been in outside of jail. The drapes were so thick that the sunlight couldn't come through. Even thicker than Lorraine's. And plushy carpet, the kind that made you suspicious, like you were somewhere you shouldn't be. In the next room, short, fancy boxes stuck out of the wall, maybe for babies. Nothing else would fit.

Good thing I was sober or I'd have never made it. When the guy came back, he said, "The owner is making an exception. Sign this."

I scrawled something that looked like a signature, as illegible as I could make it. What the hell. Once I got in and out, they could hang me for all I cared. With that, I followed him down a set of back stairs that smelled of ammonia and shit I'd never smelled before. It was cold too. My flip-flops and short shorts were all I had on besides goose bumps. Lorraine would say I was showing no respect, but hell, the old lady was beyond noticing if I was wearing a G-string and cowboy boots.

The guy took me into a room that was as cold as a freezer and, after a minute, he closed the door behind him. There was one table with one body. It had to be her. Dumb me, I stood there and wondered what the hell to do. The whole place, cold as the devil, spooked me out. I edged closer to the table and, slowly, with my thumb and pointer, I lifted a corner of the sheet near what I thought was her head. Not that I wanted to see an old dried-up body, especially my mother's. But it was the only way I was going to get what I wanted. I was sober enough and smart enough and desperate enough to know that.

The plastic-like sheet felt heavier than it looked. Her old wrinkly skin and what lay under her skin spread wide across the table, naked as a jaybird and practically yellow. Talk about stripped down. I lifted the sheet higher. At first, all I saw was the dead skin on her arms and the kind of skinny that makes you look away. Sure enough, it was her and, hot damn, there were the rings!

You'd never mistake that face though—even dead, her jaw locked in place just like the last time I saw her. Her gray hair was growing into a downright bush and it stuck out thick in a way I'd never seen before. Worse, her one tit lay flattened and spread out, the weight of it falling away to her side like it had become a wing or some damned thing. The other one, weird, the nipple completely gone where she'd been sewn shut, was flat as the sheet. I'd never seen anything like it.

Her belly was caved in from being so skinny and her old veiny hands with the rings in place—I couldn't believe my dumb luck—lay folded on top like she was already in the box. For all her sitting, her legs stuck out like toothpicks and were longer than I would have thought. Then, there, between her legs and in her pubes, practically no hair, not even gray hair like on her head. It didn't seem right, even to me. Maybe she was telling me the last thing she'd ever tell me: this is what old and dead looks like.

Her left hand, the rings, the one ring. The diamond and that stinky little wedding band she'd never taken off since Daddy gave them to her—circled loose above her big knuckles, right where they were supposed to be. The butterflies in my stomach flew into my mouth, and my mouth was so dry and hot I thought I'd puke. I don't know how long I stood there staring down at her body, her wrinkled hands with dark spots and her finger bones sticking out, stiff and scratchy. Made me think again of chicken feet.

I didn't give a shit about the wedding band. It was Daddy's *real* ring I wanted; I'd just never thought about having to touch her.

When I lifted her skinny hand, it was heavy and cold and icky stiff. Yellow and blue, nothing you would ever call normal. I took her hand in mine, awful as that was. I couldn't remember the last time her hand touched me. Braiding my hair when I was eight. That was it. Later, she did anything to avoid touching me. And now, when I stood in that room with what was left of her, we were the same strangers we'd been all these years. Her scratchy hand in mine with my chewed-up fingernails and what was left of the orange nail polish I put on the night I ended up in jail. I held her shrinking hand, cold and bony as it was. Right then, her hand in mine, the whole thing was disgusting and weird, the weird that says you're finally getting what you want and now what *are* you going to do.

I started to twist the rings, tried to get them over the knuckles but, skinny as she was, her knuckles, stubborn and sharp, without any give, were big and knotted. I spit on my hand. Then I rubbed the spit between my fingers until it was good and wet and just slimy enough to give those rings a boost. There was some give. A little. But not enough.

I should have brought some oil or something, but I hadn't really pictured how this would go. I bent over the old gal and worked up more spit. Then I heard shoes outside the door and someone talking to someone else. I looked behind me and saw the doorknob turn.

"Not yet," I said. My voice was so loud I scared myself.

I leaned further over the old lady's chicken-feet hand and spit right onto her cold finger. Then I rubbed the spit all around. I gave the rings one big yank, and they were off.

The door opened just as my fist squeezed tight around the rings, and those diamond prongs dug into the fat of my palm. Leave it to me, I always screw things up. My shorts didn't have pockets, and I only had flip-flops on my feet or I would have stowed the rings in my shoes, not that I ever wear shoes. It sure as hell was the only time I ever wished I wore a bra. That would have been the best place. There was no time for any of that.

Some guy in a white coat like doctors wear, two bullet-brown eyes inside layers of fat, walked toward me.

"This is my *mother*," I said. "Can't you let me pay my respects? Or do you always walk in on people like you own the damned place?" At least I got what I wanted. That was the thing.

Those big dog eyes were on my hands, like he knew I was up to no good. The white coat came to the head of the table. He reached down and lifted the sheet to cover her. "Sorry," he said without as much as a blink. "We need to get her ready for the crematorium."

Chapter Nineteen

Julie

With Kenny gone, Becky—supposedly off booze—had become my roommate the last four nights in Mama's twin beds. She wanted to talk about her new life when she would be the receptionist at the Chamber of Commerce, an apartment for the two of us to share. Me, I wanted to strangle her, especially when she snored all night. But we had this one last thing to do; we needed to take Dotty's ashes to the orchard.

As we headed for the car, Becky insisted I sit in the back seat. "I'm a better navigator," she said. "You've been gone too long."

I walked ahead of her and, opening the passenger door of Lorraine's two-door, pulled the front seat forward. Becky, in a pastel green muumuu with an oversized green belt around her middle, having skipped her usual fashion statement of the T-shirt and short shorts, climbed into the back. She grinned in a way I didn't trust. *You win this time*, her grin told me, *but just you wait.*

If anyone should sit in back, it was Lorraine with her short legs and wide rear end. So what if this was her car? I had to stop myself. Being petty wasn't going to get us through the day.

The J.C. Penney's bag with the pine box and Dotty's ashes shared the floor with my feet. The bag's sharp folds scratched against the inside of my legs, and my knees were so cramped they bumped against the dash. "This better not be a long ride," I said. Lorraine's head rotated in my direction and she gave me *the look*.

What I wouldn't have given right then for the quiet of a warm bath. But since Lorraine had moved me into Dotty's room with its smell of Lysol, I no longer had access to Lorraine's tub. In fact, she kept her bathroom door locked. Thank heaven for two more classes in Tasha's studio and a private student. I'd be out of there soon enough. The faster I left Sunny Acres, the better. The ashes today and settling the mobile home were all that was left to be done.

Dotty's life had been reduced to a small box, the remains— what an appropriate term—resting heavy on the car's floor between my feet. It was creepy in its own way. But how do you take a lifetime—the Formica kitchen table and rooster clock, the brown corduroy recliner and her so-called beloved wall print, all the trunked memorabilia from the Third Street house—how do you take all that and cram it into the fire until it's reduced to a grayish-white powder that resembles nothing but itself?

Lorraine sat hunched over in the driver's seat behind a new pair of mirrored aviator sunglasses. She looked like a CIA agent, and when she turned, she beamed me into her view. "Joe McKenzie said Shelly's Road was best." Her tiny, thin-lipped mouth revealed no emotion, just down to business.

"There are hundreds of almond orchards," I said. "Why did you ask my old dance partner of all people?"

Lorraine raised her eyebrows just before she stuck her

nose in the air. Same as *don't ask stupid questions.* "He owns an almond orchard, or have you forgotten?"

Becky leaned toward the front seats through the middle section between me and Lorraine. "Joe's a hot guy," she said. "You should go for him, Julie. He's always been crazy about you."

"Not my type," I said. I straightened my skirt over my knees and pinched the shoulders of my blouse. *Gay* wasn't a word that found its way into our household.

"Loaded. He's hot, and he's loaded. He's anybody's type. If you don't want him, send him to my house." Becky scooted closer to the front. "Speaking of money. When do we settle up on the mobile home, Lorraine?"

I could have laughed out loud. First, Becky was smart enough not to scotch the deal by saying trailer. Second, her question had been curling inside my mouth with no exit the last few days.

The Boss's aviators veered toward the side mirror and she suddenly changed lanes. She didn't hear Becky's question or she wasn't answering.

"What did the lawyer say, Laney?" Becky said.

Lorraine half-turned toward the back seat. From where I sat, Becky had become no more than a pinhead reflection inside Lorraine's aviators. "This isn't the day to talk about it."

"When is the day, then?" Becky said.

Lorraine kept her mouth tight, chin up and aviators dead ahead. The road promised to be her best distraction. "Can't imagine why you'd be interested," she said.

Now I was confused. Was there something I didn't know? While Becky's question was blunt and dead-center, it spoke to one of the two reasons I'd stayed the summer in Sunny Acres. Mama, of course. These last days with her. The other, getting back on my feet. For once, I was glad for Becky's thoughtlessness.

She took off her seat belt and leaned further into the front seat toward me. "What'll you do with your part, Julie?" she asked. "Go back to Vegas?"

She'd obviously forgotten her drunken accusations at Stella's Landing the day I walked out on her. "Probably not," I said. Mama at my feet, the pillow still in my head.

"Please," Lorraine said. "Have a little decency, for Lord's sake. We're burying Mama today."

After two months of too much happening, I'd about had it with these two. Especially Miss Clueless in the back seat, babbling on until you wanted to stuff a rag in her mouth. Any plan Becky had left me skeptical. She'd already made a name for herself in this town, who would have her?

I turned away and stared out the window toward where the Oakdale strip mall was once nothing but orchards and smudge pots and old farmhouses with dogs running out to bark at the cars. Even today, Nyberg Road was the fastest way to get to Riverdale and the trestle. Not that I was making a nostalgia run.

From time to time, I glanced over at Lorraine. Her crazy aviators flashed in and out of the sun, but otherwise her thoughts were anyone's guess. She'd even stopped talking about Jesus. The Fresno trip must have been a bust, as predictable as the road and strip malls and traffic lights, all of it funneled into tiny distortions inside her mirrored glasses.

"You two seem pretty serious," Becky said.

"It could be that we are." Lorraine's aviators pointed straight ahead and over the steering wheel like we were landing at LAX.

"Julie, would you buy Tasha out at the dance studio if you stayed?" Becky said.

I grabbed the twine handles and turned the bag in a different direction. "Maybe," I said. I glanced toward Nordstrom. "Or start somewhere new."

Becky had scooted so close her breath warmed my neck. "Like where? What would you do?"

"Real estate. Show production," I said. Whatever Lorraine had up her sleeve, smart girl that she was, she needed to know I wasn't leaving until I had what was mine.

Lorraine turned west off Nyberg and right onto Shelly's Road. We might as well have been headed into the woods for all the trees, their narrow and prescribed dirt rows in between the carefully lined tree trunks. Always, I felt something safe about an orchard's symmetry, the order of the trees. Seasons you could feel here, smell. The old smudge pots. Diesel fuel when they hauled the almonds out for processing. Smells I'd grown up with, smells that meant home.

"What about the mobile home, Lorraine?" Becky said. "Are you at least going to let us stay there?"

"As long as you're sober," she said. "Eventually you'll need to get your things together and go back to Stella's Landing."

Lorraine didn't say another thing for the next mile, the tires' tread pounding over gravel and the usual rattles; otherwise, the car remained silent. Finally, Becky sat back against the seat, quiet for a change. Knowing her, she'd find another way into the conversation.

Not long after Lorraine headed down the gravel road, she cut straight over into one set of orchards that veered off into other orchards. The ride was now wheel-bumps and a dust cloud behind us in the side mirror, roads meant for pickups and pickers and trucks hauling almonds, not low-to-the-ground tinny sedans.

Lorraine kept her eyes straight ahead, her aviators above those golden cross earrings. She eased her foot off the gas and we slowed over the bumpy gravel. She pulled off the road just far enough so the car wouldn't be seen. Clearly, she was only thinking about where this whole charade would take us and not about how I would get out of the car.

The orchard was a smoky green that's not quite gray, the trees dense with leaves and nut clusters, the nuts' hulls not yet ready to split open. We were long past the season of new blossoms or fuzzy green husks. You could have said the same thing about the three of us crammed into Lorraine's Escort.

"Pull up," I said.

She faced me, my blonde hair just a pinpoint in her mirrors, and she gave me the look I'd seen too many times before. Without a word, she turned over the ignition again and shoved the car into first gear. The car lurched forward two more feet. "Satisfied?" she said.

I had to practically climb over the bag before I hauled it out. Once outside the car, my low-heeled sandals sank into the dirt. Becky must have given up on me taking so long to get out of the car because she climbed out Lorraine's side. The Boss, wearing her waitress-white Dr. Scholl's sandals, waited, tapping her foot on the ground. All three of us wore skirts for what appeared to be a special occasion, skirts being something I hadn't seen Mama wear in years. Becky and I tromped behind Lorraine into a forest of nut trees like we knew where the hell we were going.

The ground under my sandals was uneven with seasons of mulch and almond hulls that never made it into a truck. The smell of rot and dust and dirt combined together made you think of autumn, just around the corner. Like black stones, the almond hulls hid inside the prickly weeds threatening a dangerous misstep, something I couldn't afford after twisting my ankle downtown. Right away, some hull found its way under my foot. I bent down to remove it. Again and again I had to stop and shake stonelike hulls from inside my sandals. Add the weight of Mama's ashes bumping against my leg and pulling on my right arm, I was completely lopsided, inside and out.

That was only part of it. *I wanted your life.* That mantra and the image of Mama's cold hands and raised veins rattled inside my head like a song that plays over and over until you think you're going crazy.

I had no idea how long we walked. Lorraine, in a predictable peach gathered skirt, forged ahead in the lead while Becky, her sad excuse of a ponytail coming undone, plodded in front of me, her flip flops not working any better than my sandals. Mama, myself, and the summer's full-blown August heat.

Driving up, the trees had looked greenish gray. But once we were inside the orchard, the trees' darker green shrouded the sun except where it filtered through leaves and landed on the path in random patterns. The shopping bag's twine cut into my hand despite changing from one hand to the other. Every time I shifted the weight to the opposite hand, I had to change my purse as well.

My siren-red toes took on an odd dusting of beige gray like the ashes in the J.C. Penney's bag. I'd lifted the lid off the box in the bedroom while Lorraine showered. Inside lay a plastic bag, tied with a plastic tie, the whole thing squared off by the rectangular shape of the wooden box. The contents could have been wheat flour or plaster of Paris for all I knew, nondescript and ordinary, unlike anything I might have imagined.

The path between the rows of trees didn't get easier. In fact, the longer we walked, the more I regretted insisting on the shopping bag. My hand was just about cut in two and, of course, The Boss never turned around to check on the rest of the expedition. In front of me, Becky looked like a rhinoceros on a Sunday stroll, her back end swaying from side to side inside the green muumuu, and her black flip flops were now completely gray. That girl had to have another pair of shoes. Oh, yes, the yellow cowboy boots.

In an hour this would all be over.

"Slow down," Becky whispered.

She stopped. She struck a match and lit the end of a badly rolled joint.

"What are you doing?" I asked.

Sweat ran down her face and her armpits were dark green rings. "Cools you down," she said. She sucked the smoke into her chest just before she handed the joint toward me and nodded, like a toke would make all the difference.

I couldn't help but look at the joint for a minute, the lumpy weed rolled inside thin white paper. I reached out to take it. How odd it felt between my fingers, the heat from Becky's inhale there inside the rolled cigarette. I don't know how long I stood there holding it between my fingers like it was a museum specimen. That is, before I extended my hand back toward her. "Thanks, but no thanks."

Becky raised her eyebrows. She looked just like Daddy then, a bit of the devil, a bit of the charmer. "Sure?"

She made me smile.

Took me a few seconds to ask myself, wasn't she being urine tested? However, if that's what it took, who was I to say. "I'll go ahead of you," I said.

We stood there, sisters who'd never said much all these years and when we did, it came out wrong. Sisters who never really knew each other after a certain age, our last time at the single-wide still shapeless and heavy between us despite these last days in Dotty's bedroom. Her eyes, black pupils inside their brown irises, showed me a little something I hadn't expected. Watering that wasn't marijuana but more like the lump in my throat.

"Thanks," she said.

I kicked off my red sandals and started to set the J.C. Penney's bag on the ground. Before the bag even hit the dirt, Becky's hand shot out and took the bag from me. While I held the shoes by the straps, I reached for the bag again. I shook my head. "It's mine to carry," I said.

I stopped to put my shoes back on, then picked along the trail in my red sandals, Becky's eyes still in mine. The shopping bag bumped against my leg, my red dress, my eyes on the uneven ground and my feet wobbly on top of the dried black almond husks and crabgrass.

Lorraine's gray-white shoes stopped in front of me. "How about here," she said. "This is as good a place as any."

Mama's last place on earth, just like that. The Boss had decided: a patch of meager grass beneath a nondescript almond tree in an anonymous row. What the hell. If Mama wanted almond hulls and dirt, that's what she was going to get.

Lorraine glanced past my arm to where Becky stood behind me.

Becky had bent over the top of her hideous green belt and snuffed her joint on the ground. If she thought The Boss missed that one, she was wrong. Lorraine's brow wrinkled the way it does when she's pissed, and her hands dug into the hip pockets of her skirt. Becky was holding up her day.

"Thought we'd do it here," Lorraine said to Becky.

Do what? Open the bag and dump the ashes along the ground? Take it out in handfuls like you see in movies? Lorraine should be embarrassed. No casket, no service. Just us, Mama's unlovely muses. Never mind Lorraine wasn't laying out the cash for an urn. There'd be no ashes on the TV or beside the bed at Lorraine's tidy Sunny Acres. And, thank heaven, not in a closet where they'd live among Lorraine's neatly stacked shoeboxes, her white blouses lined up and orderly beside a wardrobe of denim skirts. Well, at least it was pretty here in the orchard, out in the country, nature. The three of us, sweat running down the sides of our faces, would have to do.

All around us the sky above the orchard was the pearl white of August heat, the afternoon sun hanging in the trees and spackling the path where we stood. For a moment the trees, with almond clusters heavy on their branches, were the same white that's not a color. Everything—the sky, the summer light, this time in almond season, and the ashes inside a pine box—was all the same color, a grayish white that's no color at all.

The plain brown box inside the J.C. Penney's bag was smooth and lined the way wood grains are lined. Mama's shapeless body against brown corduroy, her hand with the remote in the air, that's what was in the box. I'd never made peace with her growing bush of gray hair or her wrinkled face, her cold and stiff lips when I bent to kiss her in the end just before I called 911.

Lorraine leaned down in front of the J.C. Penney's bag. My shoes were now entirely gray, like Becky's once-black flip flops. The same with Lorraine's Dr. Scholl's. Our three pairs of gray shoes stood in front of us.

With her stubby fingers and their squared-off ends, Lorraine lifted the box out of the bag and held it in front of her. I knew it was heavy; I'd been carrying it. Lorraine just held it there, away from her chest and away from her waist like it was awful and sacred at the same time.

That's when Becky looked into Lorraine's face, then mine, and she stepped forward. As if her stepping forward was a signal, I turned toward my two sisters until you could say we were in a circle, close but not touching, the way we'd been these last days.

You don't just throw someone away, even in an almond orchard, without saying something. But who would do it? Not Becky. That was for sure. If Lorraine did, there'd be Jesus this and Jesus that, and we were all sinners and doomed to hell. And me? I was having a hard time just breathing.

Then Lorraine surprised me and set the box down onto last season's almond hulls lying black in the weeds between tire tracks. The brown box and almond hulls and three pairs of feet stood at awkward angles in and around the weeded tracks.

I kept seeing Mama's stick-thin legs under the purple

afghan while her veiny fingers clung to her clear tonic glass. I remembered looking into her trifocals and seeing her larger-than-life eyes, the cloudy blue around her irises both recessed and monstrous with the magnification. Before I knew it, the swelling inside my chest lay right below that little throat notch in my neck I can never remember the name of. A tear slid down my cheek, then another on the other cheek. Then the blur of more tears and not being able to see. Any words I might have said were in the morning's mascara, two streams spreading into the Tuolumne River down my face. I couldn't look at Lorraine and I couldn't look at Becky.

I felt a hand reach awkwardly around my shoulders, the fingers warm against my skin, and gentle, like they were afraid like I was afraid. I wanted to say, *Don't be nice to me, don't be tender or sweet or loving in any way.* But I didn't say any of that. Becky's hand stayed uncertain near my neck, light and almost not there.

Lorraine took the lid off the box and picked away at the wire tie, then spread the whole bag open. Behind my tear-blind eyes, it was a miracle I saw anything. To my surprise, the box wasn't really pine. Inside the lid, laminate had come away at the edge and a peek of cardboard showed through. Lorraine, all economy and practicality, couldn't relent for one moment, even with her own mother.

Well, what difference did it make now. Her good-sized fist and bare hand went into the bag. Disgusting! Shouldn't we have brought a spoon or something? But Lorraine pulled out a handful of Mama, her fist full of ash and ash all over the back of her hand. She looked down at her closed fist.

Almost too eager, Becky did the same thing. Her chunky hand with its chipped orange nail polish went deep into the opened bag. Now she had a handful of Mama.

All three of us stood there, two with closed ash-gray fists and me about as dumb as I'd ever been in my life. Dumb and flooding at the same time. My hand went down into the plastic bag. So soft, the ashes were powder until something small and sharp, prickly like a tooth or bone, poked me. The kind of sharp that made me want to gag, then throw down what I'd just picked up.

Lorraine, without a word, raised her hand up toward the tree tops. In one big motion she opened her fist and her hand swept through the air. Becky did the same. I could not, no way.

Though no one would have said there was wind, there was wind. The wind and the ashes came together in a see-through veil. In an instant, Lorraine's lips and face and hair were ashes. The same with Becky. And the look on Lorraine and Becky's faces was probably the same surprise on mine. Just minutes before, Mama was nice and tidy in her plastic bag. Now, she'd landed on the front of my red dress, on my arms and, finally, in my tears. It was Mama and the wind and, I'll be damned, a storm of ash covered Becky's mouth where her lips were wet, and the mud of Mama spread all over her face.

I held my fist tight and closed.

"My God," from Lorraine was the first thing anyone said. Then, with her eyes closed, she spit right onto the fake pine box. I wanted to laugh. Becky did. And when Becky started laughing, so did I.

There was no way to stop. Snot and tears ran down my face. Without thinking and for no good reason at all, I threw that handful of Mama up into the air and right over our heads. My mouth was open and my nose was running and Becky was beside herself with bending over from laughing. Now, Mama was in my mouth and in my eyes and all three of us were covered in ash.

Becky and I went on like that for some time. Lorraine, the squatty Queen of Sensible Shoes, stood there, her hands on her hips and her mouth screwed up in disgust. She'd never know how funny, ridiculous really, she looked.

"We'll spread them on the ground," she finally said. She didn't look at either one of us when she said that, but farther away and through the trees, up to the sky. Becky and I started to laugh again, but I knew something had changed.

"What kind of daughters would laugh at their own mother's funeral? Laugh in the very moment they should feel closest to her," Lorraine said. "There isn't an ounce of God-fearing, God-respecting, God-believing in either one of you."

Lorraine's eyes had become bigger and darker than I'd ever seen. Furious and sad at the same time. An unexpected puckering gathered around her mouth, and her chin trembled just before her blue eyes squinted.

Seeing Lorraine's eyes, mad and scared at the same time, made me want to cry all over again. Her sobs, muffled as though in a towel or something heavy, scared me. Of the three of us, you never wanted to see Lorraine lose it. But she did. Right then, whatever she'd been hanging onto came out somewhere between a wail and a coyote's lament. She grabbed at the bag of ash and pulled it against her chest, as though she could take that ash into her body and that would erase her grief.

The hilarity died as quickly as it started. So did my own sharp sorrow. Standing in the orchard that day, I felt saddest for her. Lorraine. She never wanted anything more than a husband and family. Like Rosemary Brewer. They'd shared that. Probably even talked about it. They were vulnerable that way. On the other hand, no matter how bad things got, Becky and I would survive. We were used to things starting and ending and not always the way we wanted. But Lorraine was different. Crusty as she was, it occurred to me she might not make it through this one.

Chapter Twenty

Lorraine

"Let's get going," I said. "I've had a long day."
The weariness behind those words betrayed more than
I wanted them to know. To hell with them. It was over,
done. This, an orchard and almond trees, was what Mama
asked for. We gave it to her, and now it was time to move on.

Becky, her eyes bloodshot, took several steps around me
and blocked the driver's side door of my car. "We aren't going
anywhere until we talk about the mobile home."

Julie, refusing to be forgotten, marched in front of me
and stood beside Becky. There they were, one in a flashy red
dress and, the other, in a green dress I'd loaned her—my two
wayward sisters. What a pair.

Without blinking, I looked both of them in the eye. "The
fact Mama decided to divide the mobile home between the
three of us was not my idea. It's my home. The money will
be there when I'm ready to sell."

I turned toward Becky. "As for you, you don't have a leg
to stand on. You've already cashed in your inheritance."

Julie, any trace of crocodile tears having disappeared,

glanced at Becky, then me. "What are you talking about, Lorraine?"

"You'll have to take that up with Becky," I said.

"Becky?" Julie said.

Becky's eyebrows knotted, and the set of her mouth showed a kind of dark disgust you don't want to see, the lips tight and her eyes narrow. I'd seen Becky mad, but nothing like this. "Jesus H. Christ," she said, "you selfish goddamned bitch!"

I didn't know what she'd do, her hands balled into fists and her arms tight at her side. I could see those hands flying at me without a thought.

"Watch your mouth," I said.

Becky stepped closer until I thought she would grab me. "You'll do anything to finagle us out of our share. It's all horseshit. Pure horseshit."

"That's just how you see it," I said. "You seem to forget you're the one who's been swilling your life away. You've already used up your share. Or have you forgotten?"

Becky turned in Julie's direction. The look on her face was ten years old and she'd just discovered Daddy left town. "Julie, are you going to let her get away with this?"

Miss America seemed determined to stay cool, her shoulders back and neck tall until she towered over me with that stupid ritual breathing thing she does. "Not now or ever," she said. "Even if I have to stay in River's End and sit inside a stuffy courtroom until my face turns into a prune."

"It's done," I said. "As long as it's my home. That's how I set it up with Mama." I trained my sunglasses on Julie. "Frankly, I'm surprised, Julie. I figured you were either lining up Joe McKenzie or that cowboy you reeled in."

"Damn you, Lorraine," came from Becky. She stepped closer until she was less than an arm's length from me. Becky's arms folded across the chest of my green muumuu. Her eyes were like knives and her lower lip puffed up in a way that said she was ready to kill. Somehow, Becky's rage seemed enough for both her *and* Julie.

"Look, I'm going to say this once and never again." I pointed at Julie first, then Becky. "I was there for Mama day and night. I was the one who took her to chemotherapy and radiation, to the hairdresser when she could still go, to her friends' homes for bridge when she could still play. It wasn't you, Becky, who held her when she got scared of dying. Or you, Julie, who did no more than keep her company during her TV and tonic times. No, while you were both living your sad lives, it was me, good old Lorraine, who stayed at Diego's and made the money so we had a few extras. I paid the bills—neither of you ever sent a dime—and I was the one who woke in the middle of the night to make sure she was still breathing."

I stopped. Just saying that made my knees weak. Tears crowded behind my eyes. But I needed to say this and if I stopped, I'd never get started again. "You got the flashy life in a flashy town that you wanted, Julie. And, you, Rebecca Sue, you've been a handful and one step away from hell more years than I can remember." I sucked in my breath. "It's my *home*, not a commodity, not a spangled show costume, not a case of whiskey. You can't drink up what's mine, sell it off on a whim and then drive away."

There was no Jesus anymore. No Jack Harmon. My home was the only thing I had left. No way were these two going to even come close to understanding what was rightfully mine.

Neither of them said a word. What could they say? It was all true.

Becky gritted her teeth. She opened the passenger door and pulled the seat forward for Julie. Julie, her fat lips scrunched up and sour looking and her head thrown back, forever Miss America, made me want to laugh out loud.

Julie climbed into the back. Her long legs wedged against the passenger seat until she shifted them behind me. With my green dress bunched into her lap, Becky sat her rear end down next to me. She'd finally won something, the front seat. It was the first thing that made me smile all day.

"Pull your seat forward," Julie said.

"Yes, ma'am," Becky said.

I'd barely turned over the engine when, glancing over my shoulder, I started to back down the road. Gravel in the wheel ruts spit under the tires. I concentrated on going straight back and avoided Julie who sat there fuming, her eyes glaring and her fat lips a straight line.

Once we were turned around, I caught Julie in the rear-view mirror looking out the window at the trees. For just a moment, she couldn't hide a face as wrecked as I felt after Pastor Harmon shoved me down in Fresno. I almost felt sorry for her. If she'd been banking on the immediate sale of the mobile home, her little dream just got squashed. One more confirmation she'd just been hanging around until Mama died.

Beside me, Becky raised her eyebrows, trying to catch my eye. What a sight. She had ash in her hair and even her eyelashes were white. A nasty smirk curved the corners of her mouth. "Who the hell would want to stay in that trailer now anyway," she said. "Between you and the old lady, it's cursed."

Eyes straight ahead. Mama's ash had landed on the windshield. When I turned on the windshield wipers, the ash smeared until I had to stop by the side of Shelly's Road to let the wipers clean off the muck. Once we were going again, I shifted into high gear just to get this show on the road.

Becky leaned in front of me until I couldn't avoid her. "You're seriously cutting me out of every last dime and you've known that all along," she said. "Every fucking day you've known."

From the back seat, "What the hell are you talking about, Becky? Cutting you out?"

"How the hell did you get out of jail, Becky Sue? Remember? Who paid your fine? Who signed the papers?" I said.

Eyes narrowed and straight ahead. Nothing more out of her. Becky's jaw was steel.

I glanced into the side mirror. Now that we were back onto Nyberg Road and the tires had settled down, I could hear myself think. "I want to know what happened to Mama's rings. Greenfield Mortuary couldn't find them. Said they disappeared after you were there." My glance was aimed straight at Becky.

A half smile, smirk really, crept into the side of Becky's mouth, but she kept her eyes straight ahead. "Maybe Julie took them," she said.

Julie stared into the rearview mirror. "Dotty's rings? The diamond?"

No, not Julie. Julie would have needed to borrow the car. She never even came out of the bedroom after Mama died, likely hungover and sleeping it off for a good twenty-four hours.

That left Miss Clueless.

At the funeral home, I'd immediately asked Mr. Robbins, the mortician, about the rings. He was horrified to know they were gone. Said the funeral home was licensed and bonded, and no employee had been there less than ten years. And, yes, they'd been super busy with the bus crash on 99. "You might want to ask your sister, the . . ." and he indicated wild hair.

Becky already had her hand on the door handle when I pulled onto the Sunny Acres parking pad. Her teeth were closed and her jaw was clenched. She was ready to explode.

I turned off the ignition and looked directly at her.

"I'm sorry you can't see the fairness here," I said.

"Fuck you, Lorraine," she said. "And fuck your Jesus and your trailer. I hope you rot in hell."

"Are you finished?" I said.

"No," she said. "But tearing you apart isn't worth going back to jail."

"If I ever find out that you stole Mama's rings," I said. "I'll have the law after you."

Once outside of the car, Becky snorted the kind of laugh that was nothing like the way she'd laughed in the orchard. "You and the law can come right after me," she said. "I dare you."

Julie hadn't yet unfolded herself from the back seat, her Hollywood sunglasses back on and hiding whatever was going on inside her. She'd have her turn as soon as we opened the door to the mobile home. I could count on it.

Becky gave the car door a slam, forgetting Julie was still in the back seat. Then Becky tore off my lime-green belt that was bunched around the dress. She lifted her arm and began to whack the car. The belt made a slapping sound and the metal buckle seemed ready to break something. First, she hit the door, then the roof. Julie flinched, likely glad she was still in the back seat. Becky was about to start on the windows when I got out of the car.

"Get your tail out of here before I call the cops," I said.

The words were out of my mouth before I thought about what that would do to a crazy person. Because next Becky pulled that dress over her head and threw it on the ground. After that, she jumped on it. Worse, that girl didn't have a stitch on. Her titties were drooping and bouncing up and down and her fat butt and her bush, gray inside the red, were hanging out for the whole world to see. It was not pretty.

Julie had the good sense to stay in the car. Who could blame her? There wasn't an inch of sanity between Becky and that belt.

I yanked my cell phone out of my purse and opened it before I punched in 911. Becky probably thought I hit send, but I didn't. You could call it a moment of sanity when I was smart enough to use my God-given brain.

It worked.

Without a stitch and no respect for herself or anyone else, she started to climb into that junker pickup. When she got both feet on the pickup's step, she wiggled her fat butt in my face. "Kiss this," she said.

Her bare butt hung out for anyone who might be driving or walking by, and wouldn't old man Peterson next door love that. I couldn't believe it.

Standing beside the Escort, I listened while she sped out of the drive, never stopping for the speed bumps, the truck nothing but a rattle and clunk with all the junk Kenny had left in the pickup's bed. Not until she was gone did I remember Julie was still in the car where she'd successfully stayed out of the line snapped by the flailing belt.

I walked around to the passenger side door and yanked back on the handle. Then I reached in and released the front seat so Julie could crawl out.

"Are you satisfied?" she asked. She straightened herself into her full height until her shadow fell over me.

"You've got nothing to complain about," I said. "You've still got a bed to sleep in."

Chapter Twenty-One

Becky

Keep your eyes on the road, Becky girl. The half pint of peach brandy I'd hidden under the seat went down too fast, half-gone before I'd even passed the Sunny Acres sign. My hand reached around my feet searching for anything else hidden there, the sweet after-bite of the brandy cleaning my mouth of the bile I'd wanted to spit at that bitch Lorraine. Nothing but a dog collar and choke chain lay in a knot on the floor. Not a thing to cover my naked bod. At least I had the rings locked away in the glovebox. Lorraine could go to hell.

After being straight for days, the booze hit me hard, and I was dizzy when I turned onto Texas. My fat butt sat heavy on Kenny's sheepskin seat cover, something I always thought was stupid considering this was River's End and the Central Valley heat could boil your britches. But that day it felt good against my privates and my cold behind. That's what I was thinking when a truck full of yahoos came screeching from the other direction. They pointed and laughed and pulled a U-turn, like they could see I didn't have a thread on my body.

Their truck edged too close beside me. Must have been six guys crowded into the cab, and I was scared shitless. What if they ran me off the road? Raped me? Worse, left me for dead? I was hanging out buck naked in a way you don't ever want to see yourself, even home alone in front of the mirror. All I had was Kenny's truck between me and the street and those crazy yahoos. Any truck driver or son of a bitch SUV driving past me would get an eyeful. But I couldn't speed. Not on my life.

Stay on Texas and avoid downtown, girl. Just drive along like you're sober and nothing's wrong. Forget those fuckers now behind you, easing up on your tailgate, then backing off, some kind of goddamn tag you're not playing. This is no different than any other day except you're naked as naked can be. Now you're passing CHP's favorite hideout just before downtown. They'll go after those damned yahoos before they come after you. Eyes straight ahead, girl, and just look for the left turn and make it smooth, speed under twenty-five.

There's Ernie's. They're turning into the parking lot. Lucky them. Wouldn't a damned beer go down smooth right now. Imagine going in there naked. That would give them an eyeful. Just keep going, get over the Tenth Street bridge, Becky Sue, and hope nobody's fishing. Five minutes and you're home safe. No cops, Jesus, just no cops, please.

Past Stella's shit-brown and yellow sign and into the trailer park, my ass jumped good over what used to be a speed bump. I turned left by Olson's double-wide. There was Jason in the yard waving. I nodded, nothing out of the ordinary, an advantage in riding pickup-high. So far, so good. The usual kids. I slowed down and nodded like a new Becky, not the Becky who always yelled at the little bastards to get out of the way. Six more single-wides to go and everything was quiet.

I pulled Kenny's pickup into the parking space next to our trailer, the gravel under my tires giving me away. Two doors down, across the way, Millie Hawkins was hanging her wash, if you could call it that. A dog blanket and what looked like rags.

Up on the porch behind the screen door, Johnnie barked like he was a damned orphan. I could practically see his tail wagging through the screen where the sun had already passed and afternoon shade covered the front door. No idea if Kenny was home. Didn't matter. Johnnie had waited long enough. He was through the torn screen door and onto the truck, scratching and barking his fool head off.

Where the hell was Kenny? Thought for sure he'd be home bagging weed to sell to his buddies and the neighbors. I rolled down the window and my head got woozy from the fresh air, maybe from stopping so fast and the old adrenaline not pumping anymore. Next door, they were yelling as usual.

Sunglasses on, I opened the door about halfway and felt for the pickup stair with the toe of my flip flop. I put a finger to my lips. "Shh, shh," I said to Johnnie. I sat there a second longer waiting for my head to clear. You can do this, Becky girl.

One last glance behind me and to either side, the coast seemed clear. I scooted off the seat until I was standing. That's when the brandy hit me full-on. Damn, I hadn't counted on being dizzy. It took me a minute of hanging on to the truck door to get my balance and another minute to steady my legs past the spins.

Up the front stairs. I headed straight for the door, the dog licking my bare legs and bare ass, my hands keeping him out of my privates. If anyone was watching, that was their luck. Would give 'em something to talk about. The screen door creaked when it came back in my hand, but at least it wasn't locked. Goddamn miracle in itself. Hell, wouldn't that have been something if Kenny was sitting there and had locked the damned door from the inside.

Empty. Thank God, the trailer was empty. Another miracle when you thought about it. I'd never been so glad to see the damned laundry piled on the sofa or smell week-old trash. My cats rushed at me, meowing, and Johnnie wouldn't let me out of his sight. But it was all home, and it was safe, even with the yelling going on next door.

But the spins wouldn't let me go, and I had to grab onto the kitchen counter. I lit a cigarette after a couple of tries and stuck it in an ashtray. Had to get my head clear, get food for the critters. Yes sirree.

I flopped onto the unfolded laundry on the couch. I had to laugh. Becky does what Becky does. This time somebody somewhere was watching out for me. Screw Lorraine and her so-called mobile home, the way she tricked me out of my share. Julie would never let her get away with not selling, and that gave me courage. We'd get Lorraine one way or another.

That's when I heard the belt slap against skin, and the little boy next door cry out. The girl was pleading, "Please, Uncle. Please."

Shit, where the hell was Kenny when I needed him. The belt next door kept smacking skin and the boy kept yelling, his voice a mix of tears and terror, the kind that reminded me of what Rosemary must have yelled when the train hit her. I started for the screen door but I was buck naked and that guy had a gun.

The coiled cord of the green princess phone on the kitchen counter was practically buried under junk mail and bills. I shoved them aside. Calling 911 would mean cops, but I just couldn't stand to hear that kid scream, the ongoing sound of a leather belt slapping against someone's skin, especially a kid's.

I'd had it with that guy.

Cops. I had to think again. I didn't want cops after drinking that brandy. But Kenny, where was he? He'd know what to do.

I stood close to the edge of the screen door. The little girl was out on the front porch, blood on her head and matted in her hair. Holy Christ. Drunk or sober or scared straight, you have to do something.

Quick, I grabbed one of Kenny's T-shirts from the laundry pile, a pair of his boxers. Eased toward the screen.

The little girl started creeping toward my porch, listening, just like I was listening and stupid with wondering what the hell was going on next door. I wanted her to get back, get out of sight. Stay under the trailer. Something, anything. But there she was, already up on the second step and coming toward the screen door. She had to hear Johnnie barking, had to know someone was home because of the pickup. The crazy uncle would see her, sure as shit. It wasn't right. He'd get her, and who knew how long it would take the cops even if I called them, or if they'd come flying in here with their damned sirens blaring, that kid out of hiding and guns everywhere. Fuck, you can't trust anyone, not even yourself.

The little girl, still crying, had come up on the top step of my porch. I opened the screen and stuck my head and my arm out. Waved to her. "Come over here," I whispered. Loud enough so she could hear. "Come in and hide."

The belt stopped and the screaming with it. Nothing. That was almost worse. There were no boy sounds, no man sounds. Not a belch or fart or even a slamming door. Johnnie howled to beat the band in the back bedroom where I'd locked him up. He didn't like lockup any more than I did.

I couldn't stand it. The silence. The waiting. Nine, then one. Another one. The ringing to connect. Damn, what was I doing?

The little girl had opened my screen door. She stopped crying and stared at me. I motioned her inside.

"911. What's your emergency?"

"There's an incident," I said. The word sounded foreign and not my own and caused me to slur. Even I could hear it.

"Did you say incident?" It was a woman's voice, far away and cool as could be.

"Yeah," I said. I started to walk toward the little girl, but the phone cord wouldn't let me. She stood close to the door rubbing her eyes.

"Guy next door beating up a couple of kids. The boy's still in the house, maybe—hurt real bad." How could I say what I really thought—the kid could be dead. At least the girl was safe. Looking at me. The laundry. Now my cats sidled toward her.

"What's the address?" she said.

"Stella's Landing out on Riverfront Road. Trailer 44." No sign of the girl now, she'd disappeared down the hallway, probably with the cats.

"Who are you?" The voice sounded impatient and almost mad when I didn't answer right away.

"Live next door," I said. "A neighbor. And they've got a gun. I'm scared to go over."

Sorry. Immediately sorry I said gun. I don't know when I'd been so sorry. Still, they were just kids. Someone had to be grown up.

"How do you know?"

"He waved the gun at me the other day. He'll kill me if he finds out I called. He'll kill my dogs too."

"We'll have a team right there."

"Team? What team?"

"Don't hang up," the voice said.

Like a dummy, I stood there staring at the damned phone like it was going to wiggle out of my hands. Not knowing what else to do, I set it faceup on the counter in the only clear space I could find. And there I was, sitting on top of the laundry with the worst case of dry mouth I ever remembered. The kind where you know if you drink anything, even booze, you'll throw up.

I kept staring at the damned phone. I knew I should go down the hall and check on the girl, but I couldn't move. I'd pay now, one way or another, I'd pay. It would be just my luck that I'd be the one who ended up in jail. I could count on it, sure as shit.

No sound from the back of the house outside of Johnnie barking his head off. At least she was safe. Don't ask me why, I did the only thing I could think to do: I started folding laundry. It was the damnedest thing. The towels, like I cared. Kenny's boxers. My tank tops. None of it made sense. They'd pull up my record and I'd be the one back in jail again with the whole damned crying all night thing all over again. Goddamn, what had I done? I told on myself, for God's sake!

The girl came out from the bathroom holding my calico, her eyes so big and scared. The dried blood on her forehead said it all. Jesus, what did those kids do to deserve this mess? No mom to be seen unless she was inside and already dead. A crazy uncle, whoever the hell he was.

"It'll be all right," I said, knowing it would be no such thing.

What can I say? The whole damned SWAT team came just like the gal said they would. Jesus, no sirens, but red lights, like a parade. A van and two squad cars, police and a sheriff. A cop in a black, bulletproof vest like you see on TV came out of nowhere and, I couldn't believe it, outside the kitchen window they strongarmed Kenny, who had just come around the corner. Cops were pulling his arms behind his back and to the side of the trailer. Boozer snarled, then barked just before he started after the cop's leg. I held my breath and waited for the cop to shoot him.

"Get back," I heard some guy shout. Probably another cop. Who knows how many cops were out there. Johnnie was barking in the back of the house and now Boozer sounded the alarm out front. A fucking free-for-all if you asked me.

That's when the little girl started yelling her fool head off. She must have seen the cops or the guns or recognized Kenny and Boozer through the front door. She had a pair of lungs I'll never forget.

"What the fuck you guys doing?" I heard Kenny shout.

Through the kitchen window, open to the back, I heard a cop holler back, "Shut up, mister. You're why we're here. Cuff him and put him in the van, Pete."

They fastened cuffs to Kenny's wrists. "What the fuck's going on?" Kenny shouted. "This is my house. And who the hell called you in the first place?"

Holy shit. They thought Kenny was the guy. Now I was really in a jam. I didn't have a decent thing on and that little girl, here in my trailer, was hollering her lungs out like I was killing her.

I couldn't help myself, I opened the screen door and stepped out onto the porch. Though I couldn't exactly see them, I knew there were guns everywhere. And down the road and sticking their heads out from the ends and sides of their trailers, Fat Ronnie and Jessica and every low down neighbor in the place gawked at what was going on.

"Get back, lady," some cop said.

I pointed toward Kenny. "It's not him," I shouted. "He's my old man." My arm swung in an arc toward the opposite trailer. "Over there." Talk about giving yourself away. And what a mess, the little girl screaming behind me and, now, cops crawling onto the neighbor's porch and onto mine. I expected one of those guys in black to strongarm me any minute.

Someone else shouted, "Get back inside, lady."

But not before I saw those cop guys with their mean-looking faces up close, like they just ate worms, and those walkie-talkie things hanging around their necks and on their shoulders. Guns like I'd only seen on TV. Out of the corner of my eye, I caught Kenny staring at me from the bottom of the porch like he didn't know who I was. Maybe it was my outfit, maybe he was relieved. All I saw was disgust in the slits of his eyes.

That's when it got quiet. Real quiet. Until the screen door across from me opened, just a crack at first. An arm came out. A gun. Metal against wood as the gun landed on the porch. Then the uncle. His arms hung limp in the air and his gray hair was knotted in a stringy mess down his back. His shirttails were out around his fat belly, and his damned jeans were unzipped in front. I didn't want to know why.

Sirens now. A red and white medics truck. Before you knew it, that little boy was on a stretcher, but at least his head wasn't covered—meaning dead. That was a blessing. No mom. She'd just left those kids to fry with that no-good crazy man. Once the little girl saw the commotion next door, she was through the screen door in a flash and screaming on my front porch. She must have seen her big brother, out cold and lying on that stretcher.

As soon as I heard sirens, I scrambled toward the back bedroom with Johnnie. Someone's big knuckles hammered against that sad excuse of a screen door in my living room. "Lady?" I heard him say.

I watched the little girl from the bedroom window while I pulled on a pair of my shorts. Some policewoman held the girl's arm while she lifted the sobbing kid into a police car. The knocking continued on the front screen while Kenny stood at the side of the trailer trying to keep Boozer quiet. "Hey, Becky," he shouted.

I lit a cigarette fast, my hand shaking I was so nervous. Anything to kill the smell of brandy, though if I'd had even a part bottle hidden in the house, I'd have been at it right then. "Coming," I said. Cigarette in hand, I closed the door on Johnnie. Otherwise, he'd take after one of those cops and I'd for sure lose a dog.

Chain-smoking all the way to the front door like I was crossing a football field instead of a twenty-five-foot trailer.

"You made the call?" the cop asked.

He was over six feet, a whole head taller than Kenny. He'd taken off his helmet and goggles. He was bald. That's what I remembered most. Bald with real dark eyes that looked straight at me like he was trying to figure out what kind of troublemaker I was. Sure as shit, I expected him to ask me to go with him. Statement at headquarters. Then they'd get my name and figure I was on probation. Another DUI. It's only driving, I'd say. Never mind, it would be my third. I could kiss everything goodbye that hadn't already been taken away by Lorraine.

"Yeah, I made the call," I said.

My neck had never stuck out so far. But the look in that little girl's eyes when she came up on the porch stayed in front of me. I understood that kind of helpless.

The cop. A mustache too. I remembered that now. "We've been looking for Paul Charles for over a year. Damned shame to find him with someone's kids."

His saying that took some of the sting out of ratting on someone, anyone.

"What about the kids?" I said. "What'll happen to them?"

"Social services," he said. He had his notebook out and in front of him. Even while he talked to me, he was talking into that shoulder walkie-talkie of his.

"Will they be together?" I asked. "The kids?"

"No promises. Just depends on who's got room. The boy's going to the hospital."

When he walked back down the porch stairs, my knees got so weak I thought they'd fold. Just the relief of having him gone. I couldn't help but look toward the other cop car where, you could tell, the little girl was screaming even though the car doors were closed and the windows shut. I saw that cop woman's hand on her shoulder, but the girl would never remember that hand.

The cops and the ambulance left and the neighbors started gathering in the road. Kenny walked up on the porch, Boozer right beside him. Seeing them, I opened the bedroom door and Johnnie pushed past my legs and through the screen door, his tail wagging like the party was just getting started.

Inside, Kenny stood beside the sofa and rolled a joint. "You've done it again," he said. "Can't stay away from booze or the cops, can you, Becky Sue?"

He only calls me Becky Sue when he's so mad he doesn't know what else to say. He walked into the kitchen and opened the fridge, probably looking for one of those last beers I drank before I went to Lorraine's just days ago.

I didn't say a thing. Some things you learn after living with someone long enough. I also knew he'd never mention it again, straight out anyhow. He'd make me pay in his own way, mostly by not saying anything. Just that down-at-the-corners-of-his-mouth look that said *shithead* without saying it. "Gonna go get some beer," he said. "I want you gone by the time I get back."

I sat down on that pile of laundry. That was it. Forty-nine years old and my life was so fucked up I couldn't see straight. Two kids practically left for dead and my old man had just told me to take a hike.

Through jail and The Portals and losing out on Lorraine's trailer, now Kenny—the only person besides Lorraine who'd been steady in my life since I was sixteen. Now, no Kenny. No trailer. No job in town. No computer course. No insurance policy with Lorraine and Julie standing by. Just, be gone. Not like he was leaving me, but I was supposed to leave him. Shit. Shit. Shit. He all but twisted the knife.

I picked up the phone. "Need inpatient," I said to Candi. "Can't do this part-time."

Chapter Twenty-Two

Julie

If I wasn't curious by nature, I'd have never been caught dead inside that poorly lit hallway of this so-called hospital. We were barely through the front door when a fiftyish woman, the same size as Lorraine, dressed in a short black skirt and frilly white blouse, confronted us as though we were unwanted visitors smuggling in gin and reefers to the miserable girls we saw around us. While she was attractive enough, her graying hair and hunched shoulders, a caved-in chest screamed *no questions, please*, just, "You're looking for the conference room," she said. "Follow me."

How did she know who we were? I could imagine how Becky described us. One brown hair mostly silver and one blonde. One short and plump, the other an overdressed six-footer.

Outside, the recently painted building could have passed for a nice home. Oversized and Spanish in style, its peach color and standard terra-cotta rounded tiles on the roof were meant to persuade you it belonged in the neighborhood. It was larger than it looked from the outside. Inside, the exceptionally dark entryway failed the test of an ordinary home. The woman ushered us down a long hallway. Lorraine marched behind her and I trailed along. We passed an open door into what looked like a living room where a dozen women sat in a circle. The few who gazed out at us seemed more interested in who we were than whatever was going on in there. Probably a meeting: alcoholics and their blessed meetings. Of course. Past an office, a gray-haired man in owlish horn-rimmed glasses noted our passage, then stood quickly and shut his door. Further down the hall, our guide pointed toward a partly open door on the right. "In there," she said. Her expression, never changing, was that of someone sleepwalking through her job and waiting for retirement.

We entered a conference room with a long table and a few chairs. Other chairs lined the bland walls. The place was the deadly beige of Lorraine's living room. It made me laugh. Lorraine turned around and shot me her look. A whiteboard at the far end gave the room that Spartan classroom charm. Two long white posters on the wall listed AA's Twelve Steps while overhead fluorescent lights gave the sense of interrogation. No windows. Not a dot of color in the room except for the yellow shirt on the young woman sitting at the head of the table. When she stood, she was short, like the other staff I'd seen, maybe a requirement to work here. Lorraine should feel right at home.

"Becky," Lorraine said. Her eyes pointed directly across the table where Becky sat to the side of the staff person.

My mouth fell open. Becky was as cleaned up as I'd seen her since she was ten and Dotty insisted she wear a dress for my performance as the Sugar Plum Fairy. Her blue plaid blouse was actually ironed and even covered her chest. Her hair had been brushed and a purple plastic headband held it back from its usual bushlike appearance. No earrings, no eye makeup. Clear eyes. When she swallowed, her nervousness was given away by the up and down ripple of her throat. Here a week, it was clear that she didn't want to be here for this so-called meeting any more than she wanted us to be here. That made me even more curious.

Becky pointed at the young woman who sat at the head of the table in the golf shirt, her blonde hair slicked back on the sides and small gold hoops in her ears. "This was her idea," she said.

Becky sat to the young woman's right, fidgeting, likely twining and untwining her fingers under the table.

"Thanks for coming," said the woman with the slicked-back hair. Standing, her Dockers held their razor crease as she motioned Lorraine and me to the two seats opposite Becky. "My name is Janice. I'm Becky's counselor."

She took her chair. Her smile seemed practiced, automatic. A distasteful job from the looks of it. Before either Lorraine or I sat down, she asked, "Is this your first family session?"

Lorraine lowered herself into a chair. "Attempted session," she said. Her tone was grim. "You already know that." She pulled herself up to the table. "We talked a year ago, Janice, if you remember."

Lorraine's chin tipped down and her eyes drilled into Becky. In Lorraine's mind, she was likely still back at the double-wide after the ashes, and Becky was still beating her car with the belt. She clearly had little hope for this gathering. So why were we here? I didn't like it before, and I liked it even less now.

"Julie Carleton here. This is my first time," I said, extending my hand. The hand that grasped mine surprised me with the strength in her fingers. Yet a cool dampness and the quick drop of my hand told me she too was nervous.

I hesitated before sitting and glanced over at Becky. "I guess we have a lot to talk about."

Janice raised her head to make better eye contact. "We only have an hour before Becky needs to return to group."

Lorraine positioned herself closest to the counselor. Between Lorraine setting a sharp tone and the counselor's ring of a time schedule, we all sat down to business. I'd never been close by during Becky's previous treatments, so I had no idea what to expect. According to Lorraine, this was a command performance for the family and meant to help the patient. Simple as that. Becky, directly across from us, displayed the full-blown Carleton Curse as it reddened her neck and then her cheeks.

Janice opened the hard-backed maroon folder in front of her. "Let me explain," she said. "A family meeting is required for all patients prior to discharge."

Discharge? Already? I remembered a naked Becky tearing off from Lorraine's only days ago. The counselor must have seen my astonishment, because she added quickly, "Becky's a long way from discharge." She glanced at Becky, perhaps looking for agreement.

Becky, eyes on the table, had gone somewhere else. Like a captive, resignation along with annoyance played around her tightened mouth. Poor Becky kept biting her lower lip. When she realized we were all staring at her, she wet her chapped lips before she glanced at me and then Lorraine. I got it, she was on trial. I could see how booze calmed her down.

"In order for Becky to move on with her recovery, she has to heal the wounds of the past," Janice announced, like she was giving jury instructions. She glanced down at the open binder in front of her, full pages of closely typed lines with loopy signatures at the bottom. How official this whole thing was. She looked over at Becky and a half smile, as if to comfort Becky, crossed her face. Her tone dropped. "This is never easy."

Becky gave her a quick nod, then studied the table again. The only sound came from shuffling feet and the muffled voices outside in the hallway. Whatever was supposed to happen here wasn't happening or at least not fast enough to suit me. *Wounds from the past.* What the hell did that mean? We all had wounds from the past. Maybe different, but we all had them. You get over it and get on with things; you don't roll around in *poor me.*

Inside the silence, the air-conditioning clicked on and a dull, steady hum filled the room.

"Any questions before we start?" the counselor asked.

"What do you want from us?" Lorraine said. Quick and to the point, Lorraine's question seemed headed for the counselor, but it was really directed toward Becky, who wouldn't give Lorraine the satisfaction of eye contact. "We tried getting this meeting together before and it didn't work. I'm not sure why you think it will work now."

For the first time, I understood. Lorraine was the one who'd dealt with Becky's disasters. Emergency rooms and a jail cell, bail bondsmen and court-appointed attorneys. If there were family meetings before, she would have been the only one there. It wasn't me. It wasn't Dotty. I couldn't imagine holding Becky's puking head over a toilet bowl while detoxing Baby Sister at the Econo Lodge. Or all the times before that. No, in those few words, while she held her lime-green purse in her lap, her fingers opening and closing the fake gold clasp, Lorraine reminded us who had played watchdog with Miss Becky.

That's when I noticed Becky's hands on the table and Dotty's diamond on Becky's middle finger. Maybe Lorraine did too. The ring, that day in the car on our way back from the almond orchard, Lorraine confronted Becky who wore that stupid Cheshire cat grin. *Maybe Julie took them.* The gall. Even then Lorraine knew Becky had them. Now, under fluorescent lights, Dotty's ring, front and center, was the star on this stage.

"Here's my first question." Lorraine leaned toward Becky

and zeroed in on the ring, her if-looks-could-kill anger right in the middle of the table. "Where'd she get that ring?"

"Ask directly," Janice advised. She still thought she was in control.

"You got everything in the trailer, Lorraine," I said quietly. "Becky and I deserve something."

She glared at me. Good old in-charge Lorraine. No one was supposed to question her.

"Now you too?" she said. The same drilling at me she'd given Becky.

It was like the day she announced I was moving into Mama's bedroom. The hospital bed hadn't even left the living room. After that night with Mama, I'd barely been able to get myself out of bed. But there she was, escorting me down the hall and into Mama's still-smelly bedroom. If you trusted her tone now, she was claiming the ring as well.

I turned toward her. "Let's just do this and get out of here."

I wasn't expecting Becky to smile. But she did. Her beautiful white teeth, except for that one black cap line, straight on top and bottom, the best in the family even after all she'd been through—booze and weed and living poor with a biker who never kept a job, not to mention normal necessities like health insurance and dental visits. How she'd done it, I'd never know.

Becky leaned her shoulder just the slightest toward this Janice person. She smiled at Lorraine as if to say, *You can't get me now, you bitch*. I was certain that's what she was thinking. She'd said as much at the single-wide.

Janice shook her head no at Becky. This wasn't the direction we needed to go. Then the counselor gave Lorraine a nod before she glanced toward me, maybe looking for help. Good luck. She'd stepped into the middle of something bigger than she'd imagined. Not that I'm an expert on families. But to me, families are like a Venus flytrap—only entrance, no escape.

Janice closed her eyes. I was sure she was taking a deep breath. And I certainly wasn't interested in a fight between Becky and Lorraine, but I did want resolution. The ring, likely worth a good three thousand, was on the table. My cut would get me out of Sunny Acres.

Janice held the outer edges of the three-ring binder. Tension worked her jaw. "Family meetings are an opportunity to clear the air." Her scripted words traveled through the over-lighted air and fell onto the table.

Lorraine snickered. "I can't see how this is going to resolve thirty-five years of things gone wrong."

"We can thank you for your part," I said. "The lion's share of the trailer, now the ring. Easy for you to say thirty-five years. But this isn't about you, Lorraine. It's about Becky and, essentially, it's about what's fair. I know that's not something that registers in your book."

I'm happy to say Lorraine seemed about as flustered as I'd ever seen her. Chin trembling, the Carleton Curse, everything that could possibly give her away.

Becky removed her hands from the table and placed them in her lap as if eliminating the evidence. Our eyes caught each other for just a moment. Like me, she definitely didn't buy the notion that this one hour would resolve the twists and turns in family battles as old as the day Daddy left.

"Let's get on with it," I said.

Janice let out a sigh. And even Lorraine's now-smug mouth with its small *o* thinned out into a single straight line, indicating that, though reluctant, she could let go of this particular battle for now.

That day, anything we had to say to each other would be small change, not any different from those sad folks who played the nickel slots, then the quarters. Lorraine had finagled Becky out of the trailer and now refused to sell. And it was true that, except for keeping Mama company, I'd done little to claim my part. That was a fact. But Becky, drunk or sober, was as devious as Lorraine. Maybe we all were. We all wanted what we wanted and were forever trying to figure out how to get it. Desperate or deserving, that's who we were. Besides, every time the three of us were in the same room together, nothing good came of it. Sure, we were family. And maybe on some vague level, we cared about what happened to each other. But did we really? Weren't we really in this for ourselves? The drama always ended the same way: Lorraine won and Becky got drunk and I left town. How was it ever going to be different?

"Becky has some things she needs to say to you," Janice said.

The counselor's glance was directed at me. Maybe she thought I'd help steer Lorraine away from the argument about the rings.

I nodded at Becky. "Just so you all know, I'm not done with the ring business."

Janice shifted in her chair and faced Becky. She reached forward and laid her hand on Becky's arm. "This is your show."

We all stared at Becky, and Becky stared at the table. In the spotlight now, she wasn't as cocky as she'd been just moments ago, guilty hands visibly wringing under the table where she kept the ring from view. The overhead fluorescents buzzed above us and covered the worst of the silence. When Becky finally glanced up from the table, her gaze fell, not on us but on the wall behind and between Lorraine's head and mine. Her eyes seemed slightly glazed as if, without booze, she just wasn't there. The buzz of the lights joined the hum the air conditioner, and the bizarre white noise accentuated Lorraine's long sigh.

Becky folded her hands on the table and looked directly at Lorraine. "I'm sorry about the ring, Lorraine," she said. "I needed it."

"What does that mean? Needed it?" Lorraine said. Her voice, raspy and controlled, was as tight and strained as her cheekbones. Nothing soft or even close to soft peeked out from the straight line of Lorraine's mouth.

Becky's gaze stayed on Lorraine. And for the first time in a long time, something genuine, even believable, echoed in *I needed it*. The directness and sincerity around Becky's eyes took me back to the pigtailed girl she once was, playing dolls with me long ago under the Third Street oak tree.

"The ring was from Daddy. It's the only thing I have."

Becky spit the words and, for the first time since the redness faded on her neck and face, she was charged in a way I hadn't seen since after the ashes. Except this time she was truly sober. "Daddy gave that ring to the woman who was our mother. Now she's dead," Becky said. "It's all I ever wanted. The only thing of his that I have."

The way Becky said *his* had a private, intimate tone as if the ring was more than a ring. Whatever Daddy meant to her, if that ring could help her get her life back, I'd have to be fine with it. For some, it doesn't take a lot. Just the right thing.

"Whatever he was to you two, I can tell you he was my whole world. And when he went away, I thought I'd die. Except for you, Julie, I was alone in a way I never want to be alone again. Mama made it worse. I was the kid who was supposed to make everything work. And I didn't."

Lorraine sat there, her face grim with anger and resentment, her lips zipped tight, and she didn't say a word. Her arms, folded across her chest, held her breasts tight while her fingers tapped against her upper arms.

"Another thing," Becky said.

Becky's gaze fell onto the counselor's hand. She took her time before she directed her attention back to me and Lorraine. "It's about Daddy," she said. "Something you need to know." After a deep breath, she stared at Janice's hand, light on her arm. "Daddy probably left because of something I told him."

Lorraine inched back from the table, her short square fingers bracing the table's edge. Her lips trembled despite her effort to bite them. "What in the world could you have possibly told him to make him leave?"

"This is about Mama," Becky said.

Lorraine leaned forward, her tone accusing. "You don't know what you're talking about. You were just a kid."

I glanced at Lorraine, then Becky. "What am I missing here, Becky?" I said.

The puzzled look on my face was meant to cover what I knew but had never said, more than an inkling, likely true, but not a place I necessarily wanted to go. Too much like a nightmare. Once you fall off the cliff, you can't magically float back up.

Becky nodded at me, her eyes in mine, and the dip in her chin said she was counting on me. She seemed thoughtful for a moment, her mouth partly open and her white teeth shining behind her lips. She glanced at Janice and took a deep breath. She enunciated the words on her out-breath. "I told Daddy about Uncle Dale."

"Uncle Dale? That loser? Who cares about him?" Lorraine was on the edge of her chair now and ready for takeoff.

"How did you know?" I asked. I surprised myself, my tone calm and matter-of-fact. I might have held on to the question, but I didn't. Becky probably found out the same way I did, walking in on the two of them one night when Daddy was out of town and Uncle Dale hovered over Dotty's bedside. I could still see Dotty's bra and slip flung on the chair, the streetlight coming through the window and spotlighting her clothes just before I closed the door and sneaked back to bed.

For me, that was the night Mama became Dotty.

"I was there when Aunt Naomi confronted Mama," Becky said.

First, there was the shock of Becky calling Dotty *Mama*. Add that to Becky saying she was there when Aunt Naomi, Mama's sister, came calling. I could well imagine Mama trying to reason with her short, squat sister at the Formica table, cigarettes and cold black coffee between them, and Aunt Naomi having none of it. This revelation answered the question of why we never saw Aunt Naomi and Uncle Dale after Daddy left. Why we were so alone with who we'd lost.

Lorraine's mouth made the *o* shape I'd grown used to over the summer, a sure sign she'd become exasperated. "What the heck are you two talking about?" Lorraine yelled. "Whatever it is, it's a lie, and you know it."

"We probably all knew about Mama and Uncle Dale, we just never said anything. Not to each other anyhow," I said.

"Nothing happened." Lorraine, in her usual denim skirt and white blouse, was halfway to standing, her head forward and too close to Becky. "I can't believe it! You've been going on and on about Daddy leaving all these years, looking for any excuse to blame Mama."

"But it's true, Lorraine," I said. "How long was she supposed to hang on to it?"

Lorraine slammed her purse on the table. "Forever!"

At the sound of the purse and table colliding, the room went silent again, but differently this time. Not from the tension of things not said and held back, but from the mess of exposure. Because there it was. Truths covered by lies or silence, the turn of a prism. The lies about why we marry too quickly or not at all, how we need our kids to make up for what's missing in our marriages, or, like us, we don't have kids for fear of repeating the crime. Suddenly I was on the middle of a stage I'd known but didn't want to know. We, the Carleton sisters, had lived our lives walking around a secret, the same secret, forbidden to tell, either directly by Mama or by innuendo.

There was no way I could believe Lorraine didn't know. If not, she was a bigger fool than I'd imagined.

The color left Becky's face, and the bravado with which she'd confronted Lorraine was gone. She'd let go of the thing that haunted her. She was free and exhausted and done. She stood up. "No," she said, "I wasn't going to keep quiet forever."

I couldn't help but look at Lorraine. Head bent, her eyes remained hidden in the downturn of her head while the chains that held her glasses fell in a looped drape down from her shoulders. Was I the only one who thought she might be hiding tears? And if she was crying, what belief or myth or fairy tale had she been hanging onto—about our family or Mama? Whatever story she'd been telling herself had just died.

The shadows inside the room and on the table eclipsed the room's silence while the lights buzzed, more loudly now, and the air-conditioning took on the loudest voice in the room. Outside in the hallway, you'd have thought everyone left the building because of a bomb threat or fire.

"I want to go now," Becky said.

The clock reached its small hand past the twelve and the big hand toward the seven. Somewhere, not far away, the twelve-thirty from Sacramento crossed the L Street tracks, and the long groan of its increasingly loud whistle moved in our direction at the south end of town. The train, grinding toward us, would pass, and then be gone again. Day after day, like the tides, like autumn coming after summer, like our lives, melting into a pattern wherein a single thread hung down from somewhere in the middle, which Becky had just pulled.

Chapter Twenty-Three

Lorraine

I'd barely started down the row of trees, my white Dr. Scholl's covered with dirt, and me scurrying back through the orchard to the place we'd come just a week before, certain I'd find the trail of Mama's ash. Needing to find it. I had a lot to get off my chest.

Focus. Watch the sky, that late sun that says night would be here in another hour. And my feet. I didn't want to twist an ankle or fall. No one would know I was here, let alone care. The trees, gray now, the path through the trees darker and stony with rotted almonds from last season. I should have thought this through, come earlier.

In my mind, Peggy Lee's "Is That All There Is" played over and over. I could understand why crazy people took a gun and shot up the post office or bank or a Safeway. Neighborly folks. The kind you never suspect. Like me. But I no longer had Jesus in my heart. And if I'd had a gun, Pastor Harmon would have been the bullseye, that's how mad I was. All of them. Becky and Julie. Mama, the worst.

Even at work, I was fed up. Truckers and their baseball caps on the counter, big bellies full of coffee and glazed donuts, telling their stupid jokes and leaving lousy tips. I called in sick for tonight's supper. To hell with Diego. I'd given my whole life to that man and his lousy truck stop. No pension. No health insurance. A savings account with not enough to buy Julie out. Then what?

Julie had asked me at The Coffee Carousel that day if I'd ever do something different than waitressing. Actually, she'd asked why I stayed. Did I have the "hots" for Diego? Wasn't that just like her? As if we're all led around by our wayward hormones. I could just see Diego over the top of me, sweat dripping down his face, grunting himself silly. Men and sex. That's all they ever want, and next thing after that, they're out the door and on to the next gal, never taking care of what needs taking care of.

My foot gave way and I nearly fell, a root lifting into the path I didn't see, so lost in my head and, now, crying. Damn, why was I bawling when I just wanted to stay mad. Jack Harmon. And that loser, Uncle Dale. What the hell was wrong with Mama?

The last sun streaked through the trees and a piddly breeze hardly swayed the evening heat. It was that time of day you can usually anticipate a little wind, but not today. Birds darted through the tree branches and squawked their fool heads off. "Shut up," I said out loud. I cut over from one row to another, my teary eyes scanning the ground for any trace of ash I'd poured around the base of that one tree.

I walked along one row of trees, my eyes down toward their base and just a little above the dirt and mulch. But there was no sign of ash on the ground, just brown dirt and those prickly black almond hulls. We'd walked some distance from the car, but how deep into the orchard we left Mama, I couldn't remember.

Down on the ground and practically buried in the mulch and leaves, something powdery and gray looked like the trail I'd left the other day. If I could find where we stopped or even where I lifted that first handful of ash, I'd let go of this crazy search. Looking closer at what I thought was the trail of ash and thinking I was onto something, a twig, bent and gray and looking like ash, fooled me. For a minute, I thought I'd start bawling again, frustrated as I was.

I'd lived with waiting all my life. At Diego's. Mama's. Buck and his lousy hothouse roses. Damned men. For years I looked for his yellow jeep to drive up my driveway, his black beard grown out and those black eyes looking out from under his red Boilermakers cap. I knew the curl to his thick lips meant he was undressing me right there on the front porch. And whenever he came home, then left again on some construction job or other, I dreamed of him, the only man I ever wanted until Jack Harmon. I'd never gotten past wanting Buck's thick arms, the way he pulled me rough and tight against his body, those big hands on me like he'd never let me go. Those mornings on the Alaska-Canadian Highway, he'd be turned toward a window or looking outside the tent and I'd see him naked, the moles on his back and that little bit of black fuzz just above his waist. While I could see him, he belonged to me.

Before Buck left the first time, he told me I was the best thing that ever happened to him. Those were the sweetest words anybody ever said to me.

The good light was fading into night. Concentrate now, Lorraine, no blubbering. Just focus. I cut over into another row, trees all the same and the leaves their gray-green the way I felt. Still, no ash. The day we took Mama's ashes, I'd never thought about coming back. Never mind I intended to leave a piece of my mind here before I slept tonight.

Shadows fell away from the trees and the breeze had finally come up. But the leaves and seed pods were so thick and tight on the branches that it would take more than wind to rattle these trees. I'd had enough of this search. There, under one of the middle trees, a patch of grass looked like a place to sit. Not the right place, I was sure, but I bent over and picked the almond husks off the hard ground before I sat down. Rough dirt and crabgrass under my butt, I pulled my legs up tight, my skirt decently covering myself—as if anyone would be looking in this lonely and forsaken place—my shoes now the same color as the dirt.

The sun had turned orange in the trees, and that nighttime blue was about to take over. The early evening sounds of crickets and the breeze joined a screen door slamming somewhere I couldn't see. Yet the agitated feeling that plagued me since the afternoon wouldn't leave me alone, had left me lonely, the same kind of lonely that had taken over the house.

"Mama?" The word sounded thick and stuck in my throat along with whatever else I'd been keeping down. "Mama? You here?"

I waited. Birds, mostly crows, were the only answer I got back. Bees whizzed close by. Maybe there was a hive somewhere. "We've got to talk, Mama."

A high tide feeling started down in my belly and filled my chest before I could stop it. "I trusted you," I said. The sob surprised me along with the awful thought—*You can't trust anyone. Not your sisters, not your preacher, and now, not your mother. Forget Jesus.*

A second wave came, and my belly heaved in that way you can't stop. If I hadn't lost it before, I was losing it now. The sobs along with the emptiness and the end of everything.

The orange sky was gone and filled now with the blue that comes just before the day goes black and all you have is a half moon and a few stars to find your way back. Bats, something I couldn't see and too close, darted out of that same blue that wasn't yet black. My God, what if they got in my hair? I needed to hurry.

"What *did* you teach me? That men are no good and you should never give your heart away? That's what you said in the car on the way back from Oakland. Don't trust them. That was after Daddy left. The whole time you were sneaking around with your own sister's husband. How could you do that?

"I've lived my whole adult life being led around by your sin. That one misstep with Buck, and my abortion—I thought I'd never get over it. And, yes, I went after Jack Harmon and did the thing that weighs me down and won't let me sleep— the thing that made me so mad at myself I went home today and cut my Mister Lincoln nearly to the ground until that rose will likely never grow again. Mister Lincoln practically butchered and me eating nonstop in the Whitman's Sampler and Dove Bars and Marie Callender departments."

The wind settled, and even the birds quieted down. The night was as still as it could be even while the sky's blue turned darker.

"Like you, Mama, I went after someone else's husband," I said to the tree in front of me. "Are we cursed that way?"

I pulled my legs tighter and kept my eyes on the treetops and the light that was going fast, the sky darker and darker by the minute. The near-night sky overhead, the orchard around me, and the hard, stonelike dead almonds poking under my butt, my legs. "Remember that day in May when you took me to that butcher in Oakland, the back room of his house where there was nothing but a table with a white sheet and no padding. A sink at the side of the table and a garbage can. Some crazy machine on the floor that sounded like a vacuum cleaner. Except for a white coat, he didn't even look like a doctor, a week's worth of whiskers and his hair shaggy. Like he'd just come off a drunk. The envelope you handed him with the five hundred-dollar bills. You stood beside me at the table and held my hand while I waited for the machine to start and the pain to come right along with it. Then I closed my eyes before what wasn't more than two whiffs of ether.

"The whole thing was your idea, Mama. 'Quiet, out of town. No one will ever know,' you said. 'You don't want to saddle your life with an unwanted child and no husband.'

"But that wasn't true, Mama. Left to me, I'd have never gone, not to that naked table in Oakland. Not to any butcher who would leave me ashamed the rest of my life. Yes, maybe to one of those homes where they took in girls like me. Because I'd have wanted to keep the baby and you knew that. Knew you'd have to help me raise it. We never said, but we both knew."

I picked up one of the black and shrunken hulls that stabbed my little toe. I didn't throw it away. I just kept turning the rough outside shell with its sharp pointy end over in my fingers. "Because of you, I'll have no one to spread my ashes, let alone come looking for them."

The thought, the words, and a new wave, hot and filled with saliva, came up into my mouth until I was going to throw up. Yet I remained calm at the same time. It was the damnedest thing. Like what's said in a family and what isn't. But was I really like Mama? When Mama was done with someone, she was done for good. Sad but true, that's what happened with Becky. She should have the ring. Why not? Look what Mama did to her own sister, Naomi. That wasn't me.

The road at the edge of the orchard was so blue it was nearly black by the time I pulled myself to my feet. I dusted off the back of my skirt and walked around the tree a time or two before my foot was right enough to walk between the rows again. Watch the sky, Lorraine. I had to find my way out of there and I hadn't thought to bring a flashlight.

I walked past a dozen trees before I turned around and looked back. I tried to find the particular tree with the patch of weeds and grass, but it was just like all the other trees. I'd never find it again, just like I didn't find the ashes. No matter, it was time to go home.

Chapter Twenty-Four

Julie

Both suitcases lay open on the bed, jammed with clean clothes I'd washed late yesterday before the family meeting, somehow knowing things would change. The stuff inside my suitcases—dance scrapbooks Dotty kept and family photos—would make me a new home. I even lifted from the dresser my portrait Mama always kept on the TV and packed it inside some tights. No use leaving it here, Lorraine would just throw it away.

The house was quiet. No TV, and the only radio in the kitchen was turned off. Thank heaven Lorraine was gone, some errand she said in the note she left on the kitchen table. *Won't be back until dark. Better call a cab or get Joe McKenzie to pick you up.* That was it. I could have been the maid. What did she care? She got what she wanted. Becky and I were just in her way now. Well, she could eat all her casseroles to her heart's content.

It was easier to pack without her being here. Besides, I was so damned mad that every time I saw her, it took everything I had not to trip her or lock her in the bathroom, stuff kids do. That's what she brought out in me. She'd get hers. And I'd get mine, one way or another. At least I'd landed. The dance studio, the new rental at Joe McKenzie's apartments and a loan from Tasha to furnish it. "Until you get on your feet," she'd said.

I folded my blouses, the gold lamé the last to go into the suitcase. Couldn't help but think that if Merce Cunningham was right and dancers are first-time souls, then most of life is a surprise party.

Still, in all this, good luck really, some ache just below the surface came up whenever I had a cigarette on the patio or put on my makeup, those times when things took on a different perspective or became clear. Now, a faraway twist lived in my gut while my hand traced the eyeliner on my lower lid, that last brush of mascara. I couldn't quite believe I'd accepted River's End, the dance studio, and Joe's apartment as easily as I had. Life's miracles: take what you get and turn it around, especially when you've been as stuck as I'd been.

Wouldn't you know, the clasp broke on my makeup case when I went to close it. Looked simple enough to fix if I could just get a screwdriver and ease the tongue of the lock out enough to make the catch. I had at least another hour until Joe's man, Mario, came to move me to the apartment.

In the kitchen, the light was fading to orange through the greenhouse window. It seemed strange to think I was done at Sunny Acres, a place I now knew more intimately than I ever intended. Even the smells of the place would linger in memory long after Lorraine's silk flowers faded. I pulled open the freezer door, forever hopeful. A nice gin and tonic would have been the right farewell, if not to Lorraine, at least to Dotty. But the freezer no longer housed a bottle of any kind. Of course.

I opened the cupboard in the so-called mudroom and, leave it to Lorraine, the shelves were filled with cleaned-out jars from jams and salad dressings, the creamy kinds she favored, a Crock-Pot for heaven's sake, an old coffee pot I'd never seen, her iron and the distilled water. Light bulbs and enough sponges to last five years.

On the bottom shelf at the back sat Daddy's old toolbox, the silver shining in the fading light. From the dust on the cover, it hadn't been opened for years. I'll be damned. I'd never thought about that toolbox, since none of the women in this house were mechanically minded. I'd been sure Lorraine had a screwdriver and hammer hidden somewhere until I remembered Lorraine said she called in old man Petersen next door every once in a while. He must bring his own tools.

Seeing that toolbox, I could see Daddy all over again, his red hair falling forward as his head bent over the top, that squinty look in his eyes while searching for something in particular. The women in the house had been warned to never go anywhere near his toolbox for fear he wouldn't find what he was looking for. One thing out of place and the roof would come down.

Miraculously, Daddy didn't have a padlock on it and the clasp hadn't rusted. I hesitated for a moment, almost afraid to open it. This was the closest I'd come to Daddy outside of a photo. I set the toolbox on the washing machine after placing a towel underneath. The last thing I wanted to do was rile the owner of the house.

It took me a minute to work open the catch. I lifted the lid back. Sure enough, a top tray held the screwdrivers and a small hammer, some spackling compound that had to be nearly forty years old. Was that how long he'd been gone?

Curiosity being my middle name, I lifted out the top tray and set it to the side on the towel. A second tray held measuring tapes and a utility knife, small boxes of screws and nails, the usual stuff men keep in their toolbox, I guess. I lifted that tray out as well. Beneath the second tray were all sorts of wrenches, all neatly placed so they fit together and didn't interfere with the two top trays. At the side, a manila envelope, aged with a rusted clasp and long settled beneath the tidy array of wrenches, caught my eye.

I couldn't help but think of that Las Vegas brochure I'd found in Daddy's underwear drawer all those years ago. How that Flamingo brochure gave me a different direction and set the bar for where I was headed. While I saw the envelope there, I was almost afraid to slip a fingernail beneath it for fear of what I'd find. First, why would Daddy keep an envelope in his toolbox unless he wanted no one to see it? Second, if it meant anything, I was surprised The Boss hadn't lifted it out and disposed of it, especially if it incriminated anyone, controlling as Lorraine was.

But who was going to know? The lid was so dusty when I reached for the box that it obviously hadn't been opened for years. I turned on the overhead light and picked up the screwdriver with the longest and smoothest head, then eased the head under the envelope so I could lift it out with the least disturbance. Holy mackerel. There was no way to do it without disturbing the orderly arrangement of wrenches. Now I did feel like a snoop. At least years ago I'd been able to put Daddy's boxers and socks back the way I found them, and I never did tell anyone what I found the day I recovered the Las Vegas brochure.

If the envelope had ever been sealed, the glue had worn off so long ago that it had lost its hold. I eased my finger under the flap so as to not disturb what hadn't been disturbed in all these years and, of course, there was no way to do it without a further tear at the center, the only place the glue held. It didn't matter. Maybe I'd take it with me. Whatever was inside was useless lying around here.

As my fingers slipped inside, I felt what seemed like scraps of paper, not a lot but enough to create a small bulk of contents. I pulled them out and, taking the envelope with me, I carried them back into the kitchen where I turned on the overhead lights and sat at the kitchen table. I glanced quickly at the clock. I had maybe forty-five minutes before Mario would be here. If the lock didn't get fixed, he could help me with it.

The contents fell onto Lorraine's white tile table, an odd assortment of folded notes. But what caught my eye, then made me suck in my breath, was the word *Rosemary* on the outside of one of the notes, then another as I shuffled through them. Tom, Daddy's name on several others.

I sat back in the chair, my bare feet on the floor and my hands in my lap. What had I gotten myself into? Did I want to know? Rosemary, the babysitter, her body left on the railroad tracks. Daddy, the one who paid her, then drove her home before he disappeared. Rosemary's boyfriend, Sal, off to the Philippines with the Navy.

One breath. A second. What we know and what we don't know. What we tell and what we don't tell. Families and their secrets.

I unfolded the first note with *Rosemary* written on the outside. *Seven o'clock Tuesday, the south door at the roller rink. T.* That was it. The same with another. Tuesday the night. The roller rink the place, somewhere none of us went. Not me or Mama or Lorraine or Becky. Tuesday nights when he always went to the union hall on McDowell about a block from the roller rink.

The notes with *T* outside. *Babysitting Friday for Alice McKay. They're playing music at Cliff's. They won't be home until after two am.* If not the McKays', then somewhere else. All the notes setting up their trysts, what was obviously an affair.

The shock of the notes was one thing. Putting the meaning together was something else. The pregnancy we all blamed on Sal. Except when you thought back and counted the months, Sal, the one she talked about all the time, had been gone nearly a year when Rosemary killed herself. That was Daddy's baby. Why hadn't we figured that out? But how would we, could we? We were just girls and we trusted Rosemary. We *trusted* Daddy.

I leaned into the table. I'd stopped breathing and my fingers were digging into my palms. That wasn't just Daddy's baby; that could have been a sister or the brother we never had. The whole sordid exploration on the railroad tracks with Lorraine who adored Rosemary came flooding back. My near-glee in finding clues. The whole time we missed the big picture, that connection to Rosemary so much more than any of us expected. Did Dotty know? Suspect? Had Daddy known about Uncle Dale? Which came first?

I no longer cared about the broken clasp on my makeup bag. I glanced up at the rooster clock. I had maybe fifteen minutes to get ready. Fifteen minutes in which to leave behind more crimes than I cared to think about. Fifteen minutes before walking away from where I started. Each step forward was now loaded with more meaning than I could have imagined, until I could find that space inside, that closet really, where I could tuck away this information and try to forget I knew. It was one thing to know about Mama and Uncle Dale through Becky's revelation. But that wasn't why he left. Maybe his heart was broken when Rosemary killed herself. Herself and his baby. Maybe he was afraid of getting caught. How ironic, it was only a couple years later when Lorraine found herself in the same boat, just more innocently, more appropriately with someone we all knew she loved, if you can call it love at seventeen.

Gathering the notes together, I slipped them back into the envelope. But I knew I couldn't put the envelope back. Knew I never wanted anyone else to find it. I went to Lorraine's pristine cupboard and lifted out one of her Pyrex storage bowls. Took it to the patio where it was already dark and I was sure to see the headlights of Mario's van. Sat at the picnic table and lit a cigarette. I spread the notes, crumpled them really, inside the bowl. Shredded the envelope. Taking my silver Zippo, I touched the flame to the first note and placed it in the center of the bowl. Waited until the other slips ignited. Waited for Mario's lights in the driveway. It was already late, and what if Lorraine got to Sunny Acres first?

I threw my cigarette into the bowl and watched the flames engulf all the contents, smelled the burning tobacco and the acrid odor of the filter. Saw the lights on the paved drive just as the last paper curled inside the flame and became the ashen gray of the other papers. My breath caught in my throat. To find what you find and don't want to know. Don't want anyone else to know either.

Chapter Twenty-Five

Becky

Cab fare. That's what they gave me. One stop, two hours to pack, Kenny needs to be gone. Then straight to the sober living home out on Hartman Road. "This is stupid," Kenny said. "Afraid I'm going to get you loaded? Is that what those bitches think?" What do you say to that? Nothing. That's what I was learning: keep my damned mouth shut.

I couldn't remember the last time a cab drove into Stella's Landing. You'd have thought it was a one car parade, every yokel in the place suddenly hanging out wash or pulling their trash and garbage out of the house. Kids, ragged as ever, stood beside their moms and stared. Hell, you'd have thought I was Britney Spears. "Hey, Becky, how you doin'," from just about everywhere. Who knows what Kenny had been saying, if anything. You could tell he'd been partying by the garbage bags bunched up on the small porch. He must have been in heaven not having to consider his drunk wife and the cops or jail. He could drink his beer, smoke his weed, and be loaded every day of the week if he damned well pleased. No wonder he wanted me out of there.

Millie, the old lady two trailers over who had the two mangiest dogs I ever saw, was the bravest. She walked right over as soon as the cab pulled away. "You had anything to eat, girl? Look damned skinny, if you ask me."

I had to smile, but it must have looked like a dumb smile, pasted on in a way that made me think of Julie. I wasn't exactly used to people being nice to me. "Thanks, Millie," I said. "Just had lunch and I won't be here long enough for dinner."

"You movin'?" she asked.

"Yeah, you could say that." Lucky for me, the treatment center had taken my other stuff, mostly the Goodwill clothes and bathroom stuff they'd given me, over to Mary's Place—the halfway house where I'd have my own bedroom along with five other gals in the same house. Janice arranged it. Said they had a special scholarship that would pay for the first six months until I got a job.

Two empty banker's boxes in hand, I pulled back what used to be the ratty screen door, and that should have been my first clue. No tear at the bottom, a new screen, silver in color and neatly nailed in place. Inside the trailer, I about died of shock. I'd expected the place to look the way I left it, which was pretty much in shambles, laundry piled on the sofa and my cowboy boots scattered on the floor. I'll be damned. The place was all cleaned up. The ratty sofa was gone and a single recliner had taken its place, plus a small table with two chairs for eating. Every last plant was gone. The kitchen cleaned up, not a dish in sight anywhere and the counters cleared. The TV had come out from the bedroom, and when I went in there, the bed was made with a new blue bedspread and even a single pillow. I swear, it looked like Lorraine had stuck that blue-green satin pillow right in the middle of the tucked-away bed. I couldn't believe my eyes. That son of a bitch. He'd put up with my nonsense for years, and now look what he'd gone and done.

"How long you going to be there?" he'd asked on the phone. "Long enough to get my stuff," I said.

Who was she? Some biker chick? Hell, we hadn't even divorced, let alone talked about it. If it wasn't some gal, this was a side of Kenny I never suspected.

Now I was almost sorry. Goddamn. Gone a month and look what happened. Had I known, I might have gotten sober sooner. Though Becky doing what Becky does, that was likely a lie. It took his kicking me to the curb and nowhere to go to straighten me out. God knows I wasn't ready for the streets, but that's where Lorraine would have let me go. Her feeling guilty only went so far. Hell, it wouldn't hurt my feelings if I didn't see her ugly puss for a long time. Except she can never leave anything alone. Here it was, only September and she'd already sent me a note asking if I wanted to come for Thanksgiving. Janice said, "Don't just tear it up, Becky. She's trying." Trying, my ass. Already turned Mama's bedroom into a TV room. Truth was she'd taken over the whole damned house so no one could come and bug her. Julie, just as bad. A one-bedroom. *All I can afford*, she'd said. Message from both of them: no room at the inn for you, Becky Sue. Even Janice said, "Wreckage of your past. You'll have to live with it."

So what the hell was I doing here? Spent the last week wracking my brain with what I'd do with all my plants in that small room at Mary's Place. Now, no plants. And the kitchen? What was I going to take? My favorite drinking glass? Same in the bedroom. My clothes? They were probably too big now. That was about it. I'd left such a trail of crap behind me everywhere Kenny and I lived, I didn't really have anything anymore, maybe a few pictures. I didn't see them anywhere.

Looking around, you'd have thought I never even lived here. Aluminum foil off the windows. *To keep out the sun*, I always said, but truth be told, I didn't want anyone watching me, seeing me drink. Even new curtains, I'll be damned.

Before I could stop myself, I felt the ruffle on the bottom of the curtain over the bed; it was stiff, like new things are stiff when you first buy them. The one time we went to Chadron, Nebraska, where his folks lived, Kenny's mom was as big a pig as me. I turned to leave the bedroom, then started to go toward the closet thinking I might see her clothes. But when I put my hand on the door to slide it open, I stopped.

Kenny and I'd been together since I was sixteen. He was the only guy I ever knew. Not Danny, like he thought. Danny was just for drinking, company when Kenny was out of town. I flopped back on the bed, but pulled myself up fast before I lay down. Crap, if there was another woman, I didn't want to know. Might be a reason to drink again, Becky Sue.

In the living room, I lingered by the recliner, my hand against the green velvet-like fabric on the arm, feeling the back where an extra piece made a headrest. No, it wasn't new, but it was like new. Shit. We hadn't had anything new in so long, I couldn't remember. That got me going, the heat in my belly that says resentment is catching fire, is going to flare up and take over. It was hard enough I had to walk into this Lorraine-like double, especially sober. I didn't need to get a mad-on right then.

I leaned forward, feeling the fabric seat with my hand. I bent over and sat down. There was nothing left of me in this place, not a goddamn thing. I leaned back far enough in the chair that the footrest came up. Damn. The weed business must be really good. This was nice. The TV straight ahead where you could see it. If he had a gal living here, she had to be skinny if she was going to sit beside him. The afternoon sun came at a slant through the screen door and onto the carpet. New carpet for God's sake. That oatmeal color Lorraine likes. Would show every damned spot, especially with Boozer and Johnnie eating off the rug and slobbering the way dogs do. Would serve Kenny right.

Where were the dogs? Damn. No barking, no slobbering, nothing.

Sitting back, comfortable in the chair, cozy really, it was way too quiet. No dogs barking. No cats. Not one. Anywhere. Strange, really strange. Too neat, too quiet. The cats. That's why I'd come. I knew it right then. I'd come to see *my* cats. Spanky and Buster and Lucille. Where the hell were my cats? Goddamn, did he give them away too? Send them to the pound?

They were *my* cats. I'd picked them out. I got the cats, Kenny got the dogs. Heat burned behind my eyes and now there was a quick feeling in my chest. The one thing that was mine, really mine. The cats.

I kept seeing that little girl come out of the bathroom holding Spanky around the neck. I just knew she'd been in there hiding with those cats. Those cats taking care of her, the way they'd taken care of me.

I kept looking around the put-away living room. This was my home, the place where I'd kept secret the longing that finally took me out and over the edge. That great, ever-widening canyon of despair, the awful loneliness I'd lived with all these years and never been able to name until now. Until Janice took me into that conference room each and every afternoon. Until she bent toward me and asked, "What was it like when you were a kid, say four, five, six years old? Who was the person you counted on most?"

I just sat there, my fingers twisting around each other to keep from biting my nails, my white blouse too small but the only one that came close to fitting, the leftover pile down to purple shorts I could swim to Cabo in and a tank top that went with the shorts. "I dunno," I said to Janice. When I stopped twisting my fingers and glanced up at her, I said, "Probably my dad."

I waited for the question I expected, the one they always asked, "Why do you drink?" The question I'd have to answer again the same way I always did. But Janice didn't ask. Instead, she asked, "What was it like to be alone?"

When I looked at her blonde hair, the small gold hoops that defined Janice day in and day out the last four weeks, I said, "Guess it was lonely."

I shouldn't have said that. It felt too raw and numb at the same time. *Lonely* a word I didn't say—in fact, laughed when one of the gals said she felt lonely in the dorm even though there were six of us altogether. Like a secret, lonely was the same as hiding under the army blanket.

How long I'd been crying, I don't know. But if I sat there any longer, I'd die from crying. I threw myself out of the chair. In the kitchen I found and grabbed the green princess phone. Punched in the numbers. "Janice? Now. Come now," I said trying to carry the phone into the living room to find tissues that weren't there.

I opened the refrigerator door, and the light came back at me. No beer. I was sure he'd have a beer in there. Under the sink. A bottle maybe.

"I'll call the cab," Janice said. "What's going on, Becky? Is Kenny there?"

Nothing. Not a goddamned thing. Cleaned out! Empty!

"No, he's not here. No one's here." When I said that, a belly sob caught hold in my throat, something thick and too big that I didn't want to feel. "That's the problem," I said, practically exploding into the phone. "My cats, they're gone!"

The minute I said *gone* it was there. Everything I ever loved, gone or disappeared. And what was there after that? The choking feeling. "Can you come?" I asked.

I don't know where the hell that came from. I'd never asked a question like that in my whole life, let alone when I was sober. "Can you come, or can you send someone?" I was clear-headed enough to know Janice had a schedule, responsibilities, what she told me time and again I had to be.

Responsible. But I just couldn't leave the place alone. Not then, not like that. The same beat-up feeling as that day, right in this house, I asked Julie why she didn't take me with her. Drunk off my ass. I guess I had to be in order to ask an honest question.

Nothing on the other end of the phone. I could just see Janice thinking, maybe rolling her Holy Mother eyes at me without me seeing. "Sure," she finally said. "I'll send Patsy in the van. Will that work?"

My tears and nose kept running and the phone was still stuck in my hand. I held it away from me as though I'd never seen a phone before. The tears clouding my eyes, running down my cheeks. If I'd learned anything from Janice, wrecked as I was seeing my home had disappeared, I pulled the phone to my ear. "Thanks." Then I hung up.

I stood there. Empty, just like the house. Empty and stupid and that crazy, stupid AA word *change* pounding in my ears. Had to get out of there, move. The front porch. Close the door. The steps, I could wait here. Think for a minute. Change is what happens. And not a damned thing you can do about it. Except live with it. Fuck.

Chapter Twenty-Six

Lorraine

eopardy. Alex Trebek was right where I wanted him, volume-wise, his voice all the way from the new den into the living room and kitchen. It could have been any night, supper waiting, except it wasn't. My iced tea rested next to the sugar bowl on the counter. Five or seven teaspoons of sugar. What the hell. I didn't need to hide it anymore. There was enough tuna casserole for two in the fridge, maybe a salad. A nice piece of apple pie in the freezer. Why did I need to cook? No one else was here.

There was nothing like *Jeopardy* when you were winding down the day. Iced tea. Muffies on my feet and needlepoint in my lap here on the new chair. I didn't know why, but *Jeopardy* and iced tea and needlepoint always made me feel better.

Wednesday, Bible Study night. Now that I could go, I wouldn't. Blue eyes right to the bottom of my soul. That was Pastor Jack Harmon. Every time I thought about him, my chin quivered. All that talk about what you have to give up to be a good Christian. Living for the afterlife.

Damn the afterlife.

Tropical islands. That was one I didn't know much about. If Mama was here, she'd be the first to say *Eleuthera*, though I never knew it was part of the Bahamas. Just like I was learning a lot of things I didn't know.

What a relief, Julie finding a place to live. Becky in a halfway house. And there I was, calling and inviting them for Thanksgiving, still two and a half months away.

I was just as well off alone. Church and Mama and Diego's. That had been enough for me. Until Jack.

I turned the volume louder. Put the remote back on the TV tray by the recliner. Never noticed before, but Alex Trebek looked a little like Jack Harmon. Funny how Trebek only wore his glasses once the show had started. From the looks of his chin, he'd had a facelift too. Even men.

I pushed my needle down into what would become grass. Always the boring parts at the end. You do the fun stuff like the church and steeple and cross and flowers first, just to keep yourself going.

I looked up when I heard *Bali*. There was something in the room I hadn't smelled before. Not rubbing alcohol or pee. But it was definitely something, and it was definitely Mama. Not cologne, she didn't wear the stuff. Her clothes, all gone to Goodwill. The recliner? What was it? I'd scrubbed myself raw getting her out of the house.

My hand reached for the iced tea just to feel something cold and wet. After I picked up the glass, I glanced at the brown corduroy recliner just thirty degrees in the other direction. My head not wanting to go there, but doing it just the same.

For the first time, Mama's chair was empty. Really empty. The brown corduroy arms bare and the good beige towels used as arm protectors stored away in the hall closet. They weren't needed anymore.

To think she stabbed me in the back with her secret. Humiliated me, really, in front of Becky and Julie. I'd never forgive her for that. Never. Like I didn't know my own mother, the one I confided in and thought she confided in me. Thought we knew each other better than most folks ever do. How would I have known that even while I tried to keep our home together, it was falling apart. That I was the only one who never saw it. The smell, again. Like lilac soap or lilacs, something sweet, but faded. Her face powder? She hadn't used it for years, not since Daddy left. A lump, big as a fist, gathered in my throat and my eyes burned like it was allergy season, which it wasn't.

She *betrayed* me. That same big, fat word she used against Daddy. And I believed her. Cheered her on. Believed every word she said. She knew she was lying. All along, she knew. Made me look the fool. And everything I did for her, believed in her. That fist again in my throat, the sob I didn't want to come up.

Mama was company, someone to take care of. I just never knew it would be so hard. Not just cleaning up after her, especially toward the end. It was the way she used to cry when it was time to go to bed. Afraid she would die in her sleep, she said. Then she couldn't use the porta potty anymore. Those tears when she had an accident or needed help just hoisting her legs over the edge of the bed. I couldn't get upset, not really.

But Mama and Uncle Dale, her own sister's husband. That was wrong, so wrong.

No different than what I tried with Jack Harmon. Don't forget that, Lorraine. Another woman's husband. How could I? Jack and his daily visits when Mama got so sick. The way he'd wink at me sometimes or, when he was leaving the house, he'd put his arms around me and hug me at the front door. I should have known something was strange, the way he shook my hand after church with his wife standing there. Then the whole business in Fresno with Denise. Maybe he'd planned on staying with her in the church basement all along, maybe he'd planned a little nookie with her when the kids finally went to sleep. He had me fooled.

Up out of nowhere, a sob big enough to choke me erupted with a saved-up life of its own. No longer did supper or Bible study or islands mean anything. There I was, a little girl holding baby Becky in my arms on the sofa. "This is *your* baby," Mama had said. The weight of Becky in my arms, her small, breathing body now in my charge. Mama did that to me, my sobs so loud and deep they could have robbed me of breath. Dear God, what was happening to me, where was I going in all this mess?

My apron was now soaking wet, and I was rocking in the new chair. I needed to quiet down and stop bawling.

What is love really? Even with Buck, I wanted to *think* I loved him. We had sex. If I didn't love him but had sex, maybe an abortion was the worst sin of all. But I did love him. At least, that's what I thought. Maybe real love is only love for God. Noble love. Except that kind of love never holds you, never fills the chair across the room, never laughs at stupid things like Java and Bali. What kind of love was that?

The smell again and Alex Trebek with presidents. Mama sitting right there against brown corduroy with the remote in her bent hand. Like she was turning up the volume at the same time she reached for her tonic. *Lorraine, it's Eisenhower.* Me, here in my chair. Where we belonged. Sunny Acres Mobile Home Park, Number 15, fifth space on your right, after the swimming pool and cabana. It's what I planned for, what I said I wanted.

Chapter Twenty-Seven

Thanksgiving 1999

Lorraine

Becky set the pumpkin pie down on my clean countertop. She started to move away in the direction of the dining room where Julie and Arthur had already migrated. "Wow, that's a big pie," I said. "Looks like you had a little trouble getting it here." I pointed to the aluminum rim where the crust had broken off.

"Arthur's fault," Becky said. "He stopped too fast at the train tracks and the pie must have hit the bottom of his seat."

I dropped my chin and smiled. "Nobody will notice by the time we load it with whipped cream."

"Thought you'd be happy. Costco and all." Becky looked down at the floor when she said this but the flush on her neck crept into her face and gave her away.

This was the first time I'd seen Becky outside of a quick visit to Mary's Place, where she'd been living now for over three months. Her hair, shorter and shiny, was revealing more of her natural red. Another three months and the dyed stuff would be gone.

"I'm happy you're here," I said. "Hope you are too."
Becky pulled on the lower edge of her white top. "Yeah,"
she said. Then, quickly, "Yes, I mean."

"Go join the others," I said. "You've done your part."

Becky's smile was strained when she adjusted the shoulder strap of her purse and left the kitchen. I shook my head.
The wonders of staying sober amazed me. Even in four short
months, Becky's body had smoothed out—though an over
blouse can hide a multitude of sins. I counted myself an expert
on that one.

The roast turkey, wrapped in dishtowels, was resting on
the counter. My mouth watered just from the smell, combined with candied yams and the excess dressing baking in the
oven. Mama's orange-and-walnut cranberry relish already sat
on the table beside black olives and dill pickles. Name cards
tented above each plate. I'd made them by cutting up index
cards and coloring them with Magic Markers. Like a rainbow;
orange for myself, purple for Becky to my left, red for Julie
across from her, and blue for Arthur at the other end of the
table. Not because Arthur deserved the head of the table, but
he was the only man to carve a turkey since Daddy left home.

"Nice table, Lorraine," Julie said. She reached out and
took my shoulders in her hands, pulling me closer, tighter. A
glad-to-see-you hug and not the pretend hug offered when
she first arrived from Las Vegas.

Fifty-plus didn't look too bad on Julie. As tall as she was,
she'd probably never give up those red high heels, the big
gold earrings and all those bracelets. But there was something else about her. Was it love that made those beginning
wrinkles around her mouth and eyes disappear? Was that
because of the cowboy? If that's all it took, I might have to
think twice about Marty Simmons's invitation to a movie and
dinner. Whenever he came into Diego's with his brothers, I
could feel his eyes follow me from booth to booth.

"Thanks for inviting me," Arthur said. He stood beside Julie now, close but not touching. "Feels kinda like home."

He gazed toward Julie's hair. Julie told me on the phone that the Almond Growers decided their best bet was to put him on their staff. He was considering a small ranch around Ceres, where he could keep a couple of horses. Her voice was matter-of-fact when she said that, like it meant nothing to her. Whatever was going on between those two, she wasn't giving it away. Except you could tell. The way he stood beside her now, how he'd opened the door, following her when they came in. A man who didn't want to lose someone.

"Ready for me to have at that bird?" Arthur said.

"Sure." I handed him an apron.

"You think I need that?"

"Don't want to stain that gingham shirt, do you?"

"True. I might have to take you ladies out for a nightcap afterward." He flushed when he caught Becky's eye. "Maybe a dance or two. I've never had my own harem."

"Fat chance," Julie said. "We'll be so stuffed that you won't be able to get us up off the couch." She gave him a nudge with her braceleted hand. A playful nudge like you'd see in a couple who'd gotten past those beginning jitters and were finally at ease with each other.

I'd never had that. Not with Buck who seemed to walk out of any given door in sight. Pastor Harmon? After the one time he bounded up the stairs in his navy-blue golf shirt and khakis to pick me up for Fresno? Guess I'd just wanted to see something that was never really there in either one of them.

Becky stood at the table looking at her name card. "What's this under my plate, Lorraine?"

At first I didn't answer. The hot flush on my neck crept into my face. Would we ever outgrow the Carleton Curse? "A little something to get you. . ." I searched for the right word. I didn't want her to get the idea that I'd forgotten the two thousand I paid for her fine. But I wanted her to know I was proud of her for nearly four months in recovery, the longest she'd ever stayed sober. Not that I was counting the days. "Something to help you get back on your feet."

Her hand on the envelope. "Can I open it?"

"Think you can wait until after we say the blessing?" I asked. Quiet-like, not the old Lorraine's scolding tone.

"Sure," she said. She quickly turned away. I'd embarrassed her.

"Hey, Lorraine, there's something under my plate too," Julie said.

I tended to forget that neither of my sisters were around when Mama asked me to refinance the mobile home and immediately give Julie her share. I was madder than a bear trapped in a cage that day. No way was I giving in to Mama.

"Why don't you two wait in the living room while we get dinner on the table?"

When I turned into the kitchen, Arthur had the carving knife poised above the turkey, the wadded towels crumpled to the side. He patiently severed a slice of white meat off the breast, then carefully placed it on the platter I'd set there for that purpose. "Need help?" I asked.

"I can smell the rosemary and butter," he said. "There's something else."

"My secret touch," I said to his golden-brown eyes. "Just enough fresh thyme, then I cook it hot and fast so the juices stay in."

Arthur smiled, then licked the end of his mustache, not because he had turkey there, but as a way to prove his appetite. It was something I'd noticed other men do before they dove into Diego's famous hash.

Arthur's eyes never left the knife in his hand, his concentration on that platter of white meat, the big legs to the side. All those slices piling up. "You do this every year?"

"Not since high school," I said. "In fact it's been too long since I've seen a man in the kitchen outside of Diego." I waited a breath. "Julie always said that Thanksgiving was too big a holiday in Las Vegas to come home." I nodded toward the living room where I could hear my sisters laughing. "Becky, well, you already know about Becky."

He glanced at me. "She's looking good, don't you think?" Then he stopped and held the carving knife away from the bird and closer to his chest. "You and Julie really did good by her."

He stood tall, gazing at me from those golden-brown eyes. His Adam's apple bulged when he swallowed. "Truly, can't thank you enough for including me, Lorraine."

There was something swollen and bittersweet in those few words. Sad and tender in the way he said them. Like someone who had been alone too long, someone who hadn't known what it was like to sit around the table with family and friends and feel welcome—welcome in that way that says, *you're a part of us and we're a part of you.* None of us had that once Tom Carleton grabbed the handle of his lunch pail and walked out the kitchen door that last time. Even while I watched Arthur, I couldn't help but think of Mama sitting in her brown corduroy recliner and eating her dinner off a TV tray. Maybe she didn't want to risk the grief of knowing she'd never again have family around the table.

"We needed you to be here, Arthur."

Where that came from, I don't know. But sometimes you tell the truth even when you don't know you're telling the truth. It just bolts out on to your tongue and you don't know what you've said until it's over.

That day Julie and I had coffee downtown at the Coffee Carousel, she told me about Arthur's daughter dying. She didn't know how or when, just that it had left its mark on him the way tragic and unexpected things do.

Without thinking, my hand found his knife arm. My warm hand against his forearm where the muscle was tight and as lean as he was. Not that I expected him to, but he put his hand with those rough cowboy fingers on top of mine. Then, too quickly, I turned toward the living room and erased the one tender moment I'd known in way too long. That touch sitting deeper than my hand. There in my throat. "Time for dinner, girls," I said.

I could just see Mama hollering those words from the back porch.

Julie and Becky found their places and Arthur arrived with the turkey platter. I followed behind with mashed and sweet potatoes, green beans, and gravy. Once we were all seated, I bowed my head. The others did the same.

How do you pray when you've lost faith the way I had? When your heart's been busted and you realize you did it to yourself? That awkward silence between the thought and the words. You say the only thing that makes sense. The only thing that covers past misdeeds and the joy—yes, joy—of this moment. "Thank you," I said. "Thanks to all of you."

I waited for a moment, maybe two. "Let's eat."

"Can we open the envelopes now, Lorraine?" Becky said. She'd already pulled hers out from under the plate and had her finger under the seal. An old irritation sat on my tongue. Would Becky ever learn to wait for anything?

A smile I didn't feel. "Of course," I said.

Julie nodded toward me with the same question in her raised eyebrows—waxed, I was sure. But, again, that was none of my business. That's what they told me in Al-Anon, now that I'd finally gone. *Breathe, Lorraine. Smile like you mean it.*

"Wow," Becky said, "five hundred bucks." She dropped the envelope to the side of her plate, her spontaneous smile suddenly left her face. "Why?"

Instead of answering Becky, I nodded toward Julie.

Hers was the face I wanted to see. The moment I'd antic-ipated since I walked into the bank and asked for the loan. A small, insignificant amount to most. Yet inside those plain white envelopes hid a lifetime of grudges and resentment and, yes, jealousy wanting to be erased.

Julie sucked in her breath and her eyes became shiny in a way I hadn't expected. Emotion a stranger in this home until recently. This was not the I'll-do-it-my-way Julie. Not even the Julie who'd had all the breaks. The big life in a big town on everyone's map. The Julie who, maybe like me, never let her guard down. Yes, I'd hoped for appreciation, maybe even resolution. I hadn't counted on emotion.

"Thanks, Lorraine," she said. "I wasn't expecting. . . this." She waved the check at me.

"It's yours," I said. "What was agreed on."

I swallowed hard. Dropped my hands into my lap. Neither of my sisters needed to know that Mama wanted to cut Becky out of the will. In truth, Becky received her fair share after all. You could call it making amends, but I'd rather say it was a change of heart. Partly what I'd learned from Mama's dying. From Pastor Harmon shoving me through the door of that Motel 6. Not just the lies we tell ourselves but the stories we make up about those lies, always refusing to see what we don't want to see. Still, the truth has a way of finding us anyhow.

"I'll hand you my plate, Arthur, if you'll be so kind," I said. "Only white meat. Plenty of gravy on the dressing."

Arthur's eyes on mine, my plate held steady in his hand. He must have been inside my head because that's what was in his eyes. His smile. Not a big howdy smile. But a smile like he knew what was what. "Of course," was all he said. I reached in front of me and passed the candied yams to Becky.

A Note from the Author

S everal incidents conspired toward the writing of this
book. First, my sister's very different perspective on
our family prompted wondering on my part. Following
that, a friend was eager to remove breast implants following
notice that leaking breast implants were toxic. This made me
ponder our cultural obsession with women's breasts. When
I thought about who symbolized this obsession, I thought
first of Hollywood. No, too cliché. It was easy to turn my
head east, toward Las Vegas—but having grown up in a small
farming community in western South Dakota, I wanted to
write a small-town story. If I was to have a topless Las Vegas
showgirl, the town had to be close enough that a bus ride
wouldn't be extraordinary. (I chose a bus versus a plane; the
cowboy had to be there.)

While this book is fiction and the characters are imagined,
my imaginary town of River's End is patterned after Modesto,
California. I'm deeply indebted to the generosity of that
community for welcoming me, answering my questions, and
allowing me to wander anonymously in the almond orchards,
the library, and the town's streets. Thanks to the reporters
of the Modesto Bee, who interviewed me early on while we
sat drinking coffee downtown. Thank you, Modesto, for

allowing me to "borrow" your streets and for the very spirit of your lovely town.

Additionally, I'm grateful to the archival librarians at the University of Nevada, Las Vegas. They allowed me access to valuable resources, particularly taped interviews with the production assistant and company manager, Fluff LeCoque of Donn Arden's JUBILEE production. The librarians also introduced me to Nancy Hardy, one of the Jubilee dancers. She shared her life story, including her years of classical ballet training. She in turn provided an introduction to Diane Palm. Simultaneously, the E! channel ran a series on the Jubilee dancers, revealing their personal as well as their professional stories. These experiences humanized the performers, both women and men, who prove to be not only dedicated to their work but also accomplished athletes. Thank you so much for allowing me "backstage."

Acknowledgments

From California's Zaca Lake to Portland, Oregon, my deepest thanks to all who have supported and participated in the twenty-five-year emergence of this novel.

First, my teachers: Janet Fitch has been there every step of the way. Tom Spanbauer and the Dangerous Writers taught me to risk.

Thanks to Judy Reeves, my writing pal and faithful friend, and Laura Stanfill, for love of writing and friendship. To the Henry Writers—Kathleen, Liz, Steve, Robert, Gigi, and Laura—who patiently heard draft after draft of this story. To the Lincoln writers/sisters for their encouragement.

To my sister, Peggy, who provided the original inspiration through helping me understand that each family member has a unique and often different experience of family. To my sons, Brian and Craig Frary, and their families—Baron, Linnea, Grace, and Madison—always there for me. To the Portland reading and writing community, especially the independent book stores, which cares so deeply about writers and readers. To the Rowenas—Mary, Cherlyne, Janine, Elizabeth (my BFFs). Without my AA and Al-Anon friends, none of this would have happened. To the San Diego Thursday Writers, past and present. Thanks to all of you who gave me a safe house where I could write: Brian, Jan and Vicki, Judy, McLaren, Anne and Bill. Everyone's generosity of spirit and kindness has been my greatest reward.

Thank you to Suzy Vitello for the brilliance of your developmental edits and your encouragement. To Gina Walter, my copyeditor. A special thanks to Laura Stanfill, woman of many hats, who is also my marketing and publicity coordinator. To my assistant, Elise LeSage, for managing the social media campaign. Thank you, Brooke Warner, Publisher of She Writes Press, always available to answer questions. As well to my She Writes managing editor, Shannon Green. To Rebecca Lown and the She Writes Press art department. To my community of She Writes Sisters. Gratitude to all my readers: Judy Reeves, Peggy McMillen, Joe Rogers, Kathleen Lane, Robert Hill, Laura Stanfill, Chin-Sun Lee, Roger Aplon, and Valerie Ryan, now passed. To anyone I may have missed, my apology. You are all in my heart.

About the Author

Photo © Sarah Eastland

Though Dian Greenwood started her life in the Dakotas, she has been a West Coaster since adolescence. She studied both writing and counseling psychology in San Francisco. An early focus on poetry led her to fiction. She has published personal essays in *The Big Smoke*, a weekly online magazine. *About the Carleton Sisters* is her debut novel. She writes and works as a family therapist in Portland, Oregon.

You can find Dian on her website,
www.DianGreenwood.com.

Selected Titles From She Writes Press

She Writes Press is an independent publishing
company founded to serve women writers everywhere.
Visit us at www.shewritespress.com.

The Best Part of Us by Sally Cole-Misch. $16.95, 978-1-63152-741-8. Beth cherished her childhood summers on her family's beautiful northern Canadian island—until their ownership was questioned and a horrible storm forced them to leave. Fourteen years later, after she's created a new life in urban Chicago, far from the natural world, her grandfather asks her to return to the island to see if what was lost still remains.

Appearances by Sondra Helene. $16.95, 978-1-63152-499-8. Samantha, the wife of a successful Boston businessman, loves both her husband and her sister—but the two of them have fought a cold war for years. When her sister is diagnosed with lung cancer, Samantha's family and marriage are tipped into crisis.

Profound and Perfect Things by Maribel Garcia. $16.95, 978-1-63152-541-4. When Isa, a closeted lesbian with conservative Mexican parents, has a one-night stand that results in an unwanted pregnancy, her sister, Cristina adopts the baby—but twelve years later, Isa, who regrets giving up her child, threatens to spill the secret of her daughter's true parentage.

Revelation by Bobi Gentry Goodwin. $16.95, 978-1-63152-606-0. When Angela, a social worker, discovers her father's picture alongside a dead body, she becomes determined to uncover the truth. Her sister, meanwhile, is struggling with infertility and her brother is navigating the shoals of substance abuse. In the end, all three must lean on their faith and family to help them through.

The Happiness Thief by Nicole Bokat. $16.95, 978-1-64742-057-4. Happiness is relative. For single mother Natalie Greene, that relative is her stepsister, Isabel Walker, known as The Happiness Guru. But even with Isabel's guidance, Natalie can't control her recently re-triggered PTSD over her mother's death in a car crash years ago. The old dread. The nightmares. And that all-consuming, terrifying thought: *I think I killed my mother.*

Fire & Water by Betsy Graziani Fasbinder. $16.95, 978-1-93831-414-8. Kate Murphy has always played by the rules—but when she meets charismatic artist Jake Bloom, she's forced to navigate the treacherous territory of passionate love, friendship, and family devotion.